Acclaim for

FIREBREAK

"An exhilarating space opera from master storyteller Kathy Tyers, *Firebreak* blends political intrigue, technology, faith, deft prose, and an incredible cast of characters to whisk readers away on the year's most exciting sci-fi adventure. Readers, rejoice: *Firebreak* is Tyers's triumphant return to the Firebird universe."

—TOSCA LEE, *New York Times* best-selling author of *The Line Between*

"Tyers creates science fiction with true heart and soul. Her characters drew me along on space voyages and planetary dangers, confronting me with universal questions and challenges that were amazingly relatable to this earthbound reader. Truly an extraordinary book, with powerful and deep thoughts, convicting and beautiful."

—SHARON HINCK, Christy Award Hall of Fame author

"A glorious return to the Firebird universe! Compulsive and riveting, *Firebreak* is a powerful probe of loyalty to one's beliefs, the power of love and faith, and a daring foray into what it means to be human—and inhuman. Kathy Tyers is a master storyteller, and this story has perfect pacing and utterly addictive characters. There is a reason Tyers is my writing hero—and this spells it out page by immersive page. Absolutely enthralling!"

—RONIE KENDIG, award-winning author of The Droseran Saga

"*Firebreak* is a masterwork of science fiction. As a longtime fan of the Firebird series, it defied my expectations. The premise is fascinating and unique, the narrative is compelling and thoughtful, and the characters are well-drawn and lifelike. I enjoyed it from start to finish!"

—KERRY NIETZ, award-winning author of *Frayed* and *Amish Vampires in Space*

"The Firebird series is one of a handful of grand space opera stories that spurred me to embrace my dream of writing science fiction. What a delight, then, to revisit Firebird herself, Sentinel Brennen Caldwell, and the same beloved cast of characters from Netaia and the Federate Worlds in this fantastic tale. Tyers's heartfelt characters merge seamlessly with bold, effortless worldbuilding that brings this fictional universe to life. *Firebreak* is a breathtaking showdown between old traditions and a sinister new threat that could spell the end of human life as the galaxy knows it."

—STEVE RZASA, award-winning author of *The Face of the Deep* and the Vincent Chen series

"*Firebreak* is a thrilling fusion of action, intrigue, and heartfelt emotion. With strong themes of spirituality, mercy, and grace, this story grips you from the first page and refuses to let go—whether you're new to the Firebird series or a longtime fan."

—CLINT HALL, author of *Steal Fire From the Gods* and *Echo Nova*

FIREBREAK

Firebreak
Copyright © 2026 Kathy Tyers

Published by Enclave Publishing, an imprint of Oasis Family Media, LLC

Carol Stream, Illinois, USA.
www.enclavepublishing.com

All rights reserved. No part of this publication may be reproduced, digitally stored, or transmitted in any form without written permission from Oasis Family Media, LLC.

This is a work of fiction. Names, characters, places, and incidents are products of the author's imagination or are used fictitiously. Any similarity to actual people, organizations, and/or events is purely coincidental.

ISBN: 979-8-88605-250-3 (printed softcover)
ISBN: 979-8-88605-252-7 (ebook)

Cover design by Kirk DouPonce, www.DogEaredDesign.com
Typesetting by Jamie Foley, www.JamieFoley.com

Printed in the United States of America.

FIREBIRD INTERLUDE TRILOGY | BOOK 1

FIREBREAK

KATHY | TYERS

Whether you grew up with Lady Firebird or recently met her,
thank you for reading. This book is dedicated, gratefully,
to every one of you, especially to those who were disappointed
that *Wind and Shadow* wasn't about Firebird and Brennen.
You know who you are!

NOTE FROM THE AUTHOR

The Firebird Interlude Trilogy can be read and, I hope, enjoyed, whether or not you have read the original *Firebird* series (or if it has been a few years!). *Firebreak*, in particular, is written as a stand-alone tale and point of entry. The Characters in Order of Appearance pages, right after the Table of Contents, will get you up to speed in a hurry.

On the other hand, if you would much rather read the full series in sequence, here is a hint: The Firebird Interlude Trilogy begins shortly after Book #3, *Crown of Fire*.

TABLE OF CONTENTS

1. Call	recapitulation	1
2. Netaia	*mezzo piano*	12
3. Elector	*allegretto*	28
4. The Night Sky	modulation	43
5. Launch	*poco agitato*	54
6. Sparring	*rondo*	66
7. Contact	second movement	81
8. One Stranger	*misterioso*	94
9. Noblest and Best	*dissonance*	108
10. Shekkah	the Ehretan service for the dead	118
11. Noblewomen	*stringendo*	130
12. Iarla	*deciso*	141
13. In Blood	*subito agitato*	155
14. Seeds	*con forza*	165
15. Three Esmes	*appassionato*	180
16. Silence	*lamentoso*	188
17. Recusal	*martellato*	198
18. Two Bare Hands	*piu allegro*	203
19. Copilot	*con anima*	215
20. Into Darkness	*risoluto*	224
21. Four Saboteurs	*sotto voce*	236
22. Strike	*affrettando*	247
23. Phoena's Fop	*con fuoco*	257
24. Two Heirs	*cantabile*	265

CHARACTERS IN ORDER OF APPEARANCE

Second Commander Lady Firebird Mari Elsbeth Domita Angelo Caldwell: Her names and titles tell her story in *Firebird*, *Fusion Fire*, and *Crown of Fire*.

Second Commander: Her highest achieved rank in the Netaian Planetary Navy, now honorably discharged

Lady: Title given to extraneous heiresses (wastlings)

Firebird: The Angelo family traditionally gives their daughters avian names.

Mari: An incognito name she was given when taken prisoner by the Interstellar Federacy. Her husband Brennen, and only Brennen, continues to call her "Mari."

Elsbeth: Given name, an old one in the Angelo family

Domita: Heir name given by the Netaian Electorate, signifying the "holy Power" of Indomitability

Angelo: Her surname by birth. House Angelo rules Netaia.

Caldwell: Her surname by marriage

Shelevah (Shel) Mattason: Firebird's friend and bodyguard, a telepathic Sentinel. Formerly an instructor at the Sentinel College on Thyrica, she now lives with Firebird and Brennen.

Brennen Caldwell: Master Sentinel serving as Regional Battlefield Commander for the Interstellar Federacy. Married to Firebird, and they are raising twins. The Caldwell family is heir to ancient holy promises. Full name and rank: Master Sentinel General Brennen Daye Caldwell.

Kinnor Caldwell: Firebird and Brennen's son, pushing three years old. Full name: Kinnor Irion Caldwell, middle-named for Firebird's father. Considered "first conceived" on Netaia.

Kiel Caldwell: Firebird and Brennen's son, pushing three years old. Full name: Kiel Labbah Caldwell, middle-named for Brennen's father. First born from the womb.

Dara Caldwell: Brennen's widowed mother. Her older son, Tarance, was murdered by the renegade Shuhr. Nicknames: Ahma-Dara (Mother Dara) and Zahma (Father's mother).

Glin-Erris Coll: Diplomat serving the Interstellar Federacy. His aunt, Tierna Coll, heads the Federate Regional Council, headquartered on the world of Tallis.

Uri Harris: Brennen's travel bodyguard, also a Sentinel. Has diplomatic experience. Military rank: Lieutenant Colonel.

First Marshal Devair Burkenhamn: Head of the Netaian Planetary Navy

First Lord Baron Bualin Erwin: Traditionalist head of one of Netaia's noble houses, he has been consolidating financial control over the other houses. Powerful ceremonials director on behalf of Netaia's holy Powers.

Grand Duke Daken Cellen Erwin: Bualin Erwin's son, his father's favorite

Prince Daithi Drake-Angelo: Prince by marriage to Carradee Angelo, Netaia's former queen. Father of Netaia's current queen, Rinnah Elsbeth Angelo.

Carradee Angelo: Firebird's eldest sister, forced to abdicate during the regency crisis (see Esme Rogonin below). Having lost two little daughters to the Shuhr, she is glad to lead a quiet life without any formal title. Her infant daughter, Rinnah, is now queen.

Regent Kenhing: Bennett Drake, Prince Daithi's brother, currently serving as "Regent Until the Majority of Her Majesty Queen Rinnah." Officially Duke of Kenhing, he prefers that title.

Valora Erwin: Bualin Erwin's daughter and heiress

Duchess Esme Rogonin: New head of House Rogonin, one of Netaia's powerful noble families. Esme inherited headship upon the death of her father, Muirnen Rogonin, who served Netaia as regent and tried to make that status permanent by cooperating with the renegade Shuhr. He committed suicide rather than face prosecution.

Freda Tomma: The Electorate's token common-class representative, head of the Ice Miners' Guild

Prince Tel Tellai: Prince by marriage to the middle Angelo sister, Phoena. Phoena defected to the evil Shuhr, hoping to replace Carradee on the throne, and died at Three Zed.

Lieutenant Lord Leon Parkai: Young sensors technician at Citangelo Base, formerly a wastling, now an Inquirer on the Holy Path

Dodis Gering: Daken Erwin's manservant

Count Farring Rogonin, Count Kelsen Rogonin, Lady Diamond Rogonin: Duchess Esme Rogonin's younger siblings

Sentinel Dassah Cowan: Head of palace security

Paudan and Jess: Prince Tel's bodyguard-manservant, and his chauffeur

Arafel and Tsebee Hadarah: Shuhr sisters

1: CALL

recapitulation, a restatement of earlier musical themes

Firebird Caldwell leaned toward the starry wall display. "What in the Whorl is that?"

Sentinel Major Shelevah Mattason stood next to her, arms crossed. Gray-eyed with a strongly cleft chin, Shel couldn't help looking down on Firebird. She was a head taller.

Mounted in the Caldwell home's underground safe room, advanced instrumentation linked them with Regional Command down in Castille city. Firebird and her husband, Brennen, had one of the few homes on the Regional headquarters world with an authorized DeepScan watching post. On this meter-square monitor, a crosshatched image of space shimmered faintly.

Something odd was approaching the Federate Whorl of star systems, traveling out of the vast, empty spaces between galactic arms. Astronomers had tracked it for months, predicting that it might actually graze the Whorl. Whatever it was, it seemed to be heading almost directly for Firebird's distant home world, Netaia. Roughly moon-sized, the zone resisted scanning, as if other energies simply ceased to exist in its proximity.

But it did not warp space. It was not a black hole.

The freshest data was several days old, due to the enormous distances. Still, Firebird had followed daily updates. It was good to be distracted from her recent bureaucratic failures. Four years ago, Federate calendar, she'd been a Netaian fighter pilot, desperate to die heroically. Instead of honorable death, she'd been captured.

By Brennen.

For good.

So she ought to be accomplishing something besides motherhood, right?

Pushing a long strand of auburn hair back over her shoulder, she eyed the odd blur on the DeepScan image. It could be harmless. But she was a defender, with the warrior's calling to protect her people. "Netaia's a long way out there," she murmured.

Shel pocketed her interlink in slim blue shipboards. "Yes, and you can stop worrying about home security for another ten days. That's my job, anyway." Doubling as bodyguard and household staff, Shel had felt more like a friend than an employee since that last frightful trip back to Netaia.

Firebird's former home world might be in danger, or it could be ground zero for a marvelous new discovery, and the Netaian regent had recently asked her and Brennen to return in order to introduce their twin sons—toddlers, now—to the noble Electors.

She tapped a foot on the duracrete floor. Netaia was too distant for casual travel. If only she were closer to home—

No, she told herself firmly. Wherever Brennen was, that was home, and this world of Tallis was where she had belonged for the last two years. Federate calendar.

Two foot-taps later, she felt Brennen's unmistakable presence on the pair bond that joined them. He'd come home for the evening. In this soundproofed safe room, she hadn't heard him brake the cirrus jet.

She glanced out through the safe room's heavy metal door and spotted him striding toward them through the training area. With him came the telepathic sense of wholeness, strength, and satisfaction, his emotions balancing hers beneath all feeling and thought. Hastily she adjusted her emotional state. She'd had disappointing news today. She didn't want to welcome him home with a sense of frustration.

Trim, with piercing blue eyes, and still wearing his midnight-blue uniform, he stepped close and wrapped both arms around her shoulders. "Mari," he said. It was the incognito name he'd given her after Federate forces took her prisoner.

And there was no deceiving her psi-gifted bond mate. Plainly, he offered comfort. Leaning into his embrace, she shut her eyes and let him smooth her concerns. She was no telepath, but together, they were strong. They'd saved each other in battle and ambush and assassination attempts. A tendril of his unspoken epsilon presence reached deep, assuring and soothing. As a particularly gifted Sentinel, he would sense the pleasure he gave her. It was the tender circle of pair-bonded marriage, fully healed after its temporary breaking.

"Thank you," she whispered.

The mental touch dissipated, his body shifted, and he turned to Shel. "Regular security check?"

"All family systems are operational, including the eps-proof locks."

Family. Firebird's own patched-together little family. Looking toward the future, not noble martyrdom. Together. "Have they said anything today about that odd energy zone approaching Netaia?" she asked.

His arms loosened as Shel drew away, and a shift of focus tickled the Brennen-place deep in her mind. "No new observations," he said, "but a new speculation. A radiation echo from some supernova out between the galactic arms."

"It couldn't be related to the Shuhr, could it? Something out of Three Zed?"

"Mikuhr," he softly corrected her. He'd sat on the committee to rename that conquered world.

"Mikuhr. Right." It was a prison planet now, holding only a remnant of villainous Shuhr. Thanks to Firebird and Brennen's close-formation attack and a supernatural geologic catastrophe, the threat Three Zed posed the Federacy was considered ended, and the world had received a new official name. Its few survivors, many of them untrained children, deserved a chance to start over.

Firebird and Brennen were growing into new roles for the Federacy, too, although Brennen had sacrificed a portion of his abilities, while Firebird carried an ugly scar over her collarbone.

And in her mind, the Shuhr world would always be Three Zed. Promoted to Battlefield Director for this Federate region, as only the second Sentinel in Federate history to hold such a high post, Brenn's number one priority was making sure that miserable volcanic world never again became a battlefield. "The blockade is holding," he said. "Mikuhr is quiet."

Shel walked toward the room's heavy exit door. "I'll leave you two," she said. "Dara and I have a surprise for you." Her footsteps receded toward the home's central lift.

Brennen's emotions shifted back to the deep concern that Firebird had felt on the pair bond as he held her. "So," he said. "Today was your deadline. I'm thinking you didn't hear from the Bishdan government."

Her spirits sank, despite her effort. Firebird was attempting to create and lead a new Federate cultural exchange. It would be glorious to knit all these worlds together by sending musicians and other artists on interworld tours, sharing their different cultures while emphasizing humanity's common dreams and hopes. Over the past two years, she'd sent proposals to twenty worlds' cultural ministries, hoping that her governmental analysis studies would guide her.

Here on Tallis, there'd been enough movement to warrant hiring an aide. But no real progress in any other planetary system. Not even on the world she once called home. Even within the cooperative Interstellar Federacy, it all came down to funding.

"No," she said simply. "Bishda didn't respond."

Another wash of deep acceptance flooded her, and she sent Brennen a grateful smile. Firebird Mari Elsbeth Domita Angelo Caldwell loathed failure. She hated it with a passion so strong that only Brenn could possibly understand. As an intelligence officer, he'd been deep in her mind immediately after her capture.

She pulled a deep breath. "I always thought I could do anything I set my mind to. Plainly, I'm not an organizer. I always despised bureaucrats. Now I am one. It's hard work."

"It subjects us to other people's judgments. I know." He sank down on a wooden stool next to the safe room's stack of folded cots and clasped his hands between his knees. His dark uniform tunic looked startlingly blue against the dull gray duracrete wall. Light from the security display glinted off the star on his shoulder.

There were eight points on that star again. One, two, three, four, five, six, seven, eight. Here, truly, she had a reason to smile. He'd been terribly psi-disabled when the Shuhr captured him. Although he never might regain the extraordinary abilities he once wielded, he'd gotten back enough epsilon-energy strength and abilities to be ranked as a Master Sentinel once more.

Firebird shut her eyes and declared, "Sometimes, when I'm trying to talk sense into some stingy governmental committee, I find myself wishing for a good, honest fight against a real enemy."

When she looked again, intense blue eyes pierced her defenses. "Be careful what you wish for, Mari. Not all your enemies will end up loving you."

"I know." For Brenn, keeping the peace and maintaining public boredom—making his own position look superfluous—constituted a splendid success.

Still, she meant it. A real fight—

On second thought, no. She didn't, and she knew Brennen well enough to know that he would not have tried to steer her thoughts. Only her feelings, and only by letting her share his emotions via the pair bond. He controlled himself uncannily well, thanks to years of Sentinel training and intelligence work.

In that moment, she sensed an odd quiver in him. He squelched it instantly.

"What?" she demanded.

"Business." He glanced aside. "Regional matters."

And she was not invited to trespass there. She'd been military. She understood need-to-know. She caught a whiff of dinner through the vent duct and let the topic drop.

Brennen must have smelled it too. "Dakma!" he exclaimed. "Ahma and Shel cooked Thyrian again."

To Firebird, who was not raised on a world nearly covered by ocean, it simply smelled like fish. Still, it cheered her to sense his delight. "Then let's go up," she said. "The boys have asked for you all day."

Brennen followed her to the lift, carefully stepping around the training room's black floor mats while maintaining that affective control. As the eldest Caldwell heir, heir to prophecies older by centuries than the Interstellar Federacy itself, he'd been privileged to hear the holy Voice now and then. It did not usually bring good news.

This time, apparently, he only had to arrange a few things: transport, escort, etc. Why should this be important to the Holy One, important enough to call him once more? Unless it had to do with that odd spatial phenomenon slowly approaching Netaia.

He leaned against the back wall as the lift rose. The ground-level subfloor seemed to sink. From uplevel came an aroma from his childhood and the roar of another generation of small boys at play.

Perhaps they should answer the Netaian regent's call and bring the twins. Apparently, despite genetic confirmation, some of her kinfolk still didn't believe that an Angelo heiress had birthed two sons. They were the first male children in that family for more than a century. Meeting the twins in person was a very Netaian request from the Netaian nobles. A military escort would be in order, of course.

He stepped off the lift and headed into a spacious living area, toward a litter of colorful toys and his sweet sons, fresh heirs to the Caldwell family's holy promises. Cautiously, he dispersed the epsilon-static shields that protected him from constantly sensing others' emotions. He mentally touched each of the boys.

There was no sign of epsilon-power activity in either of them. Not yet. Good.

He flung his arms wide.

Firebird paused just off the lift as Brennen hurried in. The house's main level had broad glasteel windows providing a view across the open spaces she loved down into Castille, capital city of this Federate region. Castille's MaxSec tower shone like a lighthouse beacon over a rippling city sea. Much closer, that scent of cooking fish emanated from the house's full kitchen.

Her nearer son steered his black-and-silver jet-scoot toward Brennen. Curly, darkening auburn hair and a sharply pointed chin: This was Kinnor, whose small throat and lungs filled the house with joyful noise. He did a pretty fair imitation of Brenn's cirrus-class racing jet. "Ahpa's home," he shouted.

Kneeling, she blocked his path. "Intercept!" she sang.

Kinnor's brother Kiel reached Brennen from the other side. Chortling at the game, Kinnor steered around Firebird and roared on. Brennen sat down, cradling Kiel on his lap. Tumbling over them both and shoving the scoot aside, Kinnor joined a three-way embrace. Kin also tried to seize a child-sized scanbook reader out of Kiel's hands.

"No, Kinnor," Shel called out of the kitchen.

Kin stopped mid-reach and raised his dark eyebrows at Brennen instead of Shel, probably sensing a fatherly reprimand. Already, Brennen could speak to them subvocally. Kinnor reached away from the scanbook and squeezed Brennen instead.

Little Kiel shoved the reader almost into Brennen's face. Firebird saw a screen full of animal images, some real and some make believe. Kiel pointed down at a three-dimensional bird and spoke. "Kiel, Ahpa?"

Firebird's heart flooded joyfully.

Ahpa. Father.

Family.

Raised by palace staff, Firebird had had no close family except her eldest sister, Carradee. No bond at all with their mother, the queen. Their father had died young, possibly her middle sister Phoena's second victim, after the "accidental" death of the second-born sister. Now, Firebird's chief battle was parenting without a loving example to fall back on. Wrangling almost-three-year-old twins gave her an intense daily workout too. Sometimes, she imagined it would be easier to die for them than to teach them to honor each other and herself. They already adored their father.

Who wouldn't?

"That's right," Brennen said, drawing her thoughts back to the present. "Kiel."

Kinnor remounted his jet-scoot and roared away. Firebird fingered the little bird-of-prey medallion that hung on a fine chain around her throat. Brennen had given it to her years ago, a remembrance of his own childhood. Its wings swept back almost to touch each other. She'd worn the adjustable chain long today. "Kiel, like you," she told her quieter son. "A fierce hunting bird."

"Like you, Ahma?" Kiel widened his sapphire-blue eyes.

"That's right. I was named for a fierce bird too." Her whole family had bird names. It was an ancient tradition. Someday the boys would probably call it ridiculous.

Kinnor circled back and butted his father's knee with the jet-scoot's nose. "Fly me, Ahpa. Please?"

Brennen raised and flexed a hand, eyeing Kinnor mock-sternly for several seconds. Brennen could play as only a Sentinel could, but his kinetic powers had been the last to heal after his disablement at Three Zed, and each time a Sentinel used his epsilon powers, those abilities aged slightly. Eventually came the dreaded, shieldless waning.

Abruptly Kin's jet-scoot did a pushback, rose off the wood floor, and then—plainly directed by Brennen's hand—it arched upward toward the broad window, a meter in the air. Kinnor shrieked joyfully and clung to the scoot's little control yoke.

Firebird glanced back at the lounger, close to the kitchen. Silvered hair pulled back in a bun, Dara Dickin Caldwell returned her glance with a wink. Brennen's mother had lived in a spiritual retreat center for two years, driven there by the Shuhr's murder of Brenn's elder brother. She'd joined them here on Tallis—temporarily, they'd all agreed. She'd proved adaptable, respectful, and helpful. So far, no one wanted to conclude her "temporary" stay.

Kinnor landed in front of Brennen and Kiel and demanded, "Again, Ahpa. Again!"

Nearly three, but still such a two-year-old.

"Come now," Shel called from the dining room through a transparent, decorative firebay. Dancing artificial flames inside the bay's chamber distorted Firebird's view of Shel's tall, muscular body.

Still mounted on his jet-scoot, Kinnor careened around the firebay out of sight. Firebird eyed the colorful chaos of toys, reminded herself that put-away time came after dinner, and scrambled to her feet. Brennen also stood, carrying his square-chinned son on his hip. The resemblance was actually uncanny. Sometimes, Firebird wondered if Kiel carried her chromosomes at all.

Brennen had hinted, lately, that perhaps their family was incomplete. He would love to raise a daughter—"another red-haired woman to love," he'd teased.

Her pregnancy memories did not tempt her to repeat the experience anytime soon, even if she didn't carry twins the next time. On the other hand, she loved Kinnor and Kiel so fiercely that sometimes it hurt.

Mayhem prevailed over dinner. The boys were now big enough for repulsor chairs. Rocking side to side, bumping the adults' stationary chairs, was the newest twin game. Brenn, Ahma-Dara, and Shel—born Thyrian, all of them—obviously relished the spiced main dish. Firebird found it tasty, but she needed the pair bond to really enjoy one more variation on fish.

A few minutes into the meal, Brennen sent Ahma-Dara a long, significant glance. Firebird straightened, startled. Subvocal communication in front of the non-gifted was considered rude, but she decided to ignore it. After all, they were a mother and son who genuinely loved each other, and they both treated her with absolute respect.

Still, when she caught them at it a second time, and then a third—with visible changes of facial expression—she frowned at Brennen and said in a warning singsong, "I'm right here."

He nodded slightly and glanced toward the master room. *We'll speak privately,* she understood, and the meaningful glances stopped.

Patience wasn't her strong suit, but this looked like a good chance to practice it, and it wasn't long before she joined Brennen in private. Apparently, she'd left the music on when she followed Shel around on the security check. She was glad. Soft, classical Netaian winds and strings always helped her feel grounded on this relatively new world.

She lowered the volume with a wave. Blue-and-green tapestry drapes framed another glasteel window in here, and her artfully hand-carved clairsa—the Netaian small harp, her last treasure from home—stood on a pedestal behind a waist-high, twin-proof barrier. Its curving upper arch, shaped from a rare reddish Netaian wood, carried a design of intertwined knots. Half a decade ago, she'd been almost professional on the instrument. These days, she mostly used it for lullabies.

She kicked off her shoes, took a seat on a simple wooden side chair, and demanded, "All right. What was that?"

He sat down on the foot of the bed and ran a hand over his pale-russet hair. "As it happens," he said, "the one Federate world where I have not made an official inspection in my new capacity is Netaia."

After centuries of isolation, her home world had finally voted to join the Federacy. She waited for him to continue.

He stretched down and pulled off a boot. "It's been assumed that I already have a working relationship with your Marshal Burkenhamn, and that the inspection could wait for him to complete remilitarization."

"And coincidentally," she suggested, "Netaia is being approached by something the physicists haven't explained." She eyed him. "Or is this for me? For the cultural exchange? Even if I could get there in person, I'm not sure what I could accomplish. Or," she wondered aloud, "is it for the boys? Are we changing our minds about Regent Kenhing's invitation?"

He addressed the other boot and leaned back, flexing his feet. "Getting one other world to commit to your program could initiate momentum. As you've said."

She drew a deep, frustrated breath. "We've had this conversation. I'm not exactly comfortable subjecting Kiel and Kin to the Netaian insanity that almost sacrificed me."

"I understand." He looked down at the longweave carpet, then back at the door they'd closed behind them. Obviously, he was waiting for her to think past her first reaction.

The music changed key, and she knew that he had correctly focused on his responsibilities, as well as her cultural exchange. Until she could establish that program, all her glories were in the past. She even wondered if, in the Mighty Singer's eternal plans, she'd been spared for a cross-cultural purpose. Spared from her wastling destiny, to die young after her sister's children secured the succession. Spared, too, in space-and-atmosphere battlefields over Veroh and Three Zed.

She eyed Brennen again, guessing that this had to do with that quiver she'd felt down in the safe room. "Tell me."

He half smiled. "I heard the Voice again. One word. *Go.*"

"Oh." It was almost a squeak. The Angelo family's only faith had been reliance on the so-called holy Powers. These attributes had been appropriated by the ten noble families to control Netaia's wealth, but those days were over. Firebird served the Eternal Speaker now, the Mighty Singer she had learned to love. Hearing his holy Voice was the rarest of privileges. Even among Brennen's gifted people, only he and high-priestly Shamarr Dickin had the gift of hearing it clearly. So far, the holy Voice had only called him into deadly peril.

"Just . . . *go?*" she asked with a little shiver. "No explanation?"

Another slight nod. "That is his way."

True. The Mighty Singer left him to work out the details. "So what was that between you and Ahma-Dara, back at the table?"

He looked and felt slightly embarrassed. "I asked if she'd come along and take care of the boys, so that we could travel a bit once we're there. Visit old friends, like Prince Tel. Spend a few days at your old residence."

"She's willing?"

"She's curious. After all the tri-D images she studied when I'd married a Netaian princess . . ." He trailed off with a teasing smile.

"Don't call me that." She threw a small blue pillow.

He caught it midair with a flick of two fingers. It hovered a moment between them before tumbling onto the carpet, and his broad smile mirrored the way she felt. He'd suffered a terrible loss of abilities two years ago, and he'd worked hard to get his kinetics again.

"I'm not sure I'm ready to take them into possible danger," she said. On the other hand, Brennen probably believed he could protect them better than anyone else. He was probably right. Again.

She rocked the wooden chair. Maybe this time, the Mighty Singer simply was grounding them in their new administrative roles. Or possibly, she would get that wish: a good, honest fight against a real enemy. She still had several enemies among the noble Electors, to say nothing of the chance that a few of the renegade Shuhr might have made it off Three Zed.

Still, even establishing better cross-cultural relations among Federate worlds seemed too small—too minor—to warrant a holy call. Likelier, this pertained to the mystery approaching the Whorl from deep space. In that case, she was not at all sure she wanted to bring Kinnor and Kiel.

But to see home again . . . her former home, so distant . . .

"I will arrange the military inspection and our travel," Brennen told her. "You can go ahead with your culture-exchange plans. This could be our last easy opportunity to get back to Netaia in person."

She nodded soberly. He was leaving their greatest parental concern unspoken. His kindred's capacity for mental gifts could become discernible as early as age three, and there was a significant chance that one or both boys had inherited a dangerous mutation that had arisen in Firebird's family, a family that—to everyone's surprise—also had a touch of psi-gifted ancestry.

He folded his hands around one knee. "I think you can convince more of the Electors if they see that you care enough to meet face-to-face and present our sons." She heard paternal pride in his voice. "You do have allies there. *If,*" he stressed, "you believe you should go." She felt an odd amusement in him. "Anyway, it was a holy call. I don't refuse those. I can't. You of all people wouldn't resist out of fear."

"Not on my own behalf. I will not endanger Kinnor and Kiel. What else did your mother have to say?"

"She also feels it is important. But she did have two conditions."

"Oh?"

"She does not want to sleep in the palace."

Firebird laughed. "That should be easy. What else?"

The Brennen-place in her heart and mind focused on a lower, sadder note. "While we are off Tallis," he said, "Ahma wishes to visit the sanctuary world. To meet her granddaughter."

Firebird met his eyes, answering his melancholy with her own sympathy. Over a year ago, the cruel Shuhr had tried to entrap Brennen by cloning his skin cells to create a child who was genetically his daughter. Although he'd played no role in that little girl's conception, he had saved her life, along with the victimized Shuhr mother.

"I understand," Firebird said softly. "I would like to meet her, too." She pushed up out of the chair and waved off the music. "Very well. We are going back to Netaia."

2: NETAIA
mezzo piano, somewhat softly

The Tallis-Netaia run took nineteen days via governmental transport. The twins adapted well to travel after hard acceleration eased off, and they didn't seem to mind the odd, vibrational sensation of slip-state, traveling with every atom of their bodies turned sideways to normal space so the transport could exceed light speed.

A passenger from the diplomatic corps had also accepted Brennen's offer of free transportation, graciously tolerating the twins' soprano arguments and enthusiastic sing-alongs. Brennen often extended his privileges to cultivate goodwill for the Sentinel kindred. Sentinels were respected but feared, and Brennen was going to be the first Sentinel to serve on the Federate High Command someday. Firebird just knew it. He set ambition aside when need arose, but someday, all the Whorl would honor him. If that was pride, transferred to him instead of herself, so be it.

Anyway, Ahma-Dara agreed with her.

Cued by the pilot to take accel/decel seats in the forward lounge, she harnessed in for the long-awaited transition back into normal space. She'd taken an aisle seat so that Ahma-Dara—with Kiel double-harnessed on her lap—could see out the viewport on their left. This way, if Kiel had the same fears he'd experienced during launch, Dara could gently put him into the Sentinels' tardema-sleep.

Moments after they secured themselves and locked down their seats, a small portion of the bulkhead next to Dara seemed to dissolve. Delighted, Firebird gazed past her into a rounded rectangle of light and dark chaos. Here in quasi-orthogonal space, star-pricks turned to kaleidoscopic streaks. They wove and blended in pale-pastel shades, predominantly blue.

Ahma-Dara sighed. Her professional work as a psi-medical nurse had not required much spaceflight. She'd only traveled back and forth to Sanctuary.

"Ooh!" Kiel scattered handprints on the viewport. "Zahma, look!"

Ahma-Dara—"Ahpa's Ahma" had proved unpronounceable, so she became "Zahma"—smilingly added a fingerprint.

"Secure your harnesses," the pilot's voice chanted from overhead. "Drop point in thirty seconds, mark."

"It is beautiful," Firebird breathed.

Behind her, Brenn answered, "Truly," while Kinnor exclaimed, "Wow, wow, wow!"

This was a multiplied delight, all of them experiencing drop point together. Across the wide aisle to Firebird's right, Shel sat with Brennen's own Sentinel bodyguard, his second cousin, Lieutenant Colonel Uri Harris. Rather aristocratic and raised in political circles, Uri had befriended the diplomatic passenger during their passage—Glin-Erris Coll, nephew of the Regional Council's elegant Head.

Firebird turned back to the viewport, not wanting to miss a moment. The dancing swarm of sky streaks wriggled and whirled. Maybe the Mighty Singer perceived space and time like this. She imagined a choir of Bright Ones, his holy messengers, singing praises in complex harmonies like the visual array beyond their viewport. A line from one of the Adorations sprang into her mind. *Holy, three times holy!*

"Ten seconds," the pilot's voice rang through the lounge. "All passengers, assume and maintain a relaxed position. This is important for your comfort."

And didn't she know it. Back at the NPN Academy, cadets had done drop point while bracing themselves. Just once. She'd ached for days.

She imagined herself as an invertebrate. At least this wouldn't be as violent as combat drop point.

"Three. Two. Mark."

She fell against her flight harness. In a fighter, the harnesses hadn't been anywhere near this plush. Kiel grunted softly, but he seemed calmer this time.

The pressure ended. Finally able to turn her head and look out again, she smiled. Their pilot would have left slip-state in a zone precisely charted for this maneuver. The star streaks focused into familiar pinpoints and Netaia's largest moon.

"Ah." Ahma-Dara's voice rose and fell as if she were singing. "Amazing."

The craft rotated for its decel orbits. The magnificent arc of Firebird's homeworld filled the viewport. She tried to twist her body, stretching her harness. "Look, Kiel," she said. "Here's where Ahma was born."

He stared out the viewport, rapt. Learning, always learning.

At the planet's far north, Arctica glimmered white on the dayside and then dark, icy gray-blue under starlight. Within moments, they circled back into daylight, and she made out the long shadows of the mountainous North Reach at sunset. This far north, might she spot rocky Hunter Height in the Aerie Range? No, here came the sea again. Looking out and aft, she spotted the slender nose of their military escort ship. Another memory surged: dropping slip-shields over Federate Veroh, harnessed snugly into the fightercraft in which she intended to die.

She'd been so proud, so very proud.

Giving her head a shake, she touched her broad armrest. What had happened while they traveled incommunicado in slip-state? At the top of the little screen that appeared, her sister Carradee's message took priority. She offered palace accommodation in Phoena's old rooms, as before. Their request for on-base housing had also been accepted, details to follow.

On the pair bond came a pulse of attentive concern. Brenn would fill her in, depending on his messages' security levels. *Patience*, she reminded herself, looking down again. It might be an update on that mysterious energy zone.

Prince Tel, her sister Phoena's widower, confirmed that her presence was expected at an emergency Electoral meeting this very afternoon. The boys would not be presented until a later date. Also, her legal counsel—the aged and courageous Solicitor Merriam—sent greetings.

She straightened and stretched her back. Fortunately, the governmental transport was so comfortable, including a gradual shift of their day-cycles to Citangelo time, that she felt rested enough to face the noble Electors. They had probably never read the cultural exchange proposal she sent a year ago. She would present it again, in person, this very day. Then, she could show the boys where she'd grown up. And, maybe, the Holy One would show Brenn why he was called.

The transport kept dropping, decelerating toward the North

Continent's eastern shore. Kinnor emitted an occasional whoop, and Brennen's subvocal buzz of concentration remained strong. They swooped out over vast Middlesea and the blue-and-white swirl of an ocean storm.

Hearing a soft cabin-wide click of unlocking seat swivels, she turned hers aisle-ward. Brennen already sat facing Uri and Shel, leaving Kinnor to gape outward from the window seat. Wordlessly, Brennen passed her his secure interlink.

Priority-One alert, she read. *To General Caldwell, B.D., via DeepScan.*

DeepScan still was the only way to outrun faster-than-light messenger ships with information. Precious few places used it, including Regional Command back on Tallis. She read rapidly. Apparently, while their transport traveled in slip-state, that mysterious energy zone had resolved, on Federate scans, into a single unidentified spacecraft with uncannily powerful energy shields.

Regional Command had also picked up a garbled transmission. Brennen played it for her. It sounded like a synthesized female voice. "Distress, please . . . delegation to . . . low on power . . . ation."

She raised her eyes to Brennen's. "A ship in distress?" she asked. "From out of the dust zone—maybe even across the void in another arm? Are they even human?" Instantly, she wished she hadn't asked that last question. On Netaia, children inhaled a fear of imaginary non-humans with the very air they breathed.

"They use human language," he said gently. "And we never have seen any sign that the Holy One created other intelligent life."

It made sense. All Firebird's life, she'd heard rumors that other human settlers had survived outside the known, settled Whorl, an area rich with G-class stars. A peaceful society might have sent out an exploratory craft.

Across the aisle, Uri's and Shel's faces also looked serious. Plainly, Brennen had already communicated subvocally with them.

"Just one ship." Uri's voice had a cultured lilt. "That's no menace."

"Not yet," Firebird suggested. "But what was that about unusually powerful shielding? Something more advanced than our technology, something that made one ship look like . . . like a mysterious energy zone?"

Brennen raised a dark eyebrow.

Maybe Netaia was threatened, after all.

She shot off a prayer. *So, is this why you called him?* A shiver danced across her shoulders. The Mighty One cared for all people. She'd sung that dozens of times. All people. That had to include mysterious arrivals.

Shel glanced aft, toward the diplomatic guest. Ambassador Glin-Erris Coll still sat staring out his viewport. Firebird couldn't blame him. "They could be refugees on a generation ship," Shel speculated, "or a war party setting a trap. Either way, we appear to have a first contact."

"Regional Command's going to full alert on Tallis," Brennen said, "and they've notified the High at Elysia. I'm to focus Netaia's long-range scanners along a particular vector, but I suspect that's already been done."

And undoubtedly, this meant setting her exchange program aside. Trying to sound cheerful, she said, "I guess we're headed to the base, not the palace."

Brenn lifted a hand. "I'll send you on to Carradee as soon as we pay our respects to Marshal Burkenhamn. Refreshing your mission is one of our immediate priorities, and you are expected."

Glory, she loved this man. "But once Netaia's on board," she declared, "I'll be with you on this new discovery. Whether we're on diplomacy or defense."

"Diplomacy, I hope," Uri said. He too glanced aft, toward the ambassador. Once again, Firebird spotted Uri's resemblance to his cousin Brennen in their fine cheekbones.

Brennen glanced at her. "Now, Mari, please excuse us." He leaned toward Uri and Shel.

There was nothing rude about their subvocalizing this time. She imagined Brennen bringing his impressive communication, discernment, and command skills into a first contact. During these months at Regional Command, he had definitely grown into the higher level of authority.

Warmed by the thought, she brought her seat back around. They were dropping over an uninhabited part of the North Continent, keeping the boom and roar of their re-entry away from cities. Judging by the clumps of wild filomen trees in full orange bloom, it was springtime below.

Netaia. Lush and beautiful, a masterpiece of terraforming. Its resources were estimated at almost a quarter of the Federacy's.

"Ahma?" Kiel pointed out the view panel. "What's that bare stripe down in the trees?"

Leaning in over Dara and Kiel, she glimpsed what he'd seen. "That's a firebreak, Kiel. Some trees are cut down to protect the rest of the forest—or people's homes—if there's ever a dangerous fire."

"Oh," he said. Always observing. What would he grow up to be? Did she dare hope that there on his grandmother's lap sat Boh-Dabar, the promised Word to Come, who would renew all worlds, and who was prophesied to be born into Brennen's family?

For now, she must simply treat him as a serene, intelligent child.

They cruised over another cloudbank. The transport's shadow shrank and re-grew crazily. Behind her, Kinnor whooped again.

They would buckle back in soon. The civilian spaceport, where they would touch down, adjoined the Planetary Naval base.

To Firebird's delight, the on-base quarters they were offered adjoined the spacious home of First Marshal Devair Burkenhamn and his wife Norann. "Our children are grown and gone," Norann sent to Firebird's interlink. "I would love to hear young voices again." Dara, Kiel, and Kinnor went there directly. Meanwhile, Firebird and Brennen headed for the three-level military headquarters building.

A black-haired young woman wearing a second major's single ruby on each side of her cobalt-blue collar escorted Firebird, Brennen, Uri, and Shel to the circular command and control center. Its instrument walls, mostly darkened or shrouded, surrounded a tall tri-D well, and it had an odd odor. Abruptly Firebird realized that after breathing cleansed shipboard air for nineteen days, she was catching normal scents of cleaning chemicals, subtronics, and the staff of controllers and techs. Soon, she would stop noticing. She'd been honorably discharged from Netaian military service at Brennen's request, but obviously, the alert level was low. First Marshal Burkenhamn was still allowing her access to this secure area. The tall, muscular marshal also greeted her by her highest-achieved rank, Second Commander, which put a warm glow in her middle. The silver fringe of the big man's hair had not thinned or receded from the last time she saw him.

The mysterious arrival was immediately discussed, but even the marshal had little more information than Brennen's communiqué, which was probably several days old.

Netaia did have current scanning data. "Probably about two days out." Marshal Burkenhamn tapped the transparent tri-D well at the room's center. Inside that two-meter-wide cylinder, she saw the familiar green spheres of Netaia and its eleven companion worlds, surrounded by the silver dots of satellites and deep-space modules, and the gold pinpoints of friendly cross-space ships. A single red bogey hovered north-spinward of the Netaian system, well beyond two semitransparent, concentric globes indicating distances from the home world. "There's time to mount the personal rendezvous that they seem to be requesting, but just barely." The marshal's clipped-vowel Netaian accent sounded both strange and delightfully familiar to Firebird. "Long-range comm would be easier, but they're not responding to requests for more information. There was an ebb in that remarkable energy shielding when they sent the distress call, but the shields are back up again. Apparently, that shielding is what we picked up months ago."

Firebird glanced back over her shoulder. Their young escort had lingered behind a seated sensors tech, not far behind Brennen. Uri and Shel also hung back, next to the guarded double doors. The Netaian major called, "Their FTL drive could be quite different from ours too."

"They seem to speak Old Colonial," Firebird observed. "Maybe they monitored our transmissions and broadcasts as they approached."

Brennen gazed into the tri-D well. "They claim to be in distress, but we must always consider the possibility that this is a ruse. We should send senior representatives. I shall certainly volunteer. We also traveled with—"

Marshal Burkenhamn turned toward him. "You can't, General. The Federacy has invested too much in you now. You've got the authority to do pretty much whatever else you like, but not the authority to risk your life in potentially precarious situations."

Firebird bristled and backstepped away from the tri-D well. "That would be a very silly waste of our most gifted individual."

Brennen raised a hand. "I'm afraid he's right." He saluted the marshal.

"Sirs?" called the sensors tech. "You'll want to see this." The tech wore Carolinian khaki. This really was a Federate installation now, mostly manned by Netaians in cobalt blue, but also staffed by soldiers from other worlds.

Firebird sent Brennen a *We'll talk later* look and fell silent as they and the marshal hustled toward a large, square subtronics board. A tri-dimensional image filled this too.

The Carolinian tech pointed at the center screen. Immediately, a smaller zone magnified, with a greenish blur at one edge.

"Subspace detail," the marshal said. "There appears to be something else coming on behind the bogey that dropped out of slip-state."

Brennen frowned slightly. "It looks to be just slower than the point ship. Very loose formation. Makes sense if they're losing power."

Firebird considered the image. "I see two more objects. Not very many, are there?"

"Too early to tell," Sensors insisted.

Whatever was coming, this seemed suspicious. Firebird stared at the image. There could be still more of them behind these three.

Marshal Burkenhamn rested both of his large hands on the sensors desk surface. On the pair bond, Brennen felt so alert that it was getting hard to concentrate. "Could that be an . . ." She caught herself before speaking. *Invasion fleet? A decoy, asking for assistance?* These senior officers would have more accurate guesses, and she didn't wish to sound foolish.

Brennen straightened and addressed her by rank. This was going to be an order, whether or not he phrased it that way. "Commander Caldwell, I'm sending you on to the palace. We need to clear the room of non-active duty personnel. Take Shel, and I'll see you at the Electoral meeting."

She understood. The weight of this higher level of command had fallen on him with his promotion. "They offered us Phoena's suite again," she told him. "I'll see if I can snatch a moment with Carradee. What would you think of spending one night there?" After all, it had been her home for twenty Netaian years.

"Yes." His kiss was only a distracted peck, but he broke uniform protocol to give it.

She saluted both men. Shel stepped into position behind her.

"We have a government groundcar for you," the Netaian aide said. "Follow me."

Brennen watched Mari and Shel pass the door guards. Mari's stride was brisk and determined on the floor tiles, and to his satisfaction, the guards saluted her. Still, he felt strangely disappointed. Marshal Burkenhamn had accurately quoted standard procedure, which he disliked but understood.

He'd already risked himself more than a senior officer ought. Friend or foe approaching, his job would be here on the ground.

He turned back to the glowing tri-D well and the massive marshal. Somehow, this man had squeezed into a tagwing fightercraft. Did he too miss the adrenaline rush of battle-speed flight?

"So," Brennen said, "these strangers seem to be requesting a delegation. We came with a member of the diplomatic corps." *Thank you, Holy One.* "We must send effective communicators, to see if they actually need our help."

Marshal Burkenhamn stared into the well. "Yes."

"My right hand, Lieutenant Colonel Uri Harris, has mind-access specialist training. Sending him will ensure a truthful exchange." Brennen glanced around the command center again. Netaia had been demilitarized as a punitive measure after they invaded Federate Veroh. He'd ordered Netaia's full remilitarization, and he did like and respect Marshal Burkenhamn. The rebuilt base's tech upgrades also looked excellent.

They studied the blurred zone, now appearing in the well as a double-lobed red cloud behind the red bogey. Brennen wished he could will it to focus. Subspace was hard to interpret. "Shielding," he said, "is purely defensive. What kind of weapons do these people usually need to defend against?" On his orders, an experimental second escort craft had shadowed their civilian transport to Netaia. It was already hangared and shrouded in a secure area, and he'd seen no sign of its arrival on the sensors, which was good. He had mentioned it to no one here but Uri and Shel, and they were both under Sentinel voice-command not to speak of it. Even within Regional Command, Sentinels protected some information.

Keeping military secrets from Mari was among his more difficult jobs.

"We need to be ready," the marshal declared.

Brennen straightened his back. "We don't need to be hasty," he said, "but yes, we need to be ready. The Ituri and Carolinian navies are close. I can request additional defense." How long might it take backup to arrive? Netaia's splendid isolation made it vulnerable. He did a mental calculation and did not like the rough answer: upward of two ten-day dekia, even utilizing the FTL Messenger service.

"We still don't know these are hostiles." Marshal Burkenhamn pointed at the blurred red cloud. "But in a best-case scenario, this second group could also need refuel. Also, that shielding must require an insane amount of fuel."

"Yes." Brennen faced his subordinate. "Marshal, for this official inspection, I want to observe how quickly you can bring the Netaian Planetary Navy to full combat readiness."

First Marshal Burkenhamn saluted crisply. "You may start timing us now." He strode to the comm station and started giving call-up orders.

Brennen eyed the red bogey. *Holy One, these too are people of your creation. Give us the wisdom to keep from making them enemies, if they need our help.*

Firebird stepped out of the government groundcar onto the palace's long, white front portico, feeling weirdly vulnerable here without Brennen at her side. Shel already stood at the back of the car, probably glad to be working guard duty instead of serving as household staff. Two red-collared House Guards, sworn to protect the Angelo family, backed away from their pillars to open the tall east-wing doors.

It had been so long! Her mother, the queen, had died during the Veroh war. Her elder sister, Phoena, died at the hands of the Shuhr, and so did her eldest sister Carradee's firstborn daughters, Iarlet and Kessaree. The former regent had forced Carradee to abdicate in favor of a third child, still unborn at that time. Until Carradee birthed a fourth child, Firebird stood first in line to the Netaian throne . . . not that the noble Electors would ever give it to her, and not that she wanted it. She had a new life. With Brennen.

Pausing, she let the citrus scent of blooming fayya trees call up a cascade of memory: Academy studies, music lessons, learning to fly, and games with other wastlings, always watching over their shoulders for the other noble houses' heirs with hazing on their minds.

After savoring the trees' scent a few moments longer, and admiring a row of scarlet-and-gold marit blossoms along the white marble façade, she stepped into the old familiar foyer. High overhead, five ancient chandeliers still shed pale golden light on the walls' ornate moldings. Centered at pride of place, on a florally carved leta-wood easel, stood a new portrait of former Queen Carradee, cradling a somber infant in Angelo-scarlet velvette, her tiny chest crossed by a gold sash that she might have actually worn for ten seconds. Little Queen Rinnah Elsbeth also wore a miniature crown, probably painted in by the artist who'd made the infant seem to glow with a faint scarlet light. *Nicely done,*

Firebird observed, feeling slightly disrespectful for having arrived in a loose gray traveling suit.

So many memories—but so many victories since she left Netaia. She had no intention of staying. Shaking tension from her shoulders, she glanced left. Across the foyer's white marble floor loomed the Electoral chamber's golden double doors, framed by scarlet-and-gold liveried Redjackets in their weird half gloves. These Electoral Police had haunted every wastling's nightmares. Heir limitation was outlawed now, thanks to the Federacy. They never would inject her with Tactol again.

"My lady?" A tall man, whose midsection strained the white cummerbund of a palace servitor, strutted toward her and bowed. She answered his bow with a proper nod. How quickly palace formality came back, and how disappointing not to be met by her old friend Paskel. "I shall take you to see Her Majesty," the new man said.

"Thank you." She resisted the urge to ask what happened to Paskel. She had little time before the Electoral meeting. Hopefully, Paskel had been released from servitor status to low-common class, or even into Netaia's high-common majority. "Please have my luggage taken up to our accommodations." He signaled another servitor, who stood in the shadows.

Firebird and Shel followed the tall man past another pair of House Guards, up a curving stair and down a long, marble-walled hallway. They passed, on their right, the familiar door of her childhood rooms. Old habits and a jab of homesickness almost steered her inside. At Phoena's former apartment, Shel left her to run a security check on the rooms where they planned to stay the night. The servitor stayed with Shel.

Firebird walked on alone.

Up the hall, past another door and beyond the long stretch of apartments where Carradee had lived as crown princess, two four-point-star Sentinels guarded the largest suites. They saluted as Firebird approached. She returned the gesture. One of them pressed the panel to open a heavily carved wood door. "Please wait in the sitting room," he said.

Firebird appreciated their presence. For one thing, they eased the tension she still felt about entering her mother's long-forbidden quarters. Additionally, she could not forget that Shuhr had attacked Carradee here during her brief reign. Some of those Shuhr renegades had undoubtedly been off Three Zed when its judgment fell. They would stop at nothing to protect themselves. Hopefully, they would stay safely hidden for a long, long time.

Carradee's recent trouble conceiving another heir was probably behind the Electorate's rationale for acknowledging Kinnor and Kiel as Angelo descendants. Poor Carrie already had lost one family to the Shuhr. Little Queen Rinnah would be the most closely guarded child in Netaian history, but Kinnor and Kiel should be acknowledged, anyway.

How strange to stand here, wearing a high rank and hoping to give it away.

She took a seat on a dark-green upholstered chair near a slender pole lamp. Carradee's sitting room had the spicy perfume of cinnarulias. On four spiral-legged side tables sat several crystal vases full of those enormous white flowers. Each window was crossed and framed by sheer pullback curtains that matched the flowers, and a collection of landscape paintings created false windows on several marble walls.

One of the inner doors opened. Firebird stood.

It was Carradee's husband, Prince Daithi Drake-Angelo. His thick brown curls and prominent widow's peak made his round face look almost heart shaped. She'd last seen him at the Sentinels' sanctuary world, confined to a mobility chair. It was wonderful to see him up on his feet again. "No, no. Please sit down," he said. "Welcome back, Lady Fi. Dee is giving Her Majesty the breast, which gives me the opportunity to deliver a long-overdue thanks."

"Oh?" After the Shuhr attacked them here, Daithi and Carradee had fled to the Sanctuary. There, they'd declared themselves Inquirers into the Sentinels' ancient faith. He probably meant that. "It's Brenn you'd want to thank."

"No. I spoke with Prince Tel some time back." He sat down across from her, the deep blue of his casual shirt a perfect complement to the conservative upholstery.

Puzzled, she said, "Yes?"

"He tells me that years ago, you and one of your friends helped our wastling brother Alef leave Netaia. Apparently, Bennett has known about it for years."

She went cold. Geis refusal—the rejection of that noble destiny of an early death—had been a capital crime under the old law of heir limitation.

So was helping a wastling escape that fate. Had the new regent known but never accused her? What had he seen? Or heard? How did he know?

And might Daithi accuse her now? All things considered, she probably was safe, but she might as well answer honestly. Still, she stumbled for words. "Your other brother . . . knew all along?"

"Apparently so."

She took a breath. She'd rather liked the whole Drake family. Now, she liked Bennett Drake—now known as Regent Kenhing—even better, and maybe she owed him her life. Few wastlings had survived the days of heir limitation.

Daithi went on, "Bennett felt the traditional punishment was too harsh simply for saving a life, however extraneous that life may have been."

She still felt chilled. She and her wastling friend Corey had been so, so careful. They could have been publicly executed, or at best, ordered to suicide in private. Daken Erwin and his coterie of young heirs would have drunk South Continent wine to celebrate.

She found words. "Have you . . . ever . . . heard from Alef and Jisha?"

"No, no. Have you?"

She shook her head. Apparently, Daithi's brother and his commoner bride had vanished effectively.

Good for them.

The inner door opened. Another servitor peeped through. "Her Former Majesty will see you now." Behind the servitor came Carradee, taller than Firebird and carrying the beautiful extra weight of a nursing mother. "Come see her." Carradee smiled. "She's sleeping now. I hope."

A white canopy embroidered with cuddly looking animals surmounted Her Majesty's padded crib. Inside lay a chubby toddler in a soft sleepsuit, one fist clenched against her mouth. "Ah," Firebird sighed. "Congratulations, Carrie." Rinnah Elsbeth Angelo, acclaimed Queen before she was even born, lay dreaming, ignorant of the pressures that would fall on her one day. Firebird didn't envy that little one's future, but Carrie and Daithi would raise her with faith and love. She wished Brennen were here to wish them well too. Later on this trip, Kinnor and Kiel could meet their cousin the queen—as well as their half sister at Sanctuary, much later, at Ahma-Dara's request.

On base right now, Brenn was helping prepare for a possible first encounter. Even if the new arrivals were friendly, how might all this affect

Carradee and Rinnah? Not immediately, or so she could hope. *Please, Mighty Singer. Let Carrie have some peace. And protect my sons.*

Carradee stepped closer to Daithi, who clasped her hand. "You're going to talk with the Electorate today," Carradee said. "Are you ready to dress for them?"

"Of course."

Carradee smiled again. "Dress whites or long scarlet?"

Amused, Firebird said, "Scarlet." She fingered the little bird-of-prey medallion on its fine gold chain. "With this tucked inside. But they gave me the Triple Arrow after Three Zed, and I'm going to wear that in plain sight. To remind them I nearly died for them. Twice now."

"You always had such courage." Carradee moved to a dark fayya-wood credenza. Something limp and blue lay atop it. A pair of formal gloves, maybe, from the size of it. "I have saved this," Carradee said, "and I want you to wear it. I want you to remind them that you're just one step from . . . well, you know." She shook out a length of fabric. It was a noblewoman's sash, edged with the gold that signified royalty.

"Carrie." Firebird stepped back, barely missing the crib. "I can't take this. You were Mother's heiress."

Carradee shook her head firmly. "You can, and you must. There will be women and men down there who would have taken your life without a second thought. You served Netaia with honor, and in your new royal rank, you are here to weave us into a larger reality. We are grateful."

Firebird carefully took the sash in both hands. The glowing blue fabric felt creamy soft all the way to its gold-threaded edges. She swallowed the urge to protest again. "All—all right, then. I'll wear it, but only for you."

"Go," Carradee told her. "You've just got time to dress before the session begins."

"Will I see you there?"

Carradee laughed. "I gave up all that when I abdicated, and I don't miss it. Oh, and by the way, my will is still locked up in the courts. I'm sorry. Solicitor Merriam is still working on it. I never dreamed I'd be back, you see, when I wrote it."

Firebird felt awkward. It had been over a Netaian year. "The fortune should be Rinnah's anyway," she confessed, "although owning a venue for my cultural exchange would be a blessing."

"Done." Carradee extended a hand. "We shall not be stingy."

Firebird clasped it. "At the moment," she said, "all that can wait." Since Carrie and Daithi probably hadn't heard the latest news, Firebird filled them in.

"Your general and our marshal will take care of us," Daithi said confidently. "We aren't concerned."

Was he saying that to reassure Carrie? Probably. *Carradee the Good*, she'd been called. And *Carradee the Kind*. Their middle sister, Phoena, had called her less gracious names.

And there was no need for everyone to worry. Not yet, anyway. "The Holy One will watch over us," Firebird added. Clutching the sash, she hurried out past the door guards and back up the hall to bathe and dress.

The Erwin family's lead groundcar had the smoothest possible ride, but Grand Duke Daken Erwin felt as if something unpleasant had crawled over him. He and his father had been fighting since the midday meal. "Wastling," he declared, sweeping his black sateen breeches with a manicured hand, "to be seated on the Electorate. Her children will be royal heirs." Not his own. As a second born, he was not entitled to reproduce. But his elder sister Valora had birthed the requisite two heirs and two wastlings.

Still, Daken meant to marry soon. Furthermore, he still believed in heir limitation.

Stroking his beard, he eyed his father. First Lord Baron Bualin Erwin sat on the vast groundcar's opposite lounger. His breeches and orange-trimmed tunic gleamed dark against the richly tapestried cushions. He slumped over his jeweled walking stick. "I dislike it too." The senior Erwin's voice had gone raspy, but a youth-preserving medical implant kept him looking fairly young and moderately vigorous. His dark brown hair might even be called bushy. "We must observe protocol," he said.

"The Electorate is not powerless," Daken insisted. "Forget the Federates' policies. We can refuse to seat her."

His father harrumphed. "I know my duty. I shall do it. But we will prevail, Daken. Do nothing rash."

Daken might not be eligible to father his House's next heirs, but he was entitled to have things his own way. "We could disbar her . . . her offspring," he said distastefully. "Her blood." Wastlings never should reproduce, not unless double or triple tragedy struck the heirs of their

Houses. He cringed, imagining himself bowing to that wastling's children, sired by an offworlder he despised. A mind-crawler. The idea was almost obscene. "We can refuse to acknowledge them," he repeated, "if you won't refuse . . . her." The little Lady Fire-brat had often flaunted tradition. Hardly anyone else knew, but enrolling at the Planetary Naval Academy had saved her from a fatal hazing "accident." Heirs were not technically allowed to kill wastlings, but he and two fellow heirs had planned the event in gruesome detail, one night over a little too much joy-blossom wine.

The memory raised a brief smile.

His father leaned toward him. "We will not refuse to seat her. Let me explain this again. If we Electors alter Netaia's noble traditions, we risk losing them. Traditions keep our family strong, Daken. Show me that you remember that."

Crossing his arms, Daken stared out the rear window into the parkland surrounding the Angelo palace. His sister Valora followed in a second car. Trees, trees. Too many trees blocked the view. He wished he were back at the estate, running his hunting dogs.

The First Lord droned on, tilting his chin to address the car's figured ceiling panel. "So long as there are living Angelo descendants, they must be ranked first. Living descendants," he repeated, narrowing his eyes.

Living. For now. The car made the last turn, approaching the palace's columned portico, and Daken Erwin straightened his blue sash of honor. Back at the estate, servitor-class employees were scurrying to prepare and stock the bunker and underground kennels. Even if unknown aliens wiped the Federates off Netaia, along with the low-commoners who couldn't afford such preparedness, the Erwins—briefly demoted after the tragic Veroh war—would emerge triumphant again.

They braked in front of the portico. "Make me proud, Daken-Oaken," said the First Lord.

Tempted to sneer at the outdated childhood nickname, Daken settled for a dignified frown. "Wastling," he muttered, clenching and unclenching his fingers.

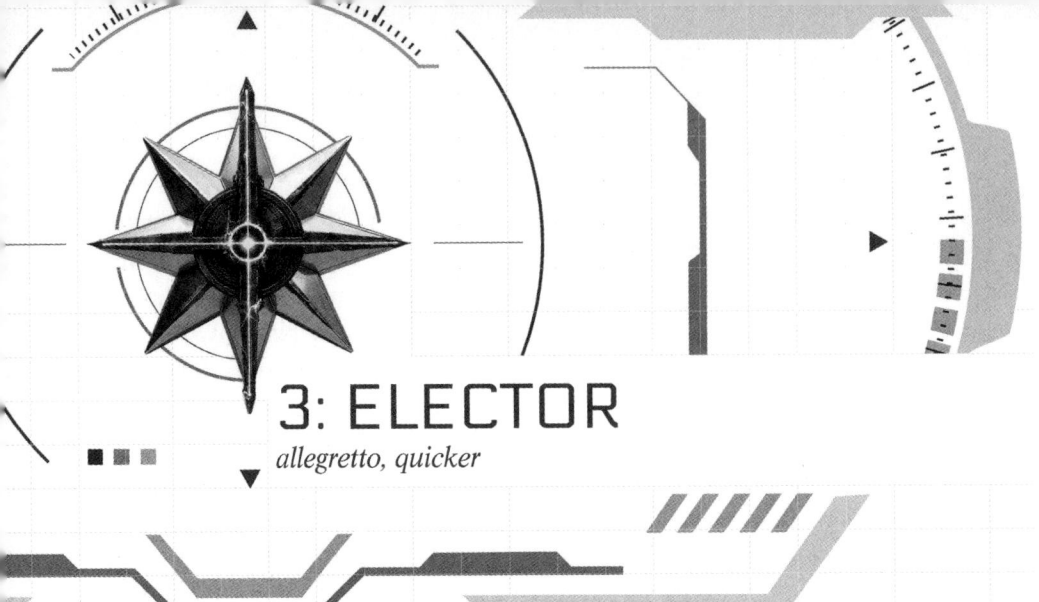

3: ELECTOR
allegretto, quicker

Two red-jacketed Electoral Policemen swept open the golden doors, and Firebird stepped onto the chamber's gold-shot black marble floor. Slowing her normally quick steps to a formal pace, she drank in the moment. Even as a wastling, she had been raised to hold her head high, proud of her impending self-sacrifice. Brennen's people had warned her that she would battle self-pride all her life. It darkened her love and trust for the Eternal Speaker. Still, that Angelo self-pride had kept her from poisoning her soul with bitterness at the unfairness of a wastling's destiny.

A U-shaped high table stood at the Electoral chamber's far end. Most of the seats were already occupied. Whispers swept the table as noble Electors' heads turned. They'd never officially draped her with the crown princess's sash. Was she offending them?

She half hoped so.

Clashing perfumes scented the room. Beneath the domed white ceiling, bas-relief wall panels bordered gilded pillars. As usual for a closed session, the tri-D newsnet transcorders wore black shrouds. A line of waiting chairs had been placed mid-floor below the high table, their backrests crusted in more gilt. First Marshal Burkenhamn stood next to one of those chairs, easy to spot by his size, especially in full dress whites. Brennen's rather dashing bodyguard, Uri Harris, had turned to speak with Glin-Erris Coll. They too wore dress-white tunics. Apparently, a military contingent had come from the base. The situation had to be stable. For now.

She'd nearly forgotten how much gilt there was in here. Ever since

Brennen returned from Three Zed, he had abhorred the glittering metal. He had to be controlling that now. She couldn't see him—hidden behind the marshal, maybe—but a sweet inrush of sensation told her he was near.

The tug of Carradee's sash across her left shoulder reminded her: Walk slowly. Look regal. On her scarlet gown's right shoulder, she had clipped the Triple Arrow, Netaia's highest military honor. It all felt like a masquerade, but today, if she played the role well, she might finally get some support for her cultural exchange.

Two men stood on the mid-chamber floor medallion, blocking her path. She shivered a little, remembering how cold that medallion had felt under her knees. She'd knelt there to receive her geis orders, a wastling's death sentence. On that awful day, these Electors had ordered her to seek an honorable end. She never would forget that occasion, so long as she lived. During the recent days en route from Tallis, she'd read up on the formal seating of a new Elector. Maybe this brief ceremony would ease some of that memory's sting.

Standing on the medallion's right edge, Prince Daithi's elder brother—Bennett Drake, Duke of Kenhing and Regent for Queen Rinnah—wore formal black under the all-gold sash of his regency. Like Prince Daithi, Regent Kenhing was quite tall.

Beside Kenhing on the medallion, darkening the chamber with a scowl that would have murdered Firebird if he could have it arranged, stood First Lord Baron Bualin Erwin. He stooped over a walking cane spiraled in multicolored jewels. The most traditional of all traditionalists, First Lord Erwin directed ceremonials and sponsored the mid-city Hall of Charity, where Netaia honored the so-called holy Powers. First Lord Erwin probably would have been delighted if the Shuhr marksman who put that ragged scar on her left shoulder had aimed just a little farther to her right.

His eyes narrowed.

The chamber fell silent as she halted. She no longer had to drop a full curtsey. A half bow sufficed.

Brennen's amusement flickered at the back of her mind. She wished she could see where he sat or stood.

"Lady Firebird," First Lord Erwin snapped, "do you come to serve Netaia?"

Excellent. He wasn't highness-ing her, sash or no sash. Wastlings of all ranks were traditionally addressed as "Lady" or "Lord." She would gladly spend the rest of her life reminding the nobles how cruelly they once treated their third- and fourth-born children.

"I do," she said. Unlike most Netaian rituals, this one was simple.

Regent Kenhing stepped forward. "After me, my lady." He turned, and as she followed him forward, she admired what she could see of the nobleman's dagger he always wore. It probably wasn't as perfectly balanced as Brennen's matched Carolinian pair, but it had a beautiful handgrip, all gold with a sculpted design of forest animals.

Crossing the chamber at this formal pace seemed to take forever. Before coming down from Phoena's rooms, she had sent her cultural exchange proposal to her place at that table. They would mostly talk about that mysterious first contact today, but she would present her proposal if they gave her the floor. It might not happen until tomorrow.

She wouldn't even bother re-presenting the other proposal she'd given them the last time she stood in this chamber. She'd asked them to relinquish much of their power to the popularly elected Assembly. What an idealist she'd been.

Maneuvering behind the gold-rimmed table at last, which was tricky in her gown, she followed Regent Kenhing almost to the central gilt chair. That central chair carried her own family crest, the Angelo starred shield, high on its back. Its armrests were carved with more stars and swirls. That had been her mother's chair, now occupied by the regent. He touched the crimson back of a chair right beside it and nodded for her to sit there.

Crown princess. This was the appalling truth until Daithi and Carradee replaced her by having another child. *Make it soon*, she prayed. The throne that Kenhing now occupied once had tempted her, briefly, before an assassin in the Hall of Charity left her with that scarred shoulder, a punctured lung, and a temporarily stopped heart. The One's words came back from her terrifying dream: *Even in tragedy, I am God. I am not surprised.*

Exhaling a sigh, she gathered her flowing skirt and sat down. People muttered and whispered up and down both arms of the table and across this center section. Years ago, as a very young honorary Elector before that geis fell on her, she had counter-voted the whole group, including her mother, the queen. She'd wanted her disapproval of the Veroh invasion to appear on the official record, where it would outlive her. But when her marshal ordered her out, she'd obeyed her geis and gone.

The invasion brought her to Brennen. It seemed like forever and yesterday.

There he sat, looking back from the middle of the row of lower chairs. She had first noticed those glacial-ice blue eyes in this very chamber, when she'd been spying with Corey on the Electors. Brennen probably remembered that, too. From her interrogation the following year.

How strange. She no longer had to fear this room.

After the usual invocation of Netaia's nine holy Powers, which Firebird ignored, Regent Kenhing reached down to a touchboard embedded near the table's gold edge. A high-toned bell sounded. Whisperings ceased. "This council shall convene," he announced, "in informal but binding session. I declare the closed emergency footing that admits only invited outsiders." He gestured toward the lower chairs. "To you, I say welcome. As you all know, we are being approached by unknowns." A holographic image appeared over the media block at center table in front of him. Within that image, Netaia and all three of its moons glimmered in traditional scarlet, the two buffer systems in traditional brown. Above Netaia's orbital plane hovered three smaller orange globes, signifying the trio of approaching spacecraft. "They have issued a distress call, and they appear to have established a parking orbit around our sun," Kenhing said, "but we must stand prepared for any menace they might pose. They plainly have superior technology. We have called this session to establish Netaia's response."

"Unknowns! Again!"

Recognizing that voice, Firebird looked left. Valora Erwin, the traditionalist First Lord's eldest daughter, glared back at her. Valora's black hair and slim figure looked impossibly young. Most Netaians carried medical implants somewhere in their bodies. Brennen's people couldn't use them.

An even younger voice piped up from beyond Valora's left. "What a wonderful opportunity. New people!" Duchess Esme Rogonin, all in green velvette, was the new head of her own House at just twenty years old. She wore her dark-blonde hair swept back from her face, accentuating her green eyes.

First Lord Erwin growled over the jeweled cane he'd laid on the table. "Plainly, this could be a threat. That second subspace wake—"

Other voices piled on top of his. "—peaceful approach."

"A scientific expedition—"

"This could be a trap—"

"Order, please." Regent Kenhing rang the bell again. His voice filled the elliptical chamber. "Emergency protocol does not justify chaos."

Silence fell, except for soft rustling noises. Keeping her posture straight and dignified, Firebird practiced her patience. According to the Sentinel Code books she'd studied, patience and faith were strongly linked.

Regent Kenhing reached down to his touchboard, and the projected image vanished. Honestly, she wished this matter was being discussed by the common-class Assembly. According to Soldane University's current simulations, Netaia's high-common majority was caught between the wealthy nobles and the restless low-commoners, desperate for peace. The threat of class warfare had eased after Three Zed fell, and—did Firebird dare hope?—after the release of a certain set of anonymous popular songs. Might another perceived threat, or her cultural exchange, tamp down the unrest even more? She had mostly neglected those simulations for two years.

While thinking of the common class, Firebird spotted a vaguely familiar face at the table's far right end. She consulted her screen. It reminded her that she'd met this woman on a prior trip. Freda Tomma was the high-common-class head of the low-common Ice Miners' Guild. Carradee had introduced a few commoners into this council. Perhaps Regent Kenhing had done the same.

"Now," Regent Kenhing said. "Discussion."

Seated halfway between Firebird and the ice miner, Prince Tel Tellai-Angelo raised a gloved hand. Black-haired Prince Tel still had delicate features, but he appeared poised and cool in his black tunic trimmed with House Tellai indigo. As usual, a feathered indigo hat lay on the table in front of him. His raised collar was split into several heavy-looking jeweled collarettes. As a princess's widower, he, too, wore the gold-edged sash of royalty. Firebird looked forward to a long talk with Tel, maybe over dinner. Officially, he still was her Netaian executor and legal representative. He'd always compensated for his boyish looks and lack of height by dressing the glamorous nobleman's part. Maybe that had attracted Her Highness, Princess Phoena the Terrible.

Tel was better off without her. He'd graciously agreed to sponsor

Kinnor and Kiel at their presentation, probably at the next regular session. That occasion would be recorded. And broadcast. Firebird had to admit that she liked the idea. She would show Netaia her beautiful sons and then whisk them back to Tallis.

"The chair recognizes Prince Tel," Regent Kenhing said.

"Surely," Tel said in an oddly airy voice, "they've picked up random transmissions. They know we are here, and their very first word to us is *distress*. Is that not correct?" As his tenor voice rose to an almost-alto, Firebird frowned slightly. Had Tel fallen back into his pathetic old ways?

Marshal Burkenhamn stood, and he, too, was recognized. "We have attempted further communication, but their original transmission is simply being replayed, so we have it in full." He raised a recall pad and read in his rich baritone, "Distress, please help. Send delegation to discuss refueling and compensation. Power too low to continue long-range communication."

A dark-bearded young man called out from next to Valora Erwin, on her left, "I don't trust that."

Those words were spoken, without waiting for recognition, in a voice that made Firebird's stomach clench. Daken Erwin, Grand Duke of Denford and the hostile First Lord Erwin's second-born, had elevated wastling-hazing to a deadly art. Years ago, he'd tried to plant a dagger in her dear friend Corey just for fun. No one would have prosecuted an heir who knifed a wastling, just so long as they weren't killed before geis orders were given. She'd shared a no-romance pact with Corey, since as noble wastlings, they both would die young. Firebird had long forgiven Brennen's squadron for Corey's death in battle, but she would never, ever forgive Daken Erwin.

She narrowed her eyes. Daken had grown a full beard, but he still wore a shifty, arrogant expression. It was tempting to imagine that face superimposed on a target in the training room back home.

Brennen lifted a hand, giving her precious moments to calm down. Regent Kenhing motioned for Brennen to speak. He stood to address the high table. "The Federacy was founded on mutual respect for all peoples. We dare to hope that this will include these . . . Strangers." He emphasized the term as if he were naming them.

Strangers. She liked it. She decided to use it.

First Lord Erwin barked, "They could be highly advanced, if they weren't sent back to the pre-technological age by the Sabba Six-alpha catastrophe that blasted this region of space. That makes them a threat."

"No," Esme Rogonin cried. "They must be delighted that we survived it. And they need our help."

"Order." Regent Kenhing reached out of the gilt throne to tap the bell again.

Again, the nobles settled. Just one chair up from Esme, Daken Erwin stroked that flawless new beard. If anything, it made him look crueler. He raised a hand. Regent Kenhing pointed in his direction. "Any moderately high technology," he said darkly, "which they plainly possess, would have shown them many habitable worlds in the Whorl. We would be rich pickings, if they intend to invade." He rested a hand on the tabletop.

Esme Rogonin reflected his gesture, something Brennen had taught Firebird to watch for. She inhaled sharply. Was pretty young Esme actually fond of that creature?

Regent Kenhing clasped his hands on the table. "They say," he said, "that they need to discuss refueling and compensation. Marshal Burkenhamn, may we assume that the Federacy intends to send a party to negotiate with these people?"

The big marshal stood up below them. "Yes. They appear to be decelerating to a rendezvous point approximately two days' travel from here, so we do not anticipate an imminent invasion. The farther away we can intercept them and discuss their request, the lower our risk. We intend to launch a diplomatic mission tomorrow morning at six hundred, sharp."

Firebird's heart sank. This, not her exchange proposal, would dominate today's closed meeting.

"Thank you, Marshal." Regent Kenhing turned slightly. "General Caldwell, if personal communication proved difficult, could one of your people speak mind-to-mind with them, using concepts instead of words?"

Whispers circled the table. They all knew what Brenn could do. He'd held nearly everyone here under mind-access, willing or unwilling, during the Federate Occupation that followed the Veroh invasion. "A fair chance," he answered. "My personal assistant, Lieutenant Colonel Uri Harris, has agreed to join the mission. If these Strangers do not come as enemies, we must not turn them against us, but we assume a certain risk to whoever we send."

Firebird spotted a tall nobleman in gray glowering down over the table: Count Wellan Bowman, the former Minister of Aquaculture and her dear Corey's father. How unfair that he lived on, still sitting at this table, after his wastling son gave his life for Netaia's greedy glory.

Regent Kenhing still wore a placid expression. He motioned toward Brennen again. "General Caldwell, it is true that a personal mission could prove risky. Could we not simply communicate from a safe location via normal channels, such as our FasScan communication satellite? Its stable-point orbit is quite close to the new arrivals."

Still on his feet, Brennen motioned to Marshal Burkenhamn alongside him.

"As I said, we have tried," the marshal responded, "and you are correct. Some risk will be involved, along with the usual requirement to see the mission through."

Brennen extended a hand. "Let me introduce our Federate ambassadors."

Regent Kenhing nodded permission.

"This," Brennen said, "is Glin-Erris Coll of your Federate diplomatic corps, nephew of the Regional Consular Head." Glin-Erris stood. So did Brennen's bodyguard, Uri, creating a shoulder-to-shoulder row of men in dress whites: the massive marshal, Brennen and his cousin Uri, and slender, short-haired Glin-Erris. On the front of Glin-Erris's white uniform and down his left sleeve, he wore the service and honor ribbons of an already respected career. As Tierna Coll's nephew, he'd been fast-tracked like Brennen. Firebird hadn't talked much with Glin-Erris en route, but she'd liked him. Smart. Well-educated. Friendly.

"Ambassador Coll has agreed to be appointed, as has my personal aide, Colonel Harris." Brennen gestured toward them. "I am posting their diplomatic credentials to your stations. The Federacy will also send an armed escort."

Armed escort—that, Firebird reflected while they all stared at the tabletop, could be the sharp-nosed heavy fighter that shadowed them here. Convenient.

Marshal Burkenhamn took a turn. "The Netaian Planetary Navy will work closely with Battlefield Director Caldwell on a strong defense while our envoy is gone, in case the diplomatic mission fails."

Brennen spoke once more. "I am authorizing the delegates, on behalf of the Federacy, to offer conditional covenance and resettlement on various Federate worlds, should the Strangers be refugees."

"You authorized them?" First Lord Erwin sneered. "There hasn't been time for a messenger to get to Tallis and back." Plainly, he was accusing Brennen of having lied.

Regent Kenhing frowned instead of calling for order. Firebird had read that House Erwin had gained considerable power lately. This felt like proof.

Brennen stood straight-shouldered. "I speak for Regional Command under these circumstances."

Glin-Erris added, "Netaia may also be represented, if it desires."

All four men sat down. Silence descended on the chamber like a gilt net. Firebird glanced left and right without moving her head and saw, in the nobles' side glances and softening postures, something she'd longed to see. Finally, they realized that this middle-sized man in dress whites, wearing the Master Sentinel's star on his shoulder, was making decisions on behalf of the Federacy.

Brennen outranked them all. By far, now.

Wishing she were free to dance with glee, she tapped a finger on her lap. Wouldn't it be amazing to participate in that mission? On the other hand, she had work to do, and Brenn was required to perform his inspection.

One person couldn't be everywhere.

Brennen looked steadily at Regent Kenhing. Again, she felt his amusement.

Regent Kenhing nodded and then said, "As the world most directly approached, we do wish to send representatives. How many, General?"

This time, Brennen remained in his seat. "Send two, as we are sending. Let there be no misunderstanding." He put on what Firebird called his "command face," dark-browed with his chin slightly raised. It gave her a glad shiver. "I will take the chosen Netaian or Netaians under mind-access. There is no guarantee that our real enemies, the renegade Shuhr, are not present among us. Even now. They are masters of masquerade."

Firebird glanced sidelong at Daken Erwin. That man certainly could have passed for Shuhr, if he'd had Brennen's abilities. She half wished they would choose him, just to make sure Brennen put him in his place, but Daken would represent only the worst sort of Netaians.

Daken Erwin's elder sister Valora's voice was pinched. "I suppose you subjected your Ambassador Coll to this indignity?"

Glin-Erris rose again, and he waited for the regent to acknowledge him before speaking. "Madam, I have given General Caldwell my full cooperation. It is known that before that Shuhr world was depopulated and blockaded, they were active here on Netaia for several months. Your prior regent even worked with them face-to-face."

True. Esme Rogonin's father, the previous regent, had suicided rather than face prosecution for that collaboration. Her mother had retired back to House Parkai.

Glin-Erris raised a hand. "Regent Rogonin was not brought to trial, but the evidence was clear, and the Shuhr must not hijack this mission."

Absolutely. Wasn't that obvious?

First Lord Erwin pushed back from the table, staring daggers again, but Regent Kenhing said, "We should accept your condition, General. A simple poll, then. Aye or nay, shall we send representatives under that admittedly distasteful requirement?"

Firebird sent Brennen a wink and reached down. On the screen over her touchboard, just two words had appeared. She touched "Aye." She couldn't wait to nominate Freda Tomma, the commoner. Really, there was no question. They would send an envoy, and he or she had better be vetted.

If only . . .

Oh, stop it, she told herself. Her place was here, to introduce her sons and present her exchange program. If Regent Kenhing didn't ring the bell to adjourn as soon as they finished this business, she might get a chance to begin.

Regent Kenhing read off, "Twenty-one *aye*, six *nay*. Very well. This session is now open for volunteers or nominations. No one shall be sent without his or her consent, including consent to General Caldwell's screening."

Firebird promptly sprang up. "Director Tomma," she declared, "would represent the Netaian people better than any of us. I nominate Freda Tomma."

Someone gasped. Eyebrows raised, Regent Kenhing turned toward his right and struck a formal pose, hand on his dagger hilt. "Madam Tomma, would you be willing to serve if this council sent you on behalf of Netaia?"

The common-class woman in plainclothes, who'd sat silent, stood to face Regent Kenhing and Firebird. "I am honored to have been suggested, Your Excellency, my lady. I would serve if this council chose me."

To Firebird's delight, the ice miner's name appeared on her inset screen. Maybe she wasn't useless here after all. Maybe with experience, she'd get better at this governmental business.

Daken Erwin stood up. "I volunteer." He glared down at Brennen. "Netaia shall not budge to foreign powers, and I shall defend its honor with my life or my death."

Firebird nearly snorted, but Daken's name appeared below Freda Tomma's. Apparently, Regent Kenhing took House Erwin seriously. Should she volunteer too?

No. No, only she could present and lobby for her proposal, and she didn't want to leave her family. Anyone here at this table could represent Netaia.

Well, maybe anyone except Daken Erwin. Brennen crossed his legs—and had he nodded slightly?

Esme Rogonin got to her feet, and her young voice pleaded. "I would go. Send me, to honor my late father. He took terrible risks to defend Netaian ways. And," she added, "I also support Grand Duke Daken." Her tone actually sounded flirtatious.

Dark-haired Valora Erwin remained seated. "Then I nominate Lady Firebird." She fairly croaked the words. "Let us reward her for taking Federate citizenship and demand that she risk herself alongside those of us whose allegiance has not wavered, or else shame her by voting her down."

Bristling—this was ridiculous—Firebird raised a hand and waited for Regent Kenhing's nod. "Noble Electors, I am no diplomat. Or negotiator." The Erwins glared, but someone chuckled, and it heartened her. "I came here for other reasons, which I hope we might discuss once we put this urgent issue behind us."

First Lord Erwin picked up his jeweled cane and pointed it at her. "For once, Lady Firebird, you and I are in full agreement. I would support either Duchess Esme or my son the Grand Duke as our representative."

That almost felt like a dare, and it brought her down hard. Stung, she realized she hadn't actually declined Valora Erwin's nomination. Maybe she could win support for her proposal by cooperating with

Electoral procedure. For once. Echoing the ice miner, she said, "I am honored to have been suggested, and I will serve if my name is chosen to represent you."

Adding *to represent you* wouldn't win her any votes. She sat down with a bump. The sash tugged, and as she smoothed it, another name appeared on the screen, the heir name they'd reluctantly granted her: Firebird Domita Caldwell.

She sent Brennen a questioning look. His steadying warmth reassured her. Surely, her cooperative gesture would be appreciated. It was only a gesture, after all.

Still. Imagine. A first contact!

Five minutes later, with seven names on the transcriber screen, Regent Kenhing stood again. "Are there any other nominations or volunteers, given the fact that we now know this intruder is not alone?" No one stirred. "Then I thank all of you who are willing. First Lord Erwin, would you ask that the holy Powers guide our deeds this day? Since we shall send two, you may each enter two votes. They shall be scored in confidence."

First Lord Erwin creaked to his feet and raised both arms. "Holy Strength, Valor, and Excellence, grant us wisdom this day—"

Firebird tuned him out. *Mighty Singer beyond space and time, only You can see the consequences of what we do now. In your love for us all, including these people now approaching us, direct this vote.* She touched only the ice miner's name, not wanting to add votes to anyone else.

A moment later, her screen blanked. Regent Kenhing stood, and she got a deep breath. Valora Erwin was right. They would love to shame her by rejecting her. Now, she must show them that she had matured enough to lose gracefully.

"Grand Duke Daken," Regent Kenhing called, and Daken stood up with his chest puffed. Unsurprised but disappointed in their choice, Firebird exhaled.

Regent Kenhing turned left, lowered his chin, and looked down at her. "Lady Firebird."

Genuinely startled, she returned his stare. *Me . . . represent them?* Shivers danced on her spine, but Brennen's warmth still came through. A disapproving buzz hummed on the table's left side. First Lord Erwin's mouth fell open. He shut it and raised his cane again.

Daken shouted before his father could speak. "Recount that, Regent Kenhing."

"It has been recounted. Twice."

Daken fell back onto his seat, visibly fuming.

Daken's father, the First Lord, called, "Then prove that you retain a sense of honor, Lady Firebird. We are not convinced that you deserve those decorations or the honor this council just bestowed on you. As for me, I am immeasurably proud of my noble son's holy Knowledge, Fidelity, and Resolve."

More Powers. Daken embodied those three, for sure.

But . . . several days shipboard . . . with *that*?

At least Daken had no idea how well she'd learned to fight back since the last time he cornered her and Corey.

Daken's eyes were still fury-wide. He pointed a finger down toward the side chairs. "Caldwell," he growled, "I subjected myself once to your mind-crawling. You know me."

Regent Kenhing shook his head. "That condition was approved before anyone accepted a nomination. We agreed with General Caldwell's reasoning."

If looks could kill, Brennen would be . . . well, certainly not dead, but defending himself. "What, Caldwell?" Daken's tone mocked him. "You think I might be one of your relatives? You don't think you finished the job at Three Zed?"

How dare he? Brennen had gone extra-vehicular into space there! He had offered to sacrifice himself, steering into a missile's path to save her life. He—

He sent her a somber look. She got hold of herself, and her doubts came clamoring in. Did he see her willingness as Angelo self-pride rearing its head again?

Was that what she'd done?

"General," Regent Kenhing said, "you will settle that single issue and nothing else. Is that correct?"

"It is." Brennen stood up and came forward. Firebird collected herself. Was he going to mind-access Daken Erwin in front of them all?

He was. She couldn't have been more pleased. If Brennen were the least bit duplicitous, he might disqualify Daken Erwin here and now.

But his people's reputation was always at stake. He stopped below the table in front of the Erwins and raised a hand, palm down. Daken scowled but stared back at him. Plainly, he remembered that eye contact would speed things along. For the next several seconds, if a greenfly had sneezed in that chamber, everyone would have heard it.

Brennen lowered his hand. "He is cleared to represent you," he said, momentarily touching the platform's edge. There was always a moment of nauseous weariness afterward. Probably no one other than Shel, Uri, and maybe Prince Tel had seen it, but Firebird actually felt it. Brennen sent a long, stern stare at First Lord Bualin Erwin before he walked steadily back to his seat and picked up his interlink.

Moments later, text appeared on Firebird's screen. *You will do wonderfully, Mari, if I am busy elsewhere. Netaia needs a better representative than that man. You will not be alone.*

No, she protested silently. *I'll be with Daken Erwin.* She looked down at Shel and addressed Marshal Burkenhamn. "Sir, these days, I go nowhere without Major Shelevah Mattason, my travel guard. Is there room for one more?" It was her last chance to gracefully refuse the appointment. Still, first contact . . . a new civilization, allies or enemies . . .

No, she would rather be here with Brennen and the twins. He probably had some way to signal the First Marshal to refuse. Would he?

Marshal Burkenhamn glanced at him, seemed to hesitate—waiting, maybe, for just that signal—and then spoke. "There is room," he said.

"Then I require one staff as well," Daken demanded. "And what about her?" He pointed at Firebird, sweeping the table with a glare. "Are we so sure that woman isn't a Shuhr impostor?"

Something rustled off to Firebird's right. Maybe somebody else thought that was a stupid remark.

"Order," Regent Kenhing called—a little late, in Firebird's opinion. He also added, "Please, Grand Duke Daken."

Brennen spoke calmly. "Send me your staff member for clearance before tomorrow morning's launch. Six hundred hours. And yes, I am certain of Lady Firebird. But if you wish . . . " He shrugged and trailed off. Firebird felt a brush of tenderness in that Brennen-place deep in her mind. She tried not to grin. If only they all knew . . . no, they never could know just how comforting it felt to touch Brennen at depth, nor even here at the surface, since they were fully connatural and pair bonded.

Regent Kenhing raised an eyebrow. "I don't believe that will be necessary." Maybe he knew a thing or two about pair bonding, even if Daken Erwin did not.

Firebird caught Brennen's answering half smile, and she vectored her focus back to what had just transpired. Regent Kenhing rang the bell that ended the session. Esme Rogonin jumped up and embraced Daken Erwin. Brennen joined the other military personnel in conversation.

Firebird stood motionless. Brennen could have silently ordered the marshal to refuse any of those requests. He had that ability too. He hadn't done it.

She'd just been made an ambassador, and to her surprise, she honestly cared whether they thought she could represent them well. She reached across her lap and fingered the silky sash.

Regent Kenhing touched her elbow, his voice warm. "We look forward to your report, my lady. Also, it seems you wished to speak about something else. Can it wait for your return?"

The last time she'd spoken to the Electorate, her speech had been characteristically impassioned and much too long. Kenhing surely remembered that. She steadied herself with a hand on the table. It shook a little with excitement. "I . . . wanted to present my cultural exchange proposal. I think I will have earned the right to speak. Later."

"Certainly." He frowned past her, toward the indignant Erwins.

She couldn't be mistaken. Brenn was sending her with his blessing, unless she was reading him all wrong. So, incredibly, were the people at this table. Were they honoring her, or did they hope to never see her again?

And what about Kinnor and Kiel?

Gathering her scarlet skirt, she hurried around the table and down the steps toward Brennen.

4: THE NIGHT SKY
modulation, a shift in key and tonality

"Tomorrow morning at six hundred," Brennen repeated. Sharp-edged snippets of conversation rose and ebbed around them as formally dressed men and women hurried toward the exit, past the side chairs where Firebird stood with him. Esme Rogonin departed with the Erwins.

Marshal Burkenhamn turned to Firebird. "Pack clothing for ten days," he said. "We'll supply everything else."

"And I'll sleep at the base," Brennen told the marshal. "Thank you again for the accommodation."

"Not at all. Norann is delighted."

Brennen touched Firebird's arm. "I'll walk you up to the rooms. Ahma doesn't expect us until tomorrow. Our plans have changed. We need to call."

Firebird still felt only his approval, but she had to allow for that affective control of his. How did he really, privately feel about her accepting this assignment? What about Ahma-Dara, Kiel, and Kinnor? And what could she do out there, anyway? As she'd said, she was no diplomat or negotiator. Maybe Glin-Erris would give her and Daken a crash course, if Daken Erwin was capable of learning anything so delicate as give-and-take. Dealing with foreign entities often required concessions. She'd never seen Daken concede anything to anyone.

Beyond the doors, other Electors gathered in the governmental wing off to her right. She and Brennen turned left and crossed the portrait gallery side by side, her skirts swishing, his bootsteps echoing. Turning, she spotted Shel and Uri a few steps back, and behind them, a flock of other nobles' massive bodyguards. She'd never seen so many of these super-sized men in one place. Whether noble-class people actually understood that there had been Shuhr onworld, or whether they were starting to accept the possibility of civil unrest, she wished she knew. Prince Tel's father, Count Eamonn Tellai, had been murdered by a disgruntled agricultural overseer.

Prince Tel stood ahead, a small, slight man next to the guarded private stairs. He swept off his feathered hat as they approached, reached for Firebird's hand, and brushed it with a polite and innocuous kiss. "Ah, my lady Firebird. You look so lovely, properly dressed. And you, General," he said airily. "So good to see you. So unfortunate that you will not be with us for several months."

Firebird felt a flicker of pity in Brennen, who'd seen Tel's despicable bride die in agony and despair. That memory obviously still bothered him. However, Firebird was glad to greet this man who'd become their ally. "It is good to see you too, Your Highness," she said in a formal tone, raising an eyebrow. Had Tel truly regressed to the genteel dandy she once knew? She glanced sidelong at the nearest House Guard, who remained at stiff attention.

Still clutching his indigo hat, Tel looked up at Brennen. Compared with Tel's fancy black tunic with its multiple jeweled collarettes, Brennen's dress whites with the single gold star on his shoulder looked downright regal. Why in the Whorl had she agreed to travel without him?

"I had thought," Tel said, "I would have more time to pay my respects. Now, however, I must gather a set of documents for our ambassadors. I have precious few moments this afternoon, but might you spare a word alone, while I am here at the palace?" He glanced up the curved stairs.

"Certainly," Brennen said with a half bow, looking and sounding exquisitely formal himself. Firebird took Brennen's arm. Followed by Uri and Shel, they made their way past the House Guards, back up the carpeted stairs in close formation. She did not miss the way that Brenn still avoided touching the gilt-ribboned banister.

"One minute," Uri said. He and Shel slipped past them into Phoena's old sitting room. As Firebird waited in the long hall, she eyed Carradee's Sentinel door guards. It was good to know she and Rinnah would be safe.

Eventually, Shel peered out and said, "Clear. We'll be in the consort's suite."

Finally inside Phoena's gaudy first parlor, Firebird longed to change back into her comfortable traveling suit, but Brennen immediately sat down on a garishly brocaded settee. Taking her cue, she claimed a dyed brownbuck lounger and crossed her ankles demurely under her long scarlet skirt.

Tel took the pale-gold velvette chair. He looked from her to Brennen and back again.

He smiled, then straightened and said in a firmer voice, "It is good to see you both again. And set aside the role of genteel cuckold."

Relieved, Firebird asked, "Why are you putting it on?"

Tel rubbed his face. "Muirnen Rogonin's gone, but the Erwins have taken his role and run with it. They've managed to get most of the Houses under financial obligation. Only a few don't toady to the Erwins. And, Firebird, besides the Tellai properties, I still am trying to administer your finances here, so I don't dare challenge them." He laid his hat aside, looking earnest. "Since Daken was the Erwin who volunteered, they all had to vote for him. And they all still think of me"—he spread well-manicured hands—"that way," he said sadly, "so why not let them keep thinking it?"

As a pathetic excuse for a man, Firebird reflected. *As Phoena's fop.*

Brennen sat back, casual at last. "So you're undercover for your own safety and on our behalf."

"Something like that."

Firebird sent Tel a sidelong smile, wishing that Tel could sense her gratitude as Brennen could.

"Thank you," Brennen said. "Still, I was sorry to see the Grand Duke selected. I would have thought you would want to send your best people."

Tel shrugged. "I believe the situation is why Regent Kenhing made that vote confidential." He glanced her way. "To make room for you as a second-place vote. They can't support you openly, but you have impressed quite a few of them. Of us."

Really? The notion baffled her. That hadn't been her read of the room.

"You have matured, Firebird." Tel laced his fingers, looking serious. "And several of us would like to see the Erwins loosen their grip. When you were last here, you mentioned a simulation you had seen, predicting, ah, instability. How does it look now?"

This was the Tel she had come to know: an alert, compassionate man who had been deeply educated in suffering. "Better," she said, "but still unstable." Civil war remained possible. Essentially, the noble electors still wielded too much power. Only the best of them, like Tel, would consider giving it up. What a quandary! "They'll send dinner up soon, Tel. Won't you join us? Then we can have a good talk."

"Thank you, but I do have a job for Kenhing." He glanced around the curtained parlor. "I'm afraid a longer visit will have to wait for your return."

Firebird followed his glance to the marble firebay. How many of the gaudy heirlooms and souvenirs on that mantel gave him painful memories? He'd lived in here, briefly, as Phoena's husband. "I am sorry," she told him. "And," she added with a cautionary look at Brennen, "it would have been wonderful to explore some of the new construction in Citangelo with you. Especially the Chapter House." She had funded that House out of her modest heir's allowance. Netaians were actually turning to the ancient faith, or so she had heard. She would have liked to meet some Netaian Inquirers. Brennen was forbidden by Sentinel law to proselytize, since their powers made them liable to charges of coercion, of forcing their beliefs on others. But after Three Zed, Firebird no longer had any such abilities and therefore no constraint on asking certain questions.

"Ah." Tel leaned back, tapping his fingertips together. "You'll know that Netaia currently has five young people who would have been considered wastlings under the old law. Three of them are training on that new Thyrian Path."

"Wonderful." She inhaled to ask the vital question—whether Tel also had reached toward the Holy One—but Tel spoke first, warning her off that private ground. She might be free to proselytize, but she was also learning to be strategic. "Carradee must never let down her guard," Tel stated firmly. "She's always been too gracious and trusting."

"We'll see to that," Brennen said. Obviously, by "we" he meant the Sentinel guards now openly deployed here. The moment had passed. Maybe when she returned, she might ascertain whether Tel still felt devoted to the so-called holy Powers.

Tel nodded, then leaned forward. "What in or beyond the Whorl do you think that is, coming toward us?"

Brennen spread his hands. "We have no more idea than you do. We can only hope the Strangers are amenable to negotiation. Perhaps they would share their shielding technology in return for a refuel."

Firebird sat upright and sent Brennen a gust of approval. Yes, that would be appropriate payment, if they didn't prove hostile.

"What if they aren't amenable?" Tel asked. "What if they just want to take without giving back?"

Tel knew the type, all right. Phoena had taken everything, whether or not she was entitled. She'd tried to take the Federate world of Veroh.

It was possible. A civilization with shielding that advanced could threaten them.

Brennen answered cautiously, military to civilian. "First Marshal Burkenhamn is bringing the Netaian Planetary Navy to full readiness, and we have two nearby planetary systems on alert."

Nodding again, Tel stood. "Yes, well, that's your job. I'm glad it's not mine. I only wanted to let you in on, well, on the act. And now I must flee." He picked up his hat off the brocade lounger.

"Wait, Tel," Firebird exclaimed. Maybe she could launch her cultural exchange on this diplomatic mission, sharing Netaian music with the newcomers. The Strangers, as Brennen called them. "My clairsa is back on Tallis, but if you could find one that I could buy or borrow before we launch tomorrow, I would be grateful. You can use my funds. I know that's asking for your time, but if you could . . ."

"I shall do my best," he said, bowing. "May your mission prove successful." His voice had gone airy again, but his expression looked somber.

Brennen opened the door. After Tel passed through. Brenn shut it and stood against it.

Firebird sat eyeing him. Silently he looked back, plainly waiting for her to speak.

Tel Tellai-Angelo descended the long stairs slowly, struggling with memories. Entering Phoena's rooms always intensified his awareness that he had never truly, honestly loved his wife, not the way those two loved and worked with each other. No, he had worshipped a woman who never truly existed, someone whom he had thought was Princess Phoena Eschelle Angelo. She actually had betrayed Netaia by instigating an unnecessary invasion, and then she'd betrayed her husband by deserting him to go to the evil, renegade Shuhr.

Near the foot of the stairs, he pushed away memories that threatened to drown him in self-pity, and he considered Firebird's request. Paudan, his knowledgeable manservant, could surely contact a clairsier before nightfall. A portable instrument of good quality could be sent to the base with his best wishes.

It was the least he could do. He stepped off the bottom stair, looking around the gallery for Paudan.

Instead, striding out of the governmental hall into the portrait gallery came Daken Erwin, who'd probably been in the sovereign's day office conferring with Regent Kenhing. Imagining his assets frozen—and Firebird's stolen—by House Erwin, Tel shortened his steps to a mincing gait. He must be meek. Cooperative.

He met Daken halfway across the portrait gallery. "Ah," Tel said, "Grand Duke Erwin. Congratulations on your appointment! May the Powers guide you to—"

"Saying your goodbyes to the wastling and the mind-crawler?" Daken asked in a low voice.

Tel clutched his hands together and studied the marble floor. "They did their best to try and rescue Princess Phoena, Daken. May the Powers have sent her directly to Bliss," he added, and then explained in cautiously pleading tones, "I must thank them at every opportunity."

Daken snorted behind his enviable beard. "You're wasting your breath. But never mind. I wanted to talk with you anyway. I have a mission for you in my absence."

"I shall do my best." Tel tried to sound eager.

Daken leveled his eyes down at him. "Look in on Esme Rogonin every day. She'll miss me. Keep her distracted. I shall probably propose marriage when I return."

Thank you for the gracious insult. Plainly, you consider me no threat. There'd been a time when Tel admired Esme Rogonin. Burning inside, he swept off the feathered hat and gave Daken a half bow. "May I be among the first to congratulate you on your impending betrothal?"

"You may." Daken strutted out through the main doors.

Feeling deflated, Tel wandered deep into the gallery until he spotted the portrait he'd personally painted of Princess Phoena Angelo, gowned in brilliant orange, before his comfortable world had turned to dust. Phoena had criticized it. *Looks too much like you-know-who*, she'd said.

In hindsight, she probably was right. Dismally he glanced up the guarded stairs, and again out the front doors, where his manservant sat waiting and the House Guards stood at attention.

Would he always love the wrong women?

Gazing down at the carpet, Firebird managed to ask Brennen, "So? Did you see that coming? Not Tel, but their electing me?"

"Yes, I did. When you walked in wearing that sash, the room's unspoken savor changed significantly. Maybe just for a moment, they saw your mother, the queen."

She cringed. He did have a gift for reading a room, but she didn't like to think of herself that way. "The sash was Carradee's idea, not mine. But . . ." She fell silent.

"You're an excellent choice. Far better than Grand Duke Daken Erwin."

"It's the opportunity of a lifetime." She felt almost guilty.

He quirked an eyebrow. "Do you remember my warning you to be careful what you wished for?"

"Yes." Her cheeks warmed. "Hopefully, it won't be a fight with anyone besides Daken." She hadn't even thought about that man in years. She'd escaped everything he represented. Or so she'd thought.

Brennen sat back down, his eyes warm. "Thinking missionally, and not about my personal feelings, you will represent Federate and Netaian humanity well. As for your wish?" He paused, glancing up at a curtained window and then back at her. "I have always loved your courage. I love it now." And he meant it. She felt it deeply on the pair bond. "You were needing a challenge. I was almost afraid you would take on something even more dangerous. You'll enjoy doing a bit of information gathering and speaking to new people." He smiled. "I have no doubt that you can deal with one spoiled Grand Duke."

She laughed her tension away. "Maybe if you're here for a dekia while we're gone, you could sniff out some Shuhr escapees. But I do wish you were coming." Almost four Fed-calendar years into this unique marriage, she never really felt whole without him. Before Brennen came into her life, she'd been proudly independent.

There was that word again. *Proudly.* "And it is my chance," she guessed, "to get the Electors' approval. For good, this time. Also," she added more seriously, "when you survived at Three Zed, I promised the rest of my life to the Eternal Speaker. You're still on this side of the last Crossing, and so am I."

"Mikuhr," he corrected her again, but he nodded. "We all must go where we are called. I would like to see Netaia in your debt. It's right to feel comfortable with that."

She stood. "Good. Then we've got to check in with your mother." She glanced around the room. "Phoena tried to run an uprising from this apartment. I wonder if there's still a media block in the consort's suite."

Trading suites with Uri and Shel took barely a minute. There was, in fact, advanced communication gear in the room where the Sentinels had waited. Shortly, she and Brennen were addressing a tenth-sized holographic image of Ahma-Dara. Her dark eyes glowed. "Don't the two of you look spectacular?"

Brennen explained the afternoon's events, and to Firebird's relief, Dara's sparkling eyes didn't narrow. "Congratulations," she said heartily. "I will tell the boys. I'm sorry you missed them, but Norann Burkenhamn is driving them around the base to look at all the wonderful spaceships. They are thrilled."

Firebird's heart squeezed. "I'm sorry I won't see them. We'll be here until late, and we're launching extremely early. Brenn will be in touch."

Dara returned a wry smile. "Children, your sons already understand that you are keeping the Whorl safe for them."

Firebird bowed her head slightly. "I can't tell you how grateful I am." She couldn't imagine her own mother stepping into the domestic role Ahma-Dara had accepted so beautifully. Now, she had an example of loving parenthood. She hoped it wasn't too late to emulate.

"We'll try not to wake you when we come in." Brennen reached for the control tab. The image vanished.

Firebird slid off one dress shoe. "Now," she sighed, "I really want to get comfortable."

"May I help?" he asked. "That is a lot of gown to manage alone. We won't have much privacy later."

Oh, the memories in those eyes. And that half smile as he reached for her hand.

And that warm sea full of incense, the sweet presence that enfolded her whenever their hearts and minds and bodies intertwined. Breathing a little quicker, she stepped toward the main parlor and called, "Shel? Please ask the servitors to delay dinner an hour or so."

Sated, comfortably dressed, and full of savory pied henny, followed by red gem tartlets and a cup of properly brewed Netaian cruinn, Firebird had one more idea. "Brenn, before we head back to the base, may I take you outdoors to one of my favorite places?"

He wore gray shipboards now. On the pair bond he, too, felt deeply contented. "Of course. We're partly here to honor your memories."

She seized his hand and tugged him back down the curving stairs, out through the palace's enormous back doors, past the sentries, across the breezy colonnade and down the stone steps. Uri and Shel might be following for security's sake, but she ignored them.

As darkness fell, long, glossy leaves on the drooping fayya trees reflected the colonnade lights in a rustling chorus. She caught the springtime scent of their blooms and the formal flower gardens, paused for a deep breath, and then led him down a pebbled path to the second reflecting pool.

"I know this place," he said, stepping onto the small wooden bridge. Its arch seemed steeper than she remembered.

She sidled closer to him, loving the warmth of his body standing next to hers in the cool evening. "You were here? Under the Occupation?" she guessed.

"No. In your memory."

"Oh." Naturally. She pointed upward, pleased that she hadn't lost her astronomical sense. Compared to Tallis's night sky, there were fewer bright, nearby stars here at the Whorl's end. She knew exactly where the springtime constellations ought to be. "Look." She pointed toward a yellow glimmer, excited to see the sun of her new home world. "Tallis."

As he squinted upward, she looked down into the water. Bulging eyes stared back, a school of finny, green-gold skitters. Some good things hadn't changed.

"Now," Brennen said softly, "let me show you what I remember. Shut your eyes." He drew away to face her, and he touched a finger to her forehead.

She closed her eyes. In her mind's eye, she saw the same stars: the bright yellow-orange light of Veroh and the dimmer yellowish spark of Tallis against a dark background. But she also felt the enormous weight of a small envelope in her breast pocket. She'd just received it from her mother. It contained a packet of fast-acting poison. She had fled outside to make peace with her impending death, and to consider the so-called Dark that Cleanses that she must endure afterward.

This was Brennen's nearly perfect memory from that long-ago interrogation.

He even remembered her thoughts from that night.

> *Fortunately, Veroh stood almost as far toward the tip of the largely Federate Whorl as Netaia itself, hopefully too far for a strong military defense to be economically feasible—so hoped the Netaian marshals. According to recent intelligence, the Veroh system had only a small self-defense installation and ten support depots . . .*

"How arrogant we all were," she whispered. "Even though it was Phoena's invasion."

He lowered his hand, eyes gleaming blue-white in the starlight. She fell back into his arms. It had felt so real, that envelope tucked into her cadet's uniform. Yet here she stood, embracing her Master Sentinel after sitting in the crown princess's chair.

"I felt how badly you wanted to see beyond Netaia's moons," he said quietly. "And already, I wanted to show you."

The breeze riffled the hair alongside her face, gently tickling. She glanced up again, looking for those two smallest moons, the little one forever chasing the larger, but never overtaking its sparkling sister.

Just like her and Phoena.

But the moons weren't up tonight, her own star outshone Phoena's now, and she would never get tired of the night sky on Tallis.

He spoke against her hair. "You will do well, Mari. Think about what you've accomplished since you stood here before the invasion. Just four standard years ago."

She had wondered, contemplating death that night, whether the so-called holy Powers existed. "Do you suppose," she mused, "that whoever's onboard that incoming ship, some of them might know the Holy One?"

"So far as we know, humanity arose on just one world. When Boh-Dabar comes, he will surely speak to the Strangers as well."

Interesting thought.

He rested his hands on her shoulders. "Show Netaia who you really are, Mari. Who you always have been, whether or not they knew it." He paused, looking down into the water. The skitters still swam circles beneath the bridge. "Phoena knew," he added. "That's why she hated you. You were a threat to her. Remember what Ottar Parkai said?"

For half an instant, she stood puzzled. Then she recalled what else Brennen probably found in her memory, something that had given her comfort during her wastling years. Years ago, the old late baron had remarked—in earshot of both Firebird and Phoena—that it was "a shame about the birth order in that family."

May her soul find rest, she prayed dutifully. She'd forgiven her sister's spite and scorn and ambition. Over and over. And over.

"Did I do the right thing today?" she asked.

"Of course you did. Go in complete confidence. May I help you?"

She hesitated. She'd committed herself, but she still had doubts, especially about leaving him behind. "I don't know," she said slowly. "It would feel a little like cheating."

He laughed softly. "My dearest friend recently said something quite intelligent about wasting their best resource person."

She laughed back at him, tilting her chin. "You're right. Thank you."

His fingertip touched her forehead once more. When she stared into his eyes, doubt and fear melted away. It felt wonderful. She pulled him close and embraced him in silence. Somewhere, a flock of cardees sang in the fayya trees. Still touching her mind with his own, he leaned his forehead against hers. "Holy One, give this courageous woman wisdom and grace." The warmth at the back of her mind grew and spread. As he broke off the contact, he whispered, "So let it be."

She exhaled, hating for the moment to end. "I guess I have packing to do." Clothes for a ten-day dekia. And hopefully a clairsa, the Netaian small harp. She'd played it seriously since she was a schoolgirl. Some of her belongings had been brought to the palace, back when they'd assumed an overnight stay. Shel would help gather and organize. She could kiss Kiel and Kinnor good night. She must—

"I will help you sleep tonight," Brennen murmured. "But I will be up very late."

Another one of his epsilon gifts: calming her mind to utter peace. "Thank you, Brenn. I'm going to need that." She took his hand and stepped off the bridge into the breeze, full of memories and hope.

5: LAUNCH
poco agitato, slightly agitated

Private feelings had no place in Citangelo Base's command center, but Brennen knew precisely where Mari was. Uri too. He had become a brother-in-arms.

Brennen stood with his back to the tri-D well, staring upward at a vertical display of local space as the diplomatic transport *Cometesse* and its Tallan heavy-fighter escort left atmosphere, vectoring perpendicular to the orbital plane. They would not slip for so short a trip but instead accelerate at a comfortable civilian rate and begin deceleration at midway. The trip out would take two days. Besides Glin-Erris Coll's diplomatic bundle, Marshal Burkenhamn's staff had procured a small but powerful remote scanning unit to deploy on board the Strangers' lead ship, since their shielding still blocked all attempts at scanning. Citangelo Base had to know more about those shields, and whatever armament the incoming ships carried, in case things went wrong.

On the other hand, if things went very right, the Federacy soon might own new and powerful shielding technology.

Uri would assist Glin-Erris and Mari in those negotiations. Shel, whose epsilon rating was nearly as high as his own, would assist Uri and keep Grand Duke Daken away from Mari.

Actually—he smiled silently—he would have liked to be there when Mari put Daken Erwin in his place.

His own place would be here on duty.

He took another long look around the command center, internalizing each monitor's location. Five controllers sat on watch. The tri-D well displaying the Netaian system gleamed, but the room felt half empty without massive First Marshal Burkenhamn. Another Netaian marshal had taken command while Marshal Burkenhamn inspected Sitree Base.

"Steady on course, sir," announced the young officer at that nearby display. *Lieutenant Lord Leon Parkai*, Brennen reminded himself. Parkai would have been a wastling under the old laws. He'd introduced himself as an Inquirer on the Holy Path.

A Netaian brother. Brennen eyed the young man in wonder. What else might the Eternal Sovereign do here?

A second thought struck him: Could it be that Boh-Dabar, now walking among them as Kinnor or Kiel, soon would be acknowledged as Netaian royalty? Could that be why they all were called here?

You delight in surprising us, Holy One. No one can stand against you.

And if that were the case, what kind of responsibility did he now carry, raising and training That One for the tasks before him?

He stepped to another sensors display. This glowing wall chart mapped current deployments. All three Netaian battle cruisers were approaching orbital launch zones. Support ships were prepping and launching from other bases: Arctica, Sitree, Claighbro. Three flight teams had loaded their new, nimble Polovia fightercrafts—replacing the older tagwings—onto carriers. The pilots were bunking in their launching chutes, on board their fightercrafts. Not perfect comfort, as he'd done it himself, but a privilege of elite pilots.

After the transport *Cometesse* and her escort fighter settled into steady acceleration, and after he caught up on the sleep he'd missed overseeing this launch, he would spend his days right here, probably napping in a secure privacy alcove. Ahma would take care of the twins. He glanced down at the darkened screen of his recall pad, where he'd loaded unfinished tasks. Later, assuming the Strangers proved peaceful and negotiations commenced, he would order the stand-down. That might frustrate eager soldiers, but the overriding goal of any defense force was to deter conflict, not to win it. Proving that they could defend Netaia against a potential invasion would be an experience to remember.

But if the ambassadors alerted him to impending conflict—the notion required his affective control because it could put Mari in danger—Netaia would be ready. He'd also called alerts on those two nearest Federate systems and sent a messenger to Tallis. If only Netaia had better out-system transmission capacity. . . .

He would manage without it, and as he'd told Mari, he did not doubt her abilities. They'd known their risks of identity and profession when they'd wed each other. Still, in the years since then, he had added a husband's concern for his sons' mother.

Clearly, he was exhausted. His thoughts were jumping like kirka frogs, and these private feelings kept intruding. He turned on one heel and faced the room's center. In the waist-high tri-D well, the Strangers' three red spheres floated amid columns of numbers: observable mass, surface components, gravidics. Many other numbers, normally provided by trans-shield scanning, still read zero. The Strangers' powerful shielding tech was radically different from anything the Federacy had yet developed. Clearly, though—judging by the floating numbers and his own eyes' evidence— "They are decelerating," he observed.

The nearest controller touched her headset. "Yes, sir. They must have observed our launch. They could be conserving what fuel they have remaining."

Even if they still had not initiated further communication, they intended to keep the rendezvous. What kind of fuel did they need? Laser-ion engines required very little of . . . what was it? Not his specialty.

He yawned before he could fight it down. He walked to the acting marshal and saluted. "Sir, I'm going to bed down for a few hours." In a real bed while he could, close to Kinnor and Kiel.

The marshal saluted back. "Very good, General Caldwell. We'll comm you if anything changes."

A fast shuttle took him to base housing and the last single-story house on Officers Row. Ahma met him at the door, smiling sympathetically. On other Federate bases, he'd seen furnished houses with this floor plan, right down to the square-cushioned loungers. His sons stampeded to grab his legs.

A man Brennen did not recognize stood several paces back. Brennen extended a hand, dragging a twin with each step. "Hello?"

His mother rested a hand on the man's shoulder and introduced him, but the man's name and homeworld slipped past. He shouldn't be this weary. All he'd done was attend an Electoral meeting on high alert, fill a night with launch preps, say farewell to Mari, and supervise the launch. He'd worked longer and under greater stresses, including deadly danger, before. He did hear Ahma call the man the new priest of Citangelo's

Chapter House and say, "I invited him to come by and meet the boys and to pray with us for the mission's success."

Trained reflexes kicked in. He clasped the man's hand and said, "I am honored to meet you."

"And I, you." The priest wore civilian clothes instead of a ministerial tunic, surely to humor the xenophobic Netaians. How marvelous to see the Holy One honored on other worlds, since he himself was not allowed to encourage others.

"Please, forgive me. I am very tired." He might as well admit it, although he owed his ahma the effort to stay awake another half hour. "We worked nearly all night. Could we pray in the dining area?" A less comfortable chair might keep him alert. "And then"—he ruffled a boy's hair with each hand—"I am sorry, my hearts, but I had better sleep awhile."

As soon as the transport's gravidics caught up with initial acceleration, Firebird and Shel unharnessed and headed aft, stepping through a wide galley to the sleeping cabin they would share overnight. Inside the tight little space, with a lower and upper bunk and room to take a few steps, Firebird dug into her issue bag. It had felt familiar to be handed one of these just before boarding. Emergency food concentrates, two packets. Stimulant capsules, containing the extract of morning kass, one packet. Bitter things. She hated them, but in a combat situation, they could be necessary. First aid supplies, one large packet. A handful of pocket lumas. A compact oxygen sniffer, fully charged. A few personal comfort items. And in hers, but not in Shel's, a bulky shock pistol. She'd been officially discharged, and this should be a peaceful encounter, but she was ordered to dress as military. As for Shel, she was more dangerous unarmed than several non-Sentinels with shock pistols.

"Looks like all we'll need." Shel tucked her bag into the right side of an overhead storage locker.

"Right. Now, let's see what Tel found me." Twenty minutes before they boarded, his manservant had arrived carrying a small musical instrument case. She unbuckled it now and carefully drew out a wire-strung clairsa by its curved and engraved upper arch. "Brand new," she observed. "He must have sent someone to buy it."

Shel straightened, so that her short, dark-blonde hair brushed the upper bulkhead. "That would be quicker than hunting for something to borrow." She sat on the gray-blanketed bunk.

Peering inside the sound hole, Firebird examined its bracing. "This is a fine instrument for its size." A hand-scribed note fell off the bank of strings. She picked it up to read, "The best we could do. My gift. May the one you worship give you success." Smiling, she ran a fingernail up the strings. A clashing discordance diminished her smile. "Definitely new," she said. "It's never been tuned." And there wouldn't be time for that. Glin-Erris expected them in the galley lounge in five minutes.

Shel shifted her seat on the blanketed bunk. "Lady Fi," she said softly, "I have never before seen you truly hate someone who was not Shuhr. We are not to hate others."

That too was in the Code books. Firebird closed her eyes for a moment, then exhaled. "Daken Erwin was the very worst abuser of wastlings. Most of the Electors never saw that. They just tolerated whatever they found out about. I think he's got a sick, ah . . ."

"I read something unbalanced on him. Almost a bloodlust."

Firebird closed the clairsa case. "Right on target." She cocked her head and regarded her bodyguard. "What would it take for you to legally voice-command him or put him in t-sleep? An attack on me, I assume?"

Shel gave a single nod. "Hopefully, very soon and very minor. Let's get it over with."

The notion stirred up a nasty memory. Daken hadn't looked like he had anything very minor in mind when he'd drawn that dagger on Corey Bowman, back when she and Corey were wastlings in their perilous early teens, and they had fled together.

She probably could handle Daken now. Still, it was a relief to be traveling with Shel. "Please stay close. I don't know anything about his servant. Maybe he's aware and keeps Daken under control. But just watch my six," she said, resorting to an old piloting expression.

"You aren't helpless." Shel sent her a knowing smile. They'd spent hours on the training mat.

Still, something could go wrong in an actual attack. "Hopefully, if I can surprise him, there's less chance I'll get hurt."

"By the way," Shel added, "this cabin locks from inside. Brennen and I made sure of it."

"Good."

They headed upship to the transport's long, oval galley. Slender

Glin-Erris already sat at the rectangular table, looking dignified and fully in charge. Cabin lights faintly reflected off his scalp under short, dark hair. Uri sat next to him. "Major Mattason," Glin-Erris said, eyeing Shel, "with us, please."

That left an entire six-stool side for Firebird and Daken, representing Netaia. She chose a spot far enough upship, on the left, that Daken wouldn't have to sit next to her, and when he appeared from the aft bunkroom passage, he took the farthest stool. His manservant, Dodis Gering, stood behind him. Gering had silvery hair and shoulders like an arctic bear, and he and Daken wore full House livery, black tunics trimmed in orange piping, with black sateen breeches.

One of their two pilots, a married couple from the Federate world of Luxia, walked in from the forward lounge. He stopped at the servo unit. "Please excuse me if I eat," he said. "I'm taking a sleep shift immediately."

None of them had breakfasted, and Firebird was eager to put something in her own belly. There was an onboard breakfast dish she'd particularly enjoyed en route to Netaia, and hopefully, the *Cometesse* carried the same menu.

"Gering, bring me something," Daken said without looking at his servant.

The pilot raised an eyebrow. "Wouldn't you want to see what's available?" He pointed at a bulkhead compartment.

Glin-Erris's Tallan duty uniform grays looked almost like the comfortable suit Firebird liked to wear for traveling, but Glin-Erris's had a crisp finish. "Please wait until we've spoken," he said. "I won't take long."

"Gering, you may remain," Daken grumbled.

Gering inclined his head. "Very good, sir."

Firebird eyed the sturdy manservant. Brennen and Marshal Burkenhamn had allowed him. Maybe he would prove better behaved than his employer. Maybe, as she'd suggested to Shel, he knew how to manage Daken.

Or maybe he was only another flunky.

"I have these for you." Glin-Erris pulled a brownbuck leather case onto the table and passed each of them a pair of small objects, taking obvious care to inspect them. "These are personal interlinks and earpieces. We can use them to speak with each other and with Citangelo

Base via Netaia's FasScan satellite. Our pilots will retain one up in the cockpit."

Pleased, Firebird picked up the earpiece and collar mike. The FasScan satellite orbited Netaia's sun at a stable point, enabling rapid communication within the system. On the mike's back, she found a small switch with three settings. One setting pointed to a small, eight-pointed star.

A private line to Brenn. Hopefully, he was catching up on some sleep. Gratefully she sent Glin-Erris a smile. She attached the mike to her collar and tucked the earpiece into position.

Daken left his on the table. "Daken?" she asked, pointing.

"Wearing that," he said loftily, "is my manservant's job." Dodis Gering had already clipped a mike to his livery tunic and was working an earpiece into place. This small, flexible model was designed to be comfortable even when sleeping.

Glin-Erris shrugged and reached into the case again. Maybe he didn't want Daken listening in on him, and maybe she understood that. "Citangelo Base, do you read us?"

After a moment's delay, a man's voice was clear and distinct in Firebird's ear. "Clear copy, Ambassador Coll. Proceed with your briefing."

Glin-Erris spread a glimmering data sheet on the galley table. "Here is our current information from Citangelo Base's scanners. Simple visual has finally picked up some surface details. Our destination craft appears to have a transport bay amidships. I assume we shall debark there," he said, touching the spot. "I shall make brief introductions. Please let me speak to them first, for several reasons." His frown was at Daken, who silently frowned back. Glin-Erris continued, "If they are a military mission, it may be difficult to tell who holds the highest rank, and that is whom I should address. If civilian, their rankings may still be important.

"At a first meeting," he continued, "we shall introduce ourselves and inquire as to their origin, destination, and fueling needs. My recall pad," he said, laying a hand over it on the table, "contains resource information for several Federate worlds, as well as current costs. I have been asked to suggest an exchange of technological knowledge as our price for refueling."

Firebird nodded. Before launch, Brennen's very words had been *Imagine if we had that shielding technology.*

Glin-Erris kept speaking. "If communication with their engineering staff proves impossible, we can suggest mental, conceptual communication."

Glin-Erris opened a hand toward Uri. "This will be done in the most non-threatening way."

Daken's small eyes flickered. He snorted.

"Precisely," Glin-Erris said in a tolerant tone. "We must demonstrate that legal limitations are always imposed on our Sentinel forces."

Uri turned to Daken and spoke with exquisite politeness. "We are governed by strict codes." Aristocrats usually took well to Uri, who moved and spoke with upper-class grace and self-confidence. "Probably stricter than you can imagine."

Daken stroked his beard. A soft "Hmm" came from Dodis Gering behind him.

"I urge you," Glin-Erris said, facing Daken and sending Gering a glance, "to support our attempt to present telepathy as a friendly way to communicate. It is on our shoulders, all of us"—he motioned, including everyone in a gesture—"to avoid making these Strangers into enemies. But," he added, "neither will we unconditionally welcome them to Whorl space until we know what they actually intend. *That* will be our second goal. To find out what, besides their fueling issue, brings them to this part of the Whorl."

"What are we really here for, if I may ask?" Firebird kept her tone respectful. "Daken and I?"

Daken glared. Glin-Erris pressed his palms together. "You and Grand Duke Daken represent the nearest planetary system, the Grand Duke as a civilian, and yourself as military personnel. Either entity might be involved in a sale of resources. When I negotiate fuel procurement and payment, you will assist with the final stages, particularly any transfer of technological data."

So, the Sentinels wouldn't represent the Federate military. Shel wore her midnight-blue duty uniform anyway, but Brennen had told Firebird to pack her dress whites. Daken stared back at Glen-Erris, apparently not understanding. But officially, if they attacked a member of Federate Netaia's military, it could be seen as an act of war.

Glin-Erris continued evenly, "Hopefully, if the language barrier remains low, each of you can identify individuals or groups willing to establish more detailed communication, so that while they await refueling, and when they travel on, they will consider us as allies."

Daken pointed at Glin-Erris. "I know what I'm going to tell them. I'll—"

"We must work as a team." Glin-Erris shot Daken a dark look. Might one of the Sentinels eventually need to voice-command Daken to cooperative silence? Glin-Erris hadn't threatened that. Not yet, anyway. At what point would it be legal under the rigid Sentinel Codes?

Glin-Erris raised his recall pad. "I am sending protocol documents for you to study en route, along with Federate resource files. The files, particularly the examples, will answer most of your questions."

Back to school, then. Firebird pictured herself studying files and practicing Tel's clairsa for the next two days. She must prove herself worthy of the Electors' nomination.

"One more thing." Glin-Erris drew up straight. "If their stance proves belligerent, we will emphasize that Netaia, as the world being approached, will be defended by the armed forces of all twenty-four Federate worlds. Three planetary navies are currently mobilizing until I personally relay an order to stand down. All known civilizations honor diplomatic immunity. We will insist on that protection if we must evacuate."

Firebird nodded, slightly distracted. At her end of the table, the Luxian pilot sat calmly eating a breakfast that smelled of sausage. Firebird's stomach gave a little flip.

"It is important," Glin-Erris finished, "in dealing with foreign cultures, to remember that innocent misunderstandings can have deadly consequences. We must assume they have good intentions. To receive the maximum benefit from any negotiation, we must be flexible."

"No," Daken barked. "We are not flexible. We find out what they want, we decide whether or not we can sell it, and we dictate terms. Most of all, we demand that they travel on, beyond Netaia, as soon as they refuel. I am the senior Netaian on this mission, and you"—he rounded on Firebird—"will cooperate in that regard."

Firebird listened hard. Daken wore no mike. Where was Marshal Burkenhamn?

"It will behoove us to be gracious," Glin-Erris said.

Something angry peered out of Daken Erwin's small eyes. "We Netaians have been invaded more than once. We shall not allow another invasion. You have plenty of room on Federate worlds. Send them past Netaia. If you won't insist, I will."

"We do not know what they want." Uri spoke up, his voice steady and reasonable. "We Sentinels will be able to evaluate whether they speak truthfully when we meet them in person. I can observe their alpha matrices—"

Daken interrupted. "Their what?"

Shel spread her hands on the tabletop. "The surface thoughts of anyone's mind create something we call the alpha matrix. Memories are deeper down."

Firebird appreciated the way that Shel—who had higher epsilon potential—distracted Daken's attention from Uri, the trained mind-access specialist.

Daken made a disgusted noise in his throat. He eyed Firebird. "I suppose they've done that to you. Multiple times."

Firebird simply said, "Yes." She had learned long ago that anything she said to Daken Erwin was ammunition for future torments. Arguing or explaining simply encouraged him.

Daken addressed Glin-Erris. "She should not be here. Neither of them," he pronounced, motioning to Shel and Uri, "should be here. I question even you, sir. All that matters is that these people travel on past Netaia, and that is all I will tell them."

Firebird spoke up. "The Planetary Navy could use that shielding of theirs, Daken."

"Grand Duke," Glin-Erris added, "by all means, tell them your preference after I introduce you. By explaining your background, I shall show them why you feel that way. You take a logical position. Assuming, again, that we are able to communicate."

Firebird had to admire Glin-Erris's even temper.

"Mister Gering," the Netaian officer's voice said in her ear, "please inform Grand Duke Daken that I am confirming Ambassador Coll's directive on behalf of the Netaian Planetary Navy."

Dodis Gering rested a massive hand on Daken's shoulder. "Sir," he said, "Marshal Lysander also asks you to cooperate with Ambassador Coll."

Daken's eyes were slits.

"That is all for now," Glin-Erris said. "Thank you." He stood and headed upship, into the forward lounge.

Toward the cockpit? Firebird followed with Shel close behind. With the hatch fastened open, it was easy to stand against its frame and peer in. The relief pilot sat relaxed in her seat, one-handing the control yoke. Her charcoal-gray Luxian uniform tunic was edged in blue green, with the short red-and-blue diagonal Federate slash over the breast.

Cometesse's instrumentation looked familiar. Shields on the console, throttle rod next to the control yoke. Simpler than the route-risk boards and multifunctional stick of a fighter. No ordnance, of course. If the pilots ever needed help, Firebird could probably fly this transport. She would enjoy that.

Glin-Erris seated himself at a side-facing station. He swept a hand up its terminal, and tiny lights winked on around the main screen. Raising a disc mike from the sloping touchboard, he spoke into it. "Unknown craft, this is the Federate transport *Cometesse*. A diplomatic delegation will be in position to speak personally, as per your request, in two standard day cycles. Please confirm."

Only a faint hiss answered for several seconds. The hiss silenced, and a voice responded. "Federate transport *Cometesse*, your delegation is very welcome."

Firebird felt her eyes widen. Voice contact. *We did it, Brenn!* To her trained ear, there was a startling lack of music to that female voice as it continued, "You shall receive landing instructions as you approach. Thank you for communicating."

Knowing that Citangelo Base would have heard every word, Firebird wrapped a hand around a grab bar and eyed the fore screen. The Strangers' spacecraft looked like a gigantic henny's egg, floating ahead of them.

Marshal . . . Lysander, was it? . . . spoke in her ear. "We copy that, *Cometesse*. Continue as ordered."

Glin-Erris pointed at a glimmering rectangle near his sideboard's left corner, glancing up at Firebird. "Marshal, we still aren't getting any lifesign readings. Their onboard shielding blocks all of our sensor waves but simple visuals."

"Confirm, Ambassador. Carry on."

As Glin-Erris cut the comm, Firebird pushed away from the door arch and looked back downship, through the acceleration lounge. Uri sat eating. Daken and Gering stood next to the warming station, reading off menu items. Daken wore a sour expression, judging by what little she could see above his beard. Those dark eyes had always frightened her.

"Hungry?" Shel asked, smiling.

"Let's wait for them to finish at the servo unit." After breakfast, she would sort her clothes and warm up her hands. She hadn't practiced diligently in months, except for those lullabies. Besides the Adorations she'd learned for Chapter meetings, she should re-polish several short classical pieces—at least two slow, soothing peacemakers, plus one flashy and virtuosic—and two or three Netaian historical suites and ballads. She wanted them memorized well enough to play without thinking about her hands. That way, she could communicate artistically to an audience, even under pressure. Music touched all human souls. Proving this would uniquely contribute to the mission, if she didn't distract her listeners with hesitations or sour notes. She hoped their little cabin was soundproofed. Serious, repetitive practice would irritate her shipmates.

Daken and Gering stepped away from the servo unit. Gering carried both trays. "Let's go," Firebird muttered, and she led Shel toward the galley.

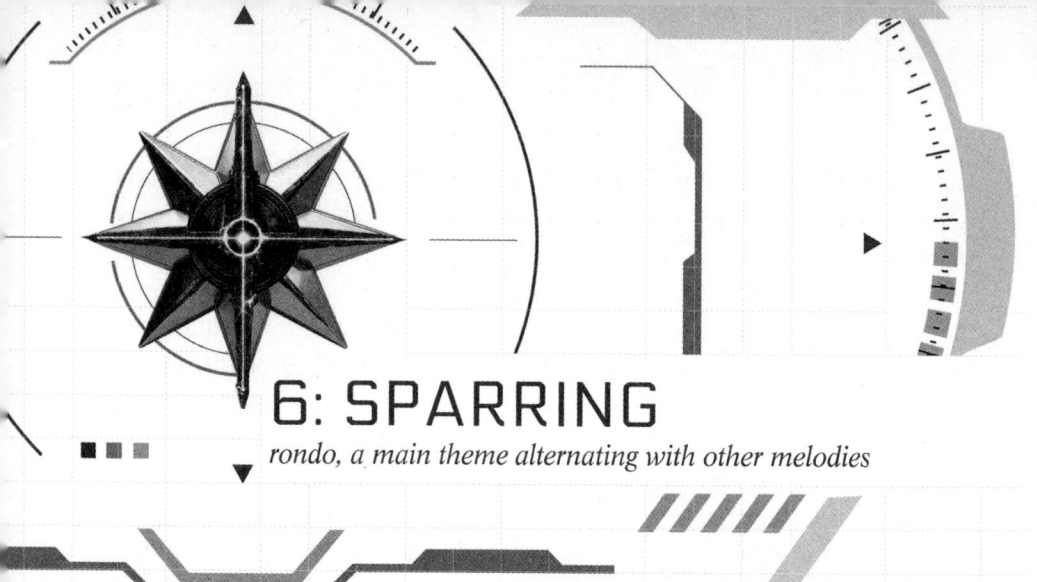

6: SPARRING
rondo, a main theme alternating with other melodies

Prince Tel Tellai-Angelo sat breakfasting on his indoor balcony, surrounded by early blossoming jantia vines and feeling wistful. He lived alone except for staff, filling his days with estate business. Spring planting was well on its way in his southern lands, and this year's crops would include essential tubers and grains for the commoners' pantries.

His interlink chimed an alert. He'd asked for updates on the ambassadors, so when he touched to receive the news, he was slightly startled to see that Claighbro House, home of Esme Rogonin, requested conversation.

Grand Duke Daken had asked him to look in on Esme. The idea of playing handmaid for Daken Erwin soured his stomach, but he'd had little contact with Esme for two years, and it would be good to see her on a more personal basis than in Electoral meetings. Perhaps enough time had passed since that terrible night when they purged the palace of Shuhr invaders and her father committed quasi-honorable suicide. Perhaps they could revisit a friendship that almost had budded.

A guard's shadow flicked across one of his skylights. Two years ago, he'd hired additional security staff. He saw no need to reduce their numbers. It was good to feel safe. Besides, he was providing worthy employment and good treatment for several Netaians whose families had been reduced to servitor status.

He delicately wiped his mouth with a cloth serviette before he touched again to converse. An unfamiliar woman wearing emerald-on-black Rogonin livery stared up at him. "Good morning, Your Highness," she said firmly but distantly, as if she were performing an unpleasant task. "My mistress the duchess is asked to see you daily, but she does not wish to travel. Might you come for a cup of cruinn at ten hundred?"

He nearly refused. Esme wasn't bothering to contact him herself. He never should have raised any hope for these visitations. He had other work to keep him busy. "I shall come," he said, making his tone of voice equally dutiful. Resigned.

"Thank you. Goodbye."

He called his tall manservant and guard, Paudan. "Have a groundcar ready at nine hundred fifty," he said. "I wish to arrive promptly."

He lingered a little longer over his savory omelet, staring up through a slanted ceiling of rose-gold framed windows into the distant sky, wondering whether Daken Erwin was trying to take command of the embassy yet. Tel could only thank the Powers—whether or not they were holy—that down here in Citangelo, Bennett Drake had been elected regent. Not First Lord Bualin Erwin.

He had Paudan dress him simply. There was no need to impress. Esme had clearly moved on, and House Tellai's children's hospital had submitted a funding request that he must address today.

The hospital was a vital concern. Still, he and Esme had shared that one terrifying night. She could not have forgotten rallying the palace servitors and begging his help.

His newest indigo groundcar waited near his ancestors' statuary garden. Nine minutes later, his driver disengaged from the city's central guidance system and turned up the Rogonins' lane. Long-leaved branches of fayya trees dangled over its main gate. They seemed poorly pruned this year. The last time he'd been here, they'd formed a perfect arch. A single sentry admitted him. Hadn't Esme's father kept at least two at the gatehouse?

On the other hand, Esme's father had been cooperating with Princess Phoena to plan an insurrection.

Tel's driver cruised past white marble outbuildings toward the familiar estate house, its blackened metal roof interrupted by the uplevel windows of staff quarters. The main entry lay between two long, low wings. In what seemed like another lifetime, he and Phoena had been fellow conspirators with Esme's father. They had plotted to put Phoena on the throne and oust Carradee. The memory shamed him. Those long wings, and the cellars below the main house, had been filled with armament. During the Federate occupation, Governor Danton's strong second, Lieutenant Governor Caldwell, had cleaned them out from roofline to subbasement.

Tel was glad that he had. Federate Governor Danton had been gone about a year. Netaia remained almost peaceful.

The chauffeur parked at the estate house's main entry and opened the car's side door. Tel slid off his seat, followed by Paudan. Pausing in front of the blindingly white door with its concealed tri-D panel, Tel breathed the sweet scent of filomen trees in full vermilion bloom. Again he looked up at the morning sky. As soon as he fulfilled this obligation, he would send a feeler to Caldwell on base. On second thought, it would be better to get his news from the palace. Kenhing would be informed, and Caldwell might not appreciate interruptions.

Impressive man, Caldwell. Getting more so every year.

Tel mounted the steps, and the ebony-framed door slid open. Beside a liveried doorman stood green-eyed Duchess Esmerield, who also had not bothered to dress formally. During the days of her father's plotting, she'd been just a girl planning her debut ball. In this loose, casual skyff and snug trousers, she actually looked rather more personable than when she'd worn an Electoral gown.

Her first words ruined the impression. "This way," she snapped.

He sighed and followed. Compared to her father, Esme seemed almost unattended. A doorman took his frock coat and gave Paudan a nod. Esme strode straight through to the long dining hall. Trophy animal heads lined both richly paneled side walls, and the massive uteh-wood table could have seated all ten of Netaia's counts, dukes, and barons, along with their spouses and heirs. He'd seen that table half-filled with conspirators. Another embarrassing memory.

Just two places were set with cups and saucers at the near end. A servant poured fragrant cruinn into gold-rimmed cups. Esme raised hers and simply stared.

He'd known not to expect cordiality, but today or tomorrow, he wanted to discuss something important. Duchess Esme, of all people, ought to understand that some of the renegade Shuhr might linger on Netaia. Esme had actually dined with some of them. She'd watched her father's bizarre behavior.

He was about to speak when footsteps tramped toward them. At the foot of the near stair, Esme's three siblings appeared. Count Farring, just past nineteen, walked up the dining hall with a dignified air. Count Kelsen, soon to be seventeen, followed close behind. The boys were dressed casually, but little Lady Diamond—now twelve—had put on a long green gown that looked like a cut-down version of Esme's Electoral attire. Lady Diamond's hips swayed as she walked, and she sent him a coquettish smile.

Tel eyed Count Kelsen. He had heard encouraging rumors about this former wastling, promoted to heir status when Esme became Duchess. It would be premature if not impolite to inquire.

"You're ready for tomorrow?" Esme addressed them firmly.

Count Farring, now her heir, half bowed to her. "Packed for autumn," he declared in a startlingly deep voice. "Ready for sport."

"The hovercraft will be here tomorrow at eleven hundred."

Lady Diamond, the family wastling, stepped up to Tel. He caught a breath of musky perfume. "Are you going to be calling on Esme?" She flicked the long skirt of her gown back and forth, back and forth. "She says you are. You may call on me instead. She likes Daken Erwin. I don't really want to go south."

Lady Diamond Rogonin was far too young to be flirting, but she probably knew that the Electors had recently ordered him to remarry and start fathering heirs for House Tellai. Wastlings no longer lived in danger, officially, but old assumptions died hard.

"Thank you, my lady," he said, "but you are obliged to obey your sister, the head of your House." He raised an eyebrow at Esme. Surely she would share his amusement.

"You're going," Esme told Diamond. "You're all going. Now, I have a guest. Go find your tutor."

Farring marched the other two back down the main-floor hallway, past a second stair. As Tel recalled, that one spiraled up past family quarters to a rooftop landing platform.

"South?" he asked delicately, sticking with polite niceties. It would be autumn down on the South Continent. All the noble Families had properties down there.

"Count Kelsen," she declared, frowning, "has become interested in that Thyrian worship house. I want him out of town for a while. If anything happens to Farring, Kelsen still might honor the Powers as the head of House Rogonin."

Ah, then, the rumors were true. The Rogonin family had a youngster interested in Brennen Caldwell's faith. Still, he mustn't interfere in their House's affairs. "You're wise," he said. That much was safe. "If our hearts turned away from the Powers, could we maintain our leadership, guiding Netaia?" It was the correct question to ask, even though he doubted the answer.

"Interesting that you would say that." Esme leaned toward him, her green eyes suddenly intense. He caught the sweet scent of her loosely coiffed hair. "Your late wife, may she dance in Bliss, turned from Netaian ways to those mind-crawling renegades on Three Zed. Forgive me, I am sure it's still a painful memory, but we all saw that it cost her terribly. And you, as well."

Her words stung, but it pleased him to hear her speak of something important. He could receive it as sympathy. "Thank you, Duchess." He opened a palm. It would have been proper to kiss her hand. Might he hope—?

She dropped both hands into her lap.

He did too. Under today's circumstances, he had no intention of telling her he'd actually landed a spacecraft on Three Zed with Lady Firebird as his passenger, trying to rescue Phoena and Caldwell. People here knew that Phoena Angelo had only married him for convenience. Sadly, this made his dandified disguise believable—even to Esme, who on that one incredible night had come with Kenhing, asking for his help. They had stormed the palace, accompanied by bodyguard staff and several Sentinels. Tel himself had shot and killed the Shuhr leader.

The memory still made his gorge rise. He'd begged his Sentinel allies to keep this story quiet. He was no killer.

He could, however, help keep Duchess Esme safe. He gestured in the general direction of Claighbro House's front gate. "After our visit, may I walk around your estate and make sure all is secure? While I walk, you could have your employees monitor your outdoor surveillance. I think that the Grand Duke would appreciate any measures we take for your safety."

"Yes, yes. Tell me about it tomorrow. When the children go south, I will have business to finish. I would go with them, but my duty is to the Electorate. I must remain on call."

He risked a small smile. There still was much to like in Esme Rogonin, including her commitment to responsibility. And those green eyes—

"Absolutely," he said, strangling the dangerous thought. That weed might blossom into trouble. "You know your duty," he said solemnly, "and you do it well." He fell back into that airy, affected voice. "I was very sorry that your name was not called for our diplomatic mission. Your optimism is a sparkling balance to those who seem consumed by their fears."

She snorted and set down her cup so hard that the saucer rattled. "Daken Erwin is smarter than all of them. He wants to send those ships deeper into the Federacy, and I agree, but I can't imagine that anyone we've deputized to that unknown vessel will welcome them with the grace that we should be showing to others—that I would have shown."

Tel furrowed his brow. Esme was daring an oblique criticism. He wished he could drop his camouflage and support her, but clearly, Esme felt no need for his support. He must live on the fringes of a society he'd once hoped to help lead, and he must make official visitations to a woman he once had admired, on behalf of a man who would not honor her.

It was tempting to be heartsick.

She picked up her interlink. "Excuse me. I must call my south-continent manager."

He'd fulfilled his obligation. He pushed back his chair, and his manservant Paudan pulled it out the rest of the way. When Tel stood, he declared, "I shall call tomorrow at ten hundred. Briefly."

One corner of her mouth twitched, and she continued to stare downward instead of looking back up.

Her big doorman reappeared, holding Tel's frock coat. Tel accepted it and walked back out the wide entryway. Paudan followed.

The indigo groundcar waited close by, but at the stairs' foot, Tel bent to address his driver. "Jess, I wish to walk the grounds for a few minutes. Wait for me."

"Very good, sir."

Stepping lightly across an overgrown night-fragrance flower bed—why had Esme's staff let the vines ramble so?—took him to an equally overgrown slope that still shimmered with dewdrops in shaded areas. Paudan followed at a respectful distance. At the hill's foot, a line of springtime-chartreuse leta trees obscured a pillared stone outwall. Beyond a maintenance gap in that wall, a streamlined groundcar almost as long as his own, but white, cruised into view. It practically stopped before it slowly, slowly drove on.

Truly, Esme needed more guards. Besides the single doorman, there'd been just one sentry at the front gate and one bodyguard out in the hallway. Did she have additional grounds staff? He stepped up onto a retaining wall and looked all around. He saw no one, particularly not—obviously, to his gardener's eye—a horticulturist. Even after two years in her new position, she was apparently having trouble finding or retaining staff.

He could not get his mind off the danger of Shuhr. At one time, the nobles had taken notice. There'd been a mass hiring of bodyguards right after the palace was stormed. There'd been no known Shuhr incidents since then, but Esme and her siblings needed more protectors. Perhaps she'd distrusted the women and men her father hired. Perhaps some had been arrested when her father's duplicity was exposed.

He picked up his pace and finished his circuit. It left him nearly out of breath and expecting to be challenged at any moment. He should have been challenged.

He was not.

Tomorrow, he and Esme must discuss something serious.

His chauffeur had glided forward to wait where Tel's path crossed the entry lane. Good man, that Jess. Tel intended to recommend him for class promotion, a privilege that the loyal Paudan had already declined.

"Home," Tel ordered as Paudan opened the side door for him.

Five hours after launch, Brennen took a stool amid several sensor screens. Careful not to spill his mug of kass, he dispersed his epsilon shields. The command center surrounded him with a stew of dread and anticipation. Netaia's powerful, planet-based probes continued to try and scan the Strangers' lead ship, but only visual data appeared. How large a force was on board, and what about those following ships?

He sipped his kass and restored his cloud of epsilon static. Netaian newsnets would demand an update soon. On the still-unclear chance that civil defense must be activated, that would be another sooner-the-better priority. Netaia's families must be protected—including, today, his own, as Mari flew toward potential danger. This was the life they had chosen, with the additional burden of sending others into peril.

He eyed the microphone controller in his hand. He'd ordered that mike-con and the detailed interlink network, including three private links or any combination of them. Using that handheld mike-con, he isolated Mari's collar mike in his earpiece. He heard only silence. She was undoubtedly studying.

He tucked the mike-con into a belt pocket.

Marshal Burkenhamn had returned. He approached to stand next to Brennen's shoulder, and Brennen dispersed his shields again. The marshal's emotional level was steady, tempered by the authority he'd worn in previous crises. Moving away from sensors, Brennen looked at the First Marshal. "Readiness?" he asked.

"About eighty percent." Marshal Burkenhamn gazed up at the central display, where the massive ovoid hovered between its twin followers. "What in the Whorl, or beyond it, is approaching us?"

Cautiously, Brennen asked, "How do you read it?"

Burkenhamn clasped his hands behind his broad back. "Even a small invasion group, with advanced enough weaponry, could do considerable damage. But it could also be easily pinpointed and destroyed. If only we had better data on those shields." Wisely, the marshal had gone straight to the worst-case scenario. That was his mission.

"Yes." Brennen set his mug on a service bench. "But it would be against Federate ideals to strike before we know who they are."

"My priority is Netaian defense."

"And mine. We have time." As they had discussed, tomorrow afternoon when the ambassadors boarded that ship and set up their scanning unit within those mysterious shields, the base should have more information.

And perhaps, soon, the ability to create similar shielding for Federate ships.

Marshal Burkenhamn turned slightly aside and lowered his voice. "Are you able to sense people—Commander Angelo-Caldwell, at least—over this distance?"

Brennen gave the standard response. "Roughly a room's width is our limit." A quest-pulse could carry mental energy farther than that, and he could sustain an epsilon wave farther than many Sentinels. Still, planetary distances were impossible, even for him, except for rare instances involving Remote Individual Amplification technology. RIA was new tech, tightly regulated by Regional Command. For good reason. Not long ago, it had been top-level secret.

The big marshal looked sympathetic. "No wonder you prefer to travel together."

Brennen nodded. He understood that others were curious. He turned the conversation back to the previous topic. "The sooner we can get tech specs on those shields, the happier I will be."

Marshal Burkenhamn shook his head. "We've tested them with visible light, sonics, ultraviolet, and low-energy laser. The bounce doesn't correspond to anything we've ever seen, anywhere in the Whorl. We can't even tell whether it's energy or particle shielding. Assuming they have to drop shields to let our people aboard, we may soon know more." He glanced at the display again. "Getting that remote scanning unit aboard should give us better data."

Better data always meant better defense. There also was *Cometesse*'s escort ship, a heavy fighter. One of those was generally deterrent enough to ensure the safety of a Federate delegation.

As for the mysterious shields, an engineering team sat beyond the tri-D well, called in to analyze data, to brainstorm and speculate. Glin-Erris would assure the Strangers that Netaia's call-up was a normal precaution against a worst-case scenario that they meant to avert. The probability remained that they were travelers in need of help.

But why, if they'd come from beyond the inhabited Whorl, had they come without adequate fuel?

Maybe they'd traveled farther than intended. Maybe their home world, like that of his distant ancestors, was destroyed. Maybe they needed fuel to get home.

Too many maybes. The Federate force needed information. They needed that scanning unit.

Marshal Burkenhamn strode away. Brennen drew out his handheld mike-con again. "I am back on duty, Mari," he said softly, "but don't let me interrupt your studies."

A few seconds later, her response came. "You're not interrupting. It's good to hear your voice."

As it was good to hear hers. "That is all for now," he said, turning back to the tri-D well. In it, the *Cometesse* was a spark slowly rising through Netaian space.

On board *Cometesse*, there'd been a peaceful midday meal. Daken had kept quiet while everyone else studied Glin-Erris's files.

As Glin-Erris gathered his utensils, Daken leaned over the dull metal table and finally spoke, sending Firebird one of his nasty smiles, barely visible through his beard. "You all are tired of studying. What might you say about letting our personal assistants have a friendly tussle?"

Surprised, Firebird glanced sideways at Shel. Maybe a friendly match—if they could keep it friendly—could create a shared memory. Also, Daken was probably feeling out Team Firebird. If he discovered that her team was strong, he might settle down and cooperate. Together, they could help the Strangers and send them on. Diplomatically, not belligerently.

So, what about his suggestion? Stocky Dodis Gering stood at his right shoulder. Firebird eyed his broad chest and sturdy shoulders. "Does that interest you, Mister Gering?" she asked.

"I am always at the Grand Duke's service," he said without emotion.

Shel rose from the table. Although tall with a long reach, she relied on skill instead of mass, and she didn't look like a Netaian bodyguard in the same way that Gering did. Firebird glanced at Glin-Erris and raised both eyebrows in a question. His hand barely opened on the tabletop, like a miniature shrug. Brennen's equally well-trained bodyguard Uri sat next to him, a motionless midnight-blue shadow.

Was there room in here? Maybe, if they moved the galley table aside.

She heard Brennen's voice, though no one else seemed to. "Let them," he said. "If you humor Daken Erwin, maybe he'll relax and be more cooperative. We can also get a read on whether Dodis Gering is trustworthy." He paused, and his tone of voice became lighter. "We could use a release here in the command center too."

Daken pointed a fork at Shel. "But no mental funny business."

"I don't think this is necessary." Firebird spoke seriously, but she knew Daken Erwin. She was consciously egging him on. "And please don't offend my friend Shelevah by accusing her of funny business."

"If it comes to blows out there," Daken said, pointing beyond the transport's bow, "shouldn't we have some idea what our people are capable of?"

Any excuse for a melee. He surely wasn't studying. He was probably bored.

Shel dropped her tray into the recycler. "I'm not offended." She looked past Daken's shoulder to address her prospective opponent. "It is good to stay in physical training, and we could dissipate some tension. Any particular rules?"

"You may set them, ma'am," Gering said in a genteel voice.

Shel didn't hesitate. "Tailbone to deck as point, three falls out of five, and a five-second limit on grappling?"

Gering's eyes widened a bit. Obviously, his opinion of Shel had just improved. He stood a little straighter. "I would find that acceptable."

Glin-Erris stepped away from the table. "There will be no injuries. We face the Strangers in only a day."

Daken puffed out a laugh. "No award to the winner?"

"Only pride," Glin-Erris returned. "Would you both agree to those conditions?"

"Shel?" Uri touched his collar mike. "He'd be good with this. Are you?" Meaning, Uri had also heard from Brennen.

Shel shrugged.

Firebird wasn't fully sold on the idea. Anyone could lose their balance for one dangerous moment. For example, there'd been that one time at home—just once—when she actually pinned Brenn. They'd both lain bewildered for the space of several gasping breaths before they burst out laughing.

Shel was good on the mat, though. She could throw a trainee without bruising her. She wouldn't harm Dodis Gering.

"On my honor," Shel said, "I will not try to cause any physical harm."

"And I," answered Gering, "will not deliberately injure this woman."

As soon as Glin-Erris gave the okay, things moved quickly. Glin-Erris and Uri unbolted the table and heaved it forward into the acceleration lounge, creating a space wide enough for a precision match. Gering switched off his collar mike and peeled off his livery tunic to stand bare chested. He ran a hand over his silvery hair.

Firebird switched her interlink to the private frequency. Immediately, Brennen's amused voice sounded in her ear. "Stay clear."

"Mm-hmm," she hummed softly, claiming a spot near the aft passway. Shel's short hair wouldn't give Gering anything to grab, and her casual shipboards wouldn't impede her motion. This would be Shel's impressive height and reach—and training—against the bulkier man's strength and weight. He might even know something about hand-to-hand.

Shel turned to Firebird. "Call the first round."

Firebird nodded. "On three."

They crouched, Shel near the servo unit where their meals appeared, and Gering under the arch of the opposite bulkhead. "Ready," he called, rubbing his hands.

Shel gave a firm nod.

"One. Two. Begin."

The bodyguards circled, hands open. Gering pointed his left shoulder toward Shel like a massive shield for eight steps, and then he lunged. Shel spun behind him, hands raised, ignoring his exposed backside. *Kicking,* she'd taught Firebird, *is risky. All your weight balances on one foot.* Kicks wouldn't even score points, according to the rules Shel had set.

Those thoughts flitted through Firebird's mind in an instant. They were circling again. This time, Shel reached for Gering's lead elbow. As if training a new fighter, she left her upper body open. Gering rotated in with a hip and grabbed her shoulders. Shel relaxed onto the deck.

"Score," Firebird said. "Gering." The big manservant raised an arm victoriously and rotated in place, but Firebird thought she glimpsed a lack of confidence in his downcast eyes.

"Hah," Daken called from near the starboard bulkhead. "One down, two to go."

In her ear: "Gift point?"

Firebird hummed again. "Mm-hmm." She kept her expression bland. Evidently, Gering knew a bit about tussling, but he was markedly slower than Shel. Firebird glanced around at the other watchers. As Daken continued to gloat, Uri pressed his palms together, looking appropriately concerned. Glin-Erris stood near the cockpit, arms crossed, frowning slightly. Behind him, a Luxian pilot peered into the galley. Almost smiling.

Actually, it was refreshing to think about something other than diplomatic responses to unexpected situations and the energy resources of twenty-four world systems. "Daken," Firebird said, trying to sound friendly. "You call round two."

This time, Shel made Gering work, turning to circle left and right, feinting and blocking, feeling out his reflexes and instinctive responses from various angles. When she finally dropped him to the gray deck with a thump, he almost looked relieved.

Daken's cheeks reddened above that perfect beard. "Score," he said reluctantly, "Mattson."

Soft cheers sounded in Firebird's ear. Was the whole command center listening? She tilted her chin and corrected Daken. "Matt-ta-son." The surname honored Mattah, the priest who rescued all those Ehretan children.

"I'll call the next point." Glin-Erris uncrossed his arms and stepped aside so not to block the pilot's view. "Unless the combatants would like a break."

Gering wiped his forehead and shook his head.

"No, thank you," Shel said calmly.

This third round ended so quickly that Firebird didn't see what happened. Maybe Uri did, but there was Gering, sitting down again. Across the galley, Daken stood with his legs planted wide and his little eyes narrowed. Maybe he was starting to realize that he'd sent Gering against the wrong combatant. Shel wasn't even breathing hard.

"Three out of five?" Shel asked, reaching down to help Gering back to his feet.

Gering glanced at Daken, got no reaction but a glower, and accepted the lift.

In the fourth round, Shel let Gering push her almost to the bulkhead before she used his own weight to flatten him.

"Match to Mattason," Firebird called happily, and again she heard faraway cheering.

"Cheating!" Daken clenched and unclenched his fists. "She's certainly using mental tricks."

"No," Uri said from his position near the cockpit. "She was not."

Daken fumed. "You Sentinels are in this together."

So much for bonding.

Shel strode toward Daken. To his credit, he stood his ground. "Do not insult me. When I give my word, I keep it. And this," she said firmly, "would have been cheating." She crouched and leaped, rising over Daken's head in a slow, tightly tucked somersault that he tracked big-eyed. She nearly grazed the upper bulkhead before gracefully landing behind him.

Silence hung in the galley. Kinetic levitation always impressed outsiders. It still impressed Firebird.

Gering stood panting, gripping one arm. Shel turned toward him. "But I taught this sport for five years, Mister Gering." She extended her palm. Gering clasped it. He said nothing, but Firebird caught his slight, respectful nod and breathed a little easier. Gering had not tried to cheat. Maybe they could trust him, but clearly Daken would not remember this as a happy moment. Maybe trying to get through to him was hopeless.

Glin-Erris raised both hands. "Very well, Grand Duke Daken. The match that you suggested did not turn out as you expected. Let there be peace among us now. Tomorrow, we face the unknown. Together."

Firebird thanked Shel and congratulated her. If Daken had any intelligence, he might surmise that his little wastling had studied hand-to-hand with someone who taught the skills. Or maybe, in his world, employees existed only to serve. Not to teach.

Troubled, she retreated to her cabin to practice her clairsa and study the files. She must be ready for tomorrow afternoon.

Alone in their cabin, Daken thrust a finger at his manservant's glistening chest. "You humiliated me," Daken growled. "Never, never do that again."

Gering gripped the edge of the lower bunk two-handed. "Sir," he offered, "you wanted to know whether the woman was to be feared. You gained valuable information." His livery tunic lay crumpled beside him.

"You made me a laughingstock." Daken paced the tiny cabin, pulse pounding. "You were hired to protect and defend me. Me, Gering."

The manservant bowed his head and stared downward. Properly humbled, from all appearances. But to Daken's mind, Dodis Gering no longer deserved the full trust that Grand Duke Daken Erwin demanded of his employees. "You will remain silent," Daken decided aloud, "until I give permission to speak. Tomorrow, when we deal with this menace to Netaia, you will remain in position and shield me from all comers. You answer to me. Not some mind-crawler's made-up rules. To me. Is that understood?"

The big man pressed his lips together and nodded.

Daken sniffed and pulled a cleansing cloth from a wall dispenser. "Here," he said. "You stink. Clean yourself."

Again, Gering nodded silently.

"And make sure that spy device is turned off. They don't need to hear what we say in private."

Gering reached for his tunic, unclipped the mike, and offered it on his palm for Daken's inspection.

The switch was rotated to the *off* position. Daken relaxed slightly. Tomorrow, all this humiliation would be worth it. He would stand before alien strangers and order them away. He would return to claim his bride and the adulation of his peers. He would accomplish what the crawling Federates and arrogant wastling could not. If he could not draw her blood anymore, at least he could shame her.

It was his birthright.

Pressing an ear to the bulkhead, he heard the irritating, repetitive tinkling of that blasted little harp. Wasn't she supposed to be studying? What did she think she could accomplish with music? This occasion called for strength. Strength of arms, strength of character.

And he was strong.

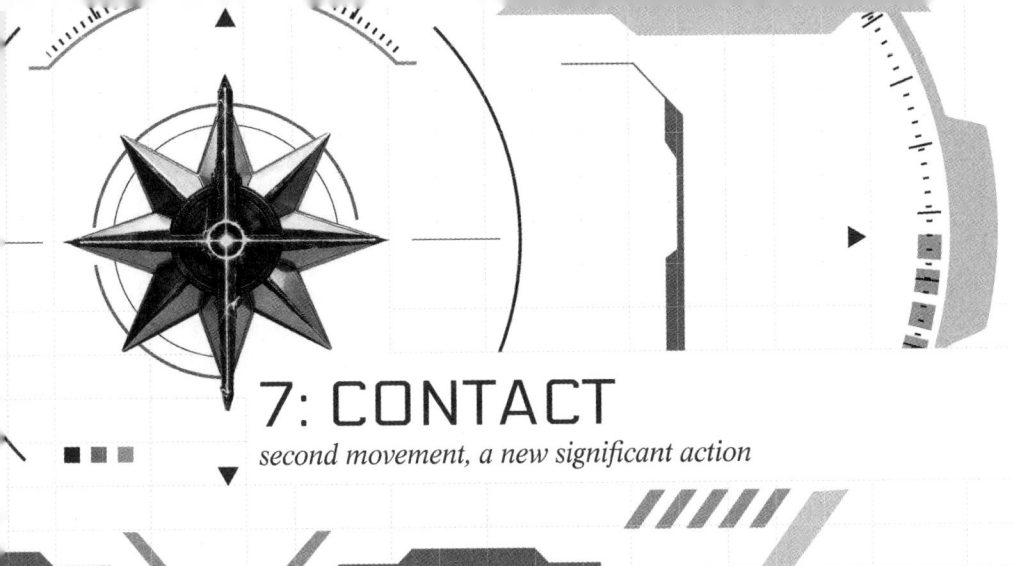

7: CONTACT
second movement, a new significant action

The second day after launch began. Upon reaching the command center, Brennen glanced at a timer on the nearest display. *Cometesse* would arrive in about ten hours. The tri-D well displayed its gradual approach to that lead object, which still was shielded in something that looked like flame.

He saluted the controllers and stepped back out into the low-ceilinged secure alcove, where he sat down on a padded bench. Equipped with sound-deadening black walls, soft floor tiles, and ceiling panels, the alcove was lit only by secondhand light from the command center. Using the mike-con, he directed his transmission and softly said, "Good morning, Mari. Are you alone?"

Rustling noises sounded in his earpiece. She was probably switching her interlink to the private frequency. "One moment," she whispered. Light footsteps tapped across a metal deck. A hatch closed with a swish and a click. "There," she said. "I'm alone. We just finished breakfast. Hello, Brenn."

"How are you? What's your read on the team this morning?"

Her hesitation might have been due to distance. "We're a little tense. We ought to figure out how to work together, but there hasn't been time to get through to Daken Erwin. Glin-Erris's tutorial is outstanding, on the other hand." Her voice took on a defiant note. "If anyone on board this transport doesn't know how to conduct a diplomatic encounter, it will be his own fault."

His. Indeed.

Her tone changed. "Now I know more about the Federacy's energy resources, and what we have to offer, than they ever taught us at the Academy. Are you impressed?"

Was she evading? He would ask for a straight answer in a few moments. First, though: "Tellai wants to know, 'Will the clairsa suit?'"

Instead of an answer, he heard a rolling arpeggio followed by the first notes and chords of a melody she had written while she was under protective custody. He smiled wistfully. With a nearly eidetic memory, one did not forget the joyous focusing of his heart into love. She had been so proud, so eager to sacrifice herself. "Tell him yes. It suits very well," she said. "And thank him."

Brushing sweet images aside, he said, "I need a report on Daken Erwin. If he is actually jeopardizing the mission, I can authorize voice-command." He reviewed some section of the Privacy and Priority Codes every day.

She sighed, making the collar mike roar. "Shel thinks he's probably going to provoke something, but I think we'll be ready. I do have that shock pistol. And Shel is Shel. Daken saw that yesterday."

Yes. They had hired Shel away from the Sentinel College. She was highly qualified in three martial arts. "You're just tense, not actually worried?"

"Right." She said it quickly. He wished he could feel her emotions instead of just trying to read her voice, as if she were some stranger. She almost convinced him. Courage didn't mean there was no fear. Often, it meant acting in spite of fear.

"You kept that cabin door locked overnight."

"Yes, sir." He knew that tease in her voice, but it was an appropriate response.

Back to business. "We will need the data from that scanning unit you have aboard," he said. "Their shields are still completely blocking us. Send confirmation as soon as the scanning unit is transferred and operational. Even before you speak with them, if possible. A white light should pulse on each of its exterior surfaces, confirming that it's operating and transmitting."

"All right. I'm sure you've got a private link to Glin-Erris too. And to Uri?"

"Yes." He tucked the controller back into his belt pocket and asked, "What will you do next?"

"Study Glin-Erris's diplomatic bundle until we board. I really am impressed with him, Brenn. And I'll practice Tel's clairsa until my fingers bleed."

Plainly, she still believed that music would move all human souls. He understood humanness rather differently, and music had not been as significant to him until he'd met her. "I assume you have not received any further comm from the Strangers." That would have been reported immediately.

"No. We're not on approach yet."

"All right. We are watching over you, Mari. So is the Holy One. Power and might are in his hand."

"Thank you, Brenn." Firebird switched off her little interlink and reopened Glin-Erris's files. Shel soon joined her. They both wore comfortable shipboards. Two hours crawled past as they lay propped on their bunks, studying. Firebird took brief breaks to practice and toughen her fingertips. She'd slept last night with strips of medicinal biotape on them.

When they returned to the galley for the midday meal, she chose *Stew #3* off the menu, a long-time travel favorite. The company was almost silent, with everyone except Daken and Glin-Erris studying. Glin-Erris tried twice to draw Daken into conversation. Daken answered in monosyllables.

Firebird frowned. They all needed to be bonding with each other, and it just wasn't happening. Still, she'd been honest with Brennen. Things were tense, not worrisome.

And since Citangelo Base was monitoring, talking did feel a little uncomfortable. So she studied, practiced, and tried to ignore the tiny time lights on her wristband, counting down hours to their arrival.

Later that afternoon, Brennen diverted epsilon energy to his aching back and feet. He had stood in the command center all day, observing as Netaia's fleet dispersed from its surface and low orbit. In the waist-high tri-D well, their gold blips and silvery targeting cones now created a defensive net around the planet's blue-green sphere. Within hours, those targeting cones would surround the Strangers' mystery ships. In just over two hours, the ambassadors would go aboard the lead ship and open in-person negotiations.

Mari. He couldn't sense her presence, but he still knew exactly where she was.

In the tri-D well, the Strangers' unusual shields still appeared as a flame-like shimmer around its ovoid surface. If those shields flickered out of existence as *Cometesse* approached, the engineers would know them for particle shields. Most Federate warships and military bases projected both particle and energy shielding.

An advanced technology might be able to create a landing breach in particle shielding, or perhaps they had a kind of shielding the Federacy had not yet developed or even imagined. He wanted that shielding. Not just for the Federacy, but for his people's sanctuary world and its defense. Shuhr forces had been soundly defeated, but survivors had doubtless scattered. They might regather and rise again, and his people were the Federacy's only defense against them.

He headed back to the privacy alcove and stretched out on a bench, thinking beyond the command center while he could. Contemplating new technology.

He had arrived on Netaia via governmental transport, shadowed by one escort fighter—but also by a second ship now hangared at a far corner of the base. The Federate Messenger service had recently developed a faster version of the small, speedy DS-212s he had ridden so many times. Back on Tallis, he had commandeered one atmospheric craft and one cross-space DS-215 for the Sentinels' Remote Individual Amplification project. On this trip, they had tested RIA's new, and still top secret, ability to travel undetected. According to Netaian instruments and records he had surreptitiously checked, it had passed the test. Stealth was not RIA's primary purpose, though. His kin had developed RIA technology to extend their epsilon powers over greater distances. Non-gifted people who knew about RIA became alarmed, and he didn't blame them. Even he had mixed feelings about enhancing Sentinels' abilities. With enhanced strengths came enhanced temptations. Even Prince Tel had warned him that some people thought the Sentinel kindred meant to take over the Federacy.

They did not. Still, the experimental ship's Sentinel pilots were camping out and standing guard at the hangar.

He eyed the time lights on his wrist. An hour and three-quarters, now. *Go with them. Protect them. Guide them. Especially—*

He squeezed his eyes shut and amended his prayer. *Protect and guide them all.*

Countdown to arrival had nearly zeroed. In her cabin on board the *Cometesse*, Firebird carefully attached to her high, white collar the three-moon clip of her Netaian rank as Second Commander, as well as the rather embarrassing Veroh Invasion service clip. Netaia's Triple Arrow for valor stood out better on Carradee's gold-edged blue sash, so she'd fastened it there. She pulled her hair into a catch at the nape of her neck.

The cabin had one slightly shining wall. Taking a deep breath, she eyed her blurry reflection. She'd seen portraits of other Houses' heirs dressed as hybrid soldier-nobles. She'd mocked them.

It was her turn. She too looked like some sort of hybrid, a slender young veteran, a Federate-Netaian traveler on the Holy Path, hoping to establish friendly contact with an unknown people. *Help!* she prayed. Short and sweet, like the little boys who'd dominated last night's dreams. She'd tucked a tri-D cube into her duffel, an image of all four of them, to show any Strangers who proved friendly.

Tel's little clairsa lay cased on her bunk too. It had half an octave too few strings at the low end, but she felt practiced and ready.

She checked the switch on the back of her collar mike—set, as Glin-Erris had directed them all, to the general frequency—and clipped it to her collar opposite the insignia. She checked and holstered her heavy-bodied shock pistol and ran her eyes over their duffels and issue bags.

Shel looked tall and sharp in her midnight blues, her strongly cleft chin showing a tiny shadow. She looked Firebird up and down and said, "No matter what Daken Erwin says, you are the senior Netaian representative. You are the Angelo. You're next in line to the throne. Don't let him talk over you, if they address you."

Firebird never wanted that gilt chair—well, practically never—and she was not at all sure she wanted today's responsibility. This wasn't going to be like going into battle against a known enemy, not the "fair fight" she'd imagined. Instead, she'd been given the honor of a lifetime. She must support Glin-Erris in negotiating for fuel supplies, try to impress the Strangers with Netaia's military capabilities and, perhaps—if they gave her the opportunity—introduce them to Netaia's high culture. Carefully she raised the clairsa case by its carrying strap.

"May I?" Shel reached out. "You'll want to keep all that decoration exposed, so they can see it. Even if they can't read what it means."

"All right. Thank you." She handed off the clairsa and picked up her bags, unlocked the hatch, and stepped into the passway, then led through the galley into the acceleration lounge.

Glin-Erris and Uri stood near the cockpit, Glin-Erris also shining in multi-decorated dress whites. Uri, officially a lieutenant colonel, matched Shel in crisp midnight blues, but Sentinels never wore insignia or decorations other than the star.

Glin-Erris gripped a handheld microphone. Firebird set her bags near the main hatch.

Uri saluted her.

Yes, at this moment, they were transitioning from shipmates to fellow ambassadors. It was the uniform he'd saluted, not the woman wearing it. She returned his salute and gave Glin-Erris the formal half bow due a Federate diplomat.

"We're catchfielded," their reserve pilot announced from the cockpit. "They're bringing us in."

Glin-Erris spoke toward his collar mike. "Citangelo, have those shields dropped?"

"Negative," she heard in her ear. "Apparently, they're energy, not particle."

Another unfamiliar voice ordered, "You are to test your interlink reception and deploy the scanning unit as soon as you're aboard."

Firebird understood. Uri had been ordered to take the portable unit out of its cargo compartment and set it down inside the landing bay. It looked heavy, so he might levitate it.

That would give Daken something else to gape at. However, the Sentinels had discussed whether to show the Strangers their unusual skills. The decision: not yet. Maybe not at all. They were not here to intimidate anyone, but to protect Glin-Erris, Daken, and Firebird.

Firebird peered past Glin-Erris, into the cockpit and through it. Both Luxian pilots sat watching the approach. The Strangers' curved hull filled the fore screen.

Daken and Gering finally strode around the galley table, wearing their orange-on-black livery. She straightened and faced them, letting them take a good look. Even if they hated her, they had to respect her rank. It wasn't just honorary.

Daken's little eyes narrowed over his freshly trimmed beard. He swept a slow, obvious stare over her, starting at her pulled-back hair and ending with her deck shoes. He glared at the Federate slash over her breast and then pointed at her waist. "She's armed," he complained toward Glin-Erris. "Why aren't we all?"

Firebird kept her voice low. "This," she said, "is a military uniform. And that," she added, "is only a shock pistol. Here." She drew it and handed it to him, butt first, then wondered what in the Whorl had compelled her to do that.

She felt Shel step closer.

He wouldn't dare fire it. Not here, not now, on approach, with Citangelo Base listening.

Daken grabbed the gun one-handed, curled his fingers around the thick chamber, and pointed it at a bulkhead. His sloppy stance revealed that he'd held energy weapons, but only casually.

Good to know.

He handed it back. "You may defend me," he sneered. "Gering has one too."

She glanced at the big man. He wore no obvious holster. Carrying concealed, was he? He remained straight-faced as usual.

"Silence in the cabin, please." Glin-Erris raised the cockpit's handheld mike and spoke into it. "This is Ambassador Glin-Erris Coll aboard the Federate transport *Cometesse*, requesting landing instructions."

The deck vibrated under Firebird's feet. Behind *Cometesse*, that single heavy fighter—their escort—would be decelerating into a parking position.

"Ambassador Glin-Erris Coll." The voice in the cockpit speaker was the same she'd heard before—low and tuneless, almost synthetic, but distinctly feminine. "Welcome, Federate transport *Cometesse*. Landing bay opening now. You shall dock within."

"Lifesigns," announced the left-seated Luxian pilot. "We're getting a large, diffuse reading."

Finally! With those shields dropped for their landing, they soon would know more.

Daken pushed past her. He twisted the cockpit mike out of Glin-Erris's hand. "I am Grand Duke Daken Cellen Erwin, also on board the transport *Cometesse*, and as I speak for Netaia, I am the senior diplomat. You will als—"

Whatever else he meant to say, he fell silent mid-word. Across the cockpit hatch from Glin-Erris, Uri had raised a hand in an unmistakable voice-command posture. Sentinels often used a modulated voice to focus their epsilon powers, and Firebird heard it now. "No," Uri said.

Clutching the mike against his chest, Daken backed away.

Uri lowered his hand, releasing Daken from voice-command.

Instantly, Daken raised the mike again. "You will listen to me," he said angrily.

Shel brushed past them all, into the cockpit. "Cut comm," she ordered.

"Already silenced." The left-seater's hand hovered over her console.

The distant woman's bland voice spoke again. "I thank you for coming in person. I will speak with you again once you are on board."

In Firebird's ear, Brennen asked, "Confirm, Erwin's trying to seize authority?"

"Yes. But we have established communication." Their real mission had begun.

Daken stepped away from the hatch, glowering. Was he back under voice-command? She tilted her head toward Uri and raised both eyebrows. Sentinels didn't always need to read minds to pick up visual and emotional cues.

Uri barely shook his head.

Firebird looked toward the cockpit again. Up ahead, a landing bay slowly opened to receive them.

The left-seat pilot softly said, "We're still unable to get any lifesign readings from their two following ships. Either they're still shielded, or for all we can tell, they could be empty."

"Copy," said a voice in Firebird's ear.

Could those be the biggest drones she'd ever seen? Glin-Erris would try to determine, quickly, whether the Strangers were military. Citangelo Base would react swiftly, if that were the case. Firebird's military role would become more vital. So would her link to Citangelo Base. She felt ready. Having Shel at her shoulder would feel like flying lead in a flight team once more.

Did the woman command the Strangers' ship, or was she simply the comm officer? *Will speaking with her be my role? Does she have family, too?*

"Everyone?" Their right-seat Luxian pilot turned his head and called,

"The landing bay is fully open. We're going inside. Seat yourselves, in case there's minor turbulence. We don't anticipate anything worth harnessing for."

Shel handed Firebird the clairsa case as they sat down. "Eternal Sovereign, watch over us."

"Amen." *Commit this day to His will and live it,* Firebird added silently, echoing her Path instructor. She cradled the instrument on her lap and got a last look into starry sky. A thick metal wall appeared. It appeared to slide behind them. A brightly lit metal cavern slowly swallowed them. Ninety-degree angles joined deck and bulkhead. A few hoses dangled. She didn't spot any of the blocky starter units that normally dotted a landing bay. Was that significant? Dust billowed as *Cometesse* pivoted 180 degrees into re-launching position. How long had the Strangers been traveling?

They settled smoothly onto a receiving grid. Dust continued to swirl in the vacuum beyond her viewport. The huge space door slid shut, now ahead of them. Brilliant panels shone overhead. She felt her heart racing.

Glin-Erris walked up to the cockpit. "We're watching for airflow now," he told the rest of them. "Still red zone, but rising."

Daken finally spoke again. "Whatever they are, they breathe what we do."

Ah, the Netaian xenophobia. Did he really expect tentacled aliens? For all his bluster, the man must be terrified. For one moment, she actually pitied him.

She didn't recognize the interlink voice in her ear. Probably a comm tech back at Citangelo Base. "We confirm your arrival, *Cometesse*. Do you still read?" The interlink had picked up a hiss and shiver, undoubtedly from the ship's massive hull and mysterious shields. Still, it was a good connection, all things considered. Another major relief. Hopefully, their scanner could also transmit out through the shields.

She heard Glin-Erris's voice in both ears, through the air and over the interlink. "We copy, Citangelo Base. Your signal strength dropped a bit, and we have a slight degradation of quality. How is your read of us?"

After a brief delay, the comm tech spoke again. "Eighty percent, good copy."

Then came the voice she loved. "You are authorized to disembark as soon as airflow reaches the green zone, and after their greeting party enters the landing bay. Citangelo Base, out but monitoring."

Firebird pushed up from her seat. Glin-Erris bent to pick up his diplomatic bundle from the seat he had left. Firebird handed the clairsa back to Shel. She gave the pilots a quick salute. They would remain on board.

"Getting air could take some minutes," Daken said stiffly. "Gering will carry duffels for us all. I shall walk in front."

He was trying again. He meant to take charge.

"No," Glin-Erris said. "That is my position. Walk alongside me."

Daken sniffed loudly.

Glin-Erris peered into the cockpit again. "As soon as they enter the landing bay, we will debark. Boarding ramp down, please."

A clank shuddered the deck under her feet. A servomotor groaned.

Minutes passed. Daken paced downship, then back up to the lounge, hands behind his back.

"Leave the boarding hatch open after we debark," Glin-Erris instructed the pilots, "in case we need to make a quick departure."

The relief pilot stood at the cockpit hatch and smiled. "We'll wait on board, powered down. We have reserves for several days. Oh," she added, raising her voice, "if any of you are wondering, we are retrofitted with ramming capacity, in case they don't re-open the space door."

Someone, back on base, had thought through several options. Firebird guessed she knew who.

The chief pilot spoke from his seat in the cockpit. "Air flow is now low green zone, rather low nitrogen. Wait a few minutes more."

Firebird sat back down. Shel stood against the bulkhead. Daken's pacing took him aft again. Uri walked to the lounge's midpoint and sang softly. "Mighty Speaker, watch over us, keep our path clear."

Firebird joined the farewell-to-Chapter liturgy. "Keep our hearts in you as we walk on." Shel hummed along. Calmed by the familiar words and reminded of the Mighty Singer's power to protect them, Firebird relaxed with the melody circling in her memory. Music had power!

The tuneless voice spoke. "Ambassador Glin-Erris Coll, on board the Federate transport *Cometesse*, I welcome you. However, I am regretfully unable to enter the landing bay at this time. Please proceed to the lounge area, where we will be able to speak at length."

Firebird jerked up straight, startled on multiple levels. *I*, not *we*, could not enter the landing bay? Why not? Was the Strangers' commander physically disabled?

"Citangelo," Glin-Erris said, "we are being asked to enter unescorted. Shall we disembark?"

The transmission lag seemed longer this time. At last, Firebird heard, "Disembark and proceed cautiously. We are noting unusual energy expenditures. Top priority to the remote scanning unit."

Firebird thought she understood. There was more at stake than refueling the Strangers. Marshal Burkenhamn—and Brennen—wanted that shielding technology. It would be a fair and invaluable exchange.

Assuming they were not hostile and this was not entrapment. *Help*, she prayed again.

Glin-Erris faced Daken. "We are a team," he stated firmly. "Please contribute to the team effort."

"Or else stay on board the *Cometesse*," Uri added, gesturing one-handed. It wasn't quite a threat to voice-command again.

Daken scowled.

Glin-Erris looked side to side, his face unreadable. "Actually," he said in a low voice, "the situation is developing oddly enough that I would like a bodyguard to enter first."

Shel saluted and edged closer to the exit hatch beside the cockpit bulkhead. Uri hung back, and Firebird recalled that he must deploy the remote scanning unit.

The hatch slid open. Glin-Erris stepped up and stood a moment, silhouetted by the brilliance outside. A faintly musky scent filtered in.

As Firebird anticipated, Daken hurried forward, not quite shoving Shel aside. Gering backed up, burdened by their duffels and bags. She read deference in the way he swept his hand forward, motioning for her to precede him. She gave him a hesitant smile.

He remained straight-faced.

Mighty Singer, watch over us.

Glin-Erris, Daken, and Shel walked shoulder-to-shoulder down the boarding ramp. Firebird followed closely. Sliding one hand along the right-hand rail, she felt as if she were stepping onto a different world. Her back might be straight, but her head seemed weightless.

No one entered from the hatch opposite the space door, the hatch that probably led in to the meeting lounge.

Daken tossed his head. "They're afraid of us."

In your imagination, Firebird wanted to answer. She held her peace.

Glin-Erris walked forward, stopping halfway across the bay. His footsteps echoed faintly. Shel stood aside, looking all around. Firebird took a position close behind Glin-Erris and stood at attention.

He spread his arms and called, "Greetings to you, Strangers in Federate space. We have come in person, and we wish to speak with you in person. You expressed a need for refueling and compensation. We are prepared to discuss meeting your needs. We would be honored to know where you come from and why you are traveling through this region of space."

Daken hustled forward to stand in front of Glin-Erris.

Glin-Erris simply pivoted forty-five degrees. Daken now stood behind him, Firebird beside him. It was a brilliant little maneuver, and she liked Glin-Erris all the more for making it.

"Please enter," the voice repeated. "Thank you. We shall speak personally." Across the wide bay, a hatch three meters by four slid open.

Something clanked behind Firebird's back. Slightly turning her head, she saw Uri step away from a meter-high black cube. The *Cometesse*'s aft cargo bay stood open. That cube had to be their remote scanning unit. Citangelo Base would be able to read this ship's specs from inside its shields and, hopefully, transmit the data back to Netaia. A small white light pulsed on its near side.

She fingered her collar mike. "Your scanning unit looks operational, Brenn."

Several seconds later, he answered, "Confirm. We're getting data. Uri, quest-pulse for presences. How many of them are there?"

Uri, who'd hurried to Glin-Erris's other side, drew a deep breath and shut his eyes. Firebird watched Uri, remembering. When she'd been trying to learn Sentinel skills, the one thing she'd managed was a quest-pulse, sending out a burst of epsilon energy. Fully trained Sentinels could accomplish precision, distance, and some communication.

Uri's eyes opened. "There is human presence," he said. "All around us. But it does not vary. It's as if only one person's alpha savor is unshielded. Others could be hiding themselves."

Daken's eyes went wide. "Their what?"

"Alpha savor," Uri repeated. "Conscious presence."

Firebird felt wide-eyed, too. If one person had cloned himself—or herself?— that might explain Uri's sensing a single alpha savor. Cloning was illegal in Federate space, but this ship had come from outside. None of their assumptions applied.

As Firebird strained for Brennen's reaction, the tuneless voice echoed in the landing bay again. "Please enter. Your assistance is desperately desired."

Firebird glanced at Glin-Erris. What would he do?

"General?" Glin-Erris asked. "We still have no greeting party, but an inner hatch has opened."

Five seconds passed. Then ten. Finally, Brennen spoke again. "Proceed with caution. We are processing your scan data now. We will update you."

Scan data, good. But nothing about Uri's quest-pulse. Brennen must also still be digesting that strange report about a single presence.

Glin-Erris motioned Shel and Uri to precede him toward the hatch. Daken stayed with Glin-Erris. Firebird sent a backward glance to the *Cometesse*, waiting there on the grid. Dodis Gering had set down the duffels and bags again to stand at attention. Now he picked them up and trudged forward.

Squaring her shoulders, Firebird followed Glin-Erris into the mystery.

8: ONE STRANGER
misterioso, mysteriously

Three young Netaian officers sat below Brennen, monitoring the tri-D well. The moment Uri had offloaded the scanning unit, it had started sending data via Netaia's FasScan satellite. Beginning at the ship's southern horizon, bit by bit and line by line, a three-dimensional image of the ovoid ship was taking shape in the well, replacing the usual view of local space. Netaian engineers would examine it from every aspect.

He glanced aside. A wall monitor would display shielding data from inside that ship, hopefully soon. Shielding remained his priority. To coordinate any defensive aggression that proved necessary, he must evaluate the Strangers' weaknesses. At Marshal Burkenhamn's order, the Netaian Planetary Navy was already dispersing into defensive positions. The room had filled, mostly with Netaian cobalt-blue uniforms. Discipline seemed tight and good.

They had boarded. *Watch over them, Holy One.*

He turned back to the tri-D well and eyed the ship's slowly growing image. An enormous void was appearing, probably the empty fuel tank.

Uri's quest-pulse reading had startled him. As a fellow Sentinel, he was more likely than most to take that impression seriously. There could be just one individual on board, unless a full crew was able to epsilon-shield against someone as gifted as Uri. Even Shuhr could not have done that. At any rate, Shuhr never had built their own ships. They always had stolen.

An odd thought struck him. Whorl civilization had long outlawed independently operating robotics. High-level pseudo-intelligence still was considered hazardous to human economy, technology, and life itself, but other civilizations might have had no such laws. The assumption had been so foundational to his thinking that until this moment, the idea had not even occurred to him. However, one individual, assisted by advanced enough robotic technology, might travel space alone.

He fingered his cuff. The short, hard handgrip of his sheathed crystace reminded him that his fellow Sentinels, Uri and Shel, were trained to handle unusual circumstances.

Brennen recognized young Lieutenant Lord Leon Parkai sitting immediately below him, facing into the well. Brennen touched his shoulder. "What are you seeing, Lieutenant?"

"Huge empty void, possibly their fuel tank," Lieutenant Lord Parkai said. "Other zones very dense with subtronics. But these"—he pointed at a dark stripe several centimeters above the slowly forming globe's south pole—"these smaller cavities could be service passageways. No, wait." He fingered his touchboard. "No, they're too narrow. Significantly less than half a meter across."

"Wide enough for service robots?"

Lieutenant Lord Parkai's hands hovered over the touchboard without moving. "Oh," he said. "Yes, sir."

Plainly, it was a new thought to the young lieutenant too.

Another Netaian spoke from his right side. "Looks like half a dozen small landing shuttles in separate chutes. But nothing leading to or out on the hull looks like a weapons emplacement, sir. Yet."

Yet. Standing back, Brennen crossed his arms. The ship would be re-scanned in greater detail as soon as the automated cycle ran a lifesigns pass. *Cometesse*'s landing bay, about forty-five percent up from that southern horizon, had just appeared as another void amid glimmering blobs and lines. The remote scanner showed as a small black cube.

They would spend hours analyzing this scan.

In his earpiece, he heard footsteps.

Firebird strode along a short, bright passageway. She'd come a long way to meet these Strangers. The files she'd studied were doing competitive aerobatics in her brain. Which would she need to draw upon? Were the Strangers potential aggressors? If not, what was the chance that she could help negotiate getting these amazing shields for Brenn and Marshal Burkenhamn?

At that moment, Daken accelerated and passed Glin-Erris. Firebird bristled, but Glin-Erris calmly kept walking, so she took that as her cue and stayed beside the Federate diplomat.

This long, bright passage led toward an equally bright opening. They emerged in a wide chamber with a high ceiling. Off to the left, past an S-shaped lounger, a curved metal bulkhead was lined with metal shelving. Mid-floor stood a multiple workstation with metal stools tucked under a dusty desk surface. Farther to the right were two closed hatches, and then a long, featureless section of bulkhead. Completing the circle, another broad metal workbench was L-shaped and also dust covered. It all looked like someone's common area, but no one awaited. There were no viewports. This chamber had to be deep in the bowels of the Strangers' ship.

Firebird exhaled sharply. She glanced aside at Shel. If Shel had dispersed her epsilon shields, she would pick up Firebird's unease.

Shel nodded slightly.

Had going deeper into the ship disrupted their link to Citangelo Base? "Testing," Firebird softly addressed her collar mike. "Citangelo, we have entered an enclosed area. No one is here."

The transmission delay seemed to last a minute.

"Read you," Brennen finally answered, his voice somewhat muffled. "Your clarity and signal strength have dropped, but we are amplifying."

Gering sidestepped closer to Daken's shoulder. Firebird came to attention again and took an attentive sniff of the musty air. Shipboard recycled, like out in the landing bay, it smelled slightly of something mechanical.

"Hello, friends." Glin-Erris spoke clearly, brandishing his recall pad. His dress whites shone under the opalescent overhead panels. "We have come, as you requested, to speak with you."

Out of the long, featureless bulkhead panel ahead of them, a soft squeal dropped erratically, like a clairsa string being loosened to its lowest pitch and then tightened up again. It took on a warbling vibrato. The acoustics in here, Firebird noted, were quite dead.

The tuneless voice spoke again. "Hello, friends," the voice echoed Glin-Erris.

Weren't they going to see someone? Were the Strangers that shy?

"Hello," Daken shouted.

Shel took a step toward Daken. Lowering her cleft chin, she barely raised a hand in warning. Daken glared and fell silent. Gering set down his double armload of duffels and issue bags. Keeping his even demeanor, Glin-Erris stood mid-cabin and addressed the bulkhead speaker. He introduced each of them by name and title, just as in the tutorial. To Firebird's satisfaction, he called her both "Lady Firebird" and "Commander Caldwell."

"We greet you," he finished, "all of us. It is our desire to know more about you, who you are, where you come from, and how we might assist you."

"I am Monu." The voice deepened into the contralto range. "I watch before I speak, and I speak before I act."

Firebird noted again the singular *I*. There couldn't be just one person on board this enormous ship. Monu must be speaking for the rest of them.

"Act now." Again, Daken raised his voice. Nobles were accustomed to being obeyed. "Or face the consequences. Come out and talk to us, Monu."

"Daken." Glin-Erris's voice dropped to an ominous tone of warning. "You will have your turn. They could have other customs. Wait."

Daken spun around to Glin-Erris. "I will not be ordered around. I—"

Shel lifted her hand higher. "Grand Duke Daken," she said. "Please wait your turn." Daken didn't finish his sentence. His cheeks and forehead turned red. He had probably never been voice-commanded before today, his body controlled by someone else. It felt eerie, as Firebird knew well.

Glin-Erris faced the vibrating bulkhead. "We wish to help you. We wish to supply the fuel that you need, in order that you may travel on. We also are authorized to discuss how you might repay us for that fuel. May we speak with you personally, Monu?"

The bulkhead took on a glimmer. A woman's form appeared, white-robed with short, dark hair. Dumbfounded, Firebird stared. The image resembled Tierna Coll, Glin-Erris's aunt, head of the Federate Regional Council.

Firebird pressed her lips flat. Tierna Coll was not on board this ship.

To Glin-Erris's credit, he spoke calmly, as if he did not see the resemblance. "Thank you, Monu," he said. "We see that you can use these bulkheads for effective communication, but in truth, we would like to speak with you person-to-person, as you really are. That cannot be your true appearance. Personal presence is important to us."

"If you find that image displeasing, I apologize. Perhaps you prefer this." The image's face widened slightly, its cheeks narrowing and its nose becoming more prominent. They now faced a stranger.

It might be Monu. It might not.

Glin-Erris still seemed unfazed. "Your culture seems very different from ours," he said. "I hope we can learn to communicate effectively, without misunderstanding each other."

"Indeed. I wish to observe you," Monu's voice said. "I desire to watch and to consider who to recompense."

Firebird let out a breath, relieved. Talks would continue, and apparently Monu—whether captain or comm officer—could ignore Daken Erwin. Would she let them see her?

Glin-Erris raised his recall pad. "Monu, Netaia and the Federacy will assist you. Depending on what kind of fuel you require, you may recompense the contributing party." He turned slowly, surveying all corners of the wide lounge. "Let us discuss your fueling needs first, so that our home worlds can begin to inventory their resources. What is it that you need?"

"Worlds, yes," Monu said. It seemed like a non-answer. *Patience,* Firebird reminded herself. *Let Glin-Erris figure out what she means. He understands diplomacy. And as he said, innocent miscommunication with an unfamiliar culture could turn deadly.* What a blessing to have an experienced diplomat on board.

Daken raised a hand. His mouth opened. "Uh," he grunted. He wheeled toward Shel, raising an arm as if to strike.

Shel opened both hands in what looked like a conciliatory gesture, but Firebird knew it for another command position. Daken's arm lowered. His cheeks and forehead darkened toward purple.

Glin-Erris transferred his recall pad to his other hand. "Monu, let me explain our Netaian representative's obvious passion. He is a high-ranking civilian on the world you are approaching most closely. Like the rest of us, he wishes to assist you quickly and send you safely on your way, but sometimes, we find it difficult to express the same facts using different words."

"I understand." Monu's voice filled the room. "Competitive others can be undesirable. Yet often, they drive us to our highest achievements."

"We agree with his feelings." As Glin-Erris began, Daken retreated to the freestanding worktable and sat down, glaring poison. Glin-Erris continued, "We, standing here, also represent twenty-three other planetary systems in the galactic vicinity, and we do all stand with the Grand Duke's home world. We will protect it from any real threat. However, we do not assume that you mean to threaten. We desire good relations with you. So, here," he said, touching the recall pad again, "I have information concerning our worlds' fuel reserves. We should be able to help you. I am also authorized to discuss compensatory payment."

Firebird had seen this tactic in Glin-Erris's files: When a vital question appears to have been ignored, simply reword and repeat. Respectfully. Assume good intentions on all sides.

As a military pilot, she'd been trained to respond to hostility.

"We would also welcome an exchange of information." Glin-Erris repeated that, too. "Where do you come from? Why are you here, in this region we call the Whorl? How might we help you on your way? We would particularly like to meet you in person, Monu, as well as the others who are on board."

"Thank you, Ambassador Coll," Monu said. "You are already meeting me in person. You have seen me for some time. You are inside the ship that I use to experience my travels. It is, essentially, myself."

Firebird straightened. Uri had sensed just one living presence. Was there just one Stranger, then, calling herself Monu? How was that possible?

Monu spoke again, her voice still tuneless. "Please, be at home for a time. I wish to return to silence and consider your gracious presence. I watch before I speak, and I speak before I act. You will be comfortable in this space." She, too, seemed respectfully repetitive.

Firebird glanced at Shel again.

Shel gave a slight shrug, also wide-eyed.

What did Brennen think of all this? Would it alter defense protocols or their mission? Hopefully, the one-sided observation period wouldn't last long. Not long enough for Daken to make more trouble, anyway. There still would be plenty to discuss. For instance, how—and why—Monu had become an apparently living spaceship.

"We thank you as well," Glin-Erris said. "But what kind of—"

The glimmering bulkhead image faded to gray metal. Apparently, this first encounter was already over.

Firebird sank onto a dusty stool, disappointed. Would those back on base blame that on Daken? She certainly did!

Glin-Erris turned toward mid-lounge. "Uri, give us that quest-pulse again. Do you really sense only one person on board, besides us?"

Uri shut his eyes for just a few seconds. Then he said, "Yes. It is a human presence. Somehow, Monu is the ship."

How bizarre. How—did Firebird dare to think it?—inhuman.

"Our mission has not changed," Glin-Erris declared. "We refuel her, negotiate payment, and send her on her way. But think of all we might learn from her." He eyed the featureless bulkhead again. "It seems," he said to his fellow ambassadors and also to Citangelo Base, "we are being asked to settle in, maybe to be observed for awhile. I fear we may have alarmed Monu with our discordant behavior."

Marshal Burkenhamn answered several seconds later. "We agree with your evaluation, Ambassador. The news, while startling, does not alter your essential mission. Learn all that you can." His voice lowered from baritone to bass. "Now, please make sure Grand Duke Erwin can hear me."

Gering hurried to the workstation where Daken sat. He pulled off his interlink and earpiece and handed them over. "First Marshal Burkenhamn for you, sir."

Daken rolled his eyes, but he tucked the little earpiece into place.

"Your Excellency," Burkenhamn said. Firebird felt slightly awkward about listening in, but she wasn't about to pull out her earpiece. "As First Marshal of the Netaian armed forces, which exist to defend you and your noble kindred, I respectfully implore you to show mannerly behavior toward every individual in your delegation." There was a slight pause. "Your Excellency, if you provoke an interstellar conflict by refusing to cooperate with Federate representatives, House Erwin must be publicly blamed."

A public shaming was the ultimate threat on Netaia. It would be rather delicious to see this man shamed.

Daken sat staring at the deck.

The marshal's voice spoke again, less harshly. "Ambassadors, now that we know that your host wishes to observe you, we are also entitled to observations. Describe for our calibrations precisely what you see in the chamber where you are being asked to wait."

Glin-Erris pointed each of them toward a different area to investigate, but Shel strode toward Daken, her midnight blues another welcome splash of color in these gray metal surroundings. Firebird blinked. Not long ago, she'd spent much of her time in monochromatic shipboard surroundings. Was civilian life turning her into a groundsider?

"I apologize," Shel told Daken as she stopped before him. "This team must cooperate, and I believe that Glin-Erris described your feelings accurately and sympathetically to Monu. Did you hear him?"

Daken glared up at her.

"Please." Shel extended a palm. "The order to quiet you came from higher up," she said. "We must work together." To Firebird's surprise, Shel still also carried the clairsa. The case's shoulder strap crossed her midnight blues at chest level. Shel probably didn't realize it, either. Firebird had heard the Ehretan modulation of voice-command once again. Daken had been freed to speak.

He still only glared. Firebird knew that man. He wanted payback.

Still trying to comprehend the idea of a person becoming a spaceship, Firebird got up and followed Glin-Erris's pointing finger toward the L-shaped workbench closest to the entry hatch. Cloth shrouds covered several box-like objects, possibly subtronics. Shel turned her back on Daken and joined her.

Firebird lifted rotting fabric to reveal a container of unfamiliar hand tools. "Construction tools here, I'm guessing," she told their listeners back on Netaia. "Or maintenance."

"Sentinel Harris?" Glin-Erris asked. "Your area?"

Uri had taken a place along the curving bulkhead to Firebird's right. "There are two side hatches, both functional, with several upper and lower bunk-sized benches inside each cabin, but no bedding. Freshing facilities, possibly operational. I agree with Lady Firebird. I believe we are in a maintenance or construction crew's living quarters with gender-separated cabins."

So Monu once had human assistants. Where had they gone when they finished working on . . . her?

"Grand Duke Daken? Mister Gering?" Glin-Erris prompted.

Gering responded, having left Daken sitting sullenly at the

workstation. "I seem to find a serving area, but it is devoid of foodstuffs, and I am not sure we should eat anything we find."

Glin-Erris raised his voice. "We conclude these quarters are not stocked for occupancy. We shall return to the transport *Cometesse* and bunk out there." Plainly, he was addressing Monu as well as Citangelo.

Monu responded. She was watching, all right. Watching before she spoke. And she would speak before she acted. "Please, Ambassador Coll." Her tuneless voice filled the chamber, but no image appeared on the bulkhead. "Remain here as guests. I can protect your fragile bodies better from the hazards of deep space in here, rather than out in a landing bay. Soon, your stay will be a brief memory."

Glin-Erris addressed the vibrating bulkhead. "Then we shall bring some comfort supplies from our craft, which is still in your landing bay." He switched smoothly from answering Monu to describing the area for those back on Netaia. "Here, I'm finding what appears to be another workstation. And, wait, here's a new hatch."

Hearing a startled catch in his voice, Firebird walked to the dark gray, S-shaped lounger and looked over it.

Glin-Erris stood near the far left bulkhead, facing an opening she hadn't seen before. Beyond it, an arched corridor disappeared into darkness. "Monu?" Glin-Erris set his face forward. "Is this the way into your personal presence?"

"It is the way to my control bridge, yes. I now believe that you are also sincere and friendly. I observe that your hand-carried information device could be helpful in bridging our cultural communication gap. We all wish to know much more about one another. You may bring your device to my bridge, Ambassador Coll."

Glin-Erris took a step toward the arched corridor.

He paused, and Firebird imagined she could read his thoughts. Even under ambassadorial protection, he shouldn't go alone into unknown territory. Different cultures might not respect ambassadors as did Federate worlds.

Daken strode forward. "I shall come too." He still sounded angry. After all, he'd been voice-commanded today, likely for the first time. "Glin-Erris and I represent entirely different entities."

"Not true," Firebird countered. "Netaia has covenanted to the Federacy. By general election."

Daken sniffed loudly. "Over valid objections from the Electorate."

"No, Daken," Shel said. "She invited Ambassador Coll, and you have shown yourself unwilling to cooperate. If anyone goes with Glin-Erris, it should be Uri or me." She glanced at Firebird. "But I will not leave you alone with that man and his servant."

Uri looked down at the deck as he spoke. "General Caldwell? I think this is that rare situation where watch-link is allowed. If Ambassador Coll is willing, would you confirm that it's code-legal?"

Watch-link? Firebird shuddered. The renegade Shuhr had done it to her. It was far more invasive than voice-command. Brennen had said that the Shuhr used it indiscriminately.

Apparently, Sentinels used it, too, sometimes, and it was probably within Uri's range of intel specialization.

Daken sidled closer, muttering, "What the Dark is he talking about?"

Shel also moved toward Firebird, silently reminding Daken that she could take him down.

"Uri could observe Glin-Erris from a distance," Firebird said quickly, moving her lips as little as possible, since the Sentinels intended to conceal from the Strangers—singular or plural—all they could do. "It's rarely allowed." Daken didn't need details. An epsilon carrier point could linger inside someone else's mind. Uri would be able to see and hear everything Glin-Erris perceived, even to read some of his surface thoughts.

"Allowed." Daken's eyes narrowed. "What do you mean *allowed*?"

"We've told you." She kept her lips tight. "These people are bound by laws. Power corrupts, and they know it." *Even if you don't.* "They spend years in training, mostly memorizing codes. The kindred walks a fine line. Always. Everywhere. They have only survived because they swear never, ever to use their abilities capriciously or selfishly. With the death penalty enforced if they do." She watched Glin-Erris, who had stepped away from the arch but stood eyeing it.

"Come now, please, Ambassador Coll," Monu intoned. "I would particularly like to discuss your compensation."

Glin-Erris looked toward Uri. "One moment, please, Monu. I am as eager as you."

"Brennen will say yes sooner or later," Uri guessed, voice low. "Glin-Erris, if you're willing to be . . ." His lips formed the words *watch-linked*, "it will take a few minutes. We may as well be ready. The link can be broken instantaneously."

"By either of us?" Glin-Erris murmured.

Uri shook his head. "Only by me, unless you leave range, which is considerable."

Considerable indeed. Firebird would not forget her and Brennen's terrifying retreat through Shuhr forces, bringing the newborn twins and trying to escape into slip-state, after the Shuhr watch-linked her. Brennen had ordered her to shut her eyes and sit on her hands. The enemy could have anticipated their escape vector and even made her fire on their own ships. A psi-med specialist could break watch-link, but they had none on board.

Glin-Erris stared at Uri a moment longer, then said, "I am willing, if that is the precaution you advise. It is within my job description, I think."

Firebird smiled slightly. Surely a Federate diplomat's job description never mentioned Sentinel watch-link. But the man seemed unshakeable. It was rare to see someone trust Sentinels this implicitly.

Uri gestured toward the lounger. "Sit down and be comfortable." Louder, he added, "We need to confer, Monu. Please allow us a few private minutes."

It was worth a try.

Firebird tried to remember how it had been done to her. Nothing came, except that she'd come up out of unconsciousness already watch-linked.

Daken retreated to the opposite bulkhead. "Those people," he growled, "will do nothing of the sort to me."

Exasperated, Firebird followed him. "Of course they won't," she said in a hushed voice. What a coward. "And you aren't going in there, anyway. Please, Daken. Keep your voice down. We're being watched."

"How much . . . that is . . . what can they . . ." Daken was actually stammering.

He seemed curious and horrified, not aggressive, for the moment. She dared to stand close enough to whisper into his ear. "Uri will be able to hear through Glin-Erris's ears and see through his eyes." He didn't need to know that voice-command also could be involved.

His eyes flicked back to the lounger and the two men sitting on it. "You live with these creatures?"

Creatures? Who was this, talking to her? "I trust them with my life," she said evenly.

Daken lifted his chin high. "You can trust me to represent Netaia to any interlopers, whoever they may be."

I trust you in no way. She kept that thought to herself, too, as she turned away. *And I will never forgive you.* She returned to the lounger. Inside one bend of its S-shape, Uri sat resting his hand on Glin-Erris's shoulder, both men keeping their eyes open while Shel gripped Uri's shoulder. Firebird hoped that Monu, and whoever else was watching, assumed a time of mutual contemplation. It certainly didn't look like anything important was happening.

Uri shut his eyes briefly, then stepped away. "There. Are you all right?"

Glin-Erris sat up. "I feel nothing."

"You won't. Please walk around the room and speak to someone, so I can hear." Uri shut his eyes and covered his ears as Shel backed away.

Glin-Erris took several steps. Firebird followed. He whispered, "Your dress uniform has acquired a bit of dust, Commander Caldwell."

Truly, their dress whites would look gray in here soon, and she did not want to smudge Carrie's sash. This was a better place for shipboards. "I'm not surprised," she said, turning back toward the lounger alongside Glin-Erris.

"Good," Uri said without opening his eyes. "As soon as the base gives us a go-ahead, we're ready."

"Watch-link is permitted." It was Brennen's voice in her ear. "We are now interpreting the Strangers' behavior as potentially aggressive, with lives at stake. Also, your eyes will catch finer details than our remote scanner when you pass through that corridor and, hopefully, reach their bridge. Go with the Holy One, Glin-Erris. We will be with you in spirit."

Brennen continued, softening his voice, "Shel, please keep an eye on Uri so he can concentrate. Uri, talk us through whatever Glin-Erris sees. Mister Gering, if you are willing to go back into the landing bay for supplies, this would be a good time. Make sure the way remains clear, in case you need to evacuate. Please tell Grand Duke Daken to be seated and be comfortable. Assure him that he will also talk with Monu. Firebird, stand down for the moment."

Firebird sat down inside the opposite curve of the lounger, twisting to watch Uri. He relaxed against the backrest, head bowed and wincing slightly. This had to feel uncomfortable. Shel followed Glin-Erris to the edge of the mysterious corridor. Striplights gleamed along its ceiling. From that post, Shel would be able to watch over Uri, but she could also hurry to Glin-Erris's aid if need be.

"I will retrieve food and bedding now." Gering touched the shoulder-high square next to the exit hatch. The hatch opened.

"As soon as you're back," Daken called crossly after Gering, "you can start cleaning." He stood mid-chamber. Trying not to touch anything dusty, Firebird guessed. Several long smudges already marred his black trousers.

"I'm going in now." Glin-Erris departed through the corridor's tall arch. "Here I come, Monu." His dress whites shone under the striplights until he rounded a slight bend and passed out of sight.

This left Firebird with Shel and Uri—who was mentally down that corridor with Glin-Erris—and with Daken Erwin, who went back to pacing. It was hard to keep an eye on him. He was probably just restless or exploring, but he could be plotting something.

Leaning slightly forward, with hands clenched in his lap, Uri narrated Glin-Erris's passage. "Long corridor. It is rather small back here. There's room for just one to walk. Machinery on both sides, but I'm not seeing any control surfaces yet."

As Daken poked his head into their presumed sleeping quarters, Firebird kept looking around. Ventilation hissed and swished. The S-shaped gray lounger ahead, and the workstation stools to her right, were plainly proportioned for human beings. Monu had obviously come from a human-inhabited world. She must have had a human body, too, once.

"It's filthy in here," Daken muttered. He was right. Everything wore that veil of gray dust.

"Deep space is relatively dust free, especially in slip-state," Shel pitched her softened voice to carry. "This has to be internal disintegration."

Firebird nodded. How long had Monu been traveling?

Uri spoke again. "Open area ahead, maybe three meters across. Dim lights, very high ceiling. Good, this must be the bridge. Hello, Monu?"

Another long pause. Firebird turned to see Daken directly behind her, looking over her shoulder. She hadn't realized he'd snuck up on her. She scolded herself for inattention. Shel couldn't stand watch all the time, not even in this small space.

Uri's voice picked up Glin-Erris's distinctly Tallan cadence. "No one is physically present in here, either, and again I see no obvious instrumentation. Hello, Monu. May we speak now? Tell us who you are, where you come from."

Firebird brushed dust off her uniform tunic, just keeping her hands busy.

Uri spoke again, relaying what Glin-Erris saw. "Monu asks me to put on a communication cap. Yes, that is all right."

Naturally, Glin-Erris gave permission. Anyone who was all right with watch-link—

"The fit is snug." Uri's hand rose. He touched his scalp. "Now," he murmured, "Monu, tell us about yourself. How may we assist . . . wait." He broke off. "Wait." His voice rose. "No, don't—" Uri's call became a cry. "Stop!"

The deck trembled under Firebird's feet. Uri flung out both arms and legs, and he slid off the lounger. Shel dashed to his side and dropped to her knees. She cradled Uri's head in her hands, squeezing her eyes closed. Undoubtedly probing his mind, his memory—and possibly checking the watch-link.

Firebird held her breath. Shel grimaced as she held Uri's face close to her own. The clairsa strap slid down off her shoulder, and the case hit the deck.

"What is it?" Daken demanded. "What just happened?"

After some time, Shel looked up and exhaled. "I think he's going to be all right," she said in a tremulous voice. "I mean, Uri's going to be all right."

She shook her head, forehead furrowed. "But Glin-Erris is not conscious—or breathing."

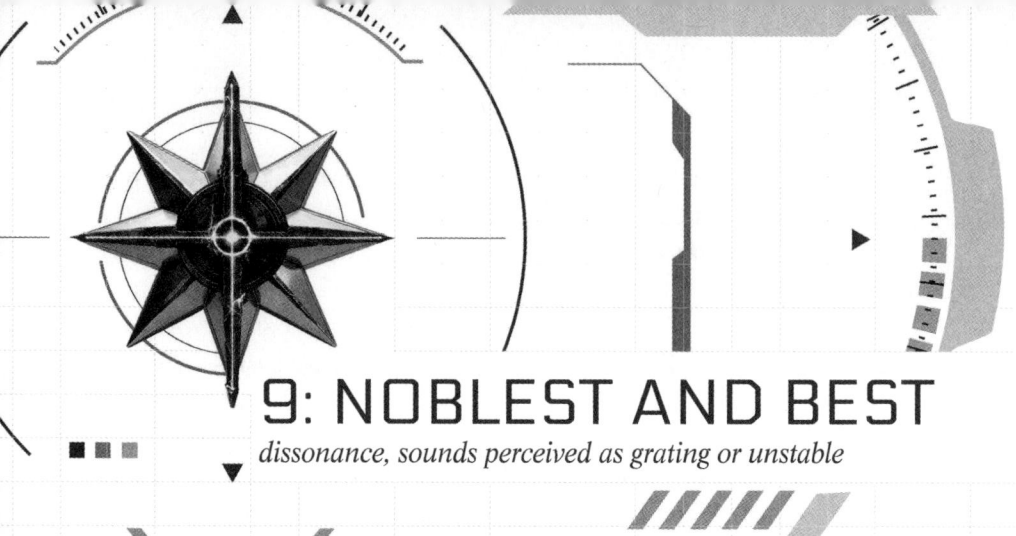

9: NOBLEST AND BEST
dissonance, sounds perceived as grating or unstable

Firebird stood near to Shel as she knelt over Uri. Why had Monu done . . . whatever she just did . . . to Glin-Erris?

Uri choked a deep gasp and started to cough. Shel stayed down on the deck with him. Brennen's voice sounded urgent in Firebird's ear. "Mari. Mari, what just happened?"

Firebird took a few steps away. "Uri went down. Looks like shock. Shel's helping him."

"Uri said—" Brennen didn't finish. The comm lag stretched out.

Firebird eyed the archway. "Shel's with Uri," she said. "I'm going to Glin-Erris." She was halfway to the arch when Brennen spoke in her ear. "Stop. If Uri doesn't snap out of shock, I need you to take charge. Stay out of that corridor. Send Shel in to quest-pulse, the moment Uri is up. He will be all right."

He would? Firebird peered down the corridor at featureless metal bulkheads. Brennen knew Sentinels' capabilities, including recovery time. Her formal uniform's collar felt tight. To prove she was a good choice for this mission, she must follow orders. Especially Brennen's.

To Firebird's relief, Uri was, in fact, moving again. Shel assisted him onto the lounger. His eyes looked dull, and he leaned hard against Shel.

"Let me, Shel." Firebird moved in. "Brenn wants you to go for Glin-Erris."

"Yes. Good." Shel gave a quick nod and vanished through the corridor's arch.

"Uri's conscious. But just barely," Firebird reported to Brennen.

Uri's limp weight was nearly pushing her over. She checked to see what Daken was doing. Still seated at the workstation he seemed to have claimed, he made no move to assist anyone. Naturally.

Please, Mighty Singer. Help us. "Monu," Firebird called. "Send us back Glin-Erris. We need to speak with him."

She heard Brennen again. "Uri's conscious? Good. I'll talk to him. See if he can walk."

She helped Uri to his feet. He steadied himself and took a halting step.

The exit hatch, back out to the landing bay, slid open. Gering returned, waddling under a burden. He dropped everything near the hatch and hurried to join Firebird and Uri. "What's wrong? Let me assist." He looked toward Daken, probably for permission. Firebird had seen all she wanted in Daken's direction. She threw another glance at the corridor before refocusing on Uri.

Gering slid an arm around Uri's waist. Could she trust the big man? Maybe, if she stayed close. She couldn't support Uri alone. "Yes, thank you. Help me keep him upright. He needs to walk a little. Base is talking to him."

Shel re-emerged from the corridor. "It's a dead end," she said, "and Glin-Erris isn't in there. I quest-pulsed. I do not find him in any direction."

Uri staggered alongside Gering, and Shel joined them. Firebird stood mid-room once more. She spoke more sharply this time. "Monu. Please return Glin-Erris to us. Immediately."

Monu's flat voice spoke from that inner bulkhead. "Do not worry for Glin-Erris, my friends. You will not find him in that way, but he is with me. Soon, he will be greater than you ever imagined."

"What?" Firebird scrutinized the corridor again. Nothing moved down there. "We need to see him. Please," she added. Glin-Erris would have asked politely. "Abduction is unacceptable in our culture, Monu."

"Ambassador Coll no longer is a crawling thing. He will be as I am, enshipped as one of my offspring. It is the highest recompense I can offer you, in exchange for my refueling."

Enshipped? Firebird held back a gasp. Was Monu trying to suck Glin-Erris Coll out of his body and turn him into . . . into one of those ships that followed her? The ships that had offered no lifesign readings?

Was that what had happened to Monu herself? According to Uri's words and gestures during the watch-link, Monu had told Glin-Erris to put something on his head. He'd thought it was a comm device. Something that fit snugly. Plainly, it had done something other than communicate.

And if Monu tried to take Glin-Erris out of his body, where was that body?

Uri walked steadily now, arm in arm with the Netaian bodyguard.

"Brenn," she said quietly but urgently. "It seems Monu is trying to make Glin-Erris into one of her companion ships. We've got to get him back. But how?"

Before Brennen could respond, Monu declared, "In return for the fuel that I need, I wish to grant your worlds the highest possible compensation. Two of your noblest and best will become my companions, much more than human, almost immortal. They shall survive long after the rest of you have died."

Much more than human? Firebird took slow breaths. The lounge's dust did suggest long travels, but that was irrelevant. They needed their leader back.

Gering eased Uri onto the lounger. Shel sat down slowly while she looked into Uri's eyes, probably subvocalizing with him.

"You shall also become my competitors," Monu announced, "and we shall challenge each other as we travel the galaxy. For I have found, at long last, that when I am alone, I weaken, and I shrink."

Daken Erwin rested a hand on the workstation. He hated playing toady to all these Federates. But more than human? "Am I hearing right, Gering?" he muttered to his servant. "She wants two of us to crew her other spaceships, or is it become her other spaceships, to travel through space alongside her? For centuries?"

Gering stood closer than he normally was allowed to approach. He leaned in. "It appears so, sir. Glin-Erris was a natural first choice. He, ah, gave the impression of being our leader, instead of you. Perhaps you have had a narrow escape, sir."

Daken raised his eyebrows, bemused. That whole Federate group, and even his loyal Gering, seemed to think that this would be some sort of tragedy. Had they no imagination? Could they not picture traveling the galaxy as an immortal mechanical? Skipping past stars, maybe ruling a solar system? Destroying whomever and whatever opposed him?

His gaze landed on Firebird, who was trying to look official and stern in that white uniform, wearing her sister's heiress sash.

There stood someone who deserved to be destroyed. For every act of defiance she ever committed, not just for her birth order.

And with Glin-Erris gone, Daken Erwin could now take up his natural role as the mission's leader.

To Firebird's relief, Uri spoke toward the vibrating bulkhead. Intelligent light had returned to his eyes. Plainly, Brennen knew exactly how quickly he could recover. "Madam, we thank you for an offer that you no doubt mean graciously, but our souls are made to live in these bodies. We cherish them. Please return our leader, Ambassador Coll, unharmed."

"When you see his new greatness," Monu proclaimed, "you will understand. He no longer has the creaturely needs that keep you crawling things short-lived and weak." Her tuneless voice became contralto again. "Simply creating the oxygenated air that you require is using some of my last seed fuel. My friend Glin-Erris will no longer need that. He will live for all time alongside me."

"What kind of fuel, Monu?" Uri asked, his voice gratifyingly steady.

Firebird sidled closer to Shel. "Try another quest-pulse," she whispered. "You've got to find him."

After several seconds, Shel shook her head slowly. "Glin-Erris is not here."

But Uri had sensed Monu when they first boarded, hadn't he? And Monu was also—what was her word—enshipped.

She felt sick. Glin-Erris must be alive. He must! "We came to help you, Monu. Colonel Harris is correct. Please return Ambassador Coll to us. We do not wish to be more than human." The second those words left her lips, she wished she could call them back. Uri, Shel, and Brennen were all more than human by some people's judgment. Her own children might be more than human.

Monu had mentioned air. As on any mission requiring space travel, there were oxygen sniffers in the issue bags. They should keep some handy, in case Monu threatened to cut them off. Could they still hope to get Monu's shields for the Federacy, without their best negotiator?

"Do not worry," Monu said again. "His essential self is more alive than you ever could have lived to expect. Like myself, although smaller."

"Explain!" Daken strode toward the resonating bulkhead, Gering beside him. "Use words we can understand!"

"I shall be busy assisting your Ambassador Coll awhile," Monu said. "When he commands his own ship, we both shall speak to you. Then, you will understand. Then, I shall select my second companion."

Firebird cringed. If they wanted to confer with the base awhile without being overheard, had they better retreat to their transport? She hated backing down, but she owed her commanding officer her thoughts. "Brenn? Should we withdraw to the *Cometesse*? Maybe mount a rescue from on board it?"

Brennen stood with Marshal Burkenhamn next to the tri-D well, staring down at the deck. Blood had drained from his face when Monu said "more than human," but Mari's repetition stung. She meant no offense, but this was exactly his ancestors' crime, trying to do more and to know more than any human was created to do or know. Their ancestors' genetic alterations had caused genocide on lost Ehret. They would pay for that crime by serving unaltered humanity until the Eternal Speaker declared their debt zeroed.

Marshal Burkenhamn loomed over him. He spoke quietly. "I defer to you, General Caldwell. Do we withdraw the mission?"

Brennen considered risk versus reward. Personnel already in place and not—for the moment—actually threatened. "It would be tragic to lose Ambassador Coll over a cross-cultural misunderstanding," he said, "but this Monu does seem to be offering something that she herself has accepted. To her, this idea of recompense probably makes a terrible kind of sense."

Yet the mission was putting Mari in danger. Mari and the others.

Still, now that they knew what Monu intended, they could resist more effectively. Resist and continue to negotiate. "Shel, Uri. Go out to the landing bay. Use the scanning unit's override to look for Glin-Erris. Link with each other if you sense him in any direction. No one," he ordered, "is to go down that corridor unless you locate him and can attempt a rescue." And then, hopefully, renegotiate. Reject enshipment but request the shielding technology.

"Sirs," a sensors tech called. "You'll want to see this."

Brennen hurried to that tech's station. Marshal Burkenhamn followed.

"I'm going to drop back about five minutes," the tech said. "That..." He pointed at a small point of light on the wall display above head level. "That is a small, near-orbit asteroid we've tracked for decades. Watch what happens as it approaches the Strangers' ship. I'll run it in quick motion."

The light point appeared to be heading dangerously close to the big ovoid when it suddenly vanished. Brennen pointed at a cluster of zeroes that flashed in place of its mass, vector, and velocity. "Nothing is there anymore, sir," the tech said. "And there was no energy release."

That made no sense.

"We normally see energy when a physical object is annihilated," Marshal Burkenhamn observed.

"Exactly, sir."

Brennen fingered his cuff. Those shields seemed an impenetrable defense. If the Federacy had them, they might never worry about Shuhr incursions again. "Send that data to the analysis team," he said. "Priority One."

"Yes, sir."

The ship also had made a slight acceleration toward Netaia. Apparently, its shields had converted that little asteroid's mass into energy and absorbed it. The Netaian fleet was near full readiness, but if Monu turned hostile, could they hope to threaten a ship with shields like that?

Marshal Burkenhamn paced several steps away, turned on one heel, and paced back. "If Ambassador Coll were to become a personified spaceship, like that creature Monu, would he have any reason to travel with Monu instead of remaining in Federate space?"

Eventually, Shel and Uri returned from the landing bay. Firebird's hope vanished when Shel shook her head. "There is no trace of him," she said. "We've told Brennen. We're starting to think the unthinkable."

Firebird sat down at a workstation, rubbing her face with her hands. If Monu was killing people, they'd better get out of here.

But then a new thought struck her. "Brenn," she said, "has it occurred to anyone that we might not be able to leave if Monu doesn't drop those shields?"

Uri's voice also spoke in Brennen's ear. "We're all exhausted," Uri said. "We arrived late in the day, and a lot has happened. I'm less than perfectly comfortable with remaining in here overnight, but I also don't like to retreat. Not yet. Lady Firebird is correct. I would rather not challenge this shielding capacity just yet."

Yes. It was growing late, and unlike spaceships, human bodies needed food and rest. Brennen gazed into the tri-D well, with its three-dimensional image of Monu's ship. What would he do if he were on board?

He would stay close to Monu. If Monu shut them out or even forced them to depart, they must give up all hope of recovering Glin-Erris and of renegotiating. The asteroid's disappearance, and Monu's acceleration toward Netaia, also were concerns. Every life in the Whorl might depend on continuing the mission.

"Strategically," he told them, "I would prefer that you stay as close to Monu as you feel is safe. Do not abandon Ambassador Coll. Monu does not seem to threaten anyone who does not approach that corridor. The possibility remains that this is a grave misunderstanding. I will have our transport pilots stand ready to bring you aboard at a moment's notice. If we reach that point, we can insist that the shields be dropped. Our heavy fighter is in position to enforce that request. Inform us immediately if you have any further update on Ambassador Coll."

He looked up to another high-wall sensor screen, which displayed local space in detail. The Netaian fleet had scattered. Cruisers, carriers, and attack ships had reached positions from which they could deploy beam weapons. They would not need the days *Cometesse* had required for personal travel. Lightspeed weaponry could strike almost simultaneously over a vast distance.

He still hoped it all proved unnecessary.

Marshal Burkenhamn also spoke through Firebird's earpiece. "Stand down for the night," he ordered. "Get something to eat. Await new orders."

Eat? She felt slightly ill.

Shel headed toward the servo unit, where she opened the bag Gering had dropped there. "Mostly concentrates," she observed. "Good choice. Easy to carry."

Sitting at the workstation beside Daken, Gering acknowledged her words with a slight nod. Shel distributed small bowls of the varicolored cubes and cups of room-temperature water. Watching Daken choke down a shipboard-style meal boosted Firebird's sagging spirits. Her own bowl smelled like a stew without spices or salt.

The marshal spoke in Firebird's ear, interrupting the impromptu meal. "Ambassadors, if we have lost Glin-Erris Coll, then you are to honor Colonel Uri Harris as your official leader."

Command, having weighed Monu's words—and Uri and Shel's inability to find him via quest-pulse—must have concluded a high probability that Glin-Erris was dead.

But the mission was not being called off.

Torn between grief, relief, and rising anger, Firebird touched her earpiece as Shel repeated the marshal's order aloud for Daken. He glared at her. Firebird was mostly relieved at Marshal Burkenhamn's order. She still felt more comfortable obeying orders than giving them.

Uri gestured at her. "If I go down again, Commander Caldwell is in charge."

Oh. So much for relief.

"No!" Daken sprang to his feet. "I am—"

Uri raised a hand. "Commander Caldwell might not want the title, Your Excellency, but she sits next to the throne."

Daken stood stiffly. "Out of respect for that throne, which stands for Netaia, and the Powers who rule there, I will honor that order."

Firebird imagined she could hear him mentally adding *for now*. He didn't look like he was worried about Glin-Erris. In fact, he was actually . . . how could that beast be smiling? She'd thought she had hated him wholeheartedly before. Now, she hated him with a cold fury that she would probably need to confess to the Holy One.

She sank down on the lounger and picked up the cased clairsa. Should she try to play music, as she had hoped, now that Glin-Erris was in peril or even dead?

Even to her, music seemed trivial at this grave moment. Still, she had to do something. She was ordered to stay put, and she wasn't sleepy.

Making music often helped her deal with negative feelings. It might even touch Monu. Wasn't that why she'd brought the harp? Did Monu sleep? She'd hoped to play for other living, breathing, walking human beings. Every human culture had its own music.

"Not again," Daken said sourly. "We had enough of that en route. For two days."

"I practiced in my private cabin," she snapped. "You didn't have to keep your ear to the bulkhead." She pulled out the clairsa's key for a hasty tuning. Moments later, her rolling arpeggio hung in the air, reverberating off metal bulkheads and a high ceiling.

She lifted her voice. "Hello, Monu. I bring an offering of music while you are busy." Might Monu respond positively? Might she distract Monu from whatever she was doing to Glin-Erris?

Shel leaned against a bulkhead. Uri sat down again. Daken and Gering vanished into the right-hand sleeping cabin.

Firebird swept left-hand chords softly against the right-hand melody of a piece she'd written for Brennen. She played it for him often, reminding him how unexpectedly she'd come to care for him. It felt natural to segue into a solemn, modal hymn that used the same tuning. The chords and harmonies tugged at her heart. Shel and Uri came over and stood close. They too knew its worshipful lyrics. Should she try to sing?

Unfortunately, she actually wanted to burst into tears. For Glin-Erris. *Don't let him be gone, Mighty Singer.* If music moved no one else, it took her by the heart. It also reminded her that she was always watched over, and not just by Brennen.

Instead of damping the strings as the hymn ended, she let the last notes ring.

"Beautiful," Uri said.

Shel gave a small smile.

Monu said nothing, neither curious nor complimentary.

"We need to sleep now," Shel said. "It is very late."

They prayed an abbreviated vespers together, including an Adoration. It promised that one day, the Sentinels' Eternal Speaker would personally enter space and time.

> I will be with that remnant.
> I will refine and test them as meteor steel

And make them a sword in my hand.
Word to Come, Mighty One, Holy King of the New Universe,
Refine all the worlds and their peoples.
Wield Your children in justice, the suns in Your truth.

Calmed and heartened, Firebird cased the clairsa. Uri joined Daken and Gering in the right-hand cabin. Surely he would be safe with them, even asleep. Daken wouldn't dare try to harm a Sentinel. If he did try, he deserved the consequences.

She and Shel slung bedding onto two of the other cabin's lower shelves, Shel near the door and Firebird further in. "Good night, Brenn," she murmured, seated on the edge of her bunk. Already, the stress and worry of her situation were returning, particularly the fact that Monu had not answered Uri's question. What kind of fuel did she require?

Shel stood over her. "You know what I'm going to ask, don't you?"

Actually, that would be better discussed when they were well rested. "Yes, please. Thank you, Shel."

Shel touched her forehead.

She was asleep almost before her face touched the pillow.

10: SHEKKAH
the Ehretan service for the dead

Firebird woke early on an uncomfortable, unfamiliar bunk with two questions flickering in her mind. First, was Glin-Erris alive, his spirit somehow extracted to inhabit one of Monu's companion ships? If so, Shel and Uri could be quest-pulsing in the wrong direction. Second, how could they establish real communication with Monu, to obtain her shielding technology without her trying to enship anyone else or otherwise threaten Federate worlds?

She dressed quickly. The white tunic she'd worn for arrival still felt fresh, but she left off her decorations. Apparently, there was just one Stranger, and decorations didn't impress her.

She and Shel met the men near the servo unit. Gering had already tested the shipboard water supply and pronounced it pure, probably distilled. Since he insisted it was his job to serve breakfast, he distributed kass and concentrates. He and Daken settled at the freestanding workstation. The rest of them sat in the soft but dusty arcs of the S-shaped lounger.

Uri spoke quietly to his collar mike. "Good morning, Citangelo. We slept undisturbed."

Marshal Burkenhamn answered. "Good morning, Colonel Harris. Thank you for the good news."

Monu spoke simultaneously, so that Firebird had to disentangle the greetings to hear, "Good awaking to you all."

Firebird wrapped her hands around her reconstituted kass. The mug's warmth felt good, and cabin temperature had not changed from moderately cool, but she hated the taste. Always. Comfortable temp, adequate light, and breathable air were basic human needs. At least the enshipped Monu remembered that.

"Thank you, Monu," Uri said, taking charge as he'd been ordered. "Most of us slept well." From the glance he threw at Daken and Gering, Firebird guessed that they'd refused his help to calm their thoughts.

"Later today," Monu said, "I plan to invite two of you to receive compensation. Every stage of the process must proceed perfectly for enshipment to succeed. It seems I am not ready yet."

Firebird's poise dissolved like the instant kass. If Monu wanted two more compensation victims, one for each of her companion ships, something must have gone wrong. Glin-Erris must be dead.

Dead.

Her stomach turned.

Uri rose from the lounger. "Must we assume that our friend Glin-Erris is no longer living?"

"Regretfully," said Monu's voice, "My first effort failed. I am terribly sorry, and I extend my deepest regrets. My intent was to reward Ambassador Coll for his courage and expertise. I am running a full systems check. I will determine at what stage enshipment faltered. As I observe you all, I shall choose whom to successfully recompense. You are your worlds' noblest and best, and certainly the most courageous. You deserve this honor, to live on when your worlds have passed into nothing."

Dead. Glin-Erris was dead, and Monu wanted two more victims.

How was it possible to transfer a living soul into a vast machine?

Brennen had just drawn the same conclusion. He had just lost someone under his authority, albeit not for the first time. He bowed his head and let the cruel, familiar wrench run its course. Years ago, when he'd led Delta Flight, a wingman had died.

He glanced around the command center. Night shift was departing, day shift tagging their counterparts and taking their places.

He rubbed his forehead, taken by a memory of Tierna Coll, Glin-Erris's aunt. Her authoritative voice always rang through the high chamber where the Regional Council met. Her nephew had now died in Federate service. It was a sad blow.

A blow to the mission, as well. Glin-Erris had been their key diplomat on board the ship that called itself Monu. Shel still had the highest epsilon strength, Uri the most experience in an intelligence capacity, and Mari's courage was unmatched.

Those still were his assets.

But Mari must not venture down that corridor, and she was the likeliest to attempt it.

They were talking. He stilled his thoughts.

Uri spoke toward the bright ceiling. "Monu, whenever we have tried to become more than human, we have always become much less." It was a gracious thing for a Sentinel to say.

And Daken plainly found it irresistible. "I agree," he said loftily.

Firebird glared.

Uri barely paused. "We must refuse that honor, as you call it," he said, "although we believe you mean it generously. There is another way in which you could repay us for whatever fuel you need. Let us begin a more meaningful discussion."

Yes, that shielding information. Firebird folded her hands and kept quiet. Uri had diplomatic experience. He would have a better chance of gathering information, including obtaining those shields for Federate engineers, while getting the rest of them back to Netaia alive.

Monu spoke again. "Two of you have already become more than human, as you call it. I have observed you speaking to each other using communication the others plainly do not hear."

Firebird sent Shel an alarmed glance. Could Monu detect subvocalizing?

Monu's tuneless voice spoke again. "Also, all of you use advanced remote technology to speak with your compatriots back on Netaia." She paused once more. "I have seen in your broadcasts that you crawling things honor the emptied shell, once the person leaves it. I shall return the shell of Ambassador Glin-Erris Coll to you. Please honor it however you wish."

Uri had gone silent, so Firebird set down her kass mug and stood up. "Are there others of your kind, Monu?"

"I am the last."

Chilled, Firebird hesitated. Daken rose, probably wanting to be the one asking questions. Shel also stood up, though, so Firebird approached the vibrating bulkhead and asked, "Where was your world, Monu?"

"Outside what you call the Whorl. I would say that you are upper galactic from it."

"Why did you leave?"

"It was seeded for fuel. For all of us."

"I don't understand."

Daken edged closer but said nothing. Apparently he'd learned yesterday that Sentinels could silence him, and he hadn't liked it.

"My size requires fuel," Monu said. "More than suns can give. You will see."

"I don't understand," Firebird repeated. Monu's people were no more? She did not use solar fuel? "What sort of fuel? Please explain." Was Brennen following this?

"I now shall be unavailable," Monu said. "I must evaluate my systems and discern what failed. I had thought that all this was ready. For the delay, I do apologize. For Glin-Erris's death, I apologize most sincerely."

Death. Glin-Erris was gone. He was a good man.

Uri seemed to have recovered. "Monu, it is imperative that we learn to speak plainly to each other. There is much about you that we wish to know, and we have an important request for compensation."

Monu did not answer this time.

Daken stopped short of Shel's reach. "You," he told Firebird, "are not our leader." He thrust a finger at Uri. "He is certainly underqualified."

Firebird held her temper. "You are not dealing with Little Lady Wastling anymore, Daken, and Uri Harris has a diplomatic background that you lack."

He snorted and turned aside.

"Brenn?" she called softly. Why weren't Brennen and the marshal reacting to this new information? Was there trouble on base?

Uri murmured, "I'm going to go quiet awhile. I'm going to quest-pulse again and see if I can establish mind-access with this Monu. We need to communicate."

"Be careful," Firebird said just as quietly. "It seems she's aware of epsilon energy. Brennen, do you think this is possible?" She wished she had him in her line of sight. What was he thinking? What was he doing?

Brennen had heard the grim threat of further so-called enshipments, but a tracking tech had demanded his attention. On a secondary board, something resembling Monu's flame-like shielding had sprung up around the heavy fighter that escorted the *Cometesse*.

"Hail the escort crew." Brennen was less concerned about this development than his people on board Monu, but this required explanation. "Are they being attacked?"

A comm officer spoke. "HF-1620, status please."

Nothing.

"Scan again," Brennen said. "Higher resolution."

"Odd." First Marshal Burkenhamn touched the comm officer's shoulder. "Keep trying to raise them."

"Yes, sir."

Brennen counted aloud Monu's energy expenditures. "She catchfielded *Cometesse*. She plainly has operative shielding, she is attempting a self-repair, and she appears to be responding to an armed craft as a potential threat."

Marshal Burkenhamn caught his drift. "She has power, and she's using it."

Brennen turned back to the tri-D well. "Her onboard adjustments, as she calls them, are not taking all her attention. She may be low on fuel, but she appears to be using a good deal of it." He lowered his voice. "So she has not been unable to communicate with us. She wanted in-person communication for other reasons."

Burkenhamn set his jaw. "Candidates for enshipment, as she called it."

Brennen stared down at the tri-D well. He wished he had taken the time to engage Glin-Erris in more conversation. He'd been a stellar diplomat and a stabilizing presence, and he trusted the Sentinel kindred. Losing him was indeed a blow.

Shutting his eyes, he prayed, *Grant him peace, and protect the others.*

Wresting his mind back to the mission, he considered how best to proceed. Uri was formerly an intelligence specialist, as he himself had been. If Uri could establish mind-access, he might be able to extract the shielding information. Most of the projected image, now complete, had a bizarre density that did suggest robotic operation.

Then, he could withdraw them all. If Monu wanted fuel, she would have to negotiate via the base's comm staff.

Also, the ambassadors probably were unaware of the other urgent matter. He pulled the mike-con from his belt and keyed it to speak with them all. "Uri," he said, though they all would hear.

Several seconds later came Uri's reply. "Yes?"

Brennen eyed the tri-D well and its image of the Strangers' ship. *Of Monu's ship,* he corrected himself. "Uri, if you can get Monu's attention or establish access, find out what she just did to your fighter escort. It's apparently been surrounded by the same field she uses to shield herself." He glanced at Marshal Burkenhamn, who raised a single finger. He nodded and continued. "Command is giving your mission one day to establish rapport with this entity 'Monu.' After that, you will be authorized to evacuate, using every power at your disposal." Uri would understand. They could reveal more Sentinel skills on their way out. "Fuel negotiations can continue off-site after that."

He waited for a response. Capable people could accomplish a great deal in one day, but thanks to the Erwin family, all three might be checked by one loose cannon.

Might Daken Erwin begin to cooperate?

Firebird had been listening hard, wondering why Brennen said so little. Uri stood back up, catching her glance. "Monu," Uri called, "if we may claim your attention for one more moment, our compatriots back on Netaia are concerned about a small escort craft that did not enter your landing bay. What did you just do to it?"

Escort craft? Firebird hadn't thought much about the heavy fighter that shadowed them here.

"It is irrelevant to your mission."

"Irrelevant?" Uri asked. Firebird certainly didn't think so.

"I have shielded it as a gesture of welcome. Its crew is unharmed."

"Unshield them," Uri called. "Immediately. They pose you no threat, since we are communicating frankly."

Shipboard noises, faint creaks and ticks, came from aft of their lounge. Was she hearing Monu make her system checks?

Daken stood up, and Firebird braced herself for more craziness. Shel angled a hand to voice-command, but Daken crossed in front of them toward the corridor, followed by Gering. "Monu," he said, "my manservant and I will retrieve the body of our companion. His emptied shell, as you called it."

Firebird frowned. Had Daken found his courage? Before anyone could object or the Sentinels could voice-command, both Netaians strode off down the corridor.

"Base," Uri said, "we might have just lost two more, both Erwin and Gering, or else they might return with Glin-Erris's body. Would Tallans object if we sang Shekkah for him?"

"Surely not," Firebird whispered. The Sentinels' service for the dead was beautifully reverent. It might even touch Monu's heart, whereas her impromptu concert last night had obviously failed. She'd played for a Shekkah service. She might remember the music.

Half a minute later, Brennen answered. "I consulted one of our controllers, who is Tallan. She had no objection. Thank you, Uri. You will have further orders shortly. Before attempting an access interrogation, wait to see whether they return from that corridor."

In another few minutes, Firebird spotted movement beyond the hatchless archway. It was Gering, shuffling toward them, carrying a limp form in dress whites. She hurried to meet him.

Gering let Glin-Erris's body slide down onto the lounger. There didn't seem to be any stiffening. Might he be alive? Crouching, she reached for his throat to check for a pulse. His throat felt cool, and no artery quivered.

Uri shook his head. She met his eyes. He shut them. A Sentinel would detect life.

So Glin-Erris was dead. Narrow red pressure stripes marked his forehead, and there was a round wound on his scalp. He'd said that Monu's device was snug, hadn't he?

Uri turned him over. More angry-looking pressure marks ran up into his short, dark hair from the base of his skull. Apparently, Monu had clamped his head.

Firebird was liking this mission less by the minute. She looked into Gering's blue-gray eyes. "Where is Daken?"

"He went on alone," Gering said gruffly. "I left him inside what I believe was the bridge." He stretched out his large hands. "It's a chamber about nine meters across. Smooth walls, round ceiling."

She had an awful thought. "Do you think Grand Duke Daken actually wants to be enshipped?"

Gering shrugged slightly. Firebird guessed the big man was conflicted. She, too, had been loyal to her Netaian family, all the way to death. But Daken Erwin was sick. Dodis Gering probably knew that better than anyone.

Uri and Shel lowered Glin-Erris from the lounger to the deck. Uri crossed Glin-Erris's hands over his chest. Seeing him laid out like a formally arranged corpse made it final. Firebird swallowed past a lump in her throat. He was not tardema-sleeping. He was gone.

Daken had passed out of the well-lit lounge. He drew his interlink to light the rest of the way. "Monu? Monu, speak to me."

The feminine voice answered. "I listen before I speak."

He reached an open area, its ceiling so high he could barely see it by the glowing screen's light. "The others are unwilling," he said, "but I would gladly become your immortal companion."

"I have not selected you. Go back." Textured bulkheads were smoothing out around him. Protrusions vanished. One obvious opening, beyond where he stood, closed in from its edges and became a bulkhead.

He would like to be able to do things like that. Impressed, he brushed off the stinging remark. "Have you selected someone else to bring on board?"

"Tentatively," she said, "Colonel Harris. Commander Caldwell also impresses me. But I am not yet certain of my repairs."

Fire-brat, ahead of him? Outrageous. Her name should have been written in her own Angelo-scarlet blood years ago, even before she'd turned traitor.

On the other hand, if Monu tested her repairs on Firebird, she might fail again. A wastling was an ideal test subject for a potentially fatal operation.

Or, if Firebird survived, he might go next. He would gladly give up fragile flesh for real power. One day, he would grow strong enough to destroy the enshipped Firebird. Maybe even Monu herself.

For now, he would placate. "What if I were your hands and feet, out there among the other ambassadors? What if I convinced them that your intentions are good?" The slight echo of his voice sounded satisfyingly compassionate. "I believe that they are."

"They are good." Her voice also echoed. "I offer the finest, most valuable commodity that humanity desires. Unending life. Encourage the others to accept this recompense for my refueling. I would thank you appropriately, Grand Duke Daken."

Satisfied, he strode back out toward the lounge, but he paused in the hatchless archway. He heard singing. It was in some other language, and that foul, tinkling little harp was playing too.

If only he were already enshipped. He would take her down. Now.

Firebird cradled the clairsa against her shoulder, one hand on its carved upper arch. She'd only practiced the Shekkah service for one occasion. Still, music usually stuck in her memory, sometimes helping her learn Ehretan words. Uri led, and Shel confidently sang the responses. Firebird kept her eyes on the vibrating metal clairsa strings. Through them, she could see Glin-Erris's still form, peacefully laid on the deck. Her eyes filled in sorrow and regret. Missions meant risks, and Glin-Erris had taken a major one, but she was glad Brennen had issued a time limit. One day. Right now, they would honor Glin-Erris and show Monu that they truly respected those who had made the Crossing.

Shel and Uri stopped singing. Caught distracted, she cadenced to a final chord in that mode.

Uri spoke. "Mighty Speaker beyond space and time, we honor the life of Glin-Erris Coll, a good man who lived a life of service. Show him mercy now." He switched to the ancient, holy Ehretan language for a liturgical prayer.

It still was hard to keep up with a fluent speaker, and motion distracted her again. Daken walked out of the ominous corridor at last. Why had he lingered, and why was he alive—the beast—after Monu killed Glin-Erris in there? She wanted answers, and she wanted them now, but not in the middle of a Shekkah service.

Daken crossed to Gering and bent toward him, whispering. He headed toward the sleeping cabin, nose in the air. Gering remained, though. Maybe he, at least, was touched by the music and words. Was Monu?

"Great is your mercy," the others chorused. Staring after Daken, Firebird managed to chant the last words with them.

Then it was time for private prayer.

Great is your mercy. It echoed in her mind. Raised in a merciless culture, she had followed that notion of mercy into a faith that Brennen was kept from explaining until she had asked direct questions and declared herself an Inquirer.

Mercy, she reflected. *Mercy for Glin-Erris,* she prayed silently. *Mercy for us all. Help us complete this mission, on behalf of our peoples.*

An odd thought occurred to her. *Show mercy to Monu, if that's possible.*

Her conscience pricked. What about Daken?

Daken deserved justice, not mercy. She would never forget—or forgive—the terror in Corey's wide eyes at the sight of Daken's gold-hilted dagger.

I can't, Merciful Singer.

No? She, who had tried to live as a sacrifice to Daken's false gods, had found mercy.

He's in your hands, she managed. *Not mine. And that's good.*

The others had raised their heads to look at her. She flung away the distracting thoughts. There was supposed to be ending music, wasn't there? "I . . . I don't remember the rest," she admitted.

Shel sang softly in OldCol, "To you we commit our brother. To you we commit our lives. Now and forever, so let it be."

Firebird did feel stronger in her spirit. She glanced at the bulkhead that had vibrated with Monu's voice. Had she heard any of that? Had it touched her soul? Might it open real communication?

Gering approached them. "This was beautiful. When we return, I shall offer appropriate Charities and Disciplines on his behalf."

A faithful Netaian was generous to offer that, since Glin-Erris had been a foreigner. "Thank you." She glanced back at the archway. "What was Daken doing in there?"

One of Gering's massive hands twitched. He glanced at the deck. Finally, he said, "He told me to wait in the corridor with Ambassador Coll's body. I confess that I disobeyed. I followed him far enough to look into the chamber, and then I carried the body straight back, instead. Leaving him lying in the walkway would have seemed disrespectful."

Shel folded her arms. "Daken was in there a long time."

Gering looked across at Shel, massive man to tall woman. "I said too much, madam. Forgive me."

"Nothing to forgive." Shel glanced toward the private cabins.

"You did well," Firebird added.

Finally, Brennen spoke in Firebird's ear. "Yes, well done, friends. Thank you, Mister Gering. We now have a full schematic scan of that ship. We are sending it via FasScan, along with analysis notes from our engineers. If you see anything today that could prove useful, or if Monu provides her fueling information, contact us immediately. Her fuel tank appears to be almost empty. You only have today," he reminded them. "Uri, continue to attempt access. Shel, lend him strength."

As Uri settled in beside Shel to try and find a way into Monu's alpha matrix—if she had such a thing, which Firebird was beginning to wonder—Firebird got comfortable on the lounger. Determined to sort through all the information available to her, she pored over the new diagrams for the next hour. Each was a slice through the spacecraft's vast interior, some cross sections running pole-to-pole and others from various angles. She had no idea what she was looking for. If engineers couldn't spot weaknesses or identify her fueling needs, how could she? Still, it would be tragic—for Monu—to send Monu back off into space, empty and alone. Their mission had been neighborly, even generous.

But it was going sour. Fast.

Daken had retreated to his cabin, but Gering produced a handheld and joined her, examining schematics. Glin-Erris's recall pad might have included additional information, but probably not what they needed now, and obviously, Daken had not brought it back out with him.

Uri seemed to be getting nowhere. She'd never seen a Sentinel so baffled. Her mind fled back to Netaia. What were her children doing? What about Ahma-Dara? Was Norann Burkenhamn showing them the city parks in springtime?

Comm with Brennen and the marshal remained appropriately terse. Near midday, Daken strutted out into the lounge. "Gering," he announced, "it's time to eat."

Gering obediently walked to the servo unit. Lunch, like breakfast, consisted of cubes and kass. It would keep them alive for a day. Daken made a disgusted face when Gering handed him a mug and a bowl.

"You stayed quite awhile in there," Shel said bluntly. "With Monu. Did she give you any more information?"

Daken held a concentrate cube between thumb and forefinger, not quite extending his pinky. He spoke down at Firebird. "If her choices are honored," he said, "she would open fuel negotiations."

Daken was never to be trusted. Was Brenn listening? "If Monu is an honorable person," she said carefully, "then naturally, we will relay her requests to Citangelo."

Daken smiled slightly.

Uri eyed the Grand Duke. "Did she tell you what fuel she needs?"

"No."

"Did you ask her?"

Daken shrugged and did not look away from Firebird. "Yes. But she only will discuss this with someone who needs the same kind of fuel. Also, she did tell me who she would like to try and process next." He lowered his chin, glaring disdainfully.

"No." Firebird stood up. Chilled, she crossed her arms. "No," she said again. Could she believe this man? How often did he tell the truth?

Daken shrugged. "Then we'll never find out what kind of fuel she needs, will we?" Perfect teeth gleamed behind that perfect beard.

Brennen's voice in her ear echoed her denial back to her. "No. Go nowhere near that corridor, Mari."

Ah. He was listening, all right. "What do we do?" she murmured. "We need information, and we haven't even opened negotiations. I don't want to give up after just one day. We've got to get her talking."

"One day," Brennen repeated. "That is all."

And according to shipboard time, the morning had passed.

Oblivious to Brennen's orders, Daken tossed his head. "Don't give up, then, Firebird. Go to Monu. Get us that information."

She clenched her teeth and spun away.

11: NOBLEWOMEN
stringendo, pressing forward

Citangelo's cloudy morning had only begun as Dara Dickin Caldwell cradled a cup of cloyingly sweet Netaian cruinn between her hands. Curious, she eyed her royal guest. Behind Her Former Majesty Carradee Angelo, in the little home's living room, Kinnor, Kiel, and their toddler cousin Queen Rinnah were running laps around furniture. Fortunately, the chairs, lounger, occasional table, and lighting looked military-grade indestructible.

The former queen, Firebird's elder sister—a tall, gentle-faced blonde—sat across from Dara at the house's small servo-dining table, under a window that looked out on spindly new trees. Meeting just after breakfast, they had opened with small talk. Abruptly, Carradee asked, "How did you ever survive losing a son and all three of your grandchildren?"

Dara had suspected this would not be a simple social call. "When Brennen, my younger son, reached me with the news that morning, I gladly would have died." The memory made her shudder.

Carradee nodded slowly. "We never knew," she said in turn, "for months, whether my little Iarlet and Kessie were alive. Of course, the Shuhr had taken them. Had"—her voice faltered—"killed them." She swallowed, then added in a distant voice, "I found by inquiring persistently that there were even tissue samples taken from their little bodies."

Dara reached out and lightly touched the younger woman's arm in sympathy. The renegade Shuhr were everything the Sentinels might have become if the Holy Speaker had not enfolded them in just, merciful laws. Shuhr thieves had stolen everything from warships to jewelry and eliminated entire families. They particularly had hated the Caldwells, even more so after her son Brennen and his Firebird destroyed their Golden City on Three Zed, the world they now called Mikuhr.

Carradee Angelo fingered her cruinn cup's rim. She wore a simple skyff and trousers, essential makeup, and simply arranged hair. Dara guessed that she was avoiding any hint of royal intimidation. Frankly, she gave off the earnest emotional sense of a supplicant.

"Labbah, my late husband, had been gone seven years." Dara's chest ached as she recalled their few happy years. "Such a good man, humble and wise. I left town after those murders. One of my cousins works at a spiritual retreat center in the mountains. Brennen and his Lady Firebird no longer needed me, so it was time to care for my own needs." The memory pained her, perhaps because she was sharing it with another woman who had also lost a family. "The Holy One looked after me. He still does."

"Ah." Carradee's face brightened. "He is as good as springtime."

Dara returned the younger woman's smile. Carradee and her husband had stepped onto the Holy Path while sheltering at the Sentinels' sanctuary world. She liked this noblewoman better than she had anticipated. There was a gentle wisdom in Carradee, a nurturing wisdom. But on the unseen emotional depth that only trained individuals would sense, Carradee was not tough enough for command, let alone for governing. She exuded a desire to be liked. Cooperative. Helpful.

"I came today," Carradee said, "not just to welcome you—though I do—" She extended a hand. A large red gemstone dominated her only ring. "But I wonder whether such intense grieving has made me unable to conceive again. Coming back to Netaia has been hard. I lost so many while living here. My dear father. My sister Lintess. Then our royal mother, and then, of course, Phoena—but then, both of my . . . first sweet babies." Her eyes thickened. "Not even dear Rinnah will ever take their place."

Changing the subject to help Carradee hold back those tears, Dara said, "I did not know you'd had a sister named Lintess. Firebird never mentioned her."

"Lintess died very young." Carradee sat upright. The threat of tears ebbed. "Some people blamed our sister Phoena, because when Lintess died, little Phoena moved into the line of succession. She was no longer a wastling. And Phoena was strong-willed, very determined, even as a young child."

In that case, grace had kept Firebird from mentioning Lintess and the suspicions regarding Princess Phoena. Dara was appreciating a new side of her son's connatural bond mate and therefore, new things about her son.

Carradee leaned in. "They tell me you are a psi healer."

"I have some experience, yes," Dara answered. How much should she say? "My elder son, Tarance, followed me into the medical profession, while Brennen longed to fly. Tarance seemed much safer." She shook her head. "How ironic. I support Brennen, now, mostly by praying. He stays in touch as he can."

"I am so sorry," Carradee said earnestly. "Now, there is trouble in our streets. Your Federacy has helped. But as a noble parent, my calling is to try and conceive again. Do you think you could help me?"

She could. First, though, she asked, "Are you a prisoner of that calling, Carradee? Like . . ." Did she dare confide in this young woman? Perhaps. "Like my son? Brennen's work could consume him, although he does it willingly. It always was his destiny, having been born with such high epsilon potential."

"Wait a moment," Carradee said as she looked down. Her Majesty Rinnah had rushed over to slap both hands down onto Carradee's lap, gasping with laughter. The twins followed, Kiel holding both hands behind his back while Kinnor wriggled ten clutching fingers. Both boys were grinning.

"Were you tickling, Kinnor?" Dara asked solemnly. He wriggled his fingers again, honest if mischievous. Dara lowered her chin and eyed him solemnly. "Did you ask permission?"

"Rinnah can't talk, Zahma." So sensible. So full of wiggles and curiosity.

"Rinnah seems all right with it." Carradee patted her daughter's blonde head. "But, Kinnor, if Rinnah starts to look unhappy, please stop."

"Okay," Kinnor pronounced. "Come on, Rinnah." He dashed away, giggling an invitation.

Her Little Majesty also dashed away, following him.

Dara watched them run off. Three beautiful children. Kiel had hung back, excited like the others but somehow distant from both. Dara wondered, not for the first time, whether she might be witnessing the childhood of the promised messianic Boh-Dabar.

That responsibility would be all-consuming. She hoped she might be able to help.

"No," Carradee answered the earlier question. "I am no prisoner. I abdicated a throne I did not want, and my call is to bear heirs whom I love."

Dara watched the Netaian toddler. "Did I hear correctly that Her Majesty's Ehretan heritage—the psi potential—has been surgically corrected?"

Carradee gave a slight smile. "Yes, and I mean your people no insult, Dara. We are simply not equipped to deal with such abilities. Your Sanctuary Master graciously traveled here to perform the surgery. He said that I would need no surgery, since I have carried a youth implant for most of my life." She touched her forehead. "How strange that we Angelos share your heritage, and that because of heir limitation, there are so few of us."

Naturally, that reminded Dara of a more immediate, more sobering concern. One or both of these beautiful Caldwell twins might have inherited a mutant gene from their Angelo mother, a gene that had created her dangerous reversed-polarity epsilon carrier. It was now publicly known that her ability to wield it had been crippled. But was that gene dominant or recessive? The twins soon would reach the age when those latent abilities often could be discerned. Dara had started carrying two child's doses of an epsilon-blocking drug in her medical kit, in case an emergency arose. Firebird usually did the same. The abilities would not fully mature until at least twelve, but trouble might come earlier. Children of high epsilon potential could be difficult. They must take no chances.

Firebird had killed, using that mutant epsilon carrier. Unintentionally, at first.

Carradee shook her head ruefully and changed the subject. "We've been told that those who want to evacuate Citangelo might do so. Will you be staying here, on Netaia, regardless? To be near your son?"

"If the children must be sent away, I shall go with them," Dara answered. "That is our agreement. My son and his wife will often need me, I think. It is good to be needed." In her private room back on Tallis, at her bedside, stood a formal portrait of them wearing royal regalia for Firebird's confirmation as an heiress.

Dara also owned a miniature portrait of a third grandbaby, a little girl who had been created by Shuhr conspirators using their own genetic stock and one of Brennen's skin cells. They had meant to entrap him. Rescued instead, little Saried lived with her Shuhr mother on the sanctuary world.

She longed to meet that child. To give her a blessing, if she could.

Carradee eyed the romping children. Dara followed her gaze. Kinnor was actually standing still, letting Rinnah take a turn tickling him. "I shall remain," Carradee said. "Daithi is working civil defense. Your son and his wife are greatly blessed by your help, I think. They are heroes."

That pronouncement required a firm answer. "You and Prince Daithi are also heroes. You protect others."

Silence fell at the table.

After several slow seconds, Carradee spoke. "Your Sanctuary Master Dabarrah helped with my grief. Could you do the same?"

It was a humbling comparison. "Master Dabarrah is our greatest healer. I could never approach his skills."

"But you are trained in epsilon healing."

"I am." Persistence should be rewarded, and Carradee—though ungifted—had been confirmed as a sister on the Holy Path.

"Will you help me?"

"Absolutely." Dara glanced at the entry. Two Sentinels stood guard outside, and inside were two uniformed House Guards. She asked the nearest uniformed Netaian, sworn to the Angelo family, "Would you watch all the children awhile, so her former majesty and I can retire to the inner room?"

After all, Kiel and Kinnor were also the House Guards' responsibility.

Tel Tellai sat at Esme Rogonin's long, heavy-looking dining table and nursed cup after cup of spicy cruinn as it went cold. His urge to warn her about her understaffed situation had to wait. On this, his second visit, she was up and down, giving orders to staff and herding her siblings into travel clothing. Count Farring and Count Kelsen complied without grumbling, but Lady Diamond had to be sent back twice before they left via hovercraft. Tel studied the long table's dark wood grain and tried not to remember his furtive conversations here with Esme's father, the prior regent. Netaia's despised and powerful Lieutenant Governor Caldwell had often been discussed, along with how to rid themselves of him.

At last Esme sat down with a sigh, looked him in the eye with an expression that silently asked *are you still here*, and rang for a fresh carafe.

Tel gathered his thoughts. "Esme," he said, "yesterday, you gave me permission to walk your grounds. They are lovely, by the way. Particularly overlooking the river." He paused to let her acknowledge the compliment.

She folded graceful hands on the table. "That's why I kept Father's gardening staff, those willing to stay. They never moved to the palace with us. Maybe someday, I shall have time to pay more attention. Kelsen will, if I marry and move to a different estate. We are in an interim situation, as you know."

He pitied her. So much potential, wasted on the Erwins—

Stop it, he told himself. "Yes," he said lightly, "and I wish you a happy match, but in the meantime, you should post additional sentry staff. A second gatekeeper, at least. We live in troubling times." He hated to mention Daken, but she already was glancing down at an interlink. "The Grand Duke would wish to see you protected."

"I'll have Pherris look into it," she said absently.

He remembered Pherris as a doddering chief of staff, more often to be found mid-nap than on duty. He risked dropping the masquerade. "Esme," he said, "look at me."

She did. Warily.

He must make her take him seriously. "Today," he insisted. "Duchess, if you don't have time to screen and hire private staff, please ask for assistance from the Enforcement Corps. You are vulnerable. It is entirely possible that one or more of the Shuhr remain on Netaia. We know that their powers allow them to masquerade with other people's faces. They can convince everyone who sees them that they really are someone else. Sentinels never would do that, but Shuhr can. And do. One of them might kill you, or imprison you, in order to steal your properties and your place at the Electoral table." He paused for breath. She'd surely heard all this before, but she needed to hear it again. Today.

"Ah," she said in a teasing voice. "So manly of you, Prince Tel. Truly, I thank you for your concern. Perhaps you have forgotten that I dealt with Shuhr some time ago. Come back in two days, and I will have started the hiring process."

Plainly, she thought his genuine concern was the playacting. It hurt to know that she thought so poorly of him. "I will be here tomorrow," he said crossly.

"The next day, if you please. That will be close enough to 'every day' to please Grand Duke Daken."

She was trying to insult him, implying that she found his presence so tiresome that she would disobey Daken in order to spend less time with him.

He eyed the mounted animal heads along the opposite wall. He, too, found the simpering old Prince Tel Tellai-Angelo tiresome. How could he convince her of danger? Turning around, he raised an eyebrow at Paudan.

His own liveried man only shrugged those square shoulders.

"And now, you have put in your time," she said brusquely. "You need not come tomorrow, Prince Tel. I shall be very busy."

That also made him wince. On the other hand, it showed—once more—an independent streak that he admired. Maybe in time, she would stand up to Daken Erwin too.

Would Daken admire her or squelch her?

Fearing that he knew the answer, he rose from the table. "Very well. Two days from now, I shall bother you briefly once more."

Her light laugh sounded hollow. Her doorman saw him out. Paudan followed. Already, probably signaled by Esme, his driver was pulling the indigo Tellai groundcar out of the coach house on his left.

As he stepped morosely down from the portico into the breezy morning, her neglected gardens depressed him further. Back at his own estate, spring bulbs were putting up blooms amid tidy beds of fine mulch. His neatly trimmed vines were covering themselves with blossoms and buds, color-matched for stunning mass displays. Here, last autumn's debris covered the night-fragrance bed. All the vines had sprawled off their trellises to wander out onto the sward.

Sighing, he slipped into the car's rear compartment. As usual, Paudan sat in front. "Home, Jess," he quietly ordered the driver, studying his hands.

What was happening out in space? As he looked up, another groundcar—long and white, like the one he'd seen cruise past yesterday—drove slowly up the Rogonin estate's lane. He saw it pass out of the corner of his eye.

Plainly, Esme had time for someone.

With the sibs departed south and Prince Tel shooed away, Esme Rogonin retreated to the ground floor sanctum that had been her father's private office. His weapons collection still hung on the wall, pairs of crossed swords displayed alongside single automatic slug-throwers. She felt like a fraud sometimes, imitating his bold reputation. She'd been schooled in Netaian ways, and she must carry on all the traditions as long as she headed House Rogonin. She'd inherited her family's Minister of Trade position and the Codex newsnet service, along with her title and properties, but she spent little time studying Trade. House Erwin, her probable future, headed the Ministry of Metals. Lacking the privilege of raising heirs, she would likely spend the rest of her life in that capacity. Daken enjoyed the hunt, so she would spend a great deal of time at home with the rest of his family. The First Lord bored her to tears, but she hoped to cultivate Daken's sister, Valora.

She lit the touchboard and was about to tell it to delete notes from the Electoral session when she spotted Lady Firebird's exchange proposal. She found its forward-looking optimism refreshing. Hadn't she told Father, the last time Lady Firebird returned to Netaia, that she rather liked the woman? She'd been striking and pretty at the Electoral table, and forthright, if a little disrespectful toward the powerful Erwins. Supposedly, she'd given House Angelo its first male heirs in over a century.

Not every noble sprig grew into their rightful title, though.

Beyond the entry hall, her front door slid shut with its usual *boom*.

That seemed odd. She shut down the console and pushed to her feet. Were those footsteps? Why wasn't the doorman announcing—

Two dark-haired women stepped into the office's open doorway. Dressed almost identically in charcoal-gray outfits that flattered their figures, they had long, young-looking faces so similar that they had to be sisters. One wore a necklace of gold beads. It looked like something Esme's mother had worn, years ago. That necklace had disappeared.

"My name is Esme," said the woman wearing it.

Esme rested a hand on her father's desktop. Had she seen these women before? She didn't think so. She laughed and answered lightly. "What a coincidence." They both had dark eyes and creamy skin that she instantly envied. However, she would have her doorman escort them out.

"My name is also Esme," said the sister who stood a little behind, on the right. "Thank you for the sweet invitation."

Esme's laughter died. She'd sent no invitation. She eyed the pair quizzically. Who would dare to enter a noble house unannounced and uninvited?

What was it Prince Tel had just said? That the Sentinel General's renegade relatives—they called them "Shuhr," strange word—might kill or imprison Electors and take their places?

She had not believed it then. She did not believe it now. The Shuhr who had taken over Father's office had made him act jocular and irreverent, but they'd never tried to kill him. They'd had no intention of taking his place, not that she could see. No, these lovely women had to have other business.

They strode forward, around the desk, one on each side.

Esme did not like that. She sat down and reached toward the alarm button under the desk's surface, near her right knee.

Her hand stopped short. A strange, warm feeling flooded through her, but her arm wouldn't move.

They *were* Shuhr. They were back, and Prince Tel was right: She was practically alone, with Farring and Kelsen gone south. She resisted a sticky-sweet emotional warmth that pressed in on her. Was this how they made Father give them state secrets? She sprang back up and opened her mouth to shout.

Her vocal cords seemed frozen.

The sister wearing Mother's gold necklace smiled, but her dark eyes retained an ominous expression. "We won't hurt you today," she said. "But we do want your memories."

Esme had never been mind-crawled. She'd been too young for the Lieutenant Governor's attention, and the Shuhr in Father's office had ignored her. Why would these people bother with her now, unless—unless Prince Tel had spoken truth? If they truly were masters of masquerade, they might want to steal her place at the Electoral table. She was no regent, no key player. They would not be obvious in her role.

Would they keep her prisoner, then? Eliminate her? "No," Esme whispered. "No, please. Let us discuss this, my friends. We can be friends, after all."

"Sit down, sweet Esmerield."

Her body complied.

The woman wearing Mother's necklace perched sidesaddle on the wide desktop. The other came around behind her back. She couldn't move or cry for help. Strong hands gripped her shoulders. Something like knives plunged into her head, and her thoughts whirled down into confusion and scattered toward insanity. The pain made her want to scream—

Until eerie peace dropped over her, a peace with the weirdest foul scent. Surreal colors painted the office walls pale yellow, orange, green.

"See?" The one who was not wearing the necklace slipped away and came around Father's broad desk. "We won't hurt you, Esme dear. You may act normally now."

"And we'll watch," the other said. "You are very much to be emulated, don't you think? Whatever were you going to do now?"

Esme tried to remember. The last few minutes, since Prince Tel departed, all felt like a blur. "I was going uplevel to the vaporbath, I think. And then, perhaps, take a stroll in the gardens. They are somewhat abandoned." Who was it that had told her that? Another idea struck her. "Wouldn't you like to see the rest of my estate?"

"Yes," said the woman wearing the necklace. "All three stories of the main house, both wings, and the cellars beneath them. Maybe we could make homes for more of our friends. Friends of us all. We have other friends here."

Esme preceded them out of the office, into the wide entry. Her liveried doorman lay on the floor, crumpled next to the front door. The surprise penetrated her uncanny peace. "You didn't . . . kill him?" she pleaded.

Esme-wearing-Mother's-necklace drew back her lips in an unflattering grin. "You don't wish to lose any more staff, do you, Esme dear? The rest of them will survive to serve us, all three of us, so long as your warm welcome lasts."

Esme tried to turn toward the doorman's body. She wanted to run. Her legs rotated her aside, instead. Had the sisters loosened their grip for a moment, proving that they could control her?

Regardless, her feet took her up the massive first stairway. It led to the family's private quarters. Uplevel, they paused at Lady Diamond's bedroom, piled with a twelve-year-old's girlish detritus. They spoke simultaneously, just slightly out of tune. The eerie effect terrified her. "Shovel it out, Esme. We shall stay here."

Something inside her was screaming. Something else was shouting, *I must escape. I must warn Prince Tel. He mustn't come back!*

The sister fingering Diamond's pale-pink window filters turned back with a sweeping gesture. "Ah, Prince Tel. The adorable little nobleman. Yes, by all means, invite him back. Tomorrow. But now." The woman's voice hardened. "Show us the east wing. Are there still military-grade weapons?"

12: IARLA
deciso, firmly

Firebird eyed Uri as he rose from the lounger. Trained as an access specialist, he'd spent most of the afternoon trying—again—to find a way into Monu's conscious alpha matrix, to learn more precisely how she shielded her massive body. This time, Shel had lent epsilon strength to the effort.

"Too diffuse," he reported after his third attempt, shaking his head. Shel mirrored the headshake.

Meanwhile, Monu made no obvious attempt to communicate. Firebird felt like a pinned insect, scrutinized by some passionless scientist. Why had Monu come to them for fuel if she ignored every attempt to compromise and negotiate? Daken's new claim, that Monu would only negotiate frankly with a fellow traveler who required the same fuel, was unanimously ignored. Apparently, they would depart at tomorrow's mission deadline, rested and ready to deal with whatever resistance Monu offered, without having helped her. Maybe that would be for the best. They still had the heavy fighter for cover, and evidently Monu had brought it inside her shields.

Stalemate.

As evening mealtime approached, Firebird reluctantly changed out of the dust-smudged dress whites she'd optimistically donned yesterday. She folded them carefully and set them on her bunk, and she pulled on comfortable gray shipboards, the only other clothes she'd brought from the transport, thinking they would spend just a few hours in here. Weary with the unfamiliar burden of failure, she folded Carrie's sash and laid it on top of the dress whites. She would pack all that tomorrow morning and give that sash back to Carrie. Wearing it had felt like a costume, anyway.

Now, for a delicious handful of concentrates—

Her conscience pricked. *Forgive me, Mighty Singer. It has been an honor to be here, even if our mission failed.* They were in Netaian space, too, orbiting a long-familiar sun. Another sweet privilege.

Shel sat down on her bunk close to the hatch. "Uri just sent me a message," she said. "Before we rest, he would enjoy some more music, if you still have the energy. It's too quiet in here."

"It would be good to feel helpful." Really, Firebird didn't have much appetite for concentrates. Out in the central lounge, she got comfortable on the S-shaped lounger as the others crafted bowls of multicolored cubes. She gave the clairsa another tuning—strings still sagging, no surprise—and searched her memory for something appropriate. Something light. Dinner music. After all, she had hoped to share music with the mysterious Strangers.

She settled on a suite of Netaian folk melodies that she'd memorized years ago. Cradling the small harp on her lap, she stretched both arms around it. Playing the opening bars loosed a flood of schoolgirl memories, and the suite—not flashy, but simple and melodic—fell into the dusty lounge like droplets of water on parched ground. The old songs predated the Coper Rebellion, of course. That infamous rising of young heirs and heiresses had precipitated the cruel laws of heir limitation. Now and then, she did reach for a bass string that just wasn't there. Hopefully, no one else noticed.

The others clapped politely. Daken set his bowl on the workstation. "I knew some of those tunes when I was growing up. Why are all the notes so high?"

For glory's sake. Of all the people who might have noticed, she wouldn't have guessed Daken. "It's a travel-sized instrument," she said. "There aren't as many low strings as usual."

"So it . . . tinkles." He sauntered closer, waving his fingers.

Shel got up from the lounger.

"We need to talk." Daken stopped a respectful distance away, raising both hands.

She couldn't remember ever hearing him sound sincere. She set the clairsa aside. Might they have found common ground in Netaian music? Had it made him willing, at last, to consider her as an equal?

"Yes," she said, trying not to hope for too much. "I think we do."

He waved toward the bulkhead that had vibrated. "How long do you think Monu has traveled alone? What stories might she have to tell? Aren't you curious?"

A little beast of suspicion appeared in the back of her mind. This wasn't a topic he would have chosen out of empathy. Not for her, anyway. "I'm very curious," she admitted. "But Monu isn't talking to us. She listens before she speaks, remember? And she speaks before she acts. She's watching us." Like a carnivore observing the herd, choosing its prey.

"I've been thinking." He crossed his arms. Shel edged nearer, and he glowered. "Leave me be, Sentinel. I only want to talk." He lowered his voice and turned back to Firebird. "Maybe she really will only talk to us as equals," he said. "To people she has elevated to her own status. Without your cooperation, Firebird, the mission seems doomed. We must send her off alone, to starve in deep space. Doesn't that make you sad?"

Her insides curdled. It was best not to hope at all, where Daken Erwin was concerned. What did he really want? And she must remember Monu was listening. "I am not going in to her. Not on those terms."

"Stand your ground, Mari," she heard in her ear. He'd kept silent while she performed. *Oh, Brenn, it's good to hear your voice.*

Daken's expression darkened to the usual glare. "You must. The Electorate chose you. So did Monu. As it turns out, this is the stance an ambassador must take. We have run out of time. Maybe if you go to her, she'll give the Federates what they want. Right? For your sake?"

He paused. Maybe waiting for her to answer.

Exchange her life for advanced shielding? "You're speaking nonsense." She frowned back at him. "I don't believe you."

"If you refuse her . . ." He gave her an even darker look. It made her recall the chill of a golden floor medallion under her knees. Suddenly, she knew exactly the word he would speak over her. The charge she'd once been sentenced to die for, *in absentia*.

He shook his head, pursing his lips. On anyone else, it might have looked regretful. On him, it was pure manipulation. "If you refuse," he said again, "then once again, I name you *traitor*."

That was no empty title on Netaia. A traitor's execution was as prolonged and agonizing as Netaia could make it. Faithful Netaians believed that the more one suffered while dying, the less he or she would suffer after death in the unimaginably terrible Dark that Cleanses.

Several retorts sprang to mind. The entire command center might be listening. She must be absolutely articulate, or else she must keep her peace.

Shel edged closer.

Mighty Singer, I'm not up to this. Guide me! Aloud, she said, "I do not accept that title. All I have done for Netaia outweighs anything you ever did."

Daken rocked away from her, twitching one side of his mouth into a sneer, but softly in her ear came Marshal Burkenhamn's reaction. "Well said, Commander."

Encouraged, she raised her voice. "But I will talk to Monu. Just not in that corridor." If Monu was watching and listening, she would hear this. "If I really am her choice, maybe she will answer me." There might still be time to redeem this mission. Daken had claimed she was Monu's first choice, but Daken served only himself. Maybe he hoped she would end up dead in another enshipment malfunction.

She picked up the clairsa and retreated to the women's cabin with just one look behind, making sure Shel followed. She closed the hatch but left it unlocked. The moment it shut them in, she murmured, "Brenn? Marshal? Advice? Just ask questions?"

"Yes," Brennen answered after the usual transmission lag. "Ask. I will be listening. The marshal was called away."

Shel sat down on her bunk again.

Firebird lifted her head. "Monu?" she called softly. "You have been watching. Will you speak?"

For several seconds, she heard only the ventilator. Then, between two bunks, a dull gray metal bulkhead turned blue. Something dark appeared at its center. Once again, a woman's head and shoulders came into focus. Her hair and eyes were reddish brown, her skin cream colored. She appeared to be in her thirties.

Once again, she looked familiar.

Startled, Firebird recognized the portrait. Her childhood heroine—her second-great-grandmother Iarla, a wastling who had survived to reign as monarch—seemed to look back at her. Clearly, Monu had searched public records, maybe using Glin-Erris's recall pad. Young Firebird Angelo had made no secret of her admiration for Queen Iarla. Iarla's amber-flecked brown eyes swept the cabin before they settled on Firebird, ignoring Shel.

"Monu?" Firebird asked, pressing her hands against her thighs. It felt right to stand at attention.

"Lady Firebird." As the image's lips moved, the tuneless voice spoke. The sync was almost perfect.

Tempted to demand that Monu show her pre-enshipped face, Firebird asked a more pressing question. "What, exactly, did you do to our friend Glin-Erris?"

"That was unfortunate," Iarla's image answered. "It has been very long since I used the enshipment function. I am close to having a repair. Then, I can welcome you and Colonel Harris. You are worthy to be made grand, like me."

Never! She wanted to scream it. But apparently, Daken had not lied. He'd just told a half-truth. Bad enough.

She rubbed her fingertips against her soft shipboards. "You know that I was a warrior," she said. "But much of my early training was in music."

"I do not see how that makes you more qualified."

Qualified wasn't what she'd meant. She explained. "I would like to honor you by putting your story into a ballad. Where did you come from? Why did you decide that you wanted to become what you are? You told us that enshipment is the highest recompense you could offer. But for us, being remembered in a song is one of the best things we could give—beyond the fueling you require," she added dutifully.

Shel nodded. As the image frowned, Brennen whispered. "Good."

Monu was already speaking. "You wish to know where I came from and why I come alone, so you can put that into music. A song, maybe."

"Yes," Firebird breathed. "Exactly." *Oh, Brenn. Listen now!* "We want to help you," she said. "Our Federacy is built on mutual respect."

Monu's image remained steady, her face devoid of expression and her voice just as tuneless. "We developed this way to become more than human when our resources declined. I was not one of the first. I worked in a laboratory. When the time came for our world's . . . " She halted and began again. "We started to compete. In time, only two of us remained. I took him, but he had been enshipped, like me, so he gave me no fuel.

My story is centuries long. I have seen nebulae and dust lanes, long empty years without the stars' warmth."

Firebird wasn't following, but maybe Brennen was. "Your story is sad," she said. Monu had rejected her own humanity.

"No," the image said. "Not sad at all. I live on. As you will live on, when your rich, beautiful world is nothing."

That sounded less than empathetic. Firebird listened for Brennen to suggest a genteel answer, because she was roiling inside.

Shel spoke up from over on her bunk. "We," she said, sweeping her hands, "would have grieved the loss of so many lives. We find death a tragic, unnatural thing."

Monu-Iarla turned toward Shel. "Death is natural. All crawling things die. I simply hastened those deaths."

Not good. Oh, not good at all. Would even music move that heart? "Aloneness is also sad," Firebird said. "We too shrink when we are alone. And," she added, "we were made for these bodies that breathe and love and, yes, that can die."

"Living without death is better than the natural."

"But you crave company now, don't you?"

Monu didn't answer.

"Perhaps we could learn to be living company for you, instead of . . . becoming enshipped." Even if so-called enshipment didn't kill her, it might mean spending thousands of years on this side of the Crossing, never hearing the Mighty Singer's galactic song. Never reuniting with Brenn or their children, when their time came.

"Show us what you need," she managed, "so we don't have to leave you here. We came on a mercy mission. There is another way you could repay us for your fueling. Would you consider—"

Interrupting her, Monu addressed Shel again. "Major Mattason, I have seen you and Colonel Harris communicate in unusual ways. Tell me what is happening then."

Firebird's breath caught. Did Monu want Sentinel powers for one of her companion ships, or was she probing for their strengths so she could take them down?

Shel spoke. "Gene work was done on our ancestors. The results were tragic. Only a few of us—their descendants—survive. We swear to serve others until our debt to humanity is paid. Then, the Mighty Speaker will set us free of this penalty."

"The penalty is illogical. All of you are the noblest and best of your worlds. Commander Caldwell and Colonel Harris will be glad to live as my companions. I am near a solution."

"Monu," Firebird said, close to exasperation, "your shields—"

The image dissolved in a haze of dark particles. The bulkhead looked like a bulkhead again.

Firebird blew out a breath. If Brenn and the marshal could come up with a way to deal with this post-human creature before tomorrow morning's departure, she would be extremely impressed. It looked like they must send her on alone. A minor-key melody might convey the sense of solitude, of aloneness, that was eating Monu alive.

Was she even alive, or was she purely mechanical?

Alone in his cabin—he had sent Gering away—Daken Erwin sat on the edge of his inadequate bunk. His duffel lay collapsed on the floor nearby, and he eyed it warily. He had brought along his dress dagger, as always. Sometimes, it called to him. Ever since he was young, something about seeing fresh blood, the essence of life, had invigorated him. He had promised the First Lord that he would not indulge on this trip. He almost regretted remembering the days when he could have written a wastling's name in their blood, a traditional prank.

He sighed.

A thought drifted up from the back of his mind, where he had tried to wall off the forbidden thoughts. There might be a simple and appropriate way to move up Monu's line of preference. What if, when all was said and done, he and Monu and Colonel Harris traveled the galaxy together? He could deal with Colonel Harris. Time and space would become his playthings. With his inescapable might, he could wipe out every strength-proud Sentinel. By moving up this way, he could slake his . . .

No. Not here, not now. His father would object.

And this wastling was guarded.

Might Monu help him? Amused by the thought, he made himself a proposition. If Monu would not cooperate, he would keep his promise and refrain. But if Monu would help, he might call that a sign from the mighty Powers. He could reclaim his birthright.

He'd been hearing Monu's voice through the bulkhead. When the harping began again, he knew that the women next door would not hear him. "Monu?" he called quietly. "Monu? Monu, are you listening?"

"Grand Duke Daken." This time, her voice seemed to come from the ceiling. "My hands and my feet. She remains resistant. I must speak with Colonel Harris instead."

"Wait." He'd gotten her attention, and the forbidden appetite pawed at him like one of his hound pups. "I have an idea that might help you. Is there some way that you could separate Firebird from that terrible bodyguard?"

"Terrible," the voice repeated.

He assumed that was a question. "I witnessed that woman fight my manservant," he explained. "She protects Firebird, and she can be violent. I will bring Firebird to you, down that hall, to your chamber. Your bridge, I mean." He stood. "But to make that happen, you would have to keep the bigger woman away."

Silence. Was she trying to decide whether he actually could overpower Firebird and drag her along? The depressing thought struck him. If that Sentinel woman had trained Firebird, he would need Gering's shock pistol to bring her to Monu.

But he had no intention of dragging anyone anywhere. He simply needed Monu to believe that he would.

He had blooded several wastlings, but they could not legally be killed prematurely. They were born, after all, to ensure their noble lines' survival. But after a geis was issued and if they resisted that fate, it was different. And Firebird had gone far beyond resistance. She mocked them all, so she was traitorous, lawful prey.

Monu remained silent. Was she considering his offer? He eyed the duffel again. Monu might be angry for a while. But she had eliminated her competitors, had she not? She would surely respect someone who also utilized that tactic.

How would it feel to cut deep enough to kill?

"Could you keep her away?" He decided to chance pressing on. "When I was in there with you, in your bridge, I saw you alter your bulkheads. Right now, you are using one to speak to me. You seem to do anything you like inside this ship—except, most unfortunately, of course, force people to come to you." He paused for effect. "I offered to be your hands and feet, and I could be that for you tonight." His voice grew stronger with his eager anticipation. "Some time tonight, if you will lock Sentinel Mattason away, open that other cabin, and wake me, I will bring you Lady Firebird." Because he could do that. He could bring Monu another body.

His father the First Lord might have objected to this deceit. But he was not going back to Netaia. He was going to travel the galaxy.

Forever.

"Otherwise," he said as a reminder, "they plan to leave in the morning."

She spoke at last. "If they leave, it will sadden me. Still, my greater need is to refuel."

"They are foul. All of them. My family is noble."

"Nobility is useless, Daken Erwin. Although, if it were useful, I now would have cause to prefer Lady Firebird even over Colonel Harris. I now know that her mother was a ruling monarch and no figurehead, and that Lady Firebird could yet be crowned."

"My father is First Lord," he reminded her tersely. When she understood what he had done, she would appreciate his precocity. The forbidden thoughts now swam in his mind on a sweet crimson flood. Such sweet and messy and delicious temptation. Yes, yes—she was going to make it happen! Rich blood, and immortality in the bargain. A delightful shiver iced down his spine.

The brat deserved to die. Many times over. He might do something truly heroic.

"They think to leave in the morning," he emphasized. "The two who wear the dark blue, the Sentinels, have not shown you all they can do."

Pause.

"That is interesting," came the response.

"You will surely outsmart them." He had Monu where he wanted her.

"Easily," she replied.

"What is it," he asked, trying to keep the petulance out of his voice, "that you see in that woman? That you want for competition and company?"

"Courage. Loyalty. A willingness to sacrifice herself for a greater good. I do not see those traits in Daken Erwin."

Sickening. He stood up to address the ceiling. "You are wrong. She is rebellious. Spiteful. She does nothing that wouldn't win a promotion."

The tinkling next door sounded mournful. It was good to know she couldn't hear him.

"I find," Monu said, "something compelling in this Commander Caldwell."

"What?" he demanded.

She didn't answer. Had he lost her after all? Disappointment drained away the sweet hope of immortality. The traitor's tinkling went on.

He tried once more. "Monu? May I bring her to you?"

Nothing.

His jaw clenched. He had come so close.

They would depart in the morning, and he would have only an imagined memory of all he might have been, traveling at Monu's side from star system to star system. "No," he groaned, sinking back down on the bunk. "Powers, no."

Firebird leaned the clairsa against her shoulder, resting. Too late in the evening, she finally had a musical assignment. Shel had gone back out into the lounge, promising to watch the door while she struggled to write Monu's ballad.

Mighty Singer, help me! This isn't just for entertainment anymore, or even for communication. This will have consequences.

But what to put into a ballad? Monu's history, yes. Might a sad, sweeping minor selection, singing about her loneliness and regrets, stir whatever emotions remained inside this vast mechanical body? Even animating Iarla, Monu's face and voice had shown no feeling. Firebird shuddered, imagining centuries in barren space. She loved the stars, but now that she'd been freed from a wastling's doom, she also loved to plant herself on a world where things grew. A home, her family. Writing all this into a song had to be possible, but no words came, maybe because she was afraid of writing clichés.

Perhaps something instrumental.

Closing her eyes, she swept her fingers up the strings and played an old hymn. It might calm her, and maybe Monu retained some memory of her world's faith.

"Don't give up, Mari." Was she hearing him, or was she imagining what he would say if he were sitting in here with her?

Alternating six- with three-minor chords sounded desperate. Could these express utter loneliness? Star lanes and centuries of solitude? Could she make Monu understand that human company could be achieved without killing someone and turning her into a spaceship?

Firebird shut her eyes, suddenly afraid. If she was wrong, and if music was not the universal language of human souls, she was about to prove it. "Help me, Mighty Singer," she whispered aloud. She might work with the clairsa until her fingertips bled, and it still might do no good.

"You are doing that again."

Iarla's face had reappeared.

"I am trying to show you that I understand loneliness."

"What you are doing shows me nothing."

By way of answer, Firebird played a rolling arpeggio. Hand strokes overlapped, coaxing the minor chord from the little instrument's longest strings up into the truly tinkling range. "This instrument is traditional on Netaia. I know it well enough to compose a little. Although it's been years since I did any songwriting. There was this." She struck up the triumphant ballad she'd written for Queen Iarla four standard years ago, near the end of another lifetime. Maybe Monu, impersonating Iarla, would appreciate the lyrics. *Iarla the compassionate, Iarla the Queen . . .* Firebird couldn't have imagined, back then, the trials and triumphs that the Holy One had in store for her. "Do you ever sing, Monu? Change the pitch of your voice and listen to your own feelings?"

"No."

No help there. She plowed deeper. "Was there ever music that moved you, long ago?"

Monu did not answer instantly this time. "When I too was a crawling thing, our music was not so different from yours. Those memories are irrelevant."

Discouraged, Firebird tried an anthem that praised the North Continent's beauty. For variety, she added a broken-heart ballad she'd learned as a teenager. She dug out the tri-D cube to show Monu the image of Kinnor and Kiel on her and Brennen's laps, and she played a lullaby.

When she finished, Monu said, "Your people still bother with nonverbal, mathematically organized, short-duration sonic units. I grew beyond such things. You were making this, this music, back in the lounge. Your fellows paid close attention. It makes little sense."

That shocked her. She blundered out a question. "Do you no longer feel anything when you hear music? Even Daken Erwin reacts. He's irritated and disgusted." Might Monu laugh?

Monu did not laugh. "Sound waves are perceived on many frequencies. Their mathematical relationship creates no meaningful experience."

Firebird sat chilled. It was very possible they were dealing with a soulless machine and that whoever programmed, and whatever occupied, the ship calling itself "Monu" actually died centuries ago. "Are you dead?" she blurted.

"Enshipment is not death," came the reply. "What happened to Ambassador Glin-Erris was accidental. It will not happen again. On the other hand, I know that you have killed."

Firebird pushed the tri-D cube aside. Since Monu knew about Iarla, she certainly knew about this. "Accidentally," she insisted, knowing there had been others. Still, the first time—

"As was Glin-Erris's death. Accidental. Do not hold me to account for that. But you killed as a warrior."

"That has nothing to do with this," Firebird said firmly, remembering Three Zed.

"Many foes."

"Yes," she confessed. Five, at least, when she and Brennen struck the renegades' world. Using the evil inside her, and the now-impossible fusion power she'd shared with Brennen, she'd taken down their entire fielding team, five supposedly invulnerable Golden City Shuhr. At other times, there had been four others in self-defense, two men and a woman whose names she knew: Harcourt Terrell, Cassia Talumah, and especially, the evil Micahel Shirak. And one Shuhr stranger, using the night-black dagger Brennen had given her. Sadly, she'd last worn that dagger during her interrupted confirmation ceremony in the Netaian Hall of Charity. Apparently, it had gone back to the palace with her blood-soaked regalia, never to be seen again.

Brennen's image smiled from the tri-D cube.

She felt dirty. Stained and scarred. She shoved down the memory and found words. "Killing wounded my soul. It is a terrible thing to rob someone of the rest of their life." Brennen always insisted, *No one is utterly good, but no one is utterly evil. The One made us all.* To exist indefinitely, always growing more tainted—more deeply wounded—would be a terrible fate. "There really is mercy and healing," she said now, "vast and forever, but we will only find it from the Holy One beyond space and time." She played another rolling minor chord. This time, she altered the last few notes to end on a leading tone. It left the arpeggio incomplete. It begged for resolution. "Do you feel nothing when you hear that, Monu? What note should come next?" Either of her boys could hum the answer.

"I hear that you show precise skill playing that instrument. That reveals many disciplined hours. Discipline is another trait I desire in companions.

Since you believe that killing wounds you, I will give you the ship with no weaponry."

Firebird slumped against the clairsa's elongated sound box. "I wanted to honor you."

"What you call music is not an honor I desire."

"What you call enshipment," Firebird argued, "is not an honor I desire. Have we reached an impasse?"

"I can take the fuel that I need," Monu said, "without recompensing anyone. I would feel that I was treating your rich world unfairly, but if it proves necessary, that will happen."

This was information, but information of the worst kind. Surely the base had heard that claim. Why hadn't she taken Netaia's fuel already? Did she possess some sense of honor, or at least of commercial exchange? "What do you mean?" Firebird demanded.

The image vanished. The ventilation's whirr was her only answer.

"Brenn?" she whispered, and she waited.

"I'm here."

"How much of that did you hear?"

After several seconds: "All, I think."

"Brenn, I don't think she has a soul anymore. Music doesn't move her. At all." It certainly didn't matter if Monu heard that observation.

His voice took on an odd, hazy hiss, as if he were lightly scrambling the transmission, taking the fewest possible chances. "She says she can take fuel without our cooperation. That's new information. Well done, getting it out of her. It's alarming, though. She has no need to give us her shielding technology if she simply can take what she wants. You are definitely leaving tomorrow."

Suddenly weary, Firebird sighed. She tucked the tri-D cube back into her duffel.

He kept speaking. "Maybe she heard you, about the Holy One's mercy. You said it well."

"Thank you." But she'd failed and she knew it.

"Sleep well, Mari. The fleet is standing ready to cover your departure."

Oh, she missed him. Missed feeling his emotions deep at the back of her mind. Missed his half smile. His warm touch. In just over two days, she would see him again.

She picked up the clairsa and got back to work.

Sobered, Brennen passed the ill news to the marshal on overnight duty. He went back to examining scans, impressing them in his trained memory—physical scans, overlaid with subtronics, over the passage of time. The engineers, with their analytical setups, kept doing the same. In his earpiece, he still heard music. She'd gone back to practicing a difficult passage of some classical piece. Over and over. Slowly. Then a little faster. A little faster yet. Any mistake required extra repetitions.

She always claimed that no one enjoyed hearing that sort of practice. She might never understand that hearing her disciplined determination was like tasting her very personhood. He had no musical training, but even when her music came in repetitive bits, it spoke to his soul.

But Monu—was her soul dead or alive?

Uri had sensed a living presence. To a Sentinel, that was proof.

A proverb rose in his memory. *Power not rooted in intimacy always leads to destruction.* Monu had given up much of her humanity, including all intimacy, to gain power. Now, she craved friendship again.

Or was this simply her idea of recompense?

Holy One, you called me here. We live only by your mercy. How may we reflect that mercy to Monu?

He wondered what kind of fuel Monu required, that she had persistently declined to name, but felt she could take without permission.

Uneasy, he called up another scan. The mission had not quite failed yet, but he would be glad when the ambassadors were safely away.

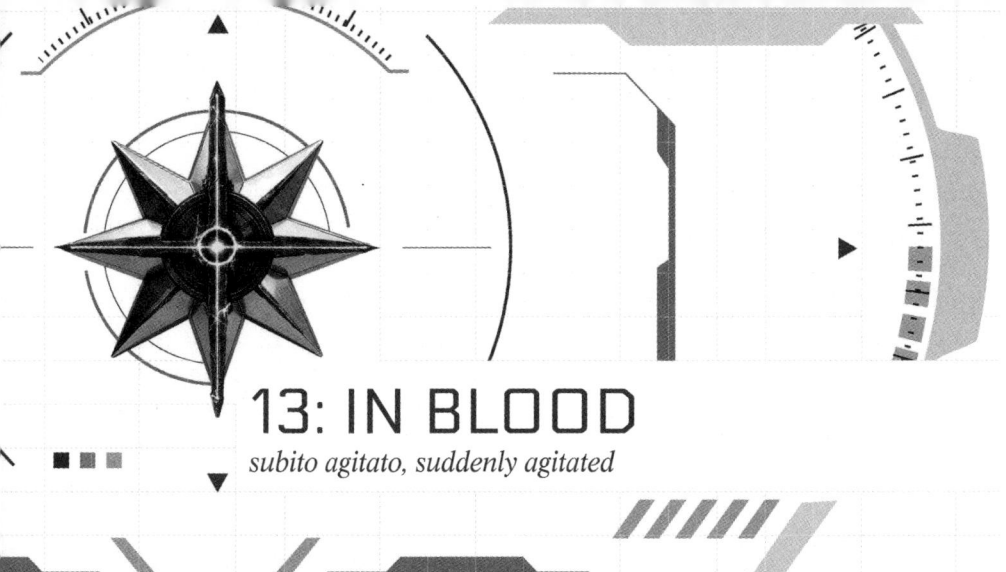

13: IN BLOOD
subito agitato, suddenly agitated

A dreamlike voice woke Daken Erwin. He rolled and rose up on his elbows. Why was he hearing a woman's voice in the men's sleeping cabin?

The voice spoke again. "Grand Duke Daken."

"What?" he snapped. Only Gering was allowed to wake him, and only when it was vitally important.

It was coming from the bulkhead next to his head. "Major Mattason is in what you call the freshing room. I am holding the door locked against her kind. Bring me Firebird. Now."

He came fully awake. Monu! Had he fooled her after all? People believed what they wanted to believe, and apparently, Monu was still human enough to illustrate that truism.

It was his sign from the mighty Powers. As he rose from his stone-hard bunk, the promise of satisfaction hit him. The cool deck under his feet did not chill his ardor. A square of dimly lit bulkhead gave enough light to see by, and he crouched to dig in his duffel. He pulled out his travel nightrobe. Slipped it on. Tied the belt.

Then he dug deeper for the heirloom dagger. He hid it against his forearm—*like those mind-crawlers hide their crystaces*, he reflected wryly—and slipped out of the men's cabin. Rounded the corner toward his right. Rested his left hand on the palm lock.

The door slid open.

He crept in, placing each foot silently. A faint line of light shone under the freshing room door. Across the cabin, another square of bulkhead glowed faintly. Monu's doing, he understood, lighting his way.

On the far lower bunk lay a blanketed form. Red-brown hair flowed over the pillow. She slept on her side, facing away. He could not have asked for an easier target.

He must make this fast, or she might stop him. Might even hurt him. A little sweet blood, the random cuts he'd given wastlings in the past, wouldn't move him up Monu's list. No, this time he was going to kill. Heart? Too well-guarded by bone.

Throat, then. Quickly. Before Monu could notice.

He accelerated forward. He flipped down the dagger's blade and reached around her shoulder.

Sudden light and a howling alarm hit him like a blow.

The shrilling howl rattled Firebird's bunk. Fully and instinctively awake, she threw herself upward.

She hit something solid and heard a grunt. Someone had been standing over her.

Every bulkhead shone white. The alarm wailed on. Shel burst out of the freshing room. Daken Erwin tottered for balance close by. He wore a black nightrobe and had a sick, hungry gleam in his eyes. He lunged a second time. A dagger gleamed.

She seized the shock pistol beside her pillow, rolled, and squeezed.

Daken slumped to the floor.

Firebird dropped the pistol, dove off the bunk, and crouched over his chest. The dagger lay in his limp hand. She seized it.

Shel halted mid-stride to stand over them.

"I stunned him." Firebird lifted the dagger. Its golden pommel was carved as a wolf's head. It had diamond eyes. It was the same one he'd pulled on Corey, a deadly work of art that had engraved itself in her memory.

Shel broke into her thoughts. "Firebird, you're bleeding."

"What?" Startled, she looked down. The left arm of her gray shipboards was soaking wet and dark red.

He'd scored on her. After all those years, threatening to blood her, he'd succeeded.

Furious, she shifted her grip and held the gleaming blade sideways, crossing his pulsating throat. Corey, poor Corey! She wanted justice, and now she could have it. Totally justified. Daken had just tried to kill her.

She always kept a shock pistol on lowest power, and though those bursts dropped a victim, they didn't always cause full unconsciousness.

"Beast," she muttered. "I have never, ever forgiven you." She'd killed others in self-defense, as Monu just forced her to remember. She'd even imagined herself in this very position, years ago, finally the victor instead of the wastling victim. It was a sweet moment, glowering into those little eyes.

Monu's tuneless voice spoke from the bulkhead. "He said he was going to bring you to me. I woke and assisted him, believing him truthful."

"Your mistake, Monu." Heart thudding, Firebird lowered the dagger another millimeter, hoping Daken retained some awareness, hoping he could feel its weight on his throat. His eyes bulged, or maybe she imagined that. "You betrayed me," she seethed. "You betrayed Monu, too, didn't you?"

"Firebird." Shel spoke softly, kneeling close by. "You're free to blood him. But not to kill him. You told me he was sick. I believe you now."

Glory, this was temptation. She had never forgiven this man, and there he lay, eyes wide and breaths shallow. Reluctantly she lifted the dagger off his neck. She'd imagined herself the victor, but she'd never imagined the actual kill. Destined to die young, she'd been shown mercy. She must show it whenever she could. The Eternal Sovereign saw everything.

And Monu also was watching. Was it possible that she was the one who'd turned on the lights and the alarm?

Firebird eyed that well-groomed beard. There were other ways of taking revenge. Not deadly, but clear to anyone who saw him—for the rest of his life. He'd done this to wastling Lord Rendy Gellison.

"Traitor," she breathed. "And coward." She flicked a traditional coward's slice across his left cheek, just under the line of his beard. For good measure, she gave him a matching one on the right cheek, letting the razor-sharp blade bite just deep enough. "You won't have scars," she informed him, "if you biotape those. But you'll have to shave off part of your beautiful beard if you want tape to stick. Your choice." Calmer now, she aimed one more verbal blow. "And when we get back to Netaia, you will face justice at the hand of my husband."

Shel straightened to stand and hurried to where their issue bags lay on an unused bunk. She reached for the nearest handle and pulled a bag open.

Firebird pushed up onto her knees. A red puddle had formed under her left hand. Blood didn't bother her, but this was more than she usually saw after a practice match. "At least it wasn't poisoned," she said lightly. "I'd know by now."

Shel pulled out a roll of pale-pink biotape. "Lie down and get out of that shirt," she said curtly. "Let's see how deep that is. And get your feet up. Higher than your head."

"He'll be stunned for ten minutes or so," Firebird guessed. She rose, relinquishing her moment of dominance. She did feel a little lightheaded.

"He won't come out of stun at all," Shel answered. "I'll put him in t-sleep. Get up on the bunk. Lie down."

Firebird complied, avoiding a wet stripe on the covers. Her left shoulder and arm felt like someone had struck her pretty hard, but there was no pain yet. That dagger was sharp. Still gripping it, she shut her eyes. When she and Brennen trained with live blades, they never sliced muscle deeply. And Brennen positively hated to blood her, so she occasionally won their first-blood matches. He'd always said he would rather protect her. She could just see his face, bending over her as she lay there. *See, Brenn? Aren't you glad you and Shel trained me?*

She shivered. She recognized the chill as shock. How badly had he cut her?

Shel would know what to do. She'd patched dozens of weapons students. Biotape worked. Worrying didn't.

Shel lifted the injured left arm and started doing things, gentle things that woke pain. "We might need both rolls," Shel said. "But he missed the veins and arteries."

"I bet he wanted my throat," Firebird managed. "Good thing I wake up quickly."

"You've got a muscle you might not want to use for awhile." Biotape hissed off the roll. Around and around it went, around her upper arm and over her shoulder.

The cut was that long?

"Why don't you go back to sleep a bit?" Shel's voice sang softly.

"Um," Firebird managed. "I'm k-keeping that dagger, you know. For the tr-trophy case, to replace the one Brenn gave me—"

Shel touched her forehead. Brilliant room light faded, and her dagger hand went limp.

Shelevah Mattason didn't recall shutting the freshing room door, let alone locking it. Furthermore she always, always locked a sleeping room's outer door.

Monu had done it all.

Firebird looked peacefully asleep, her long hair flowing over the cushion, at the edge of a pool of blood.

Brennen will be furious.

She had put Daken Erwin in t-sleep the moment Firebird faded. He lay motionless, hardly breathing. Blood barely oozed into his beard hairs, since t-sleep almost halted circulation.

Actually, she wouldn't have blamed Firebird for killing him. He deserved killing. Still, no *one* person ought to be judge, jury, and executioner. Not even for horrible people who tormented one's childhood.

"Major Mattason," the ominous voice spoke again. "I am deeply sorry for the part I played in this attack."

Monu didn't sound sorry, though. That voice was as mechanical as ever.

"Her body is damaged," Monu continued. "Simply bring her to me. I will set her free of it. I am ready now."

"You'll do no such thing, and neither will I," Shel snapped. Firebird's sliced gray shirt lay next to her pillow. For modesty's sake, Shel covered her chest with it. They were both going to need to clean up, and there was no vaporbath on board. Her hands were a slippery mess.

"When I saw the dagger, I realized his deceit. I woke her."

"Thank you," Shel muttered. But no thanks was due Monu. She'd made it easy for Daken to strike. Shel frowned. Crimson blood oozed through three wrappings of biotape. Daken's rushed, deflected slash had missed the major vessels, but minor ones could bleed a long time. Free bleeding had surely washed the wound clean. She needed to apply pressure and get it stopped. Wrapping one hand around Firebird's upper left arm and leaning hard against the left shoulder, she reached deep for her epsilon carrier, directed energy into the wound, seized muscle and vessel, and pulled them together. Wound closures would be better. Was there a complete med kit in any of the issue bags?

An unfamiliar voice spoke in her ear. "Major Mattason, this is Citangelo Base. We heard a wailing noise."

"An alarm," she answered quietly. "We had an incident. It's under control."

Uri appeared at the door, Gering behind him, both in nightrobes. "Under control," she repeated, touching his earpiece. "But it was attempted murder."

Uri knelt over Daken. "T-sleep?"

"Yes, I did." Shel sent Uri a quick information burst. His eyebrows lowered.

"What did you do to him?" Gering demanded. The big man's silver hair stood out like a mussed halo, and his white robe made him look even more bearlike. "What did he do to her?"

"Death," the bulkhead pronounced. "He deserves death."

"He is deeply asleep," Uri said simply, catching Shel's glance.

Shel understood: Tell Monu no more than they must.

The fancy dagger lay next to Firebird on the bunk. Shel picked it up. A beard hair dangled from the tip. "Mister Gering, do you recognize this dagger?" Whoever was on night duty back at Citangelo Base, they would understand who tried to kill whom. They would wake Brennen. It couldn't be helped.

Uri reached for the dagger and held it two-fingered by the ornate hilt.

"I do," Gering said tightly. "So. He tried to blood her."

Shel shook her head. "He tried to kill her."

"And he tricked Monu into helping him," Uri added. "Didn't he?"

Shel nodded once. This time, the bulkhead stayed quiet.

"You two go back to sleep," Shel said. "Take that"—she jerked her head to indicate Daken's limp form—"with you."

Ignoring her order, Gering stepped into the freshing room. He emerged with an armful of wiping materials, both wet and dry. "I will help you clean the room, if you'll let me."

Shel looked into his eyes and saw understanding. Maybe even apology. This man was not sick like his master. "Thank you," she said. Gering dropped to his knees and got to work.

When Uri was gone, Shel murmured to Gering, "He never should have gotten past me. Never." *Chaos take that man!*

"You did something to him," the bulkhead asked again.

Insistent, wasn't she? Shel answered Monu. "He's only asleep. But very deeply." Sleep. They would be short on it today, and it was time to depart. There were stimulant caps in the issue bags, bitter little purple capsules that contained the wake-up essence of morning kass. Stim caps would help them all go without sleep, if they must. In just a few hours, they might need to fight their way out of Monu's lounge, if Monu tried to keep them on board.

Maybe Monu could be put into tardema-sleep. The thought startled her.

As Gering kept cleaning, Shel found an envelope of wound closures. "Mister Gering," she said, "Daken should have more biotape in his issue bag. Please bring it to me." She would have to unwrap, clean, apply closures, and rewrap.

"Certainly." Gering rose to his feet and hurried out.

A different voice spoke in her ear. "Major Mattason, stand by for General Caldwell."

A minute later, Brennen stood in the privacy alcove, where he'd been sleeping. He rubbed the scar on his cheek as Shel answered his most urgent question. "Muscles were cut, Brennen. I am sorry. I am terribly sorry. I should not have left her unguarded, even for a moment."

He deliberately slowed his heartbeat. He should have ordered Daken to be put in t-sleep earlier. He should have ordered immediate departure, rather than waiting for morning.

Too late for those thoughts. "No one ever serves perfectly, Shel. Our bodies' needs can betray us." He was glad that Mari had taken Daken down, glad for all those training sessions, glad she'd resisted the temptation to execute justice. "There's no worrying about Daken Erwin for a while, at least." That was one positive outcome. Now, even the nobles would know t-sleep was justified.

He cut the connection and walked into the command center, where he sat staring at scan boards until he could bear it no longer. He needed to hear her voice.

Firebird woke with her left arm throbbing and Brennen's gentle words in her ear. "Mari? Mari, they woke me an hour ago. What happened?"

"I'm all right," she said, trying to sound like she meant it. Actually, there was a good deal of pain. Nearer the cabin's hatch, Shel lay on her bunk, hopefully sleeping. No, she was rolling over to sit up.

Might as well explain everything, then. She did, finishing, "Shel put him in t-sleep, and I guess she patched me while I was out cold."

He fell silent—in her interlink, anyway. Judging by Shel's eye movements, he kept talking to her. Shel answered, "Serious enough, but we know what to do." Pause. "Yes. I will." She got up from her bunk and asked Firebird, "How is it?"

"Burning," she admitted. "Throbbing."

"Inflammation means it's trying to heal. But pain won't help you. I'm going to block some nerves, and you'd better avoid moving that shoulder for a while. Let it start to heal." Shel gave the non-bloodied bedding a significant glance. "I'll tear strips and bind your arm to your side. Let me know if your fingers turn purple."

Firebird smiled weakly.

Shel bent over her again, eyes closed, undoubtedly repairing tissue as well as she could. And . . . here came the pain block. Blessed relief, instant and true. "Breakfast," Firebird said. "Let's eat early."

"Sit up. But do it slowly."

Firebird obeyed. She sat still as Shel wrapped strips of torn bedding around and over and around again. "You'll need to take these off and move a little, several times a day, until we get back to the base."

"Right."

"I'll help you." With an extra handful of bedding strips, Shel worked a clump of brown crust out of Firebird's long hair.

Brennen spoke again. "Be ready to evacuate, Mari."

"I'm not that badly hurt. Let's show Monu what courage and mercy look like." She said it boldly, but doubt niggled her mind. If Monu had no soul—if music did not move her, and if she was all programming now—would courage and mercy even matter?

She slowly got to her feet. "Breakfast," she said again, trying for enthusiasm. "Mm-mm, concentrates."

In the command center's tri-D well, a dashed arc showed Monu's new course. She was accelerating toward Netaia, and she'd said she could simply take the fuel she wanted.

Guide us, Brennen repeated. He'd been praying that ever since the aide woke him with the news that Mari had been stabbed. It was time to recall the ambassadors and warn Monu—with regrets—to come no closer. Surely the fleet's full power would overwhelm those shields, if necessary.

He paused. He needed to order a simulation, based on their observations thus far.

Two hours before day shift, the sky was still dark outside headquarters. Marshal Burkenhamn strode in, also early, carrying a cup of fragrant kass. He got his briefing from a controller and hurried over, throwing a hasty salute. "Commander Caldwell was attacked?"

"Daken Erwin brought a dagger onboard," Brennen told him.

Marshal Burkenhamn gave an exasperated grunt. "Under something like loose arrest now, I'm informed?"

Brennen nodded. "Tardema-sleep. He'll do no more disrupting." And when Daken Erwin returned to Netaia, Brennen would be waiting for him. It was tempting to imagine the encounter. He drew a calming breath.

"Badly wounded?"

"According to Major Mattason, it is serious but not life-threatening. Major Mattason is medically trained and administering aid."

The marshal turned away, rubbing the back of his neck. Brennen sensed his anger and recalled that his Mari had had a mutually respectful relationship with the marshal. "She should make a full recovery," he added. It was true, on the condition that she did not push herself too hard.

Which she probably would. Perhaps it would be best if Shel put Mari, too, in tardema-sleep, since medical cold-stasis was unavailable.

Marshal Burkenhamn stepped toward the comm station. "Any luck getting through to the escort ship?"

Monu had projected her mysterious shields to surround that heavy fighter. A comm tech answered. "No, sir. We'll try again. They could have shut down overnight."

Brennen did not like that. The escort ship's presence would be vital as the unarmed *Cometesse* launched to return. "Keep trying them," he ordered. "And we need to run some simulations," he said to the big marshal.

"Yes. Plainly, we do." Marshal Burkenhamn backed up a step. "Simulate a warning volley, I think. At one of those unmanned accompanying ships. Calculated for minor damage only."

Brennen raised an eyebrow. "Might we actually do that, with our ambassadors still on board the main ship?"

"We might merely threaten, if we knew whether Monu would take it seriously."

"We do not have full knowledge of those shields."

The marshal met his eyes. "Do not underestimate Netaian engineers."

Brennen fingered his cuff. They did need to know what to expect, based on current information, and whether any defense that Netaia might need to raise could be ineffectual. A final move in an aggressive encounter, if it proved necessary, could be entirely Monu's victory.

He turned around slowly, taking in the circle of high wall monitors, the tri-D well, the earnest personnel, and the serious-faced marshal. Officially, he had come here to make an inspection.

Perhaps he should divert Mari and the others back to Regional headquarters on Tallis, on board the *Cometesse*. Imagining Daken Erwin a prisoner in the Federacy's MaxSec tower gave him a deep sense of satisfaction.

"One more thing," the marshal said. "Monu has shown no attack capacity up until now. Under best-case circumstances, she might not possess actual ordnance."

Brennen clasped his hands behind his back and gazed at the well. "Somehow I doubt that."

"So do I."

"Warn our ambassadors," Brennen said, "before you even raise the possibility of sending a warning volley. I want to withdraw them to the *Cometesse* and then send her a warning."

Marshal Burkenhamn ran a hand over his head, then nodded. "Yes. We shall show Monu that Netaia is even more serious about defense than we are about offering aid."

14: SEEDS
con forza, forcefully

During their hasty breakfast, Firebird caught a whiff of herself on her dusty white tunic. She normally wouldn't have worn it a third time, but her sliced, bloody shipboards were unwearable. She'd needed Shel's help to slide the tunic over her bandages. She'd needed Shel's pain blocks to get on with her day.

It was time to depart, defeated. Which Electors, she wondered, might have done better? She'd boarded the *Cometesse* full of idealistic self-confidence. Daken's presence and Glin-Erris's death seemed to have doomed the mission. As she stirred up a second cup of kass, awkwardly gripping the cup against her waist with her left fingertips—maneuvering was tricky with that left arm gently bound against her side—Marshal Burkenhamn spoke in her earpiece. "Colonel Harris, inform Monu that you will be departing, and that Netaia is prepared to ensure your withdrawal is not threatened."

She sipped the bitter kass. Her whole body ached with the wound's systemic aftereffects. Still, there was almost no sharp pain, thanks to Shel. Their packed duffels and issue bags lay near the exit hatch, along with the clairsa case and two unmoving bodies, one fully shrouded and one simply wrapped with a blanket. Daken's shocked-looking face lay turned upward. She'd closed his eyes herself, still wishing she could do it for good and for always.

"Lady Firebird." Monu's voice still sounded tuneless, but Firebird detected a rise in pitch and a quicker tempo. Perhaps she was angry. "Your people apparently mean to attempt to threaten me. I have just strengthened my shields, and I can no longer afford to expend fuel creating your air. What exists on board will keep you alive until you come to me. I will make no more." A soft *whishing* that had gone on as background noise since they came onboard suddenly ceased.

No matter. They would be gone within an hour. Surely they could get out of here. There was a heavy fighter inside Monu's shields that would cover their departure.

"Do not attempt to leave this ship, Lady Firebird. Come to me. I choose you now. You only. I no longer trust or desire the Sentinel kind. You, however, owe me a life debt. I saved you from the Grand Duke. There will be no returning to your rich world."

"You only saved my life," Firebird retorted, "because you want it for yourself." She glanced at the corridor where Glin-Erris had died.

Then she froze. No returning? That had an ominous sound. "Monu," she called, "that fuel you wanted. What is it? Why can't we provide it for you?"

"I must create it myself," Monu answered in that emotionless voice, "using the world seeds that I carry."

Firebird set her cup on the work surface next to a toolbox. Was Monu finally giving the information they needed? "Organic seeds?" she asked. Surely this monstrous ship was not powered by wood. On the scans, she'd seen an enormous fuel tank.

Back on base, they were certainly listening.

"They are nanomechanical," Monu said. "They convert organic matter to biofuel. They replicate indefinitely, ceasing only when all organics are gone."

All organics were gone . . .

Firebird's breath caught. "All the organic matter on a world?"

"That is the quantity of fuel I require, for myself and my companion ships, and that is how we obtain it. I launch seeding pods before I arrive to refuel. Each pod contains multiple seeds, but I need only one to take hold. The seeds require some time to multiply and complete their work. Therefore, a multiple seeding saves time."

And Monu was only telling them now, now that they meant to abandon the mission. Something seemed to crawl at the back of Firebird's neck. "Every plant, every animal? Every living thing?"

"Also, everything made of organic material, such as wood. Harvesting Netaia will provide us with fuel for many of your years. I will soon be close enough to launch the seeding pods. There will be no returning, Lady Firebird. Come to me and live."

As she glanced at the wooden clairsa, a horrible flashback struck her. One of the Shuhr had taunted her that he foresaw Netaia as a cold cinder, spinning in orbit, due to her presence. "No," she murmured.

"I will recompense your entire world through you. You will live indefinitely. Mathematically, that will make up for many years of others' lives lost."

Her body felt frozen. "That's not the way it works, Monu."

The voice droned on. "Your people have forced me to expend too much fuel to reach any other organically living location. I shall harvest Netaia. I must live. You shall live alongside me. You are required to be grateful."

Required to be grateful? Firebird's chest burned. This monstrous thing must be destroyed. Destroyed, before it got anywhere near Netaia.

Near Kinnor and Kiel—and Brennen.

Marshal Burkenhamn's face had gone white when Monu's voice announced her plans for Netaia. White and then red. Brennen felt the same. The mission had just gone from risky to deadly. It was easy to imagine worldwide devastation if one—just one!—of those world seeds landed on fertile Netaia. Utter death. Everywhere. Converted to fuel. Everything.

An ordnance officer called across the command center, "Do we still run that simulation?"

Brennen leaned on the tri-D well, his mind racing with tactics and strategies. "Not the warning volley," he ordered. "Simulate a full-fleet energy attack, against the engineers' current understanding of that ship's shields."

"That sim is also ready, sirs," an engineer announced.

"Fire," Marshal Burkenhamn growled. "Full energy."

From every cruiser and destroyer on the simulation screen streamed a blaze of white light. Brennen blinked away the afterimage, anticipating a zone of red sparks representing damage to a target.

He saw nothing. According to the information they possessed, Monu's shields would hold against every energy weapon they could throw at her.

He fingered his cuff and controlled his breathing. Those shields must be taken down, so Monu could be destroyed before she could seed Netaia.

He shook his head, dismissing half the strategies under consideration. *Holy One, give us wisdom.* "Enlarge that image of Monu again," he ordered.

An engineer complied.

"Rotate fifteen degrees. Upward, toward me." The ovoid slowly spun.

"What are you seeing?" Marshal Burkenhamn asked.

"We thought those were launching bays for landing shuttles." Brennen pointed into the image. "But look. They are too small to carry personnel. Maybe only two meters in diameter."

Marshal Burkenhamn raised an eyebrow. "The seeding pods?"

"I believe so." It occurred to him that Netaia had not yet simulated its old, horrendous particle weaponry. He had not forgotten the siege of Twinnich, his first command. During Princess Phoena's invasion, Netaia had bombarded Federate Veroh with nuclear explosives.

Fingering a touchboard, he sent an order down to the arc of engineers. Already, they were calculating how soon Monu could effectively launch those world seeds. The engineers' variables on that attack clock included the probable mass of seeding pods, the assumption that they carried onboard drive, her rate of acceleration toward Netaia, and the momentum she could therefore transfer to them. Already, she was significantly closer than she'd been when *Cometesse* launched.

They were, in effect, creating a deadline for an attack that might not even slow her approach. Brennen rubbed the scar on his cheek, considering. They probably could not alter her course, either, not even by remote-controlling a ship of the line to ram her. A cruiser might be vaporized by her shields, as that asteroid had been.

He must get those ambassadors off that ship.

"Here you are, sirs." The engineers' preliminary estimate for a preventative attack appeared. They had just short of nineteen hours, ending well after midnight, before Monu could launch those pods to seed Netaia. They must effectively attack before then.

Effectively.

Her shields must be sabotaged. From on board.

He shook his head, hating the thought. Still, he had two Sentinels with military experience and the bravest woman he ever had known on that ship.

Holy One, not Mari. She's hurt.

Pushing aside thoughts of sabotage for the moment, he stepped closer to Marshal Burkenhamn and spoke in an undertone, "You deployed flash bombs at Veroh." It was no accusation, simply a statement of fact. "Do any remain in the inventory?" He diffused his epsilon shields to listen closely.

A low note of embarrassment rose beneath the big man's fury. If Twinnich's particle shields had failed, then-Wing-Colonel Brennen Caldwell and the young prisoner Firebird Angelo would have been killed there. By Burkenhamn's forces.

Marshal Burkenhamn's emotional sense flattened to regret. "Yes," he admitted, "we still carry them. As weapons of last resort."

With the marshal speaking so honestly, Brennen restored his shields. "Are those weapons on board your ships now?"

The marshal cleared his throat. "Yes. You ordered full readiness."

But he had not included them in the simulation.

"Monu must be stopped. This time, to save Netaia, their use would be justified."

A less ominous thought struck him, and he seized his mike-con. "Last resort" might also include using the holy Ehretan tongue as a code language, since Monu monitored all communication. Uri and Shel were fluent, and Mari had been studying. Monu never would have heard that language in a broadcast.

They must attempt that sabotage. They still had the *Cometesse* for escape.

He threaded epsilon energy around all his emotions, holding them down. "This is a last resort," he told the marshal, gripping the mike-con against his chest. "Otherwise, all the Federacy faces unstoppable destruction." Twenty-four settled, terraformed, life-giving worlds. Monu might eventually harvest them all to fill her ships' empty tanks.

How badly wounded was Mari? Uri and Shel must work while she rested and healed, saving her strength for the evacuation.

She was not going to like that.

"Sirs!" It was a different sensors officer.

Brennen swiveled leftward, to the real-time image. The oval ship glimmered inside her shielding arc. One location deep within her had taken on an ominous crimson gleam.

"I think I see," he said, eyeing columns of numbers alongside the bright image. "Help us interpret, please."

This morning's sensors officer brushed black hair out of her face. "The shields just strengthened. When they did, there was intense activity at this exact location." She reached for her slanting display and enlarged the area. "The glowing object has a trapezoidal shape, sirs. Shielding."

Shielding strengthened? Why?

Maybe to keep the team on board? Within that enlarged area, an object had two parallel sides of distinctly unequal lengths. "Circuitry at that nexus," he observed, "must control Monu's shielding. A single sabotage point." It could make the attempt simple, though not necessarily easy.

He raised the mike-con and spoke urgently. "Uri?" Monu might disrupt communication, so he must give orders quickly. Uri would understand. They worked well together. Stepping aside for privacy, he switched to the ancient and holy language. "You must destroy . . . Monu's . . . shield walls. We have found . . . a place . . ." There was no word for *instrumentation* in the holy books. ". . . where they might be . . . controlled. It is fifty-one meters above you and thirty-three aside. Sending . . . pictures now." He pointed at a comm officer and restated the data transfer order in Old Colonial, with its better and more modern vocabulary.

And if Monu did launch those seeding pods, exactly what would be coming at them? "Engineering," he called. "Analyze those six two-meter pods. Do they have propulsion? Evasive capacity? Shields?"

Several seconds later, Uri answered his communication, also using the holy language, though Uri's usage was heavily accented in Old Colonial. "Is there a passage between here and that . . . destruction location?"

Good. Uri understood what he was being asked to do. With the Mighty Speaker's help, sabotage might use less than an hour on the attack clock. The ambassadors might evacuate long before Netaia needed to strike, and if Monu's shields were down, that attack would have better chances than their preliminary simulation showed.

Brennen turned to the sensors officer and ordered, switching again to speak in OldCol, "Superimpose first image."

A gray overlay appeared over the shining blue partial image. "Yes. A direct . . . tunnel passes underneath it," Brennen said in Ehretan, "but I believe it is the way wherein Glin-Erris died."

"Then it is dangerous," Uri answered.

Brennen scrolled memory. That shielding nexus appeared inaccessible by any other passageway. "Engineering," he ordered, changing languages again, "rotate this set of images ten degrees, and then another ten, through the entire three-sixty. Send that data to our ambassadors, then examine all images yourselves. We need an accessible passage."

Imagining what he would have tried, were he on board, he addressed Uri privately again. "I have orders for you. First, put Monu in tardema-sleep if possible. You and Shel, together." That might succeed where access had failed. T-sleep dealt with a mind's involuntary beta centers, not the conscious alpha matrix. "I then . . . command . . . utter destruction of the . . . shield wall place . . . now shining on your . . . images. Destruction from below, inside that . . . bridge." Translating as he spoke was harder than he'd expected, but Uri would understand. "That will be . . . safe, if you can make her t-sleep."

Uri used OldCol. "Copy order."

"But," Brennen added, again struggling to modernize the ancient language, "we know the Stranger's special . . ." Lust? No, there was a better word. ". . . desire for Commander Caldwell. She is . . . commanded not, not, not to go into that place." *Command* instead of *order* seemed especially awkward in Mari's case, but the Ehretan triple repetition served as emphasis. "She is commanded to rest and heal."

But if sabotage took too long, they all might still be aboard when the attack clock reached zero, and when he must order the fleet to attempt total destruction.

Dread chilled him. *Mercy*, he prayed.

An engineer sprang up. She walked swiftly to Marshal Burkenhamn, who still overlooked the tri-D well. Brennen joined them without cutting his interlink connection.

"We confirmed the seeds," the engineer said, her voice near frantic. "Once we knew what to look for. They are carried inside pod-shaped drones, loaded into six excretion chutes, thirty degrees apart, along its ventral surface." As she spoke, six circles flashed white, scattered around the projected ovoid. "The drones appear to have ablation shielding for penetrating a planetary atmosphere."

Naturally. "Uri," he called. "You must also . . . try and destroy . . . six smaller . . . lifeboat ships. They carry the seeds. That is . . . highest import."

"Comm, send them that location data too," the marshal ordered.

Brennen turned to the engineer. "What about the seeds themselves? Can you analyze whatever it is those pod ships are carrying?"

"Yes, sir," the engineer said. "As we were told, they're minuscule and extremely simple. They appear to have the ability to consume, digest, and excrete—and multiply. Like mechanical viruses or bacteria. If only we understood her technology!"

Brennen tried to imagine mechanical viruses.

"And sir, we haven't detected anything like a kill switch on them. They're too simple for that. They would simply reproduce until they ran out of substrate."

Marshal Burkenhamn scowled. His nostrils flared. "Confirmed. If Monu seeds Netaia with just one of these, there will soon be nothing here but rock and fuel."

Unstoppable.

"Yes, Marshal." Color returned to the engineer's cheeks. "Netaia would be a rich resource. No wonder that creature came here."

Brennen eyed the tri-D well again, maintaining tight emotional control. Just two days ago, that ovoid image had held the hope of new allies. Maybe even advanced shielding for Federate forces. That hope was gone now. Monu was conclusively an enemy. They must destroy her. As that engineer had said, if only they understood her technology.

On the other hand, any civilization that understood Monu's technology would eventually try to duplicate it. Would the Federacy want to do that, if it led to the survival of just one strong-willed individual and the hideous death of worlds?

"Brennen," Uri spoke in his ear.

Brennen turned away as the engineer returned to her station. "Listening," he said.

Uri switched languages again. "Confirming your wishes, in order. T-sleep. Shield walls. Seed pods. We might use . . . our energy to . . . break her energy to them. But they are spread far apart."

Mentally he translated. Use epsilon force to render the pod-launching chutes unusable? "Confirm, Uri. Then depart. Immediately. It is so commanded." He looked up and around again. On every wall display's upper right corner, large red numbers had appeared: the attack clock, the countdown to their last possible moment to strike without risking Netaia's utter destruction.

The clock stood at 18.7 hours.

He pointed at the clock directly over Lieutenant Lord Leon Parkai's station. "Lieutenant, send that calculator to Colonel Harris." He then adjusted the mike-com and headed to the secure privacy alcove. "Mari. Get alone."

Firebird sank down on Shel's bunk, near the hatch, careful not to jostle her left arm and shoulder. Having recovered somewhat from the shock of finding out Monu's fueling information, she pretty much knew what Brennen must tell her. Their mission had just changed.

There also was an even greater need for cautious communicating. She listened closely as he explained the seeds. She already understood how they would multiply.

"Listen," she said, trying to muffle her voice inside a tent of long hair. "We understand. You can't let that happen. We might still be aboard, if you . . . you know. Or close enough to take damage. We accept that." She did, anyway. Maybe Brennen had gotten her alone to say their farewells, just in case. *Oh Brenn, I would have liked to hold you again.* Aloud, she said, "Holy One go with you. He gave us to each other. We never could have planned it, both of us flying what should have been our final missions."

She waited, twisting her back against the fabric that bound her left elbow close to her waist.

Finally, he spoke. "Amen, beloved. And he will go with you."

She wanted to weep, but she had to carry on. They must move quickly after a long, fruitless day. Would it have made any difference if they'd known sooner about the seeds?

Yes. They might have destroyed Monu farther from Netaia. An image stuck in her mind like a limpet mine—just one seed, doubling to two, doubling to four, and then eight. A terrible cancer spreading unstoppable across forests, fields, and cities.

Monu could hear this, for all she cared. "Someone needs to catch you if you go into bereavement shock." Pair-bonded Sentinels suffered terribly when a bond mate died. It was the amputation of half the soul.

"Remember." He spoke somberly, and she thought she heard a light scramble on his voice. "You do not need to sacrifice yourself. The final debt is paid for us."

How like him, to go straight for the state of her soul. "We are called to a higher standard," she quoted back to him.

The transmission delay seemed unbearably long. "You must depart in eighteen hours," she heard. "Go sooner, if you've done all you can. That might be right now. You mean the Whorl to me, Mari."

Uri's voice called from out in the lounge. "Data received."

"And you to me," she said. "Don't hesitate if the kill order has to be given. Meanwhile, we'll do what we can. About . . ." She lowered her voice. "Shields," she whispered.

"I am ordering t-sleep," he said. "First effort."

"Will that work if she has no soul? If she isn't even alive anymore?"

"You've suspected that for some time. Haven't you?"

"I have. It's just as I said. She has no response to music." Firebird might be one of the few people who understood this.

His voice, when it came, had taken on an edge. "You accuse her of that, just because she didn't react to your music? Many good people have nothing to do with music. You cannot judge by that criterion."

"I say that we can," she said firmly. Maybe this day was already getting to her, or the pain of her fresh wound. She shifted her shoulders again. "People love a piece or they hate it, or maybe they tolerate it, but living human beings always have some response. Monu has rejected her very humanness." Her voice was rising.

"That is not the final judgment. Only the Holy One can deliver that."

"I am not impersonating the Holy One."

"You are, in this case."

Stunned, she fell silent. Even scrambled, his voice sounded oddly angry. She was too far away to sense his feelings, but he had never used that tone with her. "We'll do what we can from on board," she repeated with deliberate calm. *Brenn, what did I say?* "We will do our best." They had no time for theological arguments. They must treat "Monu" like any other menacing machine. Destroy it quickly!

His tone softened. "You always do, Mari." The link fell silent.

Already, she wished she had used other words. Brennen had given her precious minutes in private, busy as he had to be.

But how . . . why . . . had she triggered him?

She left the room and went straight to Uri, and she touched her interlink to his, receiving the new file. Uri said nothing, possibly sensing her irritation and regret. Probably surprised by them.

Brennen thumbed off the mike-con, still grimly guarding his emotions, wishing that harsh words had not escaped him. He was too well trained to lose control under stress. Why had he done that? Of all people, why had he snapped at her?

He looked up. Eighteen hours remained. An attack would be conclusively effective if those shields were dropped. There would be time to sabotage and evacuate.

Someday, he and Mari, and a priest of the Path, must have a long conversation about human souls. Maybe they both needed a deeper understanding. Mari was still young in the faith, and he, too, could make mistakes.

He left the privacy alcove and re-entered the command center, alive with its hisses and hums. Marshal Burkenhamn intercepted him near the main double doors, out of earshot of anyone but the guards. "The Federacy," the big man pronounced, "does not allow suicide missions. Evacuation will be ordered at the first possible moment."

"Of course." At this moment, Brennen despised command and its burden. There was a deadly enemy to sabotage and destroy. Sometimes there were collateral losses. Meaningless deaths. He must not let his thoughts wander down that path. Netaia must take action or be destroyed.

"I am sorry," the marshal said, his voice deep with sincerity, "about the risk to Lady Firebird. Also, about Veroh. I do not believe I ever apologized personally."

Brennen raised his head. "Your orders at Veroh came from others, including House Erwin and House Angelo. Mari and I understand danger." He had loved and respected his brave bond mate even before she loved him back. How did she define what it meant to be human? "Someday, inevitably," he said, "one of us will reach out too far." He'd always assumed he would die first, though. He had never feared bereavement shock, the breaking of the soul-deep pair bond, until now.

Mari. Stopping Monu was a cause worth dying for. He would do everything in his power to get Mari off that ship. But if the Holy One gave them too little time, then as a commanding officer, he must grant Mari that responsibility and that final honor.

Please no!

He rested both hands on the edge of a console. He had been glad to accept command back at Veroh. His career goal had always been to reach the Federacy's High Command. He knew, now, that even a faithful soul would find that burden hard to carry with honor.

Perhaps being human, having a soul, sometimes meant being confused. Even by the one you loved.

"Sirs." The youngest-looking sensors tech, Lieutenant Lord Leon Parkai, leapt off his stool. Brennen turned toward him and looked up. A terrible sight had appeared on that wall screen. The flame-like shielding around the ambassadors' heavy fighter escort had vanished, replaced by the glowing red cloud that he'd hoped to see in that simulation ten minutes ago.

It signified "target destroyed."

Brennen went cold, instantly understanding. Monu had armament, all right. They had just lost a fightercraft and two Netaian pilots. Keeping warriors waiting was always disheartening, but these had waited only to die, and now the *Cometesse* had no fighter cover for its evacuation launch.

"Monu is destroying minor assets," Marshal Burkenhamn said. "She realizes she is vulnerable."

"Does she?" And this signaled another potential danger. Brennen inhaled sharply. "Uri," he called into his collar mike, "we just lost your fighter escort, and I'm afraid Monu might—"

Another glowing cloud billowed at a stable point in Netaia's orbit, the stable point where Netaia's FasScan communication satellite had orbited.

Brennen rested a hand on Lord Leon's shoulder. Marshal Burkenhamn stood close, looking up.

Monu had done what he feared.

"Uri?" he called.

Silence fell, blanketing the command center.

"Uri, come in."

Marshal Burkenhamn whispered an oath.

They were cut off.

Firebird, listening with her ear next to Uri's—at his invitation, hopefully providing another layer of protection from Monu's listening—heard Brennen inhale sharply just as the link went silent.

She shifted on the lounger. Her left arm was starting to seriously hurt, but that was probably just inflammation. She could manage discomfort. She'd already tucked a handful of anti-infection meds into her belt pocket.

"Brennen?" Uri asked. "Go on."

Missing the hiss of the disengaged ventilators, Firebird looked up. Shel still sat close to Uri. Gering lingered a few paces away, his massive arms crossed, his black livery smudged with dust.

Uri's eyebrows came together. "The last he said, Monu had destroyed our fighter escort. I assume she just took the system's FasScan satellite too. She has ordnance."

Firebird groaned. She might have trained with those NPN pilots. And Monu had cut off their contact with base.

Then it hit her. She might not hear Brennen's voice ever again, and their last words had been sharp. A pang of regret squeezed her chest. Why had her always-in-control bond mate sounded angry?

Or was it even anger? Was it something else?

She pushed hair back from her face. Monu's action was logical. Dividing one's enemies so they could not communicate was standard procedure.

So they were Monu's enemies now, instead of the saviors they'd hoped to be. Was their Luxian crew safe on board *Cometesse*? Alarmed, she fingered her collar mike. "*Cometesse*?"

The relief pilot answered cheerily. "We're running full checks, inside and out. We'll be ready to bring you aboard for a speedy departure."

Firebird gulped, pulled her hair back over her face, and whispered. "I, ah, don't think we'll be evacuating yet. Monu just showed us she's capable of energy fire. She couldn't miss us if we launched."

"So, we'd be in two lines of fire?"

Yes, how could they dodge both a Netaian attack and Monu's expected counter-volley? Firebird's old training kicked in. It had been years, but she'd been a passionate student. She ducked her chin and covered her mouth again. "We'd have no fighter cover. Best chance would be to get behind her and raise full particle shields, anticipating debris." That was her best guess, anyway, unless Monu's ordnance could also be found and sabotaged. She glanced up at Uri.

He nodded back. They still might escape, but Monu had shown them that it would not be simple.

And Monu was listening.

Well, they had a job to do, and eighteen hours to do it, and there was no way in the Whorl she could simply rest and heal . . . or ponder her beloved's frame of mind. He carried a heavy weight of responsibility just now.

Still, she already longed to hear his voice.

Snap out of it, she reprimanded herself. *Think. Nanotechnology.* She hadn't studied that branch of tech, but if Monu had nanomechanical world seeds, only the Eternal Speaker might know what else Monu could control. Maybe that explained all she was doing with her bulkheads—speaking through them, locking and unlocking hatches.

Firebird glanced around the lounge. Big Dodis Gering sat at the freestanding workstation, gripping his interlink. Shel and Uri sat on opposite sides of the lounger. They shaded their screens as well as they could. Uri had shown her a written note, translating Brennen's orders: attempt to put Monu in t-sleep despite Firebird's protest, take down the shields from inside that bridge, and destroy her ability to launch the seeding pods.

Firebird was specifically ordered not to engage, even though she might be better at sabotage than diplomacy. She didn't like that one bit. But who would tell Brennen if she went in there, anyway?

She could certainly help with mission prep. With ventilation shut off, they might need supplemental air soon. Their issue bags still lay piled along the bulkhead near Monu's ominous bridge corridor. She dug into the nearest bag and pulled out a masklet-and-pillar oxygen sniffer. Tucking it into the fabric that held her left arm close to her body, she went for the next bag. How long were these good for? They mustn't use them until absolutely necessary, but they had two spares. Glin-Erris's and Daken's.

"This way, Lady Firebird." Apparently seeing her close by, Monu flashed the corridor lights. "Come to me. Choose to live on. Let Netaia be remembered."

Firebird quickstepped to the others and dropped off sniffers for Uri and Shel. Sitting at the workstation, Gering looked puzzled when she handed him his. "Never used one?" she asked.

He shook his head.

After all, he'd been a planetside bodyguard. She wrapped a hand around one sniffer's compact pillar and pointed to the masklet at the business end. "These two little soft bits go into your nostrils. Inhale sharply, and you'll get a puff of oxygen."

He mimicked her gesture.

"Right." She nodded. Uri and Shel had already tucked theirs into their belts. Then, using interlinks and shielding the screens, the four of them hurried to compile an inventory. Two Ehretan crystaces. One Federate-issue shock pistol and one Netaian, still concealed on Gering's person. A gold-handled dagger. Survival gear in their issue bags. The strange tools the ancient Strangers had left them, including one with a wicked-looking saw blade. Most importantly, two gifted telepaths. Uri and Shel were almost certainly capable of dropping Monu into t-sleep, if she had a living mind.

And a transport hardened to ram a way out, if they took down Monu's shields. Firebird eyed Shel and touched her forehead, requesting access. A mild, familiar nausea confirmed mental contact. She repeated the thought to Shel.

Or ram inward? Shel's subvocalization sounded in Firebird's mind. *Destroy Monu that way?*

Firebird shook her head and replied with another carefully articulated thought. *We couldn't get up enough momentum inside the bay. We'd have to launch and circle back. She could blast us. Anyway, ramming a massive object is suicide.*

Monu flashed the corridor lights again and called Firebird's name.

Firebird ran her right hand through the blood-flecked hair over her shoulder. Here it was, the fight she'd been wanting—and the odds were awful. They were going against an enemy a thousand times their size. The Mighty Singer had seen fit to handicap her, in particular, even before the match began.

It made her feel fully alive—but this time, there were lives at stake besides her own. Millions, maybe.

Mercy, Mighty Singer!

15: THREE ESMES
appassionato, passionately

Esme Rogonin could scarcely remember feeling so relaxed and happy.

Her charming friends had been here almost a day. They had exclaimed over her elegant grounds and settled in beautifully, spending much of yesterday afternoon planning the creation of a mysterious medical lab in the south basement. Today, they'd all arisen before dawn to enjoy this half-lit view of the mighty Tiggaree River. She'd escorted them to a cluster of duracrete benches high on a bluff and ordered them all refreshments. Staff seemed oddly slow, but no matter.

"I wish you'd come sooner," she sighed, addressing the Esme who'd suggested she call her Esme Two. "We could have had such fun together."

Esme Two smiled and stirred the cruinn that had finally arrived. "We were staying at a certain South Continent property," Two said. "It seems your mother misplaced a necklace down there." She slipped a finger inside the loop of gold beads.

"Ah!" Esme reminded herself that she was now Esme One. Such an honor! "I'm so happy you found it! Does this mean I already have been hosting you all unaware?"

"Yes. Your southern lands are lovely, dear one. Once it became clear that your estate down there was being prepared for other guests, we left and came north. Ground travel is an adventure."

Esme Three lay on the lawn, wearing one of Esme's chromatic color-change gowns and staring up into puffy, brightening orange-pink clouds. "It worked out well, didn't it? Those unpleasant Federate folks—the ones you dislike so much, Esme One. They have left us alone, and so . . . here we all are, happy sisters together."

"And the springtime is such a time of awakening." Two gave a pretty little laugh.

Esme recognized her own face and voice, as if she were speaking with herself in a mirror. What a treat to be three instead of just one!

A thought occurred to her. "Where is your home, my dears? Are there rivers and sunrises there?"

Two and Three eyed each other. They did that quite a bit, as if they could speak without words. Two pursed her pretty lips, looking sad, but Three adopted an angry glower. Esme had no idea she could look so unpleasant. It was Three who answered, "Our home is lost. The shef'thet Federates ruined it."

"How terrible!" Sympathizing, Esme stretched out a hand. "How sad."

Two sighed deeply. "We have only one another now."

"A blood pact." Three's voice seemed to darken.

"But now," Esme said, "there are three of us. In this home."

"A blood pact," Three repeated. "Esme, you have not shared blood with us. Will you?"

There was the faintest recoil at the back of her mind. But why? She could not remember. "It won't hurt, will it?"

"Only a little." Three pulled something short and sharp-looking out of a pocket. "Here, give me your wrist."

Tel had awakened early with the strangest urgency driving him, and he'd been glad that Esme wanted to see him today, after all. Jess, his chauffeur, made the turn off River Way, decelerated to the Rogonins' sentry box, and stopped.

No one stood inside. *Esme, you fool.* He wanted to take her and shake her. Did her scorn for him run so deep that rather than increase her security, as he'd suggested, she would decrease it?

Or was she in trouble? His horror at that thought startled him. "Ahead, Jess. But slowly. Just bring me in sight of the carriage house."

They made the last bend beneath a clump of tall leta trees. Seated up front with the driver, his manservant Paudan raised a hand and pointed forward. At what?

The streamlined white groundcar he'd seen yesterday, driving in, still sat parked in front of the house. Who in Citangelo would be visiting Esme this early in the morning?

Caldwell had warned the Electors. *Not Shuhr. Oh, please, not Shuhr.* Tel rose on his knees to look farther ahead. Lights burned all along the upper story windows. He hadn't seen that before. It didn't seem Esme's style, particularly with her siblings sent south.

His danger sense clanged at full volume. "Jess, back up. Stop at the sentry box and be ready to make a fast escape." As Jess turned the long car, Tel brought up Esme's image on the car's crosstown link. She appeared to be outdoors, quite close. She smiled at him. "Ah, Tel, good morning. Will I see you at ten?"

So cheery, so friendly. Esme Rogonin had never behaved toward him in that way. A chill raced across his shoulders. Intruders were back in Citangelo, menacing Esme, and either they were close enough to make him see false faces, or else they were forcing her to behave unnaturally. The thought wrenched his heart. He'd tried so hard not to care. Resisting both terror and fondness, he made himself shake his head in casual regret. He must not show panic.

"Something has come up." He tried to speak with stiff, noble reserve. "I must come tomorrow, as you originally requested. I am sorry."

Before she could reply, he killed the connection and cried, "Go, Jess!"

They accelerated back up River Way, crowded now with groundcar and skimmer traffic. Tel sat gripping his interlink, staring out a window. City Enforcers would answer a crosstown emergency call, but City Enforcers would not survive an encounter with . . . with *them*. He couldn't bear to use that other terrible word again. Yes, he'd killed one of them. Yes, the memory sickened him.

If Esme was in danger, he must bring her the only help who could save her.

He put in a call to the base.

Regretfully, General Caldwell was in conference, too busy to speak with anyone. Probably, Tel guessed, something to do with those Strangers in space.

There were other Sentinels. They were onworld to guard against this very danger. Several served at the Palace, but he'd seen others at—

"Citangelo Base, Jess," he ordered. "Quick as you can."

Jess hit the override and out-sped central guidance.

Brennen sat across from Marshal Burkenhamn in the secure alcove, trying to strategize despite the loss of communication. Footsteps hurried toward the alcove. "General Caldwell?" a man called.

"Here." Brennen pushed up off the padded bench. His back and legs seemed stiff.

"Sir, a man has arrived on base saying he needs urgently to speak with you. Gives the name Tellai. That name is on your short list, or I would not have bothered you."

Was Tel up ridiculously early too? "I am sorry," he said, "but this time—"

"I have the command center." Marshal Burkenhamn stood up. "I won't order evac or attack without you."

And surely, Tel would not have come for a minor reason. "I'll meet him in Conference room One," Brennen told the aide. "Tell him it has to be brief."

"Yes, sir."

He strode up a bright hallway. Actually, it was good to escape the sudden specter of planet-wide destruction and look a nearer challenge in the face, whatever this might be.

Tel paced into the conference room, gripping his feathered hat. "Caldwell," he exclaimed, speaking rapidly, "thank you. I hope I didn't wake you. I would have settled for one of your aides. But I just came from the Rogonin estate. There could be a Shuhr on the premises. Female. I think. I just saw her on CT link, either impersonating Esme or controlling her behavior."

Shuhr? Their surviving remnant had been far from Brennen's mind this morning. Of course, they would act when Citangelo's defense was distracted. For exactly this reason, the base was controlling news releases. Nothing—yet—about world seeds had gone out. Only a general civil defense alert, effective at nine hundred hours. He frowned. "I have no time. Please give me the memory."

"Certainly." Tel stepped closer. He looked eager and offered no resistance.

Breaching Tel's alpha matrix, Brennen juggled a jumble of images: a white groundcar cruising past; a scornful Esme brushing off Tel's repeated warnings; the white groundcar, now parked at the estate; the small image of Esme looking sweetly, falsely friendly.

Tel was almost certainly correct. Brennen could not afford time this morning, but his people were always watching for Shuhr. "Yes," he said. "Only Sentinels should check that, and it will be top priority. I shall make a call."

From the hope that suddenly glimmered in Tel's wide eyes, Brennen knew that Tel had fallen in love again. With Duchess Esme Rogonin, an excellent match, but at what risk? He did not want to update Tel with the situation this fluid. If civilians found out about the risk of world seeds, they would overwhelm the spaceports. Maybe later today, a multi-stage evacuation could be ordered, allowing most civilians to escape before the Federacy put Netaia under quarantine. Ahma, Kinnor, and Kiel could leave in a first wave. Perhaps the royals should join them. Rinnah and Carradee, at least.

He shook off those thoughts. Others would take charge, if it came to that. He belonged in the command center, trying to prevent it.

"And the ambassadors?" Tel stood staring up at him. "What news?"

"Let me call Carradee's guard." Rather than answer, Brennen touched a wall panel and requested a two-way with Captain Dassah Cowan. To his relief, her face appeared almost immediately on a waist-high monitor.

With dark hair pulled back tightly from her face, Dassah Cowan had classic Thyrian features, including dark, intelligent eyes. "General," she said. "How may I help you?"

"You know Prince Tel," Brennen said with a wave.

She nodded. "Good morning, Your Highness."

"He has been to the Rogonin estate and seen evidence that a Shuhr, intending to masquerade as Duchess Esme, is in there. How soon can you strike? You have darts?"

Her eyes lit. "We do."

"Do not leave the royal family unguarded, in case we stir up something we'd rather not." He had endured Shuhr tortures, both mental and physical. He knew much of what they could do.

Tel stepped forward. "How may I help?"

Dassah's eyebrows rose. "Forgive me, Your Highness, but I do not think you can."

Tel's shoulders sagged. It felt important to let Dassah in on the masquerade. "Prince Tel is more capable than you might think." Having said that, Brennen turned to his friend. "But she is correct. No non-Sentinel should go into such a situation."

She saluted. He returned the gesture and canceled the connection.

Tel touched his arm, fear streaming off him. "I know they are powerful, Caldwell. Does Esme have a chance?"

"As good as any we can give her." *Perhaps a better chance than our ambassadors.* Horrible thought.

"They simply killed . . . Phoena . . . didn't they?"

Brennen ached for Tel. Widowed, ripped away from all he had believed in, and recently—though it would always remain a secret between them—very much in love with his own Mari. This man deserved a loving wife and the truth. "Eventually," he admitted. "They used Phoena to lure me in." About to turn and hurry back to the command center, he caught a flicker of sudden determination. He re-focused on his friend, alarmed. This man also had the crazy Netaian courage. He was, after all, Mari's second cousin. "Tel," he said sternly.

Tel's chin came up.

"Stay away. All you could do is put yourself in deadly danger."

Tel met his stare with dark, sad eyes. He saw and felt Tel's resistance.

"We must assume this is a Golden City Shuhr. Even Captain Cowan's squad might not be able to take her down. Golden City Shuhr bred for power. They were gestated in womb-banks and raised to kill each other. Few of them survived to Named adulthood." As Sentinels married out, diluting the Ehretan genes, Golden City Shuhr had only grown stronger.

"Take her down? Not . . . get her into custody?"

"They'll try, but Captain Cowan may have to use deadly force. Shuhr have no respect for lives other than their own. Not even their own children."

Tel's determination was hardening toward outright resistance.

"Tel," he said, exasperated enough to threaten, "I would like to put you under voice-command to stay away from the Rogonin estate."

Tel backed away, blinking.

"But I don't think that would be allowed by our Privacy and Priority Codes." He exhaled. "Give me your word. Sentinel Cowan will deal with the situation."

Tel drew up tall and gave him a curt nod. Brennen sensed duplicity but decided not to speak. Tel had crossed inbred boundaries to befriend him, after all.

"I need to get back." He rested a hand on the smaller man's shoulder. "But please, trust in the Holy One and psi-gifted professionals."

Tel turned without answering and hurried from the conference room.

Brennen bowed back down under the weight of command. He strode in the opposite direction, dismissed Esme Rogonin from his mind, and refocused on his own concerns: the sabotage order that just had been given, Netaia's deadly peril, and his injured, endangered Mari.

Tel Tellai hustled away, mind racing. Caldwell was right. To go back to the Rogonin estate would be foolish.

But Esme, or a woman who looked like Esme, had invited him back. If the palace guard arrived soon, he might help from the inside. Surely Esme was still alive, and by now, she could be eager to leave. A Shuhr would not do away with her without studying Esme's voice, her mannerisms, her way of thinking.

For how long? No one knew how long Phoena had survived at Three Zed before they murdered her.

He didn't remember getting back into his groundcar, but when he looked out the window, Citangelo's theater district sped by once again. City lights dimmed as daylight crept onto the highest towers.

Might he snatch her away? Making the attempt could mean his death, but who would grieve? He had no children. His parents were gone. The Electors thought him a fool. Even his sister Triona and her husband, Count Winton, rarely communicated anymore.

But he might die a hero to Caldwell and Lady Firebird. A foolish hero, but a fool with a true heart.

He stroked his chin and considered the holy Powers: Strength, Valor, and Excellence; Knowledge, Fidelity, and Resolve; Authority, Indomitability, and Pride. He might call on Valor and Resolve this day, but that was little comfort.

Port Road leaped over the Etlason River Bridge. A right turn took them onto River Way.

An odd thought occurred to him. What would it hurt to address the Sentinels' god? This god was allegedly a person, not a holy attribute. Tel glanced toward the front of the car, at his faithful staff. Paudan shadowed him everywhere, except into the heart of that military base. He really didn't want either Paudan or Jess hear him try to address a foreign god, so he darkened the glasteel privacy shield between them, and for good measure, he spoke the words in his mind. If there were such a thing as an omniscient person, his thoughts would be heard. *Sentinel God, help me. Show me what to do. Protect Esme. Protect me, and my friends, the Caldwells.*

According to his upbringing, he had just committed treasonous blasphemy. He waited, wondering whether he might feel any sense of having been heard. Nothing like that came, but then, neither did anything happen when he performed his duties to the Powers. Why might he expect that? Did he actually suspect that an infinite Person might exist?

Strange thoughts. Very well. He would continue.

River Way threaded between the Erwin and Parkai estates and crossed the Tiggaree River. Esme Rogonin's estate lay just ahead.

16: SILENCE

lamentoso, mournfully

Brennen stared into the tri-D well and fingered his cuff. *Power and might are in your hand, Holy One.* The day had barely begun, and less than an hour had passed since Monu revealed her weapons and her intent. Putting her into t-sleep might neutralize her without violence, but Uri could no longer report on their efforts. The loss of comm was not entirely unexpected. Comm techs continued to try other frequencies, but they only heard garbled, rhythmic noises at Monu's locale. She was plainly jamming across the frequency spectrum.

At least he'd been given time, after discovering the world seeds, to order sabotage. Uri and Shel must attempt t-sleep and assault the bridge. Within the bridge, they should be able to shut down shields, as well as power to the seed-launching chutes. Then they must evacuate.

Yet they might fail to achieve t-sleep. Brennen had regained enough epsilon strength to reach Master's range. He might assist.

He stood aside a moment longer, weighing a tempting thought. A speedy, stealthy little Remote Individual Amplification craft had shadowed them here. Monu's new course, while steadily decreasing the time on their attack clock, was also bringing her closer. Theoretically, he might commandeer that messenger ship and, under full acceleration, reach RIA range in just hours.

He would not know whether Uri and Shel had succeeded, though, and whether his presence would even be needed. *Go anyway*, his instincts shouted, no holy call but his own voice of experience. According to his vesting vows as a Sentinel, his place was wherever only he could serve. The Codes always allowed assisting another Sentinel in danger.

He glanced around the bustling command center. His official place was here, but his actions could decide this confrontation's outcome.

He would need an assistant pilot, since entering the RIA accord would require all his attention and make him unable to actually pilot. If he fell into bereavement shock, suddenly and utterly incapacitated, he would need even more help—

No. He could not consider Mari's death.

Yes, strategically, he must consider it.

For those two reasons, he would need an assistant if he launched. Two Sentinels had brought the messenger ship to Netaia. One or the other ought to be willing. If not, they were under his authority and could be ordered. He disliked the idea, since he was balancing at the edge of official insubordination. *Help me, Holy One. I would need a volunteer.*

Once he reached RIA range, he and Uri—no, he and Shel, since her ES rating was higher—could use the Remote Individual Amplification function to link their epsilon carriers and put Monu down. RIA would greatly increase the sabotage mission's chance of success, and the ambassadors' chance of escape.

He crossed the room and addressed the marshal. "In hangar 357 is a small messenger ship. It shadowed us here to Netaia. We were testing its stealth capability," he added, seeing the marshal's raised eyebrow. "Plainly, it passed. But it's not stealth that I need it for now. Have it prepped for launch."

Marshal Burkenhamn eyed him. His glance flicked to the Master Sentinel's star on Brennen's right shoulder. "RIA?" he asked. "We have known about it for two years. You seem to have used it very little."

"Only at Mikuhr," Brennen said. Marshal Burkenhamn looked blank. "Three Zed," Brennen explained. "And now, it appears that we could need it here." Pre-launch prep would require an hour, maybe a bit more.

There would be time. Barely. If—

The big marshal stepped close and said in a barely audible voice, "Three Zed. So that's how you got close enough to strike."

Nodding silently, Brennen eyed the tri-D well. *Monu, you have a soul. Don't you? You respond to threats as a human person would respond.* Surely she could be put into t-sleep. "Also," he told the marshal, "I must requisition a sedation dose from the med station."

Marshal Burkenhamn lifted an eyebrow again.

"For myself, sir. In case of bereavement shock."

The other man's forehead became a map of wrinkles.

Firebird touched her sniffer, making sure it still rode inside her belt—on the right side, where she could reach it one-handed. According to figures on Shel's interlink, their oxygen had dropped only a little, but carbon dioxide was building. Nitrogen remained as low as ever.

Tempted to pace while Uri and Shel prepared to make their combined t-sleep effort, she sank onto a stool she'd moved close to the lounger. She couldn't follow their murmuring in Ehretan. Monu had gone silent, except for occasionally flashing the lights in the bridge corridor. Maybe Monu was searching memory banks for transmissions in that strange language.

Firebird smiled grimly. *Good luck with that.* The Sentinels had long forbidden translation of their older holy book.

Thinking of that, abruptly she gripped the stool's edge. Had she upset Brennen at some deep level, even deeper than he knew, with her speculations about what it meant to be a human with a soul? His ancestors had tried to be more than human, and they carried that communal guilt before the Eternal Sovereign. Maybe she'd unknowingly sprinkled salt on a deep wound. She couldn't tell him that maybe she understood or ask if that's what had upset him. She could only do all that she could to make sure the mission succeeded. So, for the Sentinels' t-sleep effort, she'd offered to distract Monu with her clairsa again. She could play melodies with just one hand. She could do what she could, using her music, instead of worrying about something she couldn't fix.

"We're ready," Uri whispered. Once Monu was asleep, so they hoped, they would head for the bridge with their chosen tools. Gering had laid those out on the nearest workbench.

Firebird held back a sigh, spreading her hands. Shel had the epsilon strength, and Uri had the access skill, but she had little confidence that it would work. Eventually, Uri and Shel—and probably Gering—would walk down that corridor to meet a soulless, conscious, and angry opponent. Determination already flashed in Shel's wide-set eyes.

Gering stood close to Firebird, looking puzzled. She fingered her interlink and showed him again: *T-sleep is like what they've done to Daken. Very safe.*

He shook his head, pointed at her, and raised his eyebrows. "To you?" he mouthed.

Oh, that was what he meant. She nodded. "They did it to me at Veroh," she said aloud. Nobody cared whether Monu heard this. "I'd taken my somnus." In other words, she'd swallowed her mother's chosen poison. "The Federates used t-sleep to save me." That had been her first epsilon contact with Brennen.

Were those harsh words their final ones? She shut her eyes. *Please, no. Please give us a chance to sort things out.*

Gering understood a wastling's last duty. He nodded back. "Reports from Veroh were, ah, contradictory."

Indeed. The Federates had lied on her behalf, stating that she'd been killed. Actually, Brennen had already taken her under his protection. *Oh, Brenn. I wish we could sit and talk, sensing each others' feelings. Being pair bonded has spoiled me for mere words.*

"Firebird?" Shel called. She and Uri faced each other on the lounger, gripping hands, eyes closed, foreheads touching.

Firebird took her position at the workstation, setting the clairsa up on its tabletop instead of down on her lap. "Monu?" she called. "May I play for you again?"

Before she'd even placed her fingers, the lounge lights flickered and went out. Absolute darkness fell. Glory, had the t-sleep worked? Firebird dug in a pocket for her little emergency luma.

The overhead panels re-lit brighter than ever. Firebird braced herself. Might Monu be furious, or would she even know she'd been epsilon-touched? Had she perceived an attack?

"My lady!" Gering cried.

Hearing the alarm in his voice, she quickly steadied the clairsa, jumped to her feet, and turned. Uri and Shel had collapsed. Both of them.

She dashed around the lounge to them.

The tuneless mechanical voice wafted out of the nearest bulkhead. "Lady Firebird, you see that I can protect myself against these post-humans. You, too, will be almost invulnerable when you are like me."

So, she'd simply batted away the epsilon probe. Were Uri and Shel even alive? "I see," she said, edging closer, "that you can protect yourself." Yes, alive. Breathing, both of them.

Epsilon shock, she guessed. She'd experienced it. It could last hours, and they had only a few hours before the Federate attack. Was it still coming? Might it come even sooner, now that the base couldn't talk to them?

They would know she was alive, at least. Bereavement shock wouldn't have hit Brennen.

"By this time tomorrow," Monu said, "your air fuel will be gone. As you feel it run low and your body grows weak, you will come to me. You shall then become vast and powerful. In time, you will forget that you resisted me. I have no wish to damage you further."

Gently, Firebird pulled on Shel's shoulder to help her sit upright while her carrier re-built—but she couldn't do it one-handed. "Help," she grunted to Gering. Was there anything else she and Gering could do while the Sentinels rested, short of tearing into bulkheads? She had no desire to ignore Brennen's order and march up that corridor to Monu. An eternity traveling space would be worse than dying.

But all thought of resting and healing was gone. Gering helped her stretch the Sentinels out into more comfortable-looking sitting positions, side by side. Unlike Brenn, she couldn't lend beta energy. Might she dose them with kass-essence stim caps?

No. If this was epsilon shock, she could only wait for their carriers and beta strength to rebuild. She'd had just enough training to understand but no idea how long that might take. "We have to wait," she murmured to Gering, picking up her interlink. "Can you think of anything else to try? How do we deal with someone who uses nanotechnology?"

The big man opened his hands. Loyalty, not creativity, had been his long suit. He eyed Daken, still stretched out on the deck. "He usually makes the decisions, you know."

"I understand." She looked into Gering's broad face a little longer, pitying him. Then down at Daken. Could she pity that man too? Might Daken have become a decent human being if he'd grown up differently?

She pushed back on the thoughts. They'd been shown a locus where Monu's shielding might be vulnerable. It was right over that terrible bridge. What might Brennen do, if he were on board? Her thoughts were doing somersaults. She considered yanking out her useless earpiece and stowing it in her tunic's low pocket. The front of her dress tunic looked pale gray, unfit for formal wear, if she ever needed formal wear again. Monu could destroy them if they tried to flee now, but she had no intention of trying that.

And an odd little idea had just joined the somersaults. An old idea. Something she'd done once before, long ago.

So she kept the earpiece in place. *Come on*, she silently urged Uri and Shel. *Wake up!*

"Stop here, Jess."

Tel's driver halted at the Rogonin estate's still-empty sentry box. Tel slid out the side door that Paudan opened, and he looked up into his manservant's worried eyes. "I know what you're thinking, Paudan. No, they aren't invincible. And I do have a plan."

It probably was crazy, but he did have a plan. Tucked into his right pocket was his slim, small shock pistol. Whichever Esme he saw first, he would stun her—bring her to base in the groundcar—and trust the Sentinels to discern whether he'd brought them a normal human or a Shuhr. He didn't like considering what Esme would think of him if he stunned her. Apparently, though, her opinion of him could not get much lower. So. On with it.

He looked around in the midday sunshine. Leta trees' long leaves were still dripping off last night's fog from the nearby river.

"We aren't going to fight them," he reminded Paudan. "We're just going to stun Esme—the real one, I hope—and take her to the base. She'll be safe there."

The overgrown night-fragrance bed edged the lane all the way to the house. Tel led through overlong grass on the bed's left side. At a spot where the vines were less overgrown, he paused. Ahead, lights still burned in the main house's upper story.

Esme? If he were one of Caldwell's kin, he might have been able to send her that thought. *Come down. Get away from here!* He waited a slow count of ten and sneaked to the nearest service door.

Paudan followed. Tel had armed him, too, but he didn't know whether Paudan was much of a marksman.

He opened the side door and slipped inside. Paudan remained at the door, holding it open.

Tel walked up the stairs to the landing and softly called, "Esme?" The moment anyone came into view, he must fire. He steeled himself and tried not to broadcast any emotion.

A slender figure appeared, wearing casual clothing that might adorn any stranger on the street. The hall was longer than he remembered, the range rather far. Quickly, he fired.

The young woman crumpled.

He hurried forward and carefully, manfully, lifted her over one shoulder. Staggering to his feet, he glimpsed her face. She still looked like Esme, which was a relief. Surely, if this had been one of their enemies, her ability to fool an observer would dissipate with the stun.

If Esme had seen him, maybe she would be furious, but she would be safe. He would get her out of here while Sentinel Dassah Cowan took down the Shuhr invader. If Esme proved ungrateful, at least she would be alive.

To marry Daken Erwin.

Stifling the depressing thought and carrying his precious load, he retreated to the stairwell. Paudan waited on the landing. The bigger man took Esme in his arms. They hurried down the back stairs. It was good that he knew this house so well.

Jess had driven the car up close. They bundled Esme into the passenger compartment and sped away. "Base, Jess," Tel exclaimed, letting himself feel triumphant. He felt almost certain he'd kidnapped the right woman, but the Sentinels would make one hundred percent sure.

Because there was always the chance that this woman was one hundred percent Shuhr. Laughing bitterly at his own pun, he tenderly straightened Esme's shoulders on the rear lounge's seat. Paudan had sat her upright. Her head lolled over onto Tel's shoulder, and he wished Esme were doing that deliberately. He could so easily imagine it.

As Jess exceeded central guidance again, the city sped past. A maglev train on the elevated track approached and was gone in a silvery eye-blink. Did a stunned individual retain any smidgen of consciousness? Just how furious was Esme going to be when the stun wore off?

He raised the glasteel barrier between front and rear compartments again and spoke softly. "I apologize, Duchess. It was the only way I could think to bring you out to safety."

He watched closely, but he couldn't discern even a flicker of response.

"Esme?" He gently nudged her.

She still did not respond. Should he alert the base that he was en route?

That would probably disturb her, and she seemed to be resting comfortably after her ordeal. Virtually certain this was the genuine Esme, he settled in to watch the city. Morning traffic was heavy midtown. Using central guidance to cross Citangelo took longer than he would have liked. Didn't he remember that a shock burst took from five to fifteen minutes to wear off, depending on range and charge? Careful not to jostle Esme, he drew the little pistol again and examined it. Nothing gave him a clue. He'd had this pistol for what, eight years? And he'd never needed it.

At last, Jess made the turn around Citangelo Base's massive steel and stone walls toward the enormous, metal-spiked gates. Two watchmen guarded each side. Behind them, a fifth guard sat on the gunner's seat of a huge energy field projector.

A sentry in Netaian cobalt blue peered into the car and asked, "Would you all mind stepping out for a moment? We are on high alert, given the situation in Netaian space."

Surprised, Tel said, "Paudan, help her," and slid out of the car. He and Paudan were known here. This would take just a minute. "We have been to Claighbro House," he explained. "Duchess Esme has been menaced by Shuhr, we believe."

Paudan got halfway out of the car with the slender young woman over his shoulder.

At that moment, she straightened both arms. She seized the car's doorframe two-handed and kicked Paudan to the ground. Startled, Tel dropped his pistol. By the time he grabbed it off the duracrete, the woman had dashed past the guards and inside the gate. One sentry dropped into a firing crouch. Shot twice. Cursed creatively.

Tel stared, appalled, as she vanished behind a gray building.

Another guard dove back into his booth.

Tel cursed, too. Cursed himself for a fool.

He'd rescued the wrong woman. She'd faked the stun and pretended not to hear him. She'd let him take her right into the heart of Citangelo's defenses.

The sentry emerged from the booth. Tel raised both hands submissively. "You might as well arrest me," he said. "This is entirely my fault."

Only one of Esme's new friends sat at the dining table at midmorning break time, heartily eating delicacies out of the pantry. Esme's staff had brought her cold toast and kass, which she did not mind. "Where is our sister?" she asked.

"Gone a'hunting," Esme Two answered. "Perhaps for another trophy head." She gestured upward, toward the old wildlife mounts along the south wall. A particularly gruesome brownbuck, disintegrating with age, hung on the wall above her.

"Oh, I hope she doesn't get in trouble. I don't think it's hunting season," Esme said demurely, not liking to contradict her gracious, noble sisters. "And it's a long way to the grazing grounds."

"Not so far." Two smiled into her kass cup. "It is always open season on vermin and pests. And their cubs." She raised the cup in a toast. "Good hunting, Esme Three."

Firebird's arm and shoulder ached as she bent over her interlink. Uri and Shel still sat stunned on the lounger. Gering had stepped to a workstation to re-examine the antique tools he'd chosen. Meanwhile, there had to be something useful in the scanner files Base had sent them, and she just couldn't find it. An inner voice taunted, *There aren't many hours left. You'd better hurry.*

A grinding noise beyond the exit hatch distracted her. "Lady Firebird." Monu's voice spoke out of the bulkhead next to her. She dropped the interlink and chided herself for nervousness. She needed to be calm. Unstoppable. Indomitable.

"I have opened your landing bay's space doors and turned on a blast fan. Your transport pilots were out in the bay, examining the nose of your ship. They blew well outside. They will not return."

"No," she cried. Her heart sank. Those Luxians had been good people. She tried to raise them on the interlink. No one answered. Chilled, she touched the sniffer to make sure it still clung inside her belt. At the very least, Monu had hinted that the *Cometesse* was intact. But had the Luxians died together?

"None of you shall survive, except as my companion ships. Choose to live on, Firebird Caldwell."

Maybe the Luxians weren't dead. Maybe Monu was lying.

All around her, the voice boomed. "Answer me, Firebird."

Shel and Uri still lay motionless. With the FasScan satellite destroyed, she couldn't tell Brennen that their t-sleep attempt had failed.

"Sirs, that landing bay has reopened."

Brennen spun around. Were they evacuating? Had they put Monu in t-sleep? If not, would Monu fire or let them depart? How would he know? "Enlarge sector," he ordered.

Marshal Burkenhamn stepped to his side. He almost dared to hope.

Instead of the *Cometesse*, two human-sized forms emerged, floating straight outward from the opening. The sight filled him with dread. "Enlarge again," he ordered. "Full magnification"

The human shapes wore Luxian uniforms but were otherwise unsuited, unprepared for vacuum.

He grieved, but he stayed on his feet. The transport pilots, he guessed. Communication was lost, and from this ground base, all he could do was pray and strategize.

It was not enough.

He glanced at an attack clock.

Its crimson display read 14.6 hours.

He eyed the marshal.

17: RECUSAL
martellato, hammered out

Marshal Burkenhamn turned back to the tri-D well and issued an order. The full-well image of Monu vanished, replaced by the normal scale image of the Netaian system. Gold pinpoints indicated the fleet's attack craft. Their semitransparent targeting cones converged on the threat-red ovoid, but there still was no targeting cone in front of Monu. They knew she had ordnance, now, but not her range.

Brennen stepped closer. They could only guess when she could launch the world seeds, but he believed the engineers' attack clock. The peril to Netaia was increasing minute by minute.

"The Forward Attack Commander is waiting," Marshal Burkenhamn said quietly. "The sooner we strike, the farther away she'll be. If they evacuate sooner, we can strike immediately."

"But we still do not know we can get through her shields." Brennen eyed the attack clock's second line. Given Monu's acceleration toward Netaia, they must attempt to strike by twenty-three hundred forty tonight, whether or not his team had taken down Monu's shields.

Whether or not his team had evacuated.

Why had the pilots been out in the landing bay unsuited, so close to the space doors that they could have blown out? *Cometesse* might be disabled, the ambassadors stranded on board. *Please, Holy One. Not that.*

He rubbed his face, imagining for the moment that sabotage had succeeded, all of the seed-carrying drones remained on board to be targeted, and the team had managed to evacuate. The fleet would begin with a simultaneous energy barrage from several angles. Deploying the nuclear flash bombs would follow. That must happen far enough from Netaia to avoid showering the world with radioactive debris from the unlaunched seeds.

Yet why had that landing bay opened? Had it been Monu's doing?

A Sentinel aide sat at one side of the room. Every time Brennen glanced in his direction, the young man averted his eyes. That aide now had orders to spring into action if he fell into bereavement shock. Sickbay had delivered his sedation dose.

An alarm startled him upright. He strode to the comm station, leading Marshal Burkenhamn.

"Sirs," the tech said, "we have a situation on base. A Shuhr individual, female, has penetrated the main gate."

Brennen groaned. Tel Tellai had last been seen heading toward the Rogonin estate . . . and, yes, there on an overhead security image, he spotted the indigo Tellai groundcar just inside the main western gate.

Tel must have tried to rescue Esme, despite an almost-direct order. A certain sentry must be questioned.

On second thought, even if the sentry scored a direct hit, that might not have taken down a Golden City Shuhr.

"All Sentinels on base," Brennen said to the comm officer, "deploy to locate that individual." A Shuhr would look for victims or hostages. This woman would be Brennen's epsilon equal at least. He folded his arms. "Do we have a trace on her? Infrared?"

"Yes, sir. She's not heading this way."

Of course she wasn't. "Where is she heading?"

"Ah, looks like base housing."

Toward his sons and his mother. Victims or hostages.

He pushed away from the comm station, eyeing the tri-D well. The Sentinel Codes actually demanded that he step into danger when innocent others were at risk, if he plainly possessed the resources to defuse that situation. His official place was here in the command center, where an attack order soon would be given, with Mari, Uri, and Shel possibly trapped on board. Must he give that order? Could he?

He did have the authority to recuse himself. If ever an officer had a vested interested in delaying an attack, he was that officer, and before the attack clock zeroed, he might make a unique difference in the strike if he commandeered that little RIA ship.

But there was a more urgent concern. His mind cleared. *My children are in danger.* He swung toward the marshal. "Sir," he said, "I place full authority to order an attack, and its timing, in your hands." Unspoken words also passed between them, not subvocalized, but surely Burkenhamn understood: *Mari and our friends are in your hands now, Marshal. Do what you can for them. What you must, for us all.*

The marshal saluted him, seemingly unsurprised. "Go," he said firmly. "Base police are after her too."

Brennen shook off the chains of command and dashed into the passage.

Just finished with breakfast, Dara Caldwell also heard the Shuhr warning. *"Kinnor. Kiel. Come to Zahma."* She glanced at the little house's main door. Two Sentinel guards stood outside this morning. Two non-master Sentinels never could stand against a Golden City Shuhr, and every Shuhr in the Whorl hated Brennen. That intruder would need no help finding this house. Dara would not wait for base security.

The boys hurried over. Most of the time, they were perfectly normal children. Still, they knew a no-nonsense voice when they heard it. "Listen," she said, kneeling at their level. "There could be a very bad woman coming here. She might want to hurt you. I want you to hide. Get inside a cupboard, under the bed, anywhere you like. But don't let even Zahma know where you are. All right?"

Big-eyed, Kiel nodded somberly. He rushed past her, behind her back.

"Shut your eyes," Kinnor demanded, "and count to five."

She complied. When she could see again, he was gone.

She hurried to the inner room and her luggage, jerked out the medical necessities kit, and eyed the small vial of DME-6. It held enough of the clear blue epsilon-blocking medication to dose both little boys, should their epsilon carriers manifest on this trip. The double child's dose would not take down an adult. Still, it might weaken a Shuhr until help could arrive.

Help, she guessed, in the person of her surviving son. Duty would not keep him away long.

But a Shuhr would hope to entrap him.

She loaded both doses into a single injector and returned to the main room.

Half a minute later, the front door crashed open. A dark-haired woman strode in. Uncannily young-faced, she was unmistakably Shuhr.

Dara drew herself up tall and hid the injector against her wrist. "You are not welcome here," she said firmly.

The woman had cold eyes and a glare that might melt duracrete. "Whoever you are, get out of my way." She raised a hand to voice-command.

Dara wore no star, but she was not helpless. She shielded herself from a hurriedly focused epsilon blow. It would have taken down a non-Sentinel.

The dark-haired woman lowered her hand, narrowing her eyes. "Incognito? No shoulder star? I thought that was not allowed."

Stalling, Dara raised her left hand. Palm down, plainly not trying to use voice-command. "I am just a civilian. Medical specialist."

The woman paused. Dara felt the quest-pulse penetrate. "Shef'th," the intruder exclaimed. "The mother, the grandmother. Excellent." Her eyes hardened. She raised her hand again. This time, Dara knew, she would use more force.

A dark-haired little hurricane hurtled out of the window well. It landed on the woman's head and neck.

Kinnor, of course.

The stranger's reflexes were fast. She whirled toward the child.

Dara plunged forward with the injector. With no time to aim for nervous tissue, she emptied it into the woman's back.

The woman screeched and shook herself. Kinnor flew off. Dara held on for dear life.

Another shadow appeared in the doorway. This one wore midnight blue. "Ahma," Brennen shouted. "Stand back." Four other Sentinels followed him, probably base police, all with hands raised to voice-command. The Shuhr woman tumbled, dragging Dara to the floor. Kinnor jumped up. Laughing and fluttering both hands in the air, he ran to the bedroom.

Dara barely saw him as she pushed back up onto her feet. Streaming off her trained, disciplined, exceptional son came a fury she'd never felt in him. His affective control was utterly gone.

She believed she understood. Marshal Burkenhamn had kept her informed. To save the Whorl, the command center might need to order Firebird's death.

But she saw death in Brennen's eyes. Right here. Right now.

She stepped between him and the prone prisoner. *Brennen Daye*, she subvocalized, mindful of the other Sentinels present.

He backstepped, catching himself. One of the other guards was already talking on an interlink. Another slipped wrist restraints onto the prone Shuhr woman. A third emptied an injector at the base of the woman's skull.

A distant voice spoke out of the link. "Prince Tel has been questioned and released. He appears to be heading back to House Rogonin."

Tel probably meant to comfort the genuine Esme. Brennen could not blame him, but the prisoner prone on her belly started to laugh.

Slightly calmer, maintaining his voice-command over the disempowered prisoner, he sent his mother a flicker of thanks and fell back on procedure. "Sit," he ordered the woman. "Right there."

The other Sentinels stood back, two of them linking to maintain a second circle of voice-command. The last time he'd had a Shuhr prisoner, she'd proved inexplicably cooperative.

This woman resisted, and her mocking laughter echoed like flame inside him. They needed physical force to roll her over and brace her against the military-plain lounger. She faced him, lips pulled back in an ugly parody of a smile.

He pulled out of the command link, and he probed for a discontinuity in her internal mental shields, where he could breach for mind-access. Like his prior Shuhr prisoner, Terza Shirak, this woman had many of these weak spots in her natural defenses. They all suffered mental abuse as part of their raising. Plunging his point of focus through that discontinuity felt like swimming in spoilage. On this first access, he only needed to find out why she was laughing.

It didn't take long.

He pushed away. "There's another one at Claighbro House," he exclaimed. "Get Dassah Cowan back over there."

Tel Tellai was headed into a trap.

18: TWO BARE HANDS
piu allegro, quicker

For Tel's sake, Brennen probed the prisoner again. Her resistance faded as the drug took full effect. She had been adult-named Arafel Hadarah, and her full-gened sister Tsebee Hadarah was still at the Rogonin estate. They had been vacationing on Netaia, plundering its rich resources, when Three Zed fell to the Federacy.

Shuhr on Netaia. Just as he'd feared. Were there others onworld?

Probably. If he'd had time, he might have performed a deep, class-three mind access.

But the attack clock was running. He released Arafel Hadarah from access and straightened to his feet, giving himself a mental-emotional shakedown. Just like his Mari, he'd come close to committing murderous justice.

"Get up," a guard said. "We'll command if we must."

Drugged and restrained, but head held high, the prisoner walked out amidst the other Sentinels.

Ahma shut the door and stood against it. Both boys clambered into his lap, Kiel clutching a reader while Kinnor grabbed for his ears, chanting, "Ah-pa! Ah-pa!"

He shut his eyes, drew a deep breath, and wrapped his arms around them both. How close had he also come to losing them? For once, Kin didn't wriggle free. He dropped those little arms to hug his Ahpa's neck. Evidently, Kin had understood—clearly—that there was danger.

The flimsy lounger shifted a little. He opened his eyes to see that Ahma had seated herself on its other end. A gentle, long-familiar epsilon pulse swept over him.

He opened his memory. That was quickest. She probably perceived no surprises, since he'd asked comm staff to keep her informed. Still, his last conversation with Mari—possibly their last words, ever—had included a strong difference of feelings that he already regretted.

Ahma and his late father surely had a few of those. Perceiving each others' feelings on the pair bond did not always mean agreeing with one another.

Whether or not she was helping him, the last of his fury ebbed away. His sons' innocent touch was also calming and healing. He held onto them for another full minute, a lifetime in two-year-old time, and another minute gone from the attack clock.

Kinnor uttered a glad cry and ran from the room at full speed, headed for the sleeping quarters, probably for some new toy to show off. Kiel, still settled mid-lap, raised a scanbook toward his face. *Wild Animals of Netaia*, Brennen read at the top of the screen.

"It's Mari," he whispered, letting Ahma understand the degree of danger. "She could be trapped there."

Her quest-pulse shifted to light access, sweeping his alpha matrix. "It has been bliss," she said tenderly, and her grief echoed his own. "But we pay dearly for that bliss. Eventually. Half of us, Brennen."

Except for those like Uri who never pair bonded. He exhaled a long, slow breath. "I'm not ready."

She straightened. "I understand. Do what you can for her, and trust the One with both your fates. If she makes the Crossing, I will be here for you. Until then, she is the most important person in your life, after the Holy One. Do all that you can, for the sake of the memories you always will carry. Not even these precious sons must come between you." She paused, frowning. "And certainly not your career."

He was ready to do something risky and unauthorized. He showed her. "And I am not what I used to be. I could fall short."

"Ahpa?" a voice piped from his lap.

His ahma murmured, "A little later, dear Kiel. Ahpa and Zahma need a moment." Gently she scooted Kiel to the floor. Her arm fell warm on Brennen's shoulder. "We have not prayed together for weeks," she said quietly. She did something about it immediately, placing his future—possible bereavement and all—in the hands of the One whose finger spun the galaxy. Whose holy promises would be kept.

He answered with a prayer for her, for Kinnor and Kiel, and then for Mari, with all his heart.

Then she rested her hand on his bowed head. It felt heavy and warm. "Son of my heart," her voice said softly, "may your faith remain steadfast. May your love go deep and always be returned. And whatever perils find you, Brennen, may the Holy One himself guide you on his bright Path."

"Amen," he whispered. Blinking, he raised his head. "Amen. Thank you." He bent and kissed Kiel, who had lingered alongside them, laying a hand on his lap as if joining them in blessing and prayer. Kinnor dashed back into the room, dragging some object that looked like an antique musical toy. "Come here, Kin," he said. He kissed him, too, holding tightly though Kinnor squirmed.

He drew a deep breath. "Hangar 357. Probably for the next hour. Then I will be gone."

"As you should," Ahma said. "Did you get breakfast?"

"No time. But thank you. There will be concentrates on board." He kissed her forehead, straightened his tunic, and headed out onto the base.

Striding across duracrete lanes with renewed energy, he raised his interlink. Crosstown net had gone active, sounding an alert. "Yes?" he asked.

Dassah Cowan's voice answered. "General, I'm sorry, but the Tellai groundcar has just turned down Claighbro House's entry lane. We're heading there now, via the rooftop."

"Carry on." This time, he couldn't help Tel. Hangar 357 lay at the end of the farthest row, a long walk, with rain threatening in heavy gray clouds. Startled by weather, he flagged down a service cart and commandeered a ride.

Alone in her crib, little Queen Rinnah had started crying for no obvious reason. Carradee picked her up and held her at shoulder height so she could look down from the palace's high windows into its gardens of drooping trees, long carpets of lawn, and shimmering reflecting pools. Bouncing side to side in the universal motherly gesture, she spoke softly. Soothingly.

Thinking Rinnah asleep, she'd turned on city news over the media block. A civil defense alert had gone out at nine hundred. Her dear Daithi was out there somewhere, assisting in the distribution of emergency supplies. In lower Citangelo, low-commoners hadn't the means to prepare for emergencies. Now that the base was admitting some degree of threat, it was vital to get foodstuffs to them, even if it was only shipboard-type concentrates. Those took up little room and never spoiled.

Maybe the newsnetter's voice had wakened Rinnah. Seeing the outdoors seemed to soothe her now. "See, little one? All is calm. All is quiet."

Rinnah raised a fist to her mouth and gnawed contentedly.

Carradee wished she could dismiss her own worries. Marshal Burkenhamn's staff generously kept her and Regent Kenhing informed, even including the awful danger of nanomechanical world seeds, as they called them. On Queen Rinnah's behalf, she'd agreed with the regent and marshal to keep that specific danger out of the general news. What would be the point? If those seeds arrived here, there would be no hiding place. They could only flee, and Netaia could not send everyone offworld. Rumors were spreading, due to increased activity in the civilian spaceports' private zones. Every noble family owned a small cross-space shuttle. Ground staff was already servicing several of them. That rarely happened simultaneously.

She and Daithi had agreed to live or die with Netaia, but they would send Rinnah offworld with some other family if Marshal Burkenhamn warned them of mission failure. She would give over the Angelo shuttle to the Chapter House.

It was her duty.

Rinnah wriggled. Carradee turned away from the window and leaned against a cold marble wall. Soon, she might be saying goodbye to another daughter. Tears gathered in her eyes. "Would you like to get down, my sweet queen?"

"Dear Esme," a melodious voice called.

Esme hustled across the hall to the bedroom where her little wastling sister once lived. Her new sister, Esme Two, stood at the door. "We have a guest," Esme Two exclaimed. "He has just driven up. We must go down and greet him."

"Lovely," Esme murmured. Her head felt thick, except when she looked into the beautiful green eyes of those two precious moving mirrors. They reflected her own beauty back to her. Following Two, she descended the broad main stairs.

She should have had a doorman helping her make this greeting. Hadn't there been maids, once upon a time, scurrying about the estate, keeping things clean?

Where had they all gone?

Hating this thick-headed confusion, she pulled the heavy door open herself and was charmed to recognize little Prince Tel.

He stood with his mouth open.

Two of her. There were still two of her, wearing the same airy blue blouses. They had the same emerald eyes in identical faces, and he realized how foolish he had been. Why had he assumed there would be only one Shuhr in Citangelo?

Esme-on-the-left sent a sweet smile and dropped an awkward curtsey. "Come in, dear Tel," she said.

Not Esme, that one. Now, could he keep them straight? That one wore slender green trousers. The other wore a short black skirt, and her left wrist looked recently wounded. "Good morning, dear Duchess," he replied airily, looking between them. "Might we walk in the garden?"

"Oh, I don't think so," the real Esme said. "Please, come in. I shall order cruinn."

He followed. The door slid shut behind him with a resonant boom. As far as he could tell, the Shuhr woman had done nothing to his mind . . . yet.

But she would. She had to be lulling Esme too. His heart pounded. He took a deep breath, trying to still it, trying to regain the emotional control in which he'd been coached by—no, no. That name must not enter his thoughts. *The one on the left, now. That's her.*

They all sat down at the long table. Real Esme sat on his left. An instant later, though, the other transformed into a black-haired, unfamiliar woman.

She leered at him.

"Esme," he exclaimed, facing the woman who sat on his left. She still had dark-blonde hair and green eyes. There was no longer any point in pretending. "Are you all right?"

She laughed, a high, artificial giggle. She tippy-tapped her fingers on the tabletop and crossed her legs under the table. He averted his eyes, unable to look at this parody of a Netaian noblewoman. "Oh, I'm wonderful, Tel. These women have been the most delightful guests. You must stay with us awhile. We all would love that oh so much."

Esme Rogonin never would have used those words. Esme could be rude, but never mindless.

The black-haired woman tipped back her head. A strange voice spoke in the middle of his brain. *Where is my sister?*

His mouth opened against his will, but he managed to speak his own words. "Let Esme go," Tel said. "Please."

"And take you instead?" said the woman. "Shall I masquerade as the noble Prince Tel at the Electoral table?" She shot the image into his mind, making him nauseous. "Ridiculous," she said. "We have our standards. But you may stay with us a while. For entertainment." *Now, where is my sister?* she demanded in the middle of his head. Along with her subvoice came a scent of spoiled meat.

These people had killed Phoena. They would undoubtedly kill Esme. But help was on the way, or was it? Not knowing there were two of them, he'd brought the "sister" to Citangelo Base—

"Hah," the dark-haired woman exclaimed. "Citangelo Base. Excellent."

Esme Rogonin sat unmoving, unblinking, plainly manipulated.

Without meaning to do anything, he found himself standing and sweeping off his hat, bowing deeply. Obviously, she could manipulate him too. She'd made none of the hand motions he usually saw. Were those motions nothing but visual cues, required by Sentinel law to warn others?

Stay close to Esme, he told himself. *Stay close to Esme.*

Esme sat still, having no need to move. Her beloved sister Esme Two had suddenly changed her appearance, but what of it? As for Prince Tel, he was plainly trying to maintain that pitiable manliness act.

Esme Two would set him straight. She had no doubt.

She loved her dear sisters.

Firebird sat on Monu's S-shaped lounger, hunched over her interlink. Her injured shoulder ached. For most of a precious hour, maybe longer, Uri and Shel had lain sprawled inside the lounger's other curve. Gering, bless him, had walked down the bridge corridor three times, whispering to her each time he emerged, "Only scouting."

And Monu had done nothing. Likely, she was simply waiting for Firebird to see the floating stars of oxygen deprivation. What was a few hours' wait to a being who'd traveled for centuries and expected to refuel shortly?

Firebird drained the bitter dregs of another cup of instant kass. Studying image after image, she was following a hunch. Apparently, Monu's last human service crew had bunked in the rooms where they had been sleeping. Therefore, there had to have been access routes to other parts of the ship, and Monu must have blocked them. Assuming that Monu's last crewers used relatively small, mechanical service bots, such passages would be too narrow to look obvious to engineers back at Citangelo Base. Logically, there might be a route to that shielding nexus through those little tunnels.

Looking for that kind of route, instead of something they could walk through, she'd painstakingly re-angled every image. The biofuel tank dominated each picture, but narrow passages permeated the rest of Monu's body like capillaries. One of them apparently ended right here in the lounge, behind a bulkhead that Monu probably created just before they arrived. The human service staff that Firebird imagined, who had wielded the tools Gering was examining—or their smaller, remote-controlled mechanical messengers—would have needed access to all parts of the ship. Including an open area right over the bridge, where the shielding nexus appeared to be.

So, could she crawl through them? They looked too narrow for hulking Gering to attempt, or muscular Uri, or broad-shouldered Shel, but she was a small woman. Her uniforms had required custom tailoring.

If she could pierce that bulkhead, she would need to carry in a shock pistol, since a shock pistol could surge subtronic circuits if fired in close contact. That also gave her hope, since if Monu tried to trap her inside there, using subtronic circuits to alter her bulkheads, Firebird might be able to surge those circuits and stop the blockages until the pistol ran out of charge. She'd fired it just once, dropping Daken. Unfortunately, the quartermaster hadn't issued fresh charge cartridges. This one should be good for about twenty more bursts. She must save one burst—no, make it four or five—to surge the shielding nexus itself, or this all would be for nothing.

Or, if Uri and Shel lingered in shock as hours fled, she might unsheathe and carry in one of their crystaces—

She balked at the thought. Those ancient weapons were the next thing to holy objects, irreplaceable, brought to Thyrica by the original Ehretan refugees. Sentinels received them at their vesting ceremonies and relinquished them upon death or retirement. Shel and Uri had offered those sonic-activated crystal shard weapons as part of their sabotage inventory, but Firebird had assumed Shel and Uri would wield them. Taking one to use, unauthorized, might rob her of the Mighty Singer's blessing on any attempt.

But wouldn't he understand the need?

She'd seen Brennen cut metal with his crystace.

Would she dare?

On the other hand, several years ago, she'd been sent with an invasion force to Veroh, aiming to secure an ore for developing a world-fouling weapon. Netaia's attack had made most of Veroh open-air uninhabitable. What awful justice, what terrible symmetry it would be, if Netaia faced that kind of destruction.

She must not let that happen. And whatever else transpired, she would not end up as one of Monu's quasi-immortal companion ships.

She wrested her thoughts back to the images in front of her. Surely, those passages would be no worse for shimmying than the solar-heated water tubes she'd followed long ago at Hunter Height.

No worse until the very end, anyway. From the chamber over the bridge, she could only return by squeeze-crawling out again. Would there be time? To save Netaia from being seeded, the fleet must strike the moment Monu's shields dropped. By then, hopefully, Uri would have revived to disable the drone-launching chutes.

The idea made her stomach twist. Noble suicide had been one thing years ago. Now she had a family to live for, if she could.

Tel lay on his back in the Rogonin estate's uplevel hallway, gasping. The Shuhr woman had thrown him around like a puppet, levitating and dropping him. She'd stripped off his jeweled tunic and feathered hat and made Esme put them on. Esme had laughed along, mocking him, pointing. They'd teased each other about masquerading as the lordly Prince Tel. They'd mocked his dandified accent.

He burned with a dark fury, imagining that Phoena had been tortured for other Shuhr's amusement. How soon would they do that to Esme? Right now, this woman plainly delighted in his misery.

Did they know, back at the base, that evil lingered at the Rogonin estate?

Even his own head sometimes felt clouded. He did not doubt that the Shuhr woman was playing with his mind, diving in and out, fishing for secrets.

He must not think of—
He must not think of—
He dropped the curtain hard, repeatedly, again and again.

If and when this woman tired of throwing him around with her poisonous epsilon powers, she would rape his mind and kill him. Cruelly. Forcing Esme to watch.

Sentinel God, is there any way out? Help us all! This woman survived the loss of her world. She is a monster, but her survival is a miracle.

Help, he called into the universe. *They're changing me. Not just me, but Esme.*

Esme laughed again. Tel bounced rather well, did he not?
Yet she found herself pitying him.
He'd come here to see her.
To try and help her?
Where had that thought come from? Why in the Whorl would she need any help?

Esme Two seemed utterly focused on Tel's torment. She herself was being ignored for the moment.

The other Esmes were doing things to her!

Shuhr. The word flitted into her mind. She'd eaten a terrible dinner with some of them, ages ago. Renegade telepaths, able to do all of the things General Caldwell's people could do. And unlike General Caldwell, unbound by their religious laws.

That made Caldwell's Sentinels remarkable, didn't it? Having that much power but refusing to use it unkindly? After all, unkindness was simple human nature.

Poor Tel. This time he bounced off the ceiling. "Whee!" Esme Two exclaimed, suddenly looking like a mirror again. "Isn't this fun, sweet Esme?"

And the strange, hostile thoughts went away. Indeed, this was fun!

The Esmes walked away arm-in-arm.
Tel.
He sat up on the dark wooden floor, aching all over. He would have spectacular bruises, if she didn't kill him before they could appear under his skin.

Had he just heard a woman's voice again, inside his head? It did not feel foul like the other one. Just a little bit tummy-stirring.

Prince Tel.

There it was again. He sat upright. Crawling on hands and knees, he reached the stairway. He scooted halfway down.

Could it be? Had Sentinels arrived anyway?

The voice came again. *Get away from her and away from the second-level stairs. We need your help.*

It was distinctly another woman's subvoice. Could this be the palace guard Sentinel who'd originally been tasked with rescuing Esme? He managed to get to his feet and then straightened his trousers. *I'm away,* he thought hard. *What can I do?*

We're right above you, on the roof. We just sent a dart pistol down a dumbwaiter into the kitchens. Get her if you can. With the words came the image of a small weapon.

It was a Sentinel, all right. *You're coming in?*

Dart her. She won't expect it from you.

His hands tingled. Caldwell had explained that certain drugs could strip Shuhr of their epsilon powers. If this woman went down, Esme would be safe. Possibly not herself, if they'd tampered with her mind, but safe and alive.

He must get to the kitchens. She'd left him alone for the moment.

He hurried the best he could up the long dining table under the trophy heads and made the left turn into servant-land, as Rogonin used to call it. The automated dumbwaiter was for bringing in supplies delivered to the rooftop port. One shelf near the enormous cold cabinets stood open. On it lay a small, dark object that matched the image they'd given him. It looked almost like a shock pistol. A non-deadly weapon. His preference. The trigger was easy to find. He tucked it into a pocket. He tried to shape his thoughts into something like what he'd felt when the Sentinel sent word to him. He thought hard once more. *Got it.*

The response came immediately. *Wait in the kitchens. Near a door.*

Footsteps crashed down the first stairwell. He drew himself up. *Do or die,* he told himself.

Esme burst into the corridor, and then another Esme. "What is it?" one of them cried. The other one seized his wrist. They'd changed into identical kaleidocolor blouses and slender black trousers. Had the

Shuhr known that help was coming? He hadn't. This time, he had not betrayed anyone.

Dragging him in tandem, the two Esmes paused at the top of the broad main steps. Then, to his horror, one Esme seized the other and lifted her overhead as easily as if she'd been a toy. Pulled her backward, grinning.

She was going to throw her! Tel drew the dart pistol and fired.

Instantly, the woman dropped Esme onto the carpeted second-level floor. She grabbed for Esme's throat, roaring and biting. She might be losing her epsilon powers, but she was astonishingly strong.

Close by, more footsteps pounded. At the corner of his vision, someone grabbed for Esme's frantically kicking legs.

The fury that Tel had held back for months and years bubbled out of him. He threw himself on the Shuhr woman. Esme screamed. Someone must have grabbed her ankles, because she slid away. The Shuhr woman pulled a deadly twinbeam blazer out of a pocket. Tel lunged in and fought her for it. He seized her wrist and slammed it against a wall. She writhed out of his grasp and dove toward Esme and the Sentinels.

Tel jumped her from behind and got both hands around her throat.

Esme screamed. Terrified, he froze. He held on. And on. He held while the woman collapsed. Held while she struggled. Held while one of the Sentinels tried to pull him away. Held after the Shuhr woman went quiet.

"Tel," one of the Sentinels said. "Prince Tel. Let go."

He couldn't. His hands seemed turned to stone around the evil woman's throat.

The Sentinel raised a hand and repeated, "Let go, Tel."

His hands went limp. Horrified, he struggled onto his knees. Esme stood embracing a woman Sentinel, weeping.

Tel pushed away from the unmoving body. "She can't be dead, can she?" he asked the Sentinel. "Can they be killed by strangulation?"

"They can, if they're darted and can't put themselves into t-sleep."

He was no killer. So he had thought. Before, he had killed from a distance. This time, he'd done it with two bare hands.

Esme was staring at him, open-mouthed. She pushed away from the Sentinel, hurried to his side, and knelt beside him. "Tel, Tel, are you hurt?"

He fought his retching throat. He must not vomit in front of Duchess

Esmerield. He looked up. One Sentinel gave him an approving thumb-high gesture.

No, no. What wickedness lived deep inside him that he could kill again, even an enemy? "Only my soul," he said ruefully. "But are you all right?"

"Tel." She rested a hand on his shoulder. "Thank you." Then she wilted into his arms. He gently pulled her into an embrace, wishing he felt less ill.

The woman Sentinel—yes, it was Dassah Cowan from the palace guards—spoke gently. "You both need to come to the base. Protective custody. Just for a while. Having been with Shuhr, you . . . you are undoubtedly mind-altered. Particularly you, Duchess."

Esme drew away from him. "Undoubtedly." She looked down. "I am not myself. I have not been myself. They made me—" Her nose wrinkled, and her frown was not pretty. "Love them." She practically spat the words.

"I just got here," Tel said. "Might she have already . . ." He trailed away.

To his relief, Sentinel Cowan walked up to him and looked directly into his eyes. He felt slightly ill, but there was nothing horrifying in the woman's mental touch. "You're pretty much all right," she said. "Thank the Mighty Speaker."

Her words touched something deep inside. Hadn't he tried, recently, to pray to the Sentinels' god? *Yes, Speaker, whoever you are. Thank you.*

This time, he seemed to feel an echo. Not a reply, and certainly not words, but a sense of having touched something larger than himself. "Wait for me," he told Sentinel Cowan. Paudan and Jess still waited outside in the groundcar.

He hurried down the front steps and sent his staff back to his own estate. Then he followed the Sentinels, and Esme, up to the windswept rooftop with tears on his cheeks.

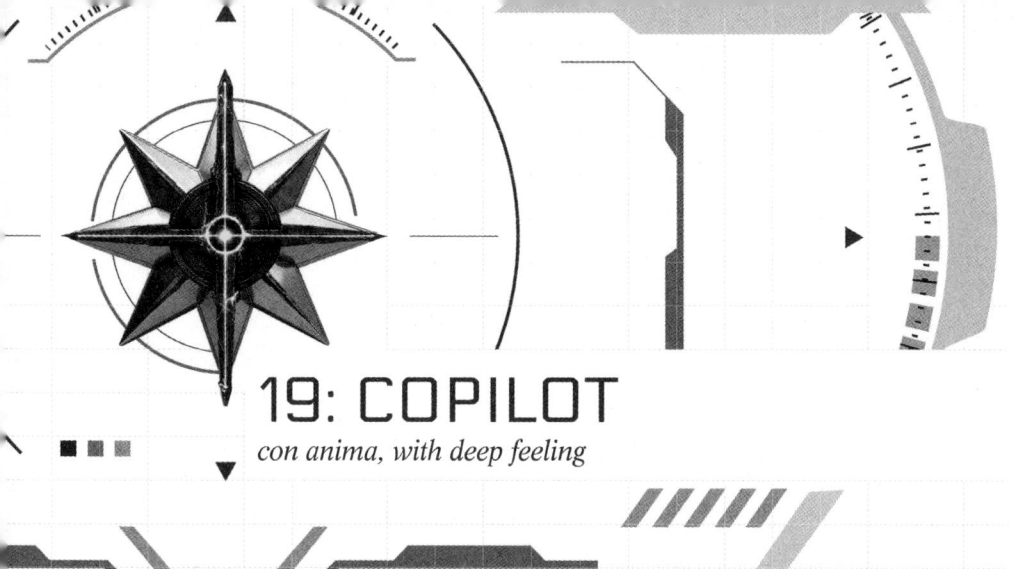

19: COPILOT
con anima, with deep feeling

The cart driver dropped Brennen at hangar 357, a broad-roofed metal building. He glanced at a security panel next to the side door, entering his security override. It let him in out of the wind. The DS-215 stood alone, a thirty-meter craft like its predecessor, and like the DS-212, it looked as if it were almost entirely stardrive engine. This one was space-black. For stealth. "Hello?" he called.

No one responded. Apparently, the Sentinel transport pilots had been called away. Maybe he'd seen them at base housing. Wherever they'd gone, they'd left a recall pad displaying the prelaunch checklist lying on a workbench.

Poor security, and he needed them back here. One of them, anyway. He eyed the screen. More than half the prep was complete. He could order the pilots to return via the command center, and while waiting, he could finish prep. First, he shut his eyes and examined his affective control. Again he threaded epsilon energy through his emotions, put a powerful pull on them, and held them down. Hard. Then he made the call.

The voice that answered was Marshal Burkenhamn's. "You're where I expected, General Caldwell."

Good. He didn't want an argument. "When can I expect these Sentinels to return?"

"They were sent to reinforce the front gate. There could be a second attack on your family."

Chilled, he weighed the possibility. The Shuhr he had seen in action rarely tried the same thing twice. He probably could go ahead with departure. Still, he must not fly out alone.

Before issuing a recall order that might be questioned, he prayed. *I am close to the forbidden line, Holy One. Help me.* Calmly he asked, "Requesting a courtesy, Marshal. If the order to fire on Monu is given, please alert me so I can be ready." *For bereavement shock.* His affective control held this time.

The marshal didn't answer for several seconds, but that was fine. Marshal Burkenhamn needed to understand that he would face whatever the Holy One, and events, determined. This enemy must be defeated. "We'll do it, son," he said at last. "I'm sorry."

"Thank you." He drew a breath. "Now, would you—"

The marshal interrupted. "One thing more. Prince Tel Tellai has just returned to base. A little worse for the wear, but essentially unharmed. He's on Pad Three with Sentinel Cowan's group."

Tel? It was not widely known that Tel had done some basic piloting. Had the marshal heard? If Tel proved unwilling, Brennen still could recall a Sentinel pilot, but he had a hunch. Perhaps the marshal was trying to save him from giving questionable orders.

"Send him over," he said. "All haste." He left the hangar door ajar.

Nine minutes later, he was working down the checklist when Tel strode in, hands clasped behind his back. The feathered hat was gone. So was the jewel-collared tunic. Wearing a simple skinshirt and trousers, Tel had a rising bruise on his forehead but a dignified set to his shoulders. Brennen hurried around the ship's rounded nose. Tel seized his hand with a wild look in his eyes. Obviously, he'd been face-to-face with a terrible enemy.

Brennen tried a light probe and found emotional chaos. Almost automatically, he returned a calming touch. "You're mentally wounded," Brennen said simply. "But you're alive, thank the Holy One. We can—"

Tel interrupted. "Caldwell." A sad, frightened resolve streamed off the smaller man. Tel cleared his throat and looked side to side. He exhaled. "I'm not sure of the proper words, Caldwell, but here it is. Whatever it is that you consider an 'Inquirer,' I need that status."

Brennen raised his head.

Tel stared at the ground. "Things . . . happened at Claighbro House. I have no explanation, except that I should not be alive. Someone or something must have, must have been looking after me. But surely I disappointed . . . him. I killed a woman. With my bare hands this time. She was one of . . . them, but she was a human being, and I might not be the kind of person that your god wants, but . . . I need . . . his help." He lifted his head. "Please, Caldwell. Tell me more."

Tel's declaration as Inquirer was cause for celebration, but Brennen was holding his emotions so tightly that he did not feel the appropriate joy. He fell back on the usual answer. "May the Mighty Speaker guide you in your questioning time." He wrapped both arms around the smaller man's shoulders, but he did not probe. "The Holy One will forgive, Tel. He called us to destroy Three Zed's Golden City to bare rock. The surviving offworld Shuhr are considered a danger to every person they meet."

And having decided to take this action, he must focus. He would barely have time to reach RIA range and assist with the sabotage. "We can talk later, Tel. I only hope Duchess Esme was not ungrateful to be rescued."

"Actually, she thanked me." Tel cringed. "Was Phoena . . . ?"

Tel had been lucky, then. "Phoena was not grateful." Powerful Golden City Shuhr had surrounded Brennen as he knelt, helpless. Phoena's energetic kick landed square in his face.

Tel shook his head and looked away, maybe seeing back in time. "Phoena had long been full of hate," he said. "And envy."

Their eyes met. Brennen felt deep understanding.

"I killed in hate, Caldwell." Tel looked at his hands, as if he did not believe he owned them. "I t-took her by the throat. Would your god want me?"

Tel Tellai, notorious dandy and fop, had killed a second enormously powerful Shuhr. Once again, he had done the Whorl a tragic but necessary service. Brennen's heart rose slightly. "Yes, Tel, he does. He wants you."

"I feel filthy." Tel's furrowed forehead showed horror. "I never could be a soldier."

"That requires training." Desensitization that he sometimes regretted.

Tel glanced around and tucked his thumbs inside his waistband. "May I have an update? They haven't told us what's happening out there."

"The Strangers are hostile," Brennen admitted. "We have seen evidence of some sort of incident in their landing bay. Our ambassadors might be stranded."

"Stranded?" Tel repeated, wide-eyed.

Brennen confirmed with a nod. "We have ordered sabotage of the Strangers' shielding, which is extraordinarily powerful, and of their attack capacity. Our attack force is in range because, if our ambassadors succeed, we must strike immediately. We must destroy that ship."

"What's the hurry?"

"I must put you under command not to repeat this."

Tel hesitated, then nodded readily. "Very well."

After voice-commanding, Brennen sent the terrible threat, along with an image of Netaia reduced to sludge over rock.

Tel gasped and stepped back.

"Finally," Brennen continued, "we lost communication with the ambassadors three hours ago. I mean to go out and assist." He glanced up at the black ship. It carried only minimal energy ordnance, but it had Remote Individual Amplification capability. "There was a time when I would have felt sure I could do this."

"You went to Three Zed because you were trying to save Phoena. You're mostly healed, aren't you? What can I do to repay you?" Tel asked.

Brennen tested the steadiness of his voice. "I need the help of a willing friend who is ready to risk his life. You might need to take over as pilot."

Tel's eyes sparked, and he drew himself up to full height. "Let me help. Details later."

This was the new Tel Tellai, abler and more courageous than anyone had realized, including Tel himself. "You piloted a RIA craft once," Brennen recalled. "Traveling with Lady Firebird."

"I did." Tel glanced up at the ship's space-black nose. "Just show me what you need. That's what she did."

He must speak plainly. Ordering a fellow Sentinel might have crossed that dangerous line, and Tel was a civilian. Guarding Tel's volition was even more crucial. He must give Tel every chance to change his mind. "If those shields are successfully sabotaged and the attack must proceed—if Firebird is killed—our pair bond will be broken. I will be helpless, in bereavement shock. That is the other case in which you would need to take control. I will coach you on how to return to base, in case that happens."

The nobleman clutched at a big tool cabinet. Apparently, he finally understood. Their own forces might kill the woman they both cared for.

Brennen looked at his friend. "This is going to be dangerous, Tel."

"We both might be killed, too?" Tel managed a smile. "I am honored. I will do whatever you need . . . Brennen."

He did not remember Tel Tellai ever using his given name. "Thank you." He inclined his head, then turned back to the checklist. "Please, we need to hurry."

"One moment." Tel pulled out an interlink and spoke quickly. "Note to Solicitor Liam Merriam. I hereby designate Regent Kenhing my backup legal executor." He sent Brennen a significant glance. "For myself and for Lady Firebird."

Yes, there was that small matter of the Angelo fortune and Carradee's contested will. Obviously Prince Tel took his financial responsibilities seriously.

A few minutes later, they were climbing into heavy life suits. "This will be a brutal takeoff," Brennen called from halfway up the boarding ladder. "This ship's predecessor rode like a missile. This is faster."

"Just what we need." Tel followed him up. "I'm sorry I delayed you this long."

Brennen closed the magnetic seal and dropped into the left-hand seat. Its acceleration padding almost swallowed him. He glanced right, confirming dual controls. "Would you rather be unconscious for launch? I can wake you when—"

"No."

"Good. Buckle in. I will answer all your questions once we are underway."

He got clearance. They taxied into position.

Firebird looked up from studying diagrams. Here came Gering once more, swinging his arms as if he were walking for exercise. He paused near the exit hatch and looked down at Daken, frowned, and circled the lounge again. Looking past him, she thought she saw something odd. Had the ceiling moved?

Apparently Gering saw it too. He stepped back and toward her. Around the lounge's edges, the ceiling had dropped half a meter. At the edge of the dropped zone, glimmering metal cascaded like an eerie waterfall, expanding the lowered area. Monu had talents they had not dreamed of.

Could she do similar things inside those little access tunnels, using subtronics to alter bulkheads and block passageways?

Surely a shock pistol would override that. It could surge circuitry.

Otherwise, there was no hope of getting to that shielding nexus.

"We are being compacted," Gering murmured. "Monu is shrinking our space." He eyed the freestanding workstation and his arsenal of ancient tools. "Shall I climb up and see if I can cut that away?"

He might be able to reach that high. "Wait until we're sure Uri and Shel won't wake in time." There was no sense provoking Monu before the Sentinels tried to assault the bridge. She didn't say that aloud, though.

"When will that be?" he asked.

She shrugged and glanced at her interlink. They had nine hours until—probably—a very quick Crossing into the holy presence. If the fleet attacked while Monu's shields remained, Monu would surely kill them all. If the shields had been dropped, well, that would be all for the best. Mentally subtracting an hour to deal with the unforeseen, Firebird reached a decision. "If the clock drops below four hours, and we can't wake Uri and Shel, we'd better assume it's up to us. Thank you, Mister Gering."

He crossed his arms, standing over her as if guarding her. "You have always looked bravely at death, Lady Firebird. I commend you."

"Thank you," she said, adding, "I don't fear the Dark that Cleanses, Gering. There's no such thing. Did you know that our people, the noble houses, only invented the Powers to keep control over the common classes?"

"I had considered the possibility." He stood stiffly as he said it.

And yet their loyalty was drilled so deeply that they were willing to die for it. What a mystery! "The Sentinels brought faith in an omnipotent God to the Whorl. There's actually hope beyond death. Hope gives us courage." She considered quoting an Adoration to him, but he was already turning away. She decided not to press him. Not yet. They still had a few hours. But before she climbed into those crawlways, if it came down to that, she must not leave Gering unready. She owed him the chance to make peace. She'd come to like him.

Once again, his head turned toward the shrouded bodies near the exit hatch.

"Your employer's only asleep," she insisted. "He's safer than Uri and Shel."

As had happened several times over the last hour, always when Gering re-emerged into the lounge, the area lights dimmed and the corridor lights flashed.

"You have less air fuel than before," Monu announced. "I have made your space smaller so you will waste less."

"I see that," Firebird answered her.

"I offer you a concession. Come to me, and the others may depart."

Empty promise. She'd killed both their pilots. Uri and Shel remained unconscious, and as far as Firebird knew, neither had flight training.

Maybe a nice, loud argument would wake the Sentinels. "There's no air in the landing bay," she called, raising her voice. "They'd suffocate out there. They'd decompress."

Movement caught her peripheral vision. Had Uri's head turned?

Monu responded. "Some air remains. When you come to me, I shall close the outer space door. Air from your lounge can disperse into the bay. Enough for them to survive while you enter enshipment."

Uri groaned softly, rocking his head side to side.

Lightened by a surge of hope, Firebird swiftly stood and came around the lounger. "Let me consider that, Monu," she shouted.

Uri's eyes opened.

"Uri," she urged, "please. Try to stay awake. We need you."

He nodded. "Awake. Yes. Need . . . a few minutes. Is Shel all right?"

Firebird looked aside, desperate to be patient, desperate to hurry him. "Shel's still out."

Gering hovered close by. "Are you going to be all right, Colonel Harris?"

"Moment," Uri said. "Self-check." His eyes closed again, but he stayed upright. "Yes," he finally said. "That was one awful epsilon blow, but I'm going to be all right."

"Epsilon blow?" Firebird asked.

"Yes. Apparently," he said, frowning, "she can repel epsilon energy back at us."

Firebird couldn't imagine. "While you were out," she told him, "Monu opened the space door. Our pilots aren't responding to hails."

"Blast." Uri turned to Shel. He rested a hand on her forehead. Firebird counted seconds. At seventeen, Shel's eyes also opened.

She shook her head and exhaled a long sigh. "Firebird," she said, "are you all right?"

"Good enough for now." Actually, her shoulder was burning.

"Never do that again, Sentinels." Monu's voice boomed all around them, rattling the deck. "Your mind-energy attacks are useless. Firebird, you will come. Resign yourself and cooperate, and I will let the others depart. It is time."

"I'm going down fighting"—Firebird met Shel's eyes—"not cooperating."

Monu called again. "Colonel Harris, if you move to depart, I shall close the space doors long enough for you to reach your transport. I no longer want your kind. I find you threatening. I offer Lady Firebird unending life. Do not rob her of this privilege." Again, the lounge lights dimmed. Briefly, they winked out to full darkness. Only the ominous corridor stayed lit.

Depart? Return to a world that Monu meant to destroy? Firebird touched her side pocket. She still had her little emergency luma. She eyed the sniffers. Uri had one tucked into his belt. Shel's lay beside her. Firebird wanted them to get moving, but surely, they were in no shape to assault Monu's bridge.

Shel spoke to Uri in Ehretan. Imitating Gering, Firebird got up and walked a lap. When she got back, the others had huddled. Shel stepped out of formation and sent an epsilon burst. *Gering let us access him. He showed us the bridge. We're going in. Distract her if you can.*

Already, Firebird marveled. Wouldn't it be helpful to wake up that quickly?

Gering gathered tools at the workstation. Another flurry of Ehretan passed between Shel and Uri. Firebird caught a few words. She almost told them about her backup plan, but they were fully focused, and she had little desire to make that one-way trip, and they must hurry. If they could take down those shields and the launch chutes from inside the bridge, she still might pilot them out to survival.

To Kinnor and Kiel. And to Brennen.

She shuffled to the bulkhead near the exit hatch, bent down, and attacked the clairsa case's latches with her free hand. Creating a diversion in deadly circumstances wasn't her style. She preferred to fly lead. Even Gering would be in on the attack while she hung back. That hurt a little.

As Shel appeared at her shoulder, Firebird got to her feet, clutching the instrument against her right arm. Shel spoke softly. "Your turn may come, if we don't come back. Even if we succeed, we will need your skills as a pilot."

"Exactly. I assume you'll maintain interlink silence."

Shel nodded. "Stay close to the exit hatch. We could be leaving in a hurry."

"Understood. I'll be right here." She glanced at the nearest workstation. "Bring me one of those stools, if you would."

Shel slid it across the floor. Firebird set the clairsa on it, since cradling it on her lap no longer would work. Not one-handed.

Gering and Uri stood close to Monu's corridor. Shel sent her a nod and joined them.

Mighty Singer, go with them.

"Monu," she called, "I have written a ballad for you. This is its melody. Please tell me what you think."

She'd done no such thing, but she doubted Monu knew long-practiced repertoire from improvising. Two-fingering a new melody wasn't difficult. It took her mind off her desire to be with Uri, Shel, and Gering.

But since Monu had little interest in music, what good was this?

The others disappeared out of her sight.

20: INTO DARKNESS
risoluto, resolutely

Shel led down the corridor, holding her drawn crystace hilt against her right wrist. Gering had shown them a round, high-ceilinged cabin with featureless bulkheads, and Uri had concocted a plan. She had not refined her kinetic skills for some time, but maintaining rate of fall had been her second-favorite part of training, after crystace work. They would keep those weapons secret as long as possible. A crystace's ability to cut metal was their best hope.

As the corridor ended in that round, high cabin, everything went dark. Monu's monotonous voice echoed. "None of you is the one person I want to see here. I will still permit you to depart, if you go immediately."

Shel looked all around. Depart to become biofuel? Not a chance. Now, how would Monu counterattack?

Gering stayed back at the corridor's end, as planned. They'd looked for a closing hatch, but there didn't appear to be one. If Monu tried to shut them in by creating a hatch, Gering had the strength to block it. Armed with all kinds of tools, he would also try to draw Monu's attention away from them.

She pulled out a pocket luma and tossed it onto the deck. Bulkheads glimmered green by its pale light.

Soft music drifted down the corridor, a melody she didn't recognize. *You stay there, Lady Fi. Whatever happens.*

Firebird's improvised melody didn't sound half bad, so she played it a second time, imagining a chord progression that she could not play. "What do you think, Monu?" she repeated.

"I see you." The answer resounded in the lounge. "I hear you. I am not pleased. Everyone I do not want for my companion has gone to my bridge. They cannot have misunderstood. You must come to me. I can do nothing for you there in the lounge."

Good. She fell back on polite repetition. "This is music, Monu. It joins all peoples." All peoples who still had souls, anyway.

"I am equipped to deal with trouble in my sanctum. You will come to me when you are the only one left alive."

But Monu still had no idea what Sentinels could do.

Another ring of dropped ceiling began at the outer bulkheads. Monu was making sure Firebird understood that she had that kind of control. "I am conserving your air fuel. Remain where you are. I shall inform you when I have dealt with the others. Then, you will come to me."

No, I won't, Firebird answered silently.

"Now," Uri muttered.

Shel felt him take a good kinetic hold. She leaped upward, drawing on her own epsilon strength. Shifting the crystace, she touched its sonic activator. By dim light she saw no particularly sensitive spot to attack, nor any obvious defenses. So she aimed the singing blade for the crest of the arc. The bulkhead might be thinnest there.

Even as she flew, Monu's voice came from all around. "I had wondered what you dangerous ones would attempt. I am learning."

Something clanged below her. Gering must have gone on the attack.

Her crystace contacted metal. She thrust it through. There at the top of her flight, she felt herself hover, felt Uri's kinetic grasp still strong.

She crouched into a pre-lunge and swept the weapon across the ceiling's arc. Metal sprang away from the wound.

"I can heal that. You will all die now."

Grid lines in the deck that Uri had barely seen came alive with electrical power. He tried to drop Shel gently. The shock struck too quickly.

And far too hot.

As Uri cried out, Shel fell a meter. She halted her drop, but that took all her concentration. Hovering short of striking range, she glanced down. Gering still stood at the corridor's opening, but Uri had crumpled into a crouch. The air over a symmetrical floor grid shimmered with heat.

So that was Monu's defense!

"What, what?" Gering called from the corridor. He stepped toward Uri, gasped, and leaped back.

She aimed her descent toward Gering. The moment her feet touched the safe zone, she spun and thrust out a hand toward Uri. Lifted him. Pulled him closer. Gering seized his flailing hand and yanked him off the grid.

Gasping, Uri struggled to his feet, but immediately he lifted one foot, balancing on the other. Something smelled hot. His soles?

He called, "We wondered what you would attempt too." Shel sensed that he was blocking pain. Lowering his voice, he ordered, "Again. Ready?"

She eyed the deck and its deadly grid. Perhaps Monu used it to guide victims into position. A palm-wide hose emerged near the crest of the ceiling. From its near end extended several long, curved tines. *The size and shape for holding someone's head*, she realized. It descended snakelike toward Uri.

"Uri!" she shouted, pointing.

As Uri spun and looked up, a pair of hands seized her from behind. Gering flung her back up the corridor, turned, and grabbed Uri too.

She would not have retreated, but Gering had decided that for them. Two steps farther back up the corridor, they stood in the pale-green light of Gering's luma. Soft music played on.

"What can we do?" she asked Uri, using Ehretan. "Two of us should have been enough."

He glanced back up the passage. "Maybe," he said softly in the same language, "Firebird could distract her . . . in here."

The music stopped. She'd probably heard her name.

"We must talk with her." Uri put down the foot he'd been elevating. He groaned.

"You're hurt," she said flatly. "How bad?"

"Delayed reaction."

Firebird came hurrying up the corridor.

"Stop!" Shel shouted. "Stay back!" Wrapping an arm around Uri's waist, Shel pushed forward, back up toward the lounge.

Firebird met them at the corridor's end. Uri was staggering. She helped Shel steady him back to the lounger.

"Electric shock," Shel said, "and probably burns. We'll do what we can for his feet."

Firebird swallowed hard and averted her eyes from the attack clock on Shel's interlink, there on the lounger. As Shel sat with Uri, pressing one palm to his forehead and one to his right ankle, Gering joined Firebird.

"Do we have a chance, my lady?" he asked.

"Yes," she said firmly. It was down to her, now. "We have a chance. There is always a chance, if we obey the holy call."

"Hmm," he said.

With each passing minute, the odds increased that she would die in a blaze of fusion fire, as her dear Corey had done at Veroh. But she would still rather be killed trying to take down those shields than helplessly waiting like a criminal for her execution. Hadn't Brenn declared that he'd never saved his life by sheltering it? Other words bubbled up out of memory: *You're a tough woman to kill, Commander Caldwell.* Coming from her old rival, Ellet Kinsman, that had been a sincere compliment.

At last, Shel stood up and joined her and Gering. "How is he?" Firebird asked.

"Recovering. Slower than last time. This is taking a toll."

Very well, then. Firebird halted near the servo unit. "I have an idea, and I want to show you." She rested a finger on her forehead, inviting access again.

Shel's familiar probe felt only slightly nauseating. Over their years together, Firebird had grown accustomed to it. She raised the set of images to mind, showing Shel what she'd found. There was a way to that shielding nexus from above. She would need a shock pistol, at least, and also—she framed the request with a sense of polite apology, knowing the request was technically illegal—but if they would let her use a crystace, even though she couldn't promise to return it, she might do the most damage in return for her self-sacrifice. While she crawled, they could focus on disabling the seed pods' launching chutes.

The sense of access melted. Shel lingered, looking directly into her eyes. As a bodyguard, it had been Shel's job to protect her. Firebird thought hard at her. *If we have just a few hours to live, that's all I am throwing away. Your Waldron is waiting beyond the Crossing. I'll wait for Brenn.*

Shel might not have caught exact words, but surely she caught the complex of emotions, because as she nodded, a faint light in her eyes softened the solemn set of her jaw. She whispered, "I'd do it, but my shoulders—"

Shel was too muscular. "You can't. Can you and Uri think of anything else?" Firebird whispered back. "Do you want to risk the bridge again, while I try this? You've got to help him disable the seeding chutes."

Uri sat with his hands clasped between his knees, blinking at the deck. Firebird followed Shel to stand over him.

Bending down, Shel spoke rapidly in Ehretan. Uri looked up at Firebird. She felt the flicker of his access probe and let him sense that she didn't honestly like the idea, but she'd done something like it before, long ago.

"You've given birth," Shel reminded Firebird. "You aren't the same size anymore."

That had occurred to her. "Nor is this Hunter Height."

Uri and Shel looked at each other.

Uri's epsilon touch felt firmer than Shel's. *Take mine*, he sent, enfolding his left wrist with his right hand.

Relief, fear, and a tingle of triumph flooded through her together. *I will do my best to return it.*

I know.

One of the Adorations—one she'd used for battling her pride—came to mind. "You give grace and true peace to the humble," she murmured, "to the contrite and obedient." She was going to need the Eternal Speaker's help now. Years ago, she'd tried to face down death by proudly imagining suffering and darkness.

This would be different.

"Yes." Shel spoke aloud as Uri got to his feet, resting most of his weight toward the left. "So there is something else that we must do," she said as she approached Daken Erwin. "We must wake him. Give him time to consider."

Startled, Firebird exclaimed, "What?"

Uri nodded. "Yes. We are all ready to make the Crossing. He is not."

"Couldn't you wait?" Firebird asked. Time was running out. "Let me get moving."

"We were born to this faith," Uri told her. "But you needed time to think it through. I think only you could hope to convince him."

"Me?" It came out as almost a squeak. "What?"

"You know Netaia's faith language."

"Well, yes." Powers. Charities and Disciplines. Bliss, and the Dark that Cleanses. Ugliness she had left behind.

Shel added quickly, "And we're forbidden to proselytize."

Truly, they were. Until Boh-Dabar came, they must show the Whorl what the obedient life looked like without ever using words. She sighed. If the fleet blew Daken into the Mighty Singer's presence, could such a sick, evil creature hope to find mercy? "Oh, all right." Her inner voice taunted her. *Move, move! Forget Daken Erwin!* "But restrain him, or he'll get in my way." She sent Gering a glance that she hoped conveyed sympathy.

"True enough." Shel sprinted for the bunkroom and returned with a bed sheet. Uri tore strips, and they bound Daken's wrists in front of him.

As they bent over Daken, Gering stood behind them, leaning forward. Irritated and impatient, Firebird paced another circuit, careful to look back and forth, trying not to eye the only metal panel that mattered, the one that might cover a way into Monu's circulatory system.

By the time she returned, Daken sat upright, rubbing his crossed hands against a scabbed cheek. He brought his hands down and looked at them. Probably checking for blood.

She stood back. This felt like a waste of precious time.

"Daken," Shel said, crouching down so not to tower over him, "it looks like Monu will win. We have nearly run out of options. We're waking you so you can make your peace with the Mighty Speaker, the Eternal Sovereign beyond time and space. His mercy is great."

"Not like the Powers," Firebird added dutifully. She stayed on her feet, two meters away. "And there's nothing you need to do except reach out and take his mercy."

Daken pressed his back to the bulkhead and used it to lever himself up to stand. Shel and Uri rose too. Even restrained, he looked evil. Uri rested one hand against a bulkhead, wincing. Standing on burned soles had to be painful.

"The Powers can't help us." Firebird tried to speak with warmth she did not feel. "Forget the Dark that Cleanses, Daken." *Because if it existed, you would have been spending eternity there.* "But there really is a promise of bliss. What Netaia made you is ugly and cruel. I forgive you, Daken Erwin." There. She'd said it, even if she wasn't sure she meant it.

"What Netaia made me"—Daken's chin rose—"is strong. I have no interest in your ugly Sentinel religion. Leave it alone." He stretched and twisted a bound wrist so he could point toward Firebird's belt. "And if you really forgive me, show me. Give that back."

She'd wrapped his dagger's blade in a strip of cloth, just under the binding that held her left arm to her chest. "Oh no," she said flatly. "That has nothing to do with forgiveness. That's a trophy, Daken Erwin. You understand that language, don't you?"

He glared, but Gering put a hand on her shoulder. She turned her head and looked into eyes that seemed to have softened. "You can just take mercy as a gift?" he asked.

"Gering," Daken shouted. The oozing cuts amid his beard gave him an even wilder look.

"That's all," she responded without thinking. Then it hit her, and her heart leapt. Gering wanted mercy.

He took his hand away. "It's too easy."

"I know how it sounds," she said quietly. "There's more to how we practice it, but we follow the Holy Path out of gratitude. Not to qualify for it. I . . ." She hesitated. Must she tell these men what she remembered?

It could be her last chance. "I was looking death in the face when I took that gift, Mister Gering. On Netaia." She glanced at Daken. "You were there. Phoena sentenced me to die at sunrise. Remember?"

Without waiting for him to answer, she looked directly at Gering. "I made a sincere request, whether or not I survived. I have never regretted it. If we get back, you can learn more. But that really is all you need to do now."

Gering shot a glance at his employer. In the dim light, Daken's scowl looked ominous.

But what could he do, bound and unarmed, to big Dodis Gering?

Gering squared his bearlike shoulders. He leaned in to Firebird and spoke in a hushed voice. "Would I have to say it out loud?"

Her breath caught. She had thought she'd have to convince him. Shaking her head vigorously, she assured him, "No. It's all between you and the Eternal Speaker, and he's omniscient. He knows our thoughts." She cast a glance at Uri and Shel. "Better than they do."

Lowering his head, Gering walked away. She felt almost sure that he was becoming one of the Holy One's children, and she rejoiced. What a moment! Even if they all died within hours, one Netaian soul would join them on the Crossing's other side.

And maybe Monu had heard the true message.

If Monu had a soul, which she doubted.

Uri stood on one foot next to the exit hatch. "Daken, if you won't ask for full mercy, it would be wise to apologize." His voice carried a note of warning.

Daken snorted. "To her?" He jerked his head toward Firebird and took a step away from the bulkhead. Shel moved toward him with angry eyes, and Daken backed off. "I," he said loftily, "am ordered to apologize. To be frank, the fit comes on me sometimes. When it does, I can't control it."

Shel raised an eyebrow toward Firebird. "Can we believe him this time? I don't think the Codes would justify probing him."

Firebird stared into his little eyes. "Maybe. Daken, I think you could have controlled it, especially at first. I was barely in school when they first warned me about you."

His lips twitched. He wanted to smile. He infuriated her. "I don't have to listen to that kind of talk from you, wastl–" He choked off the word.

Firebird had his dagger. She could repay him. He deserved it. She inwardly shook her head. She must control herself. She must release this man to the Mighty Singer, especially if she would meet him soon. He promised justice.

But letting go of her rights was hard. Daken couldn't read her thoughts, but maybe he saw the strength in her. He looked away first.

Firebird took a breath. "Help us," she said. "Please. If we get back to Netaia, I will plead with Brennen to be lenient. He'll listen to me."

She meant it sincerely, but he puffed out his chest and announced, "I will become something even more magnificent, or I will die."

Gering had rejoined the group. He stood with his head bowed.

"You." Daken narrowed his eyes at Gering. "You did it. Traitor."

Gering raised his head.

"You are no longer my employee," Daken spat. "You are a shame to

House Erwin. So, Dodis Gering, go ahead and do whatever else you want. You no longer answer to me."

Gering drew his bearlike body up tall. "I am deeply sorry, Grand Duke Daken. Eventually, we all face the eternal. I have kept all the Charities and Disciplines. I owe the Powers nothing more, and I hope that this is another way."

Firebird imagined smoke coming out of Daken's ears. He spun and turned his back on his manservant.

His former manservant.

Gering stepped toward Uri. "How may I help you?"

Uri rested a finger on his lips, and Gering nodded.

Firebird agreed. They must not say one more word until the last moment, and those moments were fleeing. Wherever they attacked Monu, Monu would strengthen her defenses.

Shel abruptly straightened, startling Firebird, and beckoned Gering close. She pointed toward his underarm.

Gering nodded again. He reached into his livery tunic, pulled out the small shock pistol he had carried concealed, and tucked it into Firebird's pocket.

Warmed, she whispered, "Thank you." Then it was time. She thought hard at Shel, *Will you try the bridge again while I crawl, or go directly for the seed chutes?*

Shel sent an uncertain glance at Uri. Gering headed toward the pitch-dark sleeping cabin, and Daken followed.

Shel touched the fabric binding Firebird's arm. "You'll probably reopen that wound and cause further shoulder damage." *Maybe never play the clairsa again*, filtered into Firebird's mind.

That didn't stop her, although she was also exhausted after the injury and early awakening. Her body was probably spending energy trying to heal. "I do need a couple of stim caps," she confessed.

Lights brightened in the deadly corridor. The massive voice echoed again. "Come in, Lady Firebird."

As Firebird fingered the knot that held her binding, Shel hurried over to the bulkhead and dove into an issue bag. She returned with two of the small purple kass capsules and a cup of water from the servo unit, and she helped Firebird unbind her arm. As Shel worked, Firebird swallowed the bitter capsules and prayed. *What else, Mighty Singer?*

The crystace.

When her arm fell free, a jolt of pain shot from shoulder to shoulder. "Shel." She grimaced. "Can you do a full pain block?"

"We normally don't. It could cause permanent damage."

The massive voice echoed. "Your air fuel runs low." Again, the ceiling waterfalled downward. It was now barely higher than Shel was tall.

Shel rested a hand on Firebird's shoulder, and oh, blessed relief, all the pain vanished as if she'd never been stabbed. Her left side felt dead from her neck to her fingertips. "I'm sorry," Shel told her. "I just did you no favor."

"It's what we need. Thank you." She tried and failed to raise her left arm. She could only lift it with her other hand.

Good enough. Angling her shoulders would give her a slimmer diameter, anyway. "Tie back my hair." She dug in a pocket for the catch she'd worn when they boarded.

Uri reached for his sleeve cuff and unbuckled his weapon sheath. They huddled together to conceal what they were doing as Shel buckled it to Firebird's left wrist. Relieved and honored, Firebird held still. It seemed a holy moment.

If only Brennen were here to see it.

She pulled the oxygen sniffer off her belt and tucked it down the front of her uniform tunic. She would need the luma and a shock pistol first, so she took the luma in her left hand. The hand felt numb, but to her relief, it would grip. She drew the pistol and thumbed a stud on one side of the handgrip, then checked the charge. Held it right-handed. All the schematics she'd studied bounced in her mind. She wished she had Brennen's memory.

No time for wishes. She had what she had, and no more.

"Ready?" Shel whispered.

Firebird glanced over at Uri. He flicked her a salute. Muffled, angry voices drifted out of the sleeping cabin.

Gazing at the bulkhead, she imagined Brennen standing there, palms pressed together. Two little people stood next to him, and she felt a smile surface. When she'd swallowed her mother's poison, she only owned pride and glory. This time, hopefully, Kinnor and Kiel would remember her. *Help me now, Mighty Singer. Give me back that old determination, but not for pride or glory. For them. For you.*

She tucked Brenn's little bird-of-prey medallion around to the back of her neck and adjusted the chain so she wouldn't have to crawl on it.

"Ready," she said.

Shel drew her own crystace. She stepped to the bulkhead and activated it. Its piercing whine sang in the thinning air as the crystalline blade emerged. Holding it two-handed, she cut into the wall with a full-body sweep. Metal zinged. Edges drew back.

Monu howled.

Shel made another slice, her body lines one with the weapon.

The howling went on.

A third slice, a powerful roundhouse kick, and an opening appeared, black and foreboding. It started to close from the edges, just as the ceiling was doing.

Firebird stepped in with her shock pistol. With a short, desperate prayer, she pressed it to the opening's edge. She fired.

The closing stopped, leaving a stub like a half-healed wound.

It worked! The shock bursts did surge Monu's local circuits.

"Go!" Shel thumbed off her crystace. She made a stirrup of her hands.

Firebird used her right hand to pick up the left, raising the luma. She kept the shock pistol in her right hand, steadied herself, and stepped onto Shel's hands. The luma shone pale green into the narrow passage.

Would she fit? Forcing her left arm and the luma ahead of her, she shimmied inward. Her hips slid in too. Encouraged, she powered forward with hips and shoulders and crawled deeper. Close places never had bothered her. Neither did darkness, but she had to see to judge distance. She must take the very first upward branch. Monu had stopped howling. She might be waiting to strike.

Daken Erwin stomped out of the sleeping cabin. Gering had refused to untie his wrists or recant his treason. The low-commoner had insisted that his mind was his own, and—worse—that Daken Erwin, his noble master and lifetime employer, had no right to trespass in his mind like . . . like a Sentinel! That untied, Daken might endanger them all.

The lounge had darkened. Only Monu's corridor gleamed. Sentinel Harris sat on the lounger, holding one foot with both hands. Sentinel Mattason stood opposite her Sentinel partner, next to a cut-open hole in the very bulkhead where Monu had first appeared to them. What had they done to her?

"Where's the wastling?" he demanded.

Shelevah glanced into the black hole in the bulkhead.

"With my dagger?"

The mind-crawler actually laughed. "Is that all you care about?"

Balling his bound fists, he marched across the lounge toward the glimmer of light.

"No!" Uri Harris dropped his foot onto the deck.

They were too slow to stop him. He passed into the arched passageway and onward, into Monu's central bridge. Something dangled from the ceiling under those brilliant lights. "I am here," he shouted. "You honor the bold, and I am the only one willing." He circled in place. "Loose me, and I can help you fight off the rest of them." Their bizarre offer—forgiveness, as if he needed to apologize for anything he ever had done—clanged in his mind like a hideous bell.

Monu's deep, feminine voice seemed to call out of every bulkhead above and around him. "You attempted to kill her."

"She deserved it," he declared. "She has always been obstinate. She still refuses to come to you. But I am here." He raised his crossed palms toward her ceiling. Now was his hour. "You will find me fine company, a strong competitor, a guide to this part of the Whorl. I know which worlds have the best resources. Make me a companion ship!"

Monu spoke slowly, evenly, as always. "Lady Firebird knows how to lay down her life for a cause. It will be a sad waste to kill her, but as soon as I take you, if she will not come to me, then I will kill her."

He laughed. "Yes, take me. And to be frank, Firebird Angelo was born to be wasted. That is why we call them wastlings. I am ready to become your companion. I will challenge and inspire you."

"You are three times a traitor," Monu said dispassionately. "To her, and to me, and now, you offer to betray other worlds in your Whorl. I was in no rush to kill the others. You are different."

Startled, he turned aside. A hatch appeared where there had been no hatch. It slid across the corridor.

Closing him in.

21: FOUR SABOTEURS

sotto voce, sung in a soft undertone

Six meters into Monu's capillary system, Firebird crawled forward, keeping her head down. Her neck was already starting to ache. She heard screaming not far away. The voice sounded falsetto. Maybe Daken finally pushed someone too far.

Daken was no longer her problem. She'd done her duty by him, more than he deserved. It felt good to stretch out her body, to hold the pocket luma aloft and push against bulkheads with her shoulders, hips, knees, and toes. She'd done a lot of this when she was a girl. Seams and slight protrusions slid past. The way was mostly smooth, but she couldn't help pressing against the sniffer's pillar. It made a long lump under her chest, and it hurt. Those midline nerves weren't blocked.

The screaming continued. Though tempted to ask Shel what was happening, she maintained interlink silence. She might be safer if Monu didn't know precisely where she was. Still, when Shel cut into that bulkhead, Monu had responded. She had to know or guess what Firebird was attempting.

There was shoulder room to keep her shock pistol high and ready. That was assuring. She had no idea how many charges Gering had used on the pistol he'd given her, so she must save at least five charges on her own to surge the shielding. She had fifteen to use and must count on no more. After what happened to Uri in the bridge, she could only hope Monu didn't have any of those electric grids in her inner parts. She also hoped that she'd guessed right about Monu only having interactive surfaces in the crew-access areas. No human could see his or her internal organs. That also gave her hope.

And Monu seemed to be busy. That falsetto screaming barely paused for breath.

A dark opening appeared overhead. *Go fifty meters up*, she reminded herself. *Then left.* She curled up tightly and shoved her uncooperative left arm into the vertical passage. Shining bulkheads vanished into darkness up there. If she slipped, it would be a long slide back down.

So I won't slip. She forced both shoulders upward, wriggled her feet against the surface behind her, and gave a push.

The screaming weakened.

Shel? Uri's subvocalization carried a note of urgency. He sat crosswise on the lounger, feet up. His right boot sole looked scorched.

Abandoning the cut-open bulkhead, Shel stepped to the lounger. *Do you need another pain block?* Unsettling screams echoed out of Monu's corridor. Apparently, she was executing justice. Whatever she might be doing to the Grand Duke, Shel had no pity to spare for him, and it meant Monu's attention was elsewhere.

Uri's glance flicked back and forth. He answered in Ehretan, "No. We must trace those . . . seeding passages now." He drew out his pad. "We have the locations."

"Do you need me yet?" she responded in Old Colonial. "If not, I will track and assist." *Firebird.* No need to tell him who she meant.

A flurry of movement startled her. Dodis Gering, who had stood near the now-blocked corridor, dashed to the freestanding workstation. He seized a long-handled heavy tool and stalked down the corridor. Seconds later, Shel heard metal bashing metal.

She admired his courage. But if Monu could use bulkheads as weaponry, she might retaliate. If that happened, Shel must break interlink silence and warn Firebird.

"Go ahead." Uri motioned. "I will signal if I need you."

Shel was tempted to call down the corridor and remind Gering to conserve air, but if Gering could keep Monu distracted, it might improve Firebird and Uri's chances. Even old-fashioned muscle was helpful.

Uri sat with his interlink, eyes closed.

She considered initiating contact, either via interlink or by quest-pulse, to let Firebird know that apparently, Monu could not use bulkheads as weapons. No, if Monu didn't try to wound or kill Firebird in there, Fi would draw that conclusion herself. The bulkhead wound Shel had carved gaped like a missile strike. Monu hadn't repaired it.

Was Monu conserving fuel?

Firebird angled her right shoulder and left hip against opposite bulkheads, braced herself, and continued upward. *Fourteen.* Brace. Push. *Fifteen.* Brace. Push. *Sixteen.* She must try to turn left—she still felt certain which way was left—after the count hit a hundred. She'd always had a good sense of direction, but if she missed the target . . .

I won't miss. Seventeen. Brace. Push.

The screaming faded to an agonized hiccupping.

It stopped.

Daken Erwin, she mocked the ritual words of a wastling's final geis orders, *your service to Netaia has ended.*

Now what would Monu do? *Eighteen.* Brace. Push.

A meter over her head, out of the shiny green-lit walls, there emerged a ring like a heart's valve. It slowly closed inward, similar to the way the ceiling had dropped.

So much for stealth. Firebird shimmied faster, touched her shock pistol to the crawlway's edge, and stroked the trigger. The narrowing stopped. Relieved, she pushed her left arm through. Right shoulder. Then her head. The numb left shoulder, and finally, her hips.

The shoulder felt weak, and it left a dark streak on and above the valve-like constriction. By the pale-green light, this didn't look remotely like blood. That helped, but the spot would be slippery, and she'd come a long way up.

"Shel," she said softly, "she knows where I am."

"Are you all right?" answered the voice in her ear.

"So far." She still could count on fourteen charges to use en route. She rested a foot on that new constriction and used it as a blessedly firm step to propel herself upward. "How's Uri?"

"All right."

I'm coming, Monu. In her mind she saw Brennen and Kiel, hunched over a scanbook.

Another constriction appeared. She shocked it away. *Thirty-two.* Brace. Push. She imagined Kinnor "flying" his jet-scoot in front of a wide window. *Thirty-three.* Brace. Push. She remembered Kiel, pointing out a viewport to ask about the firebreak, the trees cut down to protect the rest of the forest.

Let me be the firebreak for my sons, she prayed. One of those boys might be Boh-Dabar, or might father him. But if she failed, they could be turned to brown sludge.

Another constriction. Another shock burst gone. She tried to shimmy faster. "Help me, Shel?"

She felt the quest-pulse as a quick wash of urgency. Imagining Brennen back on base, falling into bereavement shock after the fleet fired through Monu's disabled shields, made her heart hurt. He was strong, though. He would live on. *This is for you!* Brace. Push. Her neck and right shoulder ached, but her whole left side remained numb, thanks to Shel.

By pale-green light, another protrusion appeared, narrowing more quickly than before. Thirteen pushes later, there came another. She surged them away, counting shock charges instead of meters. If Monu knew where she was, why didn't she just block a passage farther ahead?

Was Monu playing her like a skitter in the palace ponds?

A thunderous crash startled Shel, breaking the urgent prayer she'd settled into. Gering had not reappeared, but his clanging had stopped. Uri still sprawled on the lounger, lost in what looked like a sustained quest-pulse. He had to be tracing circuitry, looking for those pod-launching chutes, ignoring his burned feet. *Help him,* she begged the Speaker. *And Firebird. And Gering.*

From Monu's corridor came a groan. Gering emerged, wearing a look of defeat, his broad shoulders slumped, his silver hair plastered down. Tears streaked his cheeks. "Monu has killed again," he said.

"Daken?"

He nodded.

Recalling the screams, she didn't ask for details. Instead, she simply said, "I am sorry. He was your life for many years."

He covered his face with those powerful hands.

Uri straightened abruptly and said in Ehretan, "I believe I destroyed one line. I shall try for another."

"How is your energy? Are you in pain?" Could he keep this up?

"I am fine."

"How is my lady?" Gering asked.

"I'll check." Shel sent a probe deep into the ship's bowels. Feeling a flicker of satisfaction, she used the interlink. "Progress?"

A whisper answered. "About to go horizontal again. Found a passage in the right direction."

Shel relayed the message to Gering.

He shook his head sadly. "I do not think we shall see her again."

"We will," Shel answered. "On one side of the Crossing or the other."

Brennen gripped steering yoke and throttle rod. Acceleration had not eased. In the right seat beside him, Tel looked pale but kept both eyes open. Good man. Tel had proved an apt Inquirer, curious about the faith's promises and origin. Brennen wished he could mention the Boh-Dabar prophecies about his family, but by voice-command, that knowledge still was restricted to consecrants, even though the Shuhr had proved that they knew all about it.

The tearing heart-pain of bereavement had not struck. Burkenhamn had given him full sensor access from base. On the little ship's main screen, he was about to cross from one warship's cone of fire into another. Every ship had Monu in striking range.

And Mari. And Uri, and Shel.

He would have to cut acceleration to give Tel the steering controls.

Not yet, not yet. He must resist self-confidence. *Power and might are in your hand, Holy One. Great is your mercy. Do not let them suffer!*

Firebird had, in fact, found a horizontal passage that suited her sense of direction. Bracing herself to get into it without falling was tricky. Still, once she left the vertical, she didn't have to brace so hard. She crawled almost comfortably for several minutes, but either this passage was longer than it looked on the charts, or else she was tiring. Probably both. Both shoulders hurt, despite Shel's pain block. She'd wriggled Gering's shock pistol out of her pocket. She could only imagine what this must be doing to the muscles Daken sliced and the shoulder itself.

If that screaming had been Daken, he would knife no more wastlings, and poor Esme Rogonin wouldn't have to marry the beast. That thought energized her. If there'd been anything to Netaia's false faith, he might have suffered so much in dying that he could have gone directly to bliss. Supposedly.

But Monu seemed to have stopped trying to block her. Did Monu still think she was in the vertical shaft?

Several minutes later, something moved in the green glow ahead. Firebird froze, heart sinking, as a reflective metal panel began dropping in front of her. It was shiny enough to mirror the luma's green light, and it was distant enough that a shock burst would have no effect. She couldn't achieve contact.

She fired Gering's pistol anyway. Twice. But inexorably down came the panel, as if on a hinge, making a faint groan.

It was too far ahead. This time, she'd have to use Uri's crystace.

Just as well. She had only six bursts left on the reliable weapon. She pushed forward. She ought to be getting close to that central chamber.

Another mechanical groan came from behind her, its pitch slightly higher. She had no room to twist and look back, but she understood. Monu had been playing her. Now, she was stopped. Maybe at some final security barrier.

If it was, and she could get through it, she might have arrived.

The groan ahead ended with a lethal-sounding clang. Another clang came from behind.

Not just stopped. Trapped.

She drew a deep breath. Air would fail quickly in this small space. "Shel," she murmured, "she's got me. I need to use Uri's crystace."

With our blessing, Shel's voice whispered.

Arching her back, Firebird pulled her right arm close. Air came first. Centimeter by centimeter, she worked the oxygen sniffer out of the front of her shipboards. She rested it on the passage in front of her and pushed the luma down into her left sleeve cuff, dimming but not quite extinguishing its light. She shifted her shock pistol to her numb left hand and let Gering's rest next to the sniffer.

Then, carefully, she slid Uri's crystace from the sheath, praying. *I'm not entitled to this, Mighty Singer. But your people loaned it to me, and I am thankful.*

Bits of an Adoration sang softly in her memory:

> My mortal enemies surround me;
> I am caught, they have tracked me down. . . .

I am their prey.

O Holy One, save me by your hand....

She touched the sonic activator. The singing crystal blade emerged. She almost couldn't see it in this dim light.

Clenching the crystace, she pushed it into the left edge of the entrapping panel. It barely sank in. Plainly, it hadn't cut through. She didn't have the room or the strength to execute Shel's graceful full-body slices. Arching her back again, and working her elbow to the farthest angle the passage would allow, she pried the weapon back and forth. Pulled it free. Lay panting.

Monu's dreadful voice came out of the bulkheads, sounding more mechanical than ever. "You make a noble effort. You could have come to me easily. I shall enjoy traveling with you."

The crystace still sang its piercing note. A golden spark danced across her field of vision.

Low oxygen. She needed to drop the crystace to use the sniffer. Pressing it to her face, she pleaded. *Mighty Singer, is this it? Will I die trapped here, without doing the job?* How could he let that happen? She was willing to give her life for others, but what if she died and Monu triumphed anyway? For one black moment, she despaired.

Then came the turn. Self-pride had fueled those thoughts about "doing the job." Whoever promised that brave efforts would succeed? How many people had died unknown, in catastrophe or disease or in a war they might have hated, without accomplishing some noble goal? Another line from the Adorations sang in her mind: *Though the Whorl be destroyed, I will rejoice in you. You are my strength.*

She pushed the sniffer's business end into her nostrils for another deep breath. The air tasted like sunrise in a conifer forest, like the sweet air at Hesed House, where she'd been consecrated into this age-old faith.

"Shel?" She exhaled the name with a breath. Drew another deep one from the sniffer. Monu would hear this, but it didn't matter. "It's too thick to cut through."

"I'll see if I can help. Give me half a minute."

A scurrying noise came from overhead. She rotated her left arm, pushing out the pocket luma she'd tucked into her sleeve. Its pathetic light shone upward. Half a shimmy ahead, in a hand-width opening, one of the little maintenance bots they'd already suspected dropped onto the surface where she lay. She raised her left arm—it actually could move in that direction—and clubbed it with the butt of her shock pistol. The motion didn't hurt. It probably should have.

"Monu." Firebird spoke loudly. "You are too powerful to realize it, but what you need is mercy." *There, Brennen. If this creature still has a soul, at least I said something. Is it enough?* She pictured his face. It wore a slight frown.

What else would he have said? "Your soul is stained with millions of deaths. Maybe billions. But they are in the Holy One's hands. Yours is still in doubt. Ask for mercy, Monu. Ask forgiveness for your soul." Pointless, she guessed. Monu was too powerful to realize she needed mercy, and she probably had no soul.

Monu's voice buzzed above her. "There is no such thing. Do not fight me any longer. You will join me now."

"Never," Firebird retorted. "Never!" She gripped Uri's crystace.

"Then you choose to die."

"Let me go. Open the way."

"I regret your choice. It means that your world will be forgotten. Still, I will make your death easy, since I honor you. I shall also not use your empty shell for fuel. I shall launch it into your sun." Down through the overhead hatch slid a cluster of long, thin metal prongs at the end of a fat hose. Prongs that would hold a living head.

Seizing the crystace again, Firebird shrank away. "What will happen to you when you die, Monu? Someday, you will wear out." The shining prongs flexed inward and outward, grasping and releasing. At their center spun a round blade. It reflected green light. In her mind, she saw Glin-Erris's body and the strange marks on his forehead, scalp, and neck.

"I shall not die," Monu said. "You crawling things all shall die. But unlike your treacherous shipmate, I shall honor you. You have already given me inspiration. So lie still. There will be little pain."

Shel's voice came over the link at that moment, and Firebird felt a burst of energy arrive on a quest-pulse. "Try again," Shel's voice said in her ear. "Try the panel again."

She couldn't reach it, not with this thing coming toward her and blocking her way. With her knees braced against the passage walls, she had just enough room to bend her right arm. To pull it back.

The thing whirled toward her, its blade spinning faster. "Simply hold still," the voice buzzed. "I can kill slowly or quickly. You have earned quick."

Caught between faith and fury, Firebird straightened her arm, dropping Uri's singing blade across the grasping metal fingers. Three of them shattered. Bits of metal clattered into the passage.

She must strike higher up. She rolled onto her back and aimed for the hose-like line linking those fingers with the maintenance opening. The crystace cut it like butter. The apparatus clattered down in front of her. She sliced it to bits, using the flat of the crystace to push the still-spinning blade aside. She must crawl past those blades carefully, if she could get through the panel.

"Die slowly, then," Monu's voice said. "As your air fuel goes away. But there will be no pain. Then I must refuel."

Firebird wrenched and twisted her body. "I felt that pulse, Shel. Can you do it again, when I cue you?"

The sniffer had restored some energy too. She seized it again and breathed deep and managed to pocket Gering's shock pistol. Twisting her spine all the way down, and ignoring new pain between her shoulder and neck, she slanted both shoulders. Her right elbow moved. Clinging to the crystace meant losing her grip on the sniffer. She levered herself even farther backward, into a brace against the new panel behind her. The surface below now had another slippery stripe. "Now, Shel!"

She felt the gift of strength. Planting both feet, she stiffened her shoulder and spine and drove her body forward. Metal vaporized along the crystace's atom-thin line. She felt the sudden release of an exiting blade.

"Yes! It's through!" She drew the blade along the panel's low edge. Swapping crystace for sniffer, she gulped another frantic breath and made another cut up the opposite side.

She hoped the opening was wide enough. Shimmying forward, she thrust her skull against the panel, which gave. Just slightly. Not far enough. She pushed again. Twisted her neck. Tried to push upward to create herself a door.

Another glimmering star danced in her vision. Air, she needed air! Extra energy from Shel had meant burning more oxygen. Retreating half a meter, she felt the sniffer pass under her belly. Farther back, with a desperate twist of her spine, she pushed onto it one more time. Sweet air!

Struck by inspiration—literally—she closed her teeth on the sniffer's business end. She slid forward again, still gripping the singing crystace.

Hold onto them, she told herself, *or die.* She shut her eyes and made one more push. Metal gave way. She was through.

Shel sat close to Uri, lending epsilon strength. As soon as she'd helped Firebird, Uri had folded forward, questing for another launching chute. The ceiling had stopped dropping. That was no comfort, if it meant Monu was focused on Firebird.

"Where are you now?" she murmured into the interlink.

No answer came.

Barely able to see by the glow through her sleeve, Firebird crawled into a larger area with a slightly higher ceiling. Another half-meter passage led off to her right. Another opened up at eleven o'clock high.

The central chamber. What security measures did Monu have in here?

Monu's voice blasted so loudly her ears rang. It sounded higher pitched than before. "If you think life is such a holy thing, you have no right to try and destroy me."

Was that fear pitching Monu's voice toward soprano? "I have that right!" Firebird yelled back. "You destroy entire worlds—people, animals, forests, croplands—to fuel yourself. And you have yet to convince me that you are alive." She dropped her voice and murmured, "Shel, do we have any scans of that chamber over the bridge?" She couldn't remember.

Shel didn't answer. Maybe this chamber was interlink-shielded.

A shriek drowned out anything Shel might have said. It blasted out of every bulkhead around, above, and below her, no falsetto scream but a full-throated blast in several octaves. It had to be sonic security. It could leave her deaf or dead. She wanted to drop everything and cover her ears as she crawled farther into the new low chamber. The luma fell from her sleeve.

Ahead and below, a tangle of tubes and connectors protruded from a rounded object twice the size of a skull and the same shape as the ship. It was the wrong shape to be the shielding nexus, but with all those connectors, it had to be something vital.

The shrieking crescendoed.

She pushed onto her knees, lowered her hand, and seized the crystace. She sliced a connector.

The shriek became a scream. "No!"

Rattled but encouraged, she cut another connector. The shrieking dropped to a howl. "No! No!"

Silence fell. Firebird's brain stopped vibrating. Looking up and seizing the sniffer, she spotted a trapezoidal object embedded in a bulkhead. Almost exactly at eye level.

Glory! It was the shielding nexus.

Another star danced across her field of vision, but she dropped the sniffer. *Take me, Mighty Singer, and let the fleet take this thing that calls itself Monu.* She seized her shock pistol and knee-crawled to the trapezoidal object. Firing one-handed, she discharged both pistols, one after the other. A red light appeared on her own weapon's handgrip. It had died before Gering's. *There, Brenn. Strike!* She squeezed Gering's trigger once more. *Strike now, for our sons and Netaia!*

22: STRIKE
affrettando, hurrying onward

Devair Burkenhamn leaned over the tri-D well. He had loved that wastling soldier-child. She'd won a longer, better life than anyone could have expected, along with the honor she'd openly craved. He respected her enemy-turned-lover, as well. Frankly, he'd envied the way that Brennen Caldwell danced with authority, generally following but sometimes well ahead. How Caldwell had managed not to fall off the fast track baffled him. As marshal, he'd helped by sending Prince Tel to that hangar, but the burden of command lay heavy tonight. Only minutes remained on the attack clock. The order must be given, in the hope they could overwhelm those shields. Those seeding pods must not be launched.

"Sir!" An excited voice interrupted his thoughts. "Look!"

Down in the tri-D well, the flamelike net of shielding around the red ovoid was flickering. It went out.

He whirled toward the comm station.

"General Caldwell!"

Brennen had just cut full-power acceleration when the DS-215's comm shouted in his headset. For a moment, he could sit almost comfortably in his inclined flight seat. He fingered the comm, glanced toward Tel—who seemed to be handling fast flight well—and responded. "Caldwell."

Marshal Burkenhamn's voice carried a note of awe. "Monu's shields just dropped. Completely."

Mari, was that you?

"They did it!" Tel exclaimed. Brennen caught his glance. "Are we going to attack?"

The marshal was still speaking. "You're not in shock?"

"Negative." Brennen dared to hope. "She's alive, Marshal. The whole team might be alive. Can we give them ten minutes to evacuate?"

There was a short pause. "Ten minutes, but no more. Unless we strike now, Monu can launch the world seeds. Or her debris can hit the planet."

The correct response would have been *you must strike.*

Brennen managed to say, "The timing is in your hands, Marshal. I am off duty." He prayed, then. *Please, Holy One.* "The ship is yours, Tel." He swiveled away from the slanting display and reached for the splayed-finger RIA array. It fit under his flight cap. If he and Shel could put the unshielded Monu in t-sleep, Netaia's fatal strike would surely succeed. Was he close enough to link with Shel?

Probably, if Shel was listening for him.

He could only hope and pray that Marshal Burkenhamn would wait to strike.

His heart cried, *Get out of there, Mari!*

Devair Burkenhamn leaned on the edge of the tri-D well. From four small ports along Monu's ventral side, threat-red drones emerged. He felt his face go pale.

They had relied on their best estimates to calculate that attack clock, but Monu had honored no estimates. Her world seeds were on their way.

"Carriers," he shouted, "launch fighters. Sending targeting data."

With Monu's shielding disabled, returning through the tunnels seemed pointless. Firebird's sniffer was in the red zone, anyway. Just like the shock pistols.

"Your effort is for nothing." Monu's voice replaced the sonic shrieking. "I have seeded your world for your future use. Come to me and honor Netaia's memory."

"No!" Firebird screamed. She swung the crystace left and right, cutting connectors around the ovoid object that might be Monu's control module. Fury empowered her. She clenched her teeth. "This is for Kinnor."

"No." Monu's voice was no longer mechanical. "Stop!"

"That one's for Kiel." Another slice. The connectors were surprisingly accessible, most likely for the maintenance robots' convenience.

"Stop, please, stop."

Was she finally hearing emotion? "This, and this, and this is for Brenn."

A sharp yelp answered each cut.

But was this for nothing but revenge? She crawled forward to rest her full weight on the ovoid object. "And this," she panted, "is for Netaia!" She sliced through the last connector, leaning into the crystace to cut the bulkhead beneath it.

A cotillion of stars danced in the chamber's thin air, almost as bright as her fading luma. She grabbed the sniffer for a final deep breath, pulled up her feet underneath her, braced against the ceiling, and stomped on the object with her last strength. *We make the Crossing together, Monu.*

The ovoid object dropped beneath her, down into the bridge cabin below. Firebird fell with it. Down . . . slowly down . . .

Slowly?

She landed atop the object on a broad, flat deck. She bounced up again, nearly to the bridge's curved ceiling. Or what had been the ceiling.

Gravity was gone.

But so were the oxygen-starvation stars. Deactivating the crystace, she gulped air. It was thin down here, but it was thicker than it had been overhead. A hatch lay at the chamber's edge, tossed aside, twisted and bent. "Great is your mercy," she sang softly. "Great is your mercy!"

The lounge lights died. Standing next to Shel, Gering floated up off the deck. "What just happened?" he cried.

Shel clutched upholstery two-handed. "Maybe the fleet struck." She counted ten seconds, waiting for a blast of annihilation. Waiting to hear the Bright Ones singing praise.

Instead, she heard someone who was no Bright One singing weakly in the ominous corridor.

Uri gasped and opened his eyes, seeming to return to them from his quest-pulse. "She launched! She launched four seeding pods. I could only disable two of the chutes." He murmured an oath as he pulled out a luma, faced the exit hatch, and kicked off. Eerie shadows crossed the bulkheads around them. He'd always had awesome agility in zero-G.

But Monu had initiated catastrophe. Shel had to shield herself against Uri's frustration, almost despair. Her own was awful enough.

Gering floated upward again. "I can't—"

"Grab something," Shel directed, realizing that even the furniture might float.

Uri reached the exit hatch. He slapped its control panel. The hatch slid open several centimeters, sucking dust motes into the opening.

Monu had opened the space doors hours ago. She had not closed them.

Uri sent the exit hatch shut. "That singing. It's Firebird. Get her! We've got to get off this ship."

And escape—to where? Not to Netaia. The fleet might blow Monu to bits momentarily, but unless they intercepted every one of those pods, a world was about to die.

Shel pulled out a fresh luma, activated it with a squeeze, and kicked off toward the corridor.

Firebird's numb left arm wanted to float. Momentarily disoriented, she tried to grab it and sheathe the crystace. Uri should get it back, if the Holy One let them reunite before the fleet's blast arrived. She let go of the discharged and useless shock pistols and gave them a push. They floated away.

The fleet must destroy the world seeds. She had done all she could.

Another pale light floated toward her. It lit a long, arched corridor. "Shel?" she coughed. "Shel, I'm here." She just wanted to rest. *Mighty Singer, if this is the death you have for me, comfort Brenn.*

The green glimmer arrived. "Here," Shel cried. "Take Daken's sniffer. What in the Whorl is that thing?"

Firebird pushed the mechanical egg shape toward Shel. "I think it's Monu's brain. Take it to the fleet if you can."

Shel's brighter luma lit the chamber. A metal claw, like the one that had just tried to kill her, dangled out of a bulkhead. It was streaked with something dark and wet. A two-legged shape drifted against the bridge's other side, also darkly smeared, and the far end—the head end, which she couldn't see well—was surrounded in zero-G by a halo of dark droplets. Orange piping decorated the black breeches. She recalled the grim screaming. If that was Daken, he'd gotten what he richly deserved. *Please, I don't want to look any closer. I just want to rest. I am finished.*

"Breathe on this," Shel ordered. Like swimmers maneuvering underwater, they swapped Shel's proffered sniffer for the half-meter ovoid.

A helpless laugh bubbled up, along with Firebird's returning energy. "I didn't consider gravity," she managed to exclaim between rich gulps of oxygen. "I've been on ships with gravidics for so long, but there's no actual gravity out here—"

Shel dug in a belt pocket. "You're fading," she said firmly. "Get this down." She pushed something small and dark at Firebird's lips.

It was horribly bitter. She tried to spit it out.

"No," Shel barked, covering Firebird's mouth with one hand. "Swallow that, or you're dead. We're all dead. Netaia's dead. She launched seeds, Lady Fi."

"I know." Firebird felt the push of voice-command. Gagging and chewing her tongue to create saliva, she managed to swallow most of the kass capsule. It tried to come up. She swallowed harder.

Shel was already tugging her right arm and pushing them both along the corridor, shoving the control module ahead of them. It bounced off a bulkhead. "Uri's at the hatch. Help me, Firebird!"

The hatch. *Cometesse*, and a chance for survival, but where would they go?

Stim caps worked fast. Firebird felt it hit her system with a rush. The false calm she'd managed, thinking she could gratefully die, evaporated like Thyrian dew. The fleet must have delayed, maybe so that she and Shel and Uri might escape.

Now all of Netaia would pay.

No! She kicked a bulkhead, trying to help Shel keep moving.

Beyond the arch, the barely green-lit lounge seemed enormous after that close shimmying. Uri stood at the exit hatch, clutching its frame. "Got her?" he shouted.

"Yes, and something that might be Monu's brain. Can you manage Glin-Erris?"

"Yes," he shouted back. "There'll be airflow when I open this."

Shel wrapped a warm arm around Firebird's waist.

Something creaked in the darkness. A gentle breeze became a serious wind. It pulled them toward Uri, who crouched against the hatch's edge. Shel grabbed his hand. "Don't lose your sniffer," she shouted at Firebird.

Firebird tightened her grip on it, peering ahead. Beyond the hatch lay utter black. She blinked. Could they get onto the transport without blowing out into vacuum like the Luxian pilots?

Blow out, she reminded herself. *Blow out a thin stream of air, and you might survive near vacuum for longer, if the nitrogen bends don't get you first.*

On the other hand, they had been breathing pure O_2 from these sniffers, and Monu's nitrogen was low from the start.

"Go," Uri ordered, holding his sniffer close to his chin. "Firebird, Gering, grab anything you can. Try to slow down."

They bounced along the short passage that had been so bright. Dusty wind blew past, chilling her, but that wind meant there still was air. She couldn't feel her left arm. Shel seemed to have shifted her grip from her waist to that hand. Another strong hand gripped her right shoulder. That had to be Gering. Uri had mentioned Gering.

The passage ended. Shel's subvoice was loud in Firebird's mind. *Kill the lumas,* she ordered. *Maybe we can see by the stars, if our eyes adjust.*

The landing bay fell dark again. Wind whooshed past.

"Can you see it?" Uri called aloud.

Firebird clung to a bulkhead protrusion, holding the sniffer's business end against her nostrils. Gering dropped one hand from her shoulder, probably holding on, too.

That's not working, Shel subvocalized again. *Here.* She made a pitching motion. Another green glimmer sprang up and floated away. For a few moments, Firebird saw the whole landing bay, including *Cometesse*'s open hatch and extruded landing ramp. She saw Uri, too, close by. Clutching the corpse-shrouded body of Glin-Erris in one hand, Uri gripped a bulkhead protrusion with the other.

She hesitated. In zero-G, if they hit *Cometesse* too hard, they might push it right out into space. *Hurry,* she wanted to cry. *Hurry!*

Uri lowered his sniffer once more. "Grab a ramp railing if you can," he directed. "Ready, Shel? Gering?"

Firebird peered forward. Could she help, with her one good arm holding the sniffer to her face?

"Here we go," Uri called.

Firebird released her grip and lowered the sniffer. She started exhaling.

Brennen touched control panels.

She is alive.

Fighters were swooping in, targeting four pod-sized blips on his screens. Just four seeding pods? Uri and Shel must have disabled two launch chutes. Two of the pods, then, must be destroyed, unlaunched, with Monu.

And Monu's shields were down.

Get off that ship, Mari! And Uri, and Shel. He'd always been able to quest-pulse to Mari over startling distances, but he could not send verbalized thoughts that far. He made it a prayer instead. Unquestionably, she was already doing her best.

Tel's head looked small over the broad shoulders of his life suit. He sounded surprisingly confident. "Straight course, no deceleration."

Brennen activated the RIA unit and let it catch his epsilon carrier. He sent the quest-pulse anyway, touched her familiar presence, tried to send assurance. Then he sent a second epsilon pulse, this one to Shel. More than Mari's touch, he needed an update. The big ovoid's landing bay still yawned open.

Mari! This time, he tried to send it through the RIA unit. *Mari, where are you all?*

Shel's stronger epsilon savor answered instead. He felt a hot swirl of urgency and an answering mental cry. *Wait!*

Had Firebird sensed a quest-pulse?

Impossible. Brenn couldn't be out here.

Gering flailed all four limbs. Together, they sailed in dim darkness up to the landing ramp and almost past it. Firebird grabbed a railing with her good hand and curled herself into a ball. Shel caught the other railing. Pushing off ramp struts, they swam into the open hatch. Uri made it, too, pushing Gering ahead of him and pulling Glin-Erris's body behind. The transport's entry hatch shut.

The wind stopped, but Firebird kept floating. *Cometesse*'s gravidics were also non-functional. She clutched her sniffer and inhaled hard.

Slapping a panel over the hatch to slip-seal it, she hit the emergency striplights as well. Shel and the others floated at crazy angles.

Firebird seized a grab bar and hauled herself into the cockpit. "Uri," she cried, "help me!"

Shel hung back in *Cometesse*'s galley. *Wait, Brennen, wait!* she returned. *We need air!* And why in the Whorl was he close enough to subvocalize?

Dodis Gering clung to the metal table, clutching his sniffer. He would probably recoil if she subvocalized, so she lowered her sniffer to speak aloud. "Your charge is almost gone." She pointed at the yellow light near the pillar's end. "Let me put you in t-sleep. I need permission." Drat those Codes. If he didn't give it, she should put him down anyway. Every sniffer she could free up would be one more for Firebird and Uri in the cockpit.

Would Gering trust her?

He did. "You do fight fair, Sentinel Mattason," he said. "Do what you must."

Go, go, Firebird urged herself. The kass cap was kicking fully now. She seemed to see everything through a blurred haze. Dual controls, good! She slammed her right palm onto *Cometesse*'s starting cycle. Instrument lights flickered on. Wrestling herself into the nearest seat felt like trying to swim upside down. Buckled in, she felt steadier. Comm? Did they have comm? Could they let the fleet know they were alive?

Comm was on her left. Her left arm hung useless. Her right hand shook.

"Uri!" The generator's howl dropped steadily in pitch, as it should. "I need you to talk, and I can't fly one-handed!" She hit every control she could reach. Even if she'd had two good hands, this thing would be a beast to fly, compared with a nimble fighter.

Brennen finally heard Shel answer. *Monu's disconnected. We've got her control module on board. Uri's helping Firebird launch. Hold fire, hold fire!*

Naturally, Mari was piloting. Though wounded. How badly?

And . . . control module?

Monu launched four seeding drones, Brennen answered. *Get out of there!* He eyed the six pale screens representing three-dimensional space around him. The launched fighters were maneuvering crazily, chasing pods, firing and tuning their lasers.

Why weren't the pods already destroyed? Did they also have powerful shields? "I have it, Tel." He took the controls and vectored the messenger ship into a long arc out of the big ships' cones of fire, back toward the planet.

Firebird pointed at the comm panel.

Uri lunged toward it. "Netaians approaching the enemy ship," he shouted, "hold fire! This is the Federate transport *Cometesse*, now departing!" He turned to her. "Brennen's close. They know Monu launched her seeds."

Brenn was close? They'd almost escaped—but—

No time to think. Looking out the vast space door, she spotted the huge, shadowy ships of the line. She was blinking up the barrel of Netaia's firepower, and Monu, though helpless now, still might destroy her home world. *Strike!* she wanted to shout. *Forget us. Take Monu's ship! There are still pods aboard!*

The generator's howl quieted. *Cometesse*'s main engines thrummed. Firebird pointed again. "Pull that yellow lever. Grab the control yoke." Stars shone beyond the space door. Real stars, not the dancing kind.

A throaty roar surrounded her. Green go-ahead lights appeared. "We have drive! Steady the yoke! Push!" She leaned on the throttle. They only needed speed. No steering, no ability to go evasive, and this transport had no shields. Friendly fire could easily get them.

She released the brake. The space door seemed to leap toward them. More stars appeared, overhead and below, to starboard and port.

Uri shouted at the comm panel again. "Transport *Cometesse* is launching. Hold fire, this is the Federate transport *Cometesse!*"

Bracing against her seat back, she pushed all her remaining strength against the throttle. *Faster, faster!*

Uri touched his earpiece, and his voice took on a triumphant note. "Yes, yes, we're off." He leaned over to address her. "Maintain course. Fast as we can make her move."

Was she done? Surely she was done. Her body was done, but her brain was full of kass caps. She stared through the fore screen into space.

A quest-pulse brushed her again, carrying a scent and savor of comfort and warning. She melted into the sensation. *Brennen!*

An unfamiliar voice called from the comm panel, "*Cometesse,* recover on board the cruiser *Irion*. We will catchfield you when we can. We still must stop Monu's debris and four seeding drones."

Four drones. There had been six. Uri had made their job simpler. *Bless him, Mighty Singer.* And . . . the *Irion*. It was named for her father. Which of those distant shapes was the *Irion,* so she could fall into his embrace?

Marshal Devair Burkenhamn stared at the tri-D image, scarcely able to believe that even Firebird Angelo had escaped. *Bravo, Commander.* But the peril was upon them. With a deep breath he called, "Forward subcommanders, clear an avenue for the transport *Cometesse,* then attack with all ordnance. Destroy the enemy ships. All three of them. Fighter squadrons, take out those four smaller drones and vaporize all debris. Nothing must enter our atmosphere."

23: PHOENA'S FOP

con fuoco, with fire

The *Cometesse*'s fore screen went blindingly bright. The big ships were firing. Firebird shut her eyes and buckled forward to protect her sight. A shock wave threw her against her harness. Stars seemed to plunge upward as *Cometesse* pitched. Praying she'd gained enough momentum to escape Monu's debris, she cut the engines.

Again she felt Brennen's touch. This time, it sent her unconscious.

Brennen gripped the messenger ship's steering yoke. His relief over Mari's escape faded quickly. She was badly wounded and terribly weak. Nudging her down into healing sleep had been the only help he could give her.

He pressed a resolution panel. On his pale-blue visual screens, each fighter squadron was chasing a two-meter drone. Those drones seemed to have automatic sense-and-evade technology and, of course, insanely strong shielding. Energy fire bounced off, no matter how the fighters tuned their lasers.

Uri had said they had Monu's control module on board the *Cometesse*. Brennen stretched out through the RIA link again. This time, he quested for a foreign presence.

There it was. An alpha-matrix savor like nothing he'd ever felt before. "Take it, Tel!" *Monu*. He used the stern tone of command. *Monu, answer me.*

An eerily foreign-scented presence rose to answer his quest-pulse.

The remnant, maybe, of an ancient soul. It tried to resist, thrusting epsilon power away.

He focused more tightly. *Monu!*

Her defenses gave way. *You have won. Leave me alone.*

What did you do to Lady Firebird? On his prior quest-pulse, he had felt Mari at the deathly edge of her strength. Monu had wanted to steal her soul, like Glin-Erris's. Had she almost succeeded?

She took my shields. She cut me from my body.

Is she injured? He strengthened the demand, bracing himself to go deeper into a nauseatingly foreign awareness.

She is hurt, but not by me. Then, oddly, *She is a worthy opponent. I would have honored her. You know her, then?*

We belong to each other. He projected a mental image, the tri-D recently taken with their sons in their laps.

Her savor changed to surprise. *I have seen that image. You are Brenn. Are you also a worthy opponent?*

I have tried to be. You do not need to die, Monu. Let us help you.

She shifted to anger. *They are destroying my mighty body. That is not help.*

He opened his eyes and momentarily left the RIA accord. On the six screens in front of him, an enormous debris cloud had formed at one edge. Monu's "mighty body."

We defend our homes, Monu. You would have done the same. Cannot we work together? Save you, even learn from you? You are also a human soul.

I took the last other life on my world. There is no such thing as a soul.

You are a human life, then. We would help you, if you would allow it. Build you a body that did not require others' deaths.

Her anger hardened. *I am what I have chosen to be. If that has ended, it has ended.*

That is a great loss, Monu. Something else seemed to want his tongue. He gave it. He heard himself speaking—singing, actually—words that he did not know. Was this another privilege of his family's eldest heir, one he had not heard about?

When the song ended, he felt her listening with all the strength she had left. Not knowing what he had sung, he reached for the plain, obvious truth. *You and I, and Lady Firebird, were made in a resplendent image. We are beloved, despite our failings. Ask for mercy while you live.*

He heard a response as from an even greater distance. She was losing power. *I will not live in this weakness.*

Weakness can be our great strength. As he had learned, personally. *My people also tried to be more than human. The Holy One saved us, the God of Gods.*

There is no such thing as a god, either. Incongruously, she added, *Grieve me. Sing me your Shekkah.*

Shekkah for Monu? Startled, he reached further into the distance where she seemed to be fading. *If you desire it. But Monu, you have tried to kill Lady Firebird's world.*

I still will honor her. He almost could not sense that voice now. *I need no fuel for her anymore. I show you a secret.*

Into his mind sprang an image that was already hatefully familiar, one of the ovoid seeding pods. Now, though, he saw spots gleam on its hull. *Only touch,* she explained. *Hitting solid ground. It opens them. They resist energy to survive heat in atmosphere. Honor her. Remember me.*

And she was gone.

He pulled out of the link, blinking and shaking his head. Only touch? Beside him, Tel clenched the DS-215's secondary controls.

He had it! He seized the comm. "All ships," he called. "Pods are sensitive to physical contact only. Do not use energy weapons. Missiles only. Repeat, missiles only."

On his screens, he saw the scattering drones. Difficult to pick out, they were arcing toward Netaia's night side. Three of them. Three squadrons of Netaian fightercraft scattered, chasing them.

But Monu had launched four pods.

He enlarged the center screen and spotted a pod that out-sped the others, possibly struck and boosted by a chunk of exploding debris. It would reach atmosphere in minutes.

This messenger ship should accelerate faster than anything else in the Federate inventory. But he had no missiles.

Not again, Holy One. "I'm taking over," he told Tel, seizing his control yoke. "What I'm going to attempt might not be survivable. I am sorry."

Tel blinked. He had committed himself to assisting Caldwell . . . Brennen . . . for this mission, live or die. Apparently, things had not been serious yet. They were about to get serious.

Well, he had made his peace with the mysterious Holy One. He only wished he'd told Esme goodbye. That he admired her. That he loved her.

And Lady Firebird was alive. *Please,* he begged the Holy One. *Get us back to Citangelo. I will never act Phoena's fop again.* He tried to speak firmly. "I told you. I'll assist if I can."

"Be ready for your pressure suit to reactivate, and get your helmet on. We're going full speed."

Tel's helmet was under his seat. He flailed gloved, blunted fingertips down there and found something soft and limp. At that moment, pressure hurt his hips and legs. Once again, acceleration flattened him back against the reclined seat. Brennen visibly leaned against the throttle, pushing hard. He'd explained the six-screen display. Tel concentrated on the middle one. It represented the view in front of them. Apparently, that last pod was turning sharply downward, toward the planet.

"Is it trying to evade us?" He reached down again and pulled the soft object into his lap. It looked like a transparent hood. When he pulled it over his head and pressed its edges to the suit's collar, the helmet inflated off his scalp. Fascinating, if not fashionable.

"Yes, it's evading. But this," Brennen's voice said through the helmet's speakers, "is why we brought this ship to Netaia. Testing a new stealth mode." He reached aside.

They plunged.

The pod's image went to center on that middle screen. It looked like a straight shot. Tel swallowed hard. "What can I do?"

"Just be ready for a jolt."

Caldwell had ordered the other ships to use missiles. A messenger ship had no missiles.

He was going to ram it. Up here, out of Netaia's atmosphere. They had the clear advantage of size. Probably mass too. Still . . .

Tel prayed like he had never prayed before. His arms and shoulders felt chained to the seat back, but Brennen reached aside to flick a communication switch.

"Marshal Burkenhamn," he called.

The familiar voice came in Tel's headset too. "General Caldwell. Assume that was you, starting a dive after that pod. You no longer appear on our sensors."

Brennen gave a grim nod. "Confirm stealth mode. It can't see us coming. Physical contact should explode it high enough for debris to burn up on entry. Monitor every speck. Nothing reaches the ground. Consider it," he said, and his voice went wry, "a test of your ground-to-air system." He paused. "Can you get a scan on that pod? What's its mass? How many seeds, how powerful its explosive charge?"

Only a few seconds passed. This was a little awesome, watching the man do what he had been trained to do, in the kind of spacecraft where he had been trained to do it.

"Negative," the answer came. "Can't scan through its shields. Sound familiar?"

"Yes." Like Monu herself.

The pod's image remained steady, the center of a square bull's-eye. Growing.

"General Caldwell?" The marshal's voice quieted. "If you trigger it, it's likely to splatter on you. May I remind you that you are no longer authorized—"

"Affirmative." Brennen cut him off.

Tel shuddered. Splatter? Those hideous world seeds? All over this ship? Did that mean—it had to mean—that they would not be able to land on Netaia. "Will they burn off if we re-enter?" Tel asked, making sure.

"Maybe. Most of them. Can't risk the chance that one of them gets sucked into a seam."

Tel braced his head against the seat back and blinked water from his eyes. This was the end, then.

"If we succeed," Brennen said into the microphone, "we'll send the DS-215 sunward and exit. This is my pickup request. Two survivors, if we can get extravehicular."

"Copy, General Caldwell. May your god save you," said the voice in Tel's headset.

"And you."

Exit. Extravehicular. Did that mean they would . . . jump out?

Calm. Tel roused himself. He was wearing a life suit, wasn't he? *Stay calm. Panic could kill us. Both of us.*

Brennen flicked the communication switch again. "Half a minute until impact, Tel. Unless we miss."

"You won't miss." But if Tel lived to remember this moment, it would doubtless haunt his nightmares. Bulkheads vibrated around him. "Just tell me what to do," he repeated. He hated this helplessness.

"I will. Twenty seconds. Brace against the seat back."

That wasn't difficult. Moving away from it would have been the hard thing.

"Twelve. Ten."

On the center screen, Tel spotted a small protrusion. Just off center. Off center? Would this be a miss? He squeezed his eyes shut.

"Four. Three. Go limp, Tel."

The seat and deck shuddered. His eyes flew open. Everything around him seemed to be shaking. The center screen washed out with light and went dark. Something tinkled on the hull. Debris. Debris that would destroy his world if he carried it home.

Brennen's words, *might not be survivable,* echoed in his memory. Did Brennen look frightened?

No. Simply serious. A red light blinked, backlighting his profile inside the transparent helmet-hood. "We've got hull damage," he said, covering the light with one gloved hand. "Could lose cabin pressure. That's why we're suited." He seemed calm. He had to be relying on years of training. Nothing heroic. Just doing his job.

What a job.

The ship's nose pitched upward, pushing Tel down into the seat. The cockpit was getting warm. Hot, even. They must be down in the atmosphere. Tel hadn't had time to notice that he was sweating. He noticed now.

The pressure suddenly ended. He felt light again. The bulkhead behind him now felt like *down* instead of *back.* He wished his stomach and hands were steadier. The other five screens fell dark. "Have we lost power? Steering?" he asked, dreading the answer.

"Just sensors. Steering jets are behind us."

"How do we . . . exit?" Suddenly, that didn't sound so bad. The cabin's ceiling—now it felt more like a bulkhead—looked altogether too solid.

"Same way we got in. Through the hatch. This isn't a fighter, with a canopy to blow."

"Ah." He should have known that. He drew a deep breath. *Under control. Brennen has everything under control.*

"One moment." Brennen manipulated the steering mechanism again, and the nauseating lack of orientation settled out. "New course," he said. "This ship will spend eternity inside Netaia's sun."

"But isn't it a valuable prototype?" So he'd been told.

Brennen actually laughed. "We know the tech works. We'll build another, if Regional command lets us." He hit another switch. "Stealth mode off. Now, Netaia can make sure it ends up destroyed. Has to be done." He rested a gloved hand on Tel's shoulder. "I have been extravehicular before," he said. "Suited, EV is survivable. The bad bit is over. We're alive."

"Ah." Tel managed a smile. "The view will be stunning, I think."

"But there is no knowing how long we'll be out there." Brennen unspooled something that looked like a cable from his suit's exterior. He attached the hooked end to something Tel couldn't see on his own suit. "There. We're staying together."

"May I say, sir, that it has been an honor to serve with you." Tel followed Brennen back to the hatch. There was just room to stand and walk a few steps inside this messenger ship.

Brennen touched the lock panel. Nothing happened.

"Did our impact jam the mechanism?" Adrenaline ghosted through Tel's system again. He'd actually begun to relax.

"One moment." Brennen pulled off the suit's left glove. He worked something out of his sleeve cuff.

The crystace, of course. "Leap clear," he said, "when I get this open. Don't touch the hull."

"I did understand that," Tel said lightly. He'd gladly tried to assist on this dangerous mission. He'd done nothing. He'd been no help at all.

But it looked like they were going to survive.

The humming crystace bit deep. Brennen cut a square, sealed the weapon in an exterior suit pocket, then re-gloved. He kicked at the square he had cut. The cable dangled between them.

The square didn't budge. Brennen stood motionless for two seconds. Then he said, quietly, "I do need your help, Tel. Or we're trapped in here."

Actually, Tel saw the problem. Instinctively. Something about the angle of pressure Brennen was trying to apply. "Brace against that bulkhead," Tel said, "and strengthen me."

Brennen stepped away. Tel turned and felt Brennen's hands on his back. He felt the Sentinel's kinetic strength flow into him, too.

He pushed.

The metal square burst free and floated away. The push on his back diminished. Cabin air was escaping.

"Good," Brennen exclaimed. "Now, running start, and we'll leap outward as far as we can."

First Marshal Burkenhamn stared up at a tracking display. His neck ached. He had already ordered that pickup, stat. How had the soppy Prince Tel survived that ride? The notion made him smile.

Every molecule piercing Netaia's atmosphere was being tracked. Fragments of seed or of the outer pods burned as they fell.

Off to his right on another high screen, the debris cloud that represented Monu herself shrank. Catchfield officers on board the *Irion*, the *Excellence*, and the *Resolve* were corralling deadly shrapnel. Groundside controllers and at least one patrol cruiser would monitor the cloud's passage, and the contaminated messenger craft, until the sun cleansed the Netaian system.

A recently launched patrol ship decelerated toward two drifting suited forms.

"Job well done, Battlefield Director Caldwell," he murmured. "I believe we have passed your inspection."

Carradee Angelo held aside a curtain and peered into the night sky. Blue-green meteors streaked, seemingly from a single source.

Daithi stood across the room, next to the crosstown link, beside a young page in Angelo scarlet. They were poised to send Rinnah offworld at a moment's notice. Queen Rinnah Elsbeth, already dressed for travel, had fallen asleep in her crib near the credenza.

"All good, so far," Daithi said quietly. "It's vaporizing so high that I can't imagine anything hitting the ground. Not now."

Carradee bowed her head. "Praise to the Holy One, and to our friends."

24: TWO HEIRS

cantabile, in a singing style

Firebird came awake slowly, aware of a warm presence close by, oh so close by, oh it was him, oh it was him.

She lay swimming in a warm sea full of incense. Opening her eyes would be too exhausting. She managed to move breath through her vocal cords. "You're here." *Did you get the seeds?* she thought hard at him. *Did you save Netaia?* She also felt a dull ache up and down her left side, stiff pressure across her left shoulder and down her arm to the elbow and, strangely, over one leg. But warm hands held both of hers.

Yes, the answer wafted over that warm sea. *Yes. We did. Together.*

"Brenn," she whispered. *Come on, eyes. Open! He's here!*

"No." His voice sounded like music. "Don't try to speak. Just give me your thoughts. I only woke you to assure you that you're safe. You drained every cell's energy and lost significant blood, but we're back on the ground."

Energy. Blood. It all felt dreamlike. If what he was saying was true—of course it was—her body's energy reserves would take days to recover. There were probably replenishing medications in her circulatory system.

But they had defeated Monu. His satisfaction resonated on the pair bond. A shiver of victory sent her eyes open.

He wore plain shipboards, his hair stood up in several directions, and new stress lines crossed his forehead. He looked wonderful.

She exhaled a long sigh. He leaned in to kiss her.

With his smoky-sweet presence inside her alpha matrix like this, he would pick up her thoughts. *Are the twins all right?*

He spoke aloud again. "Safe with Ahma. Uri will also be all right. The meds are treating his feet."

Hand to warm hand, mind to living mind. This was so, so, so much better than trying to communicate over a distant interlink. Turning her head left a few more degrees, she saw the green-and-white arc and monitor lights of two medical regeneration field sources, one clamped over her left shoulder and arm, and the other half-covering her left thigh. She heard them too. One hummed a minor third below the other. She groaned. *Regen. Again?*

"Again." He smiled. "Your shoulder's a mess, my dear Mari, and I don't think Daken Erwin did most of the damage. Shel and I have been talking."

"Why?" she managed aloud, glancing at her leg.

"They're stimulating new blood cells."

"Oh. Sorry," she added. "Glin . . . Erris."

Somberly he nodded. He touched her lips with a fingertip. "Rest, Mari. But I would like to see how you took down those shields."

She stared into his eyes, inviting deeper access, and felt him press down into memory—oh, oh, that feeling. She retraced her passage through the ship's capillaries and felt his deep approval, even when she confessed that she had borrowed—

"Well done." He smiled again. "Uri's crystace is also safe." Then his expression grew somber. "I spent a few last moments with Monu, using a RIA unit. She is dead now. The fleet disintegrated her control module, fearing contamination."

He had a RIA unit? Here, in the Netaia system? What else had he not told her? *How did you destroy all the seeding pods? Will you show me?*

"Later. Your heart needs to rest. Also—" He released her hands and laid his head on her chest. She threaded her fingers into his hair, closing her eyes. "I'm afraid I am guilty," he said, his voice barely audible, "of proselytizing her. I'll have to report it to the Masters back on Thyrica."

Did she—

"No."

If Monu was already a dead machine, then you couldn't have coerced her. You can use that as a defense.

"Actually, she was alive." He lifted his head to speak into her ear. "She asked me to have Shekkah sung for her."

Her eyes flew back open. Beyond Brennen was the white ceiling of a medical facility. *Monu was listening when we sang for Glin-Erris? She was touched by music after all?*

"It seems she may have been," he murmured. "I think the Holy One sang to her at the last."

Then you were right. She had a soul. And I think I might know why you—

He lifted his head. "Later, Mari. I will apologize in full when you feel stronger." He slowly sat upright, and she felt his sadness. "Yes, Monu had a soul. But she turned away, even from him."

How like Brenn to have offered mercy. Firebird pressed into the pillow. What had Monu been before she became a mechanical entity, doomed to consume whole worlds?

He raised a dark eyebrow.

"Sir?" A med in a yellow tunic appeared at his shoulder. "We're moving another bed close to this one."

He touched her forehead, but this time, she needed no help to fall into healing sleep.

Firebird rested in base housing for three days. Then, she and Brennen had business to finish.

Standing in the civilian spaceport's gate area, Esme Rogonin gently touched Firebird's shoulder sling with one hand and clung to Tel's arm with the other. Tel and Esme would shortly depart for Thyrica and deep psi-healing. Apparently, a Shuhr woman lay dead, reduced to cargo. Another, Arafel Tsadarah—currently imprisoned in medical cold-stasis—would be surgically disempowered and returned, along with her sister's body, to Mikuhr. She would live out her days among their own people.

That was more mercy than Firebird would have given a Shuhr.

Esme's green eyes looked dimmer than those of the bright-eyed ingénue Firebird had known. Firebird suspected she looked equally weary. Tel, on the other hand, seemed taller than she remembered. He wore conservative charcoal gray with an indigo kerchief peering from a pocket.

"I would have married Daken." Esme's voice was distant, bleak. "Eventually, I would have been the one stabbed and bleeding." She looked into Firebird's eyes. "Thank you, Lady Firebird. I am so sorry you're hurt. I wish you a speedy recovery."

A wheeled shuttle sped across the gate area. Shel waited outside in the groundcar with Ahma-Dara, Kinnor, and Kiel. Firebird felt awkward in the public terminal, her scarlet Electoral gown attracting too much attention. Uri stood close, both feet encased in healing cocoons, surveying the crowd for danger. So did Tel's faithful manservant, Paudan, and to her delight, Dodis Gering. Esme had already hired him.

Firebird smiled at Esme and glanced at Tel. "A better man than Daken will travel alongside you," Firebird said. "I am glad for you both."

Tel stood, straight-backed, eyes clear and shining, although subtle pain lines surrounded his eyes and crossed his forehead. Glory, it was good to see those two together.

"I believe you are right," Esme said. "Prince Tel has surprised me in many ways." She tilted her head. "Shall we meet again someday?"

"I hope so." *He has surprised me, too,* Firebird reflected. He'd helped Brennen destroy the last seeding pod, and he'd declared as an Inquirer!

Firebird wrapped her right arm around Esme's shoulder in half an embrace. Her left arm remained immobilized, except for a few daily exercises. To her disappointment, even regeneration hadn't repaired all the damage. Back at Tallis—though Brennen was urging the sanctuary at Procyel—there would be surgical reconstruction. She'd had enough "fair fight" to last a lifetime.

Probably. One never knew.

A metallic voice rang through the terminal. "They're calling you," Brennen said. He looked splendid in dress whites with the Master's star shining on his shoulder. "Holy One go with you," he told Esme and Tel, raising a hand as if in blessing.

Tel gave Brennen an awkward embrace. Paudan and Gering saluted. They all strode off.

"Oh," Firebird exclaimed, "wait!" Clutching a handful of scarlet skirt, she dashed after them. "Tel, your clairsa? I'm so sorry. We didn't have time to grab anything as we were launching. Not even our duffels." Her precious Triple Arrow was gone forever. So was Carradee's sash.

She still had Daken's dagger, though. Packed away.

Tel laughed. "That was a gift. I have better gifts of my own, now, that I am far more concerned about." He took Esme's hand again, raised and kissed it. She beamed.

As their little group disappeared toward the private transportation gate, Firebird felt Brennen's warmth at her side. "Esme and Tel go well together," she said, looking up.

"Yes." His eyes sparkled down at her. "May they be blessed by the Holy One." He took a step back. "Come on. We're barely on time." He put his arm around her and propelled her onward.

Firebird stepped into the palace's foyer and stopped, startled. Dead center, at the place of honor next to the sweet image of Rinnah and Carradee, hung her own formal portrait. That star-eyed girl of sixteen stared down from the gilded stand.

Uri, Shel, and Ahma-Dara walked on, but Brennen halted beside her. She eyed the portrait, laughing softly. She'd last seen it hidden in her abandoned music room. Evidently, Netaia wanted to reclaim her.

Brennen encircled her waist with one arm. "You were very pretty," he told her, "but you are beautiful now. Go on," he added. "I'll stay out here until they call the boys."

She gathered her long skirt. Carradee had sent down a swath of silken blue fabric to cover her unlovely sling. Firebird paused outside the tall double doors, glancing at the usual gaggle of bodyguards.

Several of them saluted.

She returned a half bow. She turned back and nodded to the liveried Redjackets standing guard. Obediently, they swung open the doors.

An eerie silence fell. The chamber looked huge ahead of her. This afternoon, the tri-D transcorders were naked, unshrouded. The session was being broadcast. Low-commoners might be watching.

She walked in alone.

Regent Kenhing smiled down across the chamber, resting one hand on the empty chair next to his own. "This," he announced, "is Indomitability."

Wounded indomitability, maybe. Firebird flushed. She glanced left and right and spotted several empty seats behind the high table as she approached. Tel's and Esme's, of course—to the Electors' great displeasure, so Carradee said. They had wanted to decorate Tel. But the whole Erwin clan was also absent. Daken's funeral was scheduled tomorrow in the great Hall of Charity. His father the First Lord had demanded that he receive full honors, having died in service to Netaia. Unbelievably, the First Lord also was threatening to bring a charge of murder against Firebird, for abandoning and silencing his son and second-heir.

Actually, she did believe that he would threaten. But the Electors had denied the first request and answered the second with a flat refusal.

"Daithi and I," Carradee had said angrily over the CT link, "made sure of it. The Erwins' domination is over."

In position behind the table, Firebird sat down with a sigh. Regent Kenhing rang the bell to call the Electorate to order. "I have one item of old business," he announced. "Without our valiant Planetary Navy, and the Federacy's assistance, Netaia would now be in the throes of worldwide destruction. We offer our heartfelt thanks, Marshal Burkenhamn. Lady Firebird."

Seated in back near Uri and Shel, Marshal Burkenhamn stood. Firebird took that as a cue and rose to her feet. Amid applause and cheers, her face heated again. She sat down quickly. They ought to be thanking Brennen too. He'd finally shared memory with her. It had been thrilling. Still, he hadn't made his entrance.

"There was also a threat of renegade Shuhr penetrating this very chamber," Regent Kenhing said, "and we are submitting an official request that the Sentinel presence onworld be made permanent. We need their protection. Does anyone object?"

Blessed silence. She smiled down at Uri and Shel.

"Finally, we have two urgent items of new business, since Lady Firebird soon will be leaving us." He turned toward her. "My lady, before you left us as our ambassador, you wished to present a request. Is that still your desire?"

"Yes." She rose to her feet again. "I offer," she said, fingering the tabletop, "a revised proposal for a cultural exchange program that would honor Netaia's high culture in numerous ways." She'd rehearsed this little speech a dozen times. "Music and all the other arts lift us above ourselves." She pitched her voice louder and lower, making it ring in the chamber. "They help us see further and understand others more deeply." How tragic that Monu could not have shared that. "Netaian music still is the best, the most honest and moving, that I have heard anywhere in the Whorl. Other worlds should know what we have accomplished here, and we also owe it to them to see and hear what they have accomplished." She glanced at the transcorders along the far walls, knowing this was also being announced to the Netaian populace.

Regent Kenhing swept the table with a gesture. "You all received this proposal last night," he said, surprising her. "You all have had time to study it, along with my funding proposal. Are there any objections?"

Funding? Excellent. The Erwins really did seem to be on their way out.

"The motion passes," Regent Kenhing announced, "and this body also is prepared to consider your prior proposal, Lady Firebird."

She sent him a quizzical look.

"It has been some time," he said agreeably, "since you asked us to consider relinquishing some electoral power to Netaia's Assembly. It shall be considered in committee."

It took an effort to keep her mouth shut. She had all but given up on that older proposal from her governmental analysis studies. She gave Regent Kenhing a grateful nod. She didn't trust herself to speak.

The regent turned toward the wide golden doors. "Finally, we have a celebration." His voice lightened. "Two little boys of unacknowledged royal descent are out in the entry hall, trying to keep their finery clean."

Laughter rang around the table. In Firebird's ears, that was true music.

A Redjacket strode up to Brennen and half bowed. "You are summoned, sir."

"Kinnor," Brennen called sharply. Kin stood gripping a gilded portrait support one-handed, imitating the ancient duke's dour face by curling his lower lip. A liveried servant stood on the stand's other side, steadying the painting. Sternly Brennen subvocalized, *Must Ahpa do voice-command?*

Kinnor straightened, raised his chin, and looked almost exactly like his mother. Proud, even defiant. Could it be this environment? Kin marched with stomping, exaggerated strides back toward Brennen and Kiel. The boys matched precisely in scarlet-and-black suits from Tel's tailor, a parting gift. Hopefully, they were too young to be scarred by this brief encounter with Netaia's royal protocol.

"Go with these men," Brennen directed. "Act very dignified. We practiced."

The doors swung open. Kiel reached for his brother's hand.

Brennen slipped into the chamber behind them, watching as they paraded up the chamber toward the gold floor medallion.

There was far too much gold in this chamber. Still, he felt an echo of joy and gratitude behind his lingering uneasiness. He glanced up at the Electoral table.

Mari sat biting her lip. He sensed that she was near tears with pride. The right kind of pride, this time.

Tel had offered to sponsor the boys on this occasion, but Tel was gone. Surely, the Electors had scrambled another sponsor.

Yes. Regent Kenhing was stepping around the table, holding a knot of blue fabric. Sashes for both of them.

Brennen sat down next to his ahma, who held Norann Burkenhamn's hand. *Guess what,* Ahma sent. *Norann just registered as an Inquirer.* Beyond Ahma and the Burkenhamns, Carradee and Daithi returned his smile. He had not expected to see them. The former monarch had avoided Electoral sessions for some time.

"Noble Electors," Regent Kenhing announced, extending a hand, "today we acknowledge these children as descendants of House Angelo. May they come, in time, to a full understanding of all that this means." He shook out both lengths of fabric and draped the boys simultaneously.

Ahma nudged him and whispered, "There'll be no arguments about who became prince first."

Not really princes. Acknowledged heirs, though. He could explain later.

Kiel and Kinnor made their coached bow with a slight alteration. Each boy kept a hand on the other one's shoulder. They were already playing twin games. What would they do next?

Firebird felt as if her chest might burst. Was ever anything so adorable?

The boys straightened with enormous eyes, taking in all that gleaming gilt and polished marble. She saw the chamber anew, as if for the first time. Kinnor and Kiel would have all the choices now, and if she and Brennen raised them with the Holy One's help, surely their choices would be good ones.

And the Electors . . . were they truly willing to consider relinquishing some of their unholy power at last?

Was this why you called me here? Brennen prayed. *Not to help save Netaia, or offer your mercy to the last member of a dying civilization, but so our sons could help stabilize a world I once despised?*

He did not expect an answer. He had obeyed the call. It was enough.

Maybe his futile gesture toward Monu proved the lengths to which the Eternal Sovereign would go, and ask his people to go, to offer his mercy.

Questions remained, though. If the Sentinel kindred stepped out of the Eternal Speaker's ways, they too would deserve obliteration, like the Shuhr. Would he see either group go extinct in his lifetime?

He eyed the little boys, marching out in step, still dramatically—delightedly, like miniature performers—gripping each others' shoulders. Could one of those children be the promised Word to Come, or his father?

And was their family complete? Wouldn't he love a daughter with her mother's flaming hair and brilliant eyes?

He had not mentioned it in quite awhile. Much had changed since then. Mari needed time to heal.

Still . . .

Oddly, Firebird was having similar thoughts. *He is such a loving father. Imagine him holding a daughter on his lap.* It was easy to picture. At Hesed House, on the Sentinels' sanctuary world of Procyel II, a little girl almost Kiel and Kinnor's age was being cared for. They had promised Ahma-Dara a chance to meet her granddaughter.

Still, a daughter of their own—

As the door boomed shut, Firebird looked into Brennen's eyes, caught the warmth in him, and drew strength.

The high-toned bell dismissed the session. She worked her way around the long table, collecting careful embraces. Dukes and duchesses, counts and countesses, barons and baronesses. All wishing her a speedy recovery. All asking her to return.

Surreal. And exhausting.

Brennen strode through the mob. Gently, he took her right arm. "Thank you all," he announced. "Now, Commander Caldwell needs to rest and recover."

They turned away as if he'd voice-commanded.

Maybe he had.

Harnessed into an acceleration seat two days later, Firebird eyed her recall pad. The Electoral broadcast had yielded results. Travel applications and artists' and musicians' references—nearly all common-class, including quite a few low-common—were trickling in. Her aide back on Tallis, Clareen Chesterson, would have work at last. Not long ago, Firebird had wished for a fair fight instead of bureaucracy. Was bureaucracy the real price of victory?

That, and another set of scars. She set down the recall pad and pushed deeper into her seat. She would have her surgery at Sanctuary, and they would keep their promise to Ahma-Dara. It would be good to rest there.

Seated behind her, Brennen had already drifted off in a well-earned nap. His sleep came through on the pair bond like a weighted blanket, dragging her down to join him. Ahma-Dara and Kiel sat beside her, nearer the viewport.

"Take handholds for full acceleration," a crewer's voice warned. The travel shield beyond Dara and Kiel consolidated and went dark. They accelerated smoothly into slip-state.

"That was fun," Kiel declared. He looked up at Firebird with his father's glacial-ice blue eyes. "Ahma," he asked, "can we do it again?"

END

AUTHOR'S NOTE

The Firebird books have lived in my heart since I was a young mom. While recovering from long covid in 2023, I self-indulgently read the whole series again. That years-long gap between #3 *Crown of Fire* and the next-generation #4 *Wind and Shadow* made me wonder: What *were* Firebird and Brennen doing during that time? Encouraged by writing friends, I started brainstorming. The Firebird Interlude Trilogy has resulted. I love Firebird and Brennen and their worlds as much as ever, and I thank the Lord for those encouraging writing friends.

    Kathy Tyers Gillin, Montana 2025

ACKNOWLEDGEMENTS

Heartfelt thanks to my Monday-evening villagers and my beta readers for enthusiastic encouragement and terrific suggestions: Meg Cook, Jamie Downer, Sharon Hinck, Broose Johnson (this book is largely your fault), Carol and Charles Kankelborg, Ronie Kendig, Barbara Keremedjiev, Nathaniel McClaflin, Maren Olson, Kearen Samsel, Deborah Scheurr, Molly and Anna Wilmington, and especially, to my favorite retired pilot and genuine-but-modest hero, my love and chief cheerleader, Captain Bill Gillin. Thank you, Lisa Laube, for an excellent developmental edit; thank you again, Jamie, for managing my online presence; and thank you once more, Steve Laube, for the opportunity to share Firebird and Brennen's adventures with this world. A hearty thanks to the gifted Enclave Publishing team, too, for the excellent final polish and sparkle—especially Lindsay, Sarah, Coralie, Jamie, and Trissina!

My deepest gratitude goes to the Three-in-One whose songs I hope to sing forever, who generously gives and mightily transcends all songs and all stories. As always, any inconsistencies, impossibilities, or accidental perversions of truth in this book are mine alone.

ABOUT THE AUTHOR

Kathy Tyers is known for her award-winning Firebird series and two licensed Star Wars Legends novels, including New York Times bestseller *The Truce at Bakura*. Her messiah-in-space novel *Daystar*, the conclusive end of the original Firebird series, won a Carol Award, and her standalone *Shivering World* received the visionary Christy. A friend and mentor to several newer writers, Kathy also authored *Writing Deep Viewpoint: Invite Your Readers Into the Story*.

Besides writing books, Kathy has worked as an immunobiology lab tech, taught elementary kids, supported herself in a garden center and as a freelance editor, earned a graduate degree in her fifties, and was a semiprofessional flutist for decades. She lives in southwest Montana with her husband, retired pilot William T. Gillin, and her married son and daughter-in-love live in Alaska. If she isn't reading or writing, she might be nurturing her short-season herb and vegetable garden, plinking on her grandmother's baby grand piano, or still occasionally trying to learn to play her Irish harp, *cláirseach na hÉirann*.

Visit Kathy's website, kathytyers.com, or the Kathy Tyers page on Facebook.

TRAVEL THE
FIREBIRD UNIVERSE

ENCLAVEPUBLISHING.COM